# Arabella
### the
# Traitor
### of Mars

## TOR BOOKS BY DAVID D. LEVINE

*Arabella of Mars*

*Arabella and the Battle of Venus*

*Arabella the Traitor of Mars*

# Arabella
### the
# Traitor
### of Mars

## THE **ADVENTURES**
## OF **ARABELLA ASHBY**

### BOOK **THREE**

# DAVID D. LEVINE

**TOR**

A TOM DOHERTY ASSOCIATES BOOK
NEW YORK

ARABELLA THE TRAITOR OF MARS

Copyright © 2018 by David D. Levine

A Tor Book
Published by Tom Doherty Associates
175 Fifth Avenue
New York, NY 10010

www.tor-forge.com

Tor® is a registered trademark of Macmillan Publishing Group, LLC.

The Library of Congress Cataloging-in-Publication Data is available upon request.

ISBN 978-0-7653-8283-2 (hardcover)
ISBN 978-1-4668-8951-4 (ebook)

Our books may be purchased in bulk for promotional, educational, or business use. Please contact your local bookseller or the Macmillan Corporate and Premium Sales Department at 1-800-221-7945, extension 5442, or by email at MacmillanSpecialMarkets@macmillan.com.

First Edition: July 2018

Printed in the United States of America

0  9  8  7  6  5  4  3  2  1

This book is dedicated to my father, who taught me calculus at the dishwasher and gave me *Mission of Gravity* and *Gravy Planet* as bedtime stories.

# Arabella
## the
# Traitor
### of
# Mars

# 1

---

## EARTH, 1816

# 1

## THE VICTORY JUBILEE

Arabella descended the steps beside London Bridge in a great rush, Captains Singh and Fox and Lady Corey following behind at a more stately pace. Spread out below across the frozen river lay the Victory Jubilee, celebrating the final defeat of Napoleon at the Battle of Venus. It was night, and the lights of the festival reflected dully from the ice below, echoing the stars which winked crisply in the black sky above. "Do be careful!" Captain Singh called.

"La, sir, you are far too cautious!" she called back, coquettishly.

"But we have not yet proved your foot upon ice!" Captain Singh had been born in India, and despite being widely traveled on Earth, Mars, and Venus and the interplanetary atmosphere between, had little experience of ice or snow. His formality, caution, and intellect were at once his most endearing and most annoying qualities.

Arabella herself had little more experience with ice than her husband—her previous sojourn on Earth had not included any such phenomenon as this—but so delighted was she at the prospect of the Jubilee that she refused to be deterred. "Pshaw!" she replied, laughing. "It has functioned perfectly thus far!"

Nonetheless, she checked her pace at the bottom of the stairs, stepping cautiously onto the scuffed translucent surface. The paths were laid with sand to provide steady footing, but so great was the pedestrian traffic that the sand was constantly swept aside. But her artificial foot's clockwork mechanism was performing as designed, mimicking the natural foot's spring on each step, and she found her footing to be entirely acceptable. Though she had confidence in the design that she and Captain Singh had worked out together after her injury in the closing moments of the Battle of Venus and constructed during the subsequent voyage to Earth, she was pleased that it functioned well in this unusual circumstance.

And a very unusual circumstance it was, as the Thames very rarely froze over and had not done so in nearly twenty years. The current exceptionally cold temperatures were due to the eruption of Mount Tambora in the Dutch East Indies, whose dust girdled the globe and blocked the rays of the life-giving Sun; the planet's veil of smoke had been plainly visible from above upon Arabella's recent approach to Earth. "We are quite fortunate," Lady Corey had declared, "that our ships of the air are able to observe and report upon this and other phenomena of the planetary atmosphere. If not, we would be shivering in the dark, with no idea how long the phenomenon will persist, and not even know the reason why!"

Taking her attention away from the ice, Arabella looked out across the Jubilee. The scene reminded her in some ways of the weekly market in Fort Augusta on Mars, with rows of stalls and shops and stands selling all manner of souvenirs, food, and drinks, whose smoke perfumed the chill air deliciously. It was also reminiscent of the Mars Docks not too many miles away, with huge follies of wood and paper and vast fabric pavilions taking the place of the Marsmen and other aerial ships there assembled. In terms of population it resembled the most crowded balls she had attended during her previous visit to England, but multiplied a thousand-fold and spread out across the ice between the bridges—the babble of conversation, music, and the braying of animals was nearly deafening.

Her companions caught her up as she presented her ticket to one of the men who stood at the base of each stairway. These men, mostly watermen and lightermen unemployed by the freezing of the Thames, charged thruppence for admission to the ice and a penny to depart—it was their only income until the river should clear, and Arabella had paid it gladly. Surely such a spectacle as this would never recur in her lifetime, and she intended to take in every aspect of it that she could.

"You were absolutely right!" she cried to Captain Fox as he joined her on the ice. "It is a marvel to behold!"

"I told you," he replied with a smirk. "In celebration of our great victory, the whole city is done up like a Port Charlotte whore." He turned to his wife. "Beg pardon." Lady Corey's glare in return combined long-suffering vexation with unfeigned, deep affection.

In truth, Arabella often wondered what the Foxes saw in each other. He was a self-centered, impulsive privateer captain, a man of great and sometimes uncontrollable appetites; she was a very proper and composed lady of excellent breeding, nearly ten years her husband's senior. Indeed, it was Lady Corey who had educated Arabella in the ways of a young woman of quality—to the extent, Arabella herself was forced to admit, that such education was even possible. But both Foxes were charming, though in very different ways; both intelligent; both wealthy; both brave and decisive in a crisis. And it had been in a very great crisis, the escape from the Marieville prisoner-of-war camp and subsequent Battle of Venus, that the two of them had come together and, quite unexpectedly to all, fallen in love.

Having taken her bearings, Arabella spied her destination ahead on the right, and noted smoke and flames beginning to rise from it. "Hurry!" she called to her companions, rushing ahead. "The fireworks at the Castle of Discord are about to begin!"

The Castle of Discord was the center-piece of the fair, upon which all the lanes of shops and caravans converged like the spokes of a wheel, and a grand fireworks display was promised for the opening night of the Jubilee. Already a vast crowd had assembled on every side of it; their voices combined in an eager, anticipatory pandemonium, mingled with the music of hurdy-gurdies and the cries of vendors selling pastries and meat pies.

Arabella pushed through the thickening crowd until she reached a point where the view of the Castle was not too obscured by the hats and shoulders of those before her, then paused until her husband and the Foxes could catch her up. But as she was looking over her shoulder in search of them, a tremendous boom sounded. Startled, she turned to see what had caused it.

The Castle of Discord was an enormous structure, larger than a three-story house, built of wood and canvas and painted to resemble ancient, mossy stone. A grim and imposing edifice, it was surmounted by crenellations, behind which stood painted figures of mustachioed men in French Army uniforms with rifles, bayonets, and cannons. At the very top, a figure much larger than life, wearing a huge cocked hat worn athwartships, clearly represented Napoleon. And the boom which had drawn Arabella's attention had come from the launch of rockets all around the Castle, which burst in a fusillade of red and white fireworks in the air above to the general approbation of the crowd.

This first broadside of fireworks was answered by another fusillade from the Castle's upper reaches, this one in blue and gold, which drew in turn another, still larger response from the ground.

Soon huge flowers and sheets of colored flame were clashing in the air above the Castle, matched by sprays of sparks and Catherine wheels mounted upon its painted-canvas ramparts. The windows of the Castle now illuminated, showing colored images and moving shadows representing major battles of the wars just concluded. The crowd roared its approval of each great gout of flame and crash of gunpowder; one man near Arabella cried out that it was "the very duplicate of a real cannonade!"

Despite her enjoyment of the spectacle, this comment gave Arabella pause. For it caused her to consider the great gulf between the harmless and beautiful display before her and the grim, deadly reality of an aerial battle—the sound alone of which carried more destructive power than all the pretended violence of this entire performance—and to realize just how different her experience of the war had been from that of the people around her, most of them Londoners born and bred who had never set foot on an aerial man-of-war or a battlefield.

On and on the fusillades continued, fireworks bursting, cannon booming, and smoke rising in a choking cloud. The crowd's enthusiasm rose, and the sound and fury of the pretended assault upon the Castle of Discord doubled and redoubled. So great, in fact, was the fire and smoke that the Castle itself became completely obscured . . . and then, without warning, from the midst of this vast dark cloud sounded a mighty crash, greater than that which had gone before, accompanied by an abrupt cessation of the fireworks. The crowd stood stunned in the sudden darkness and silence, the fire and noise of the mock battle replaced by a few flickering flames and the occasional cough.

And then a cheer rose up from the front ranks of the spectators—a cheer which heightened as it spread backward and further backward. The cheer crashed like a wave over Arabella's position as the smoke cleared, revealing that the Castle of Discord had completely vanished! The painted canvas walls had fallen away under cover of the smoke, revealing a grand edifice of white marble, enlightened with stained glass windows and surmounted with a gilded dome and lofty spires. Lights glimmered on within and without, revealing to all the majesty of the structure which must have stood hidden within the Castle all along.

"Behold!" came a voice as the cheering began to die down. "The Castle of Discord has been destroyed! Behold in its place . . . the *Temple of Concord*!"

At this announcement the crowd began cheering and shouting in still greater earnest, ragged calls of "hip, hip, hurrah!" rising in competition from various parts of the vast icy plain upon which the new Temple stood, and echoing from the ice, the river banks, and the side of London Bridge close by.

Then, to Arabella's surprise, the happy crowd around her fell suddenly silent, staring behind her as though at some supernatural apparition. Furthermore, from that direction she could now hear a peculiar sound, which combined burbling, hissing, and clattering. She turned to the sound . . . and beheld an amazing sight.

George Augustus Frederick, His Royal Highness The Prince of Wales, Regent of the United Kingdom of Great Britain and Ireland, was neither as handsome and slim as his official portrait, which she had seen in Government House in Fort Augusta, nor as grotesque as the caricatures in the gazettes. Yet, despite the peculiarity of the circumstances, she recognized him immediately—and even if she had not, the deference of those about him made immediately clear that this was a personage of extreme importance.

He rode in a Merlin chair, with two large wheels behind and a single wheel in front, the latter being steered by a sort of tiller held by the occupant. This much was not unexpected—as every one knew, the Prince suffered horribly from gout. But instead of an attendant pushing, behind the Prince there was an engine of some kind. She could not see it well from here, but by the sound—which she now identified as boiling water and the hiss of steam—it must be some sort of very compact steam engine. Cables ran from it to levers on the chair's sides, presumably allowing the Prince to control the chair's forward motion. She longed to inspect the mechanism.

As to the Prince himself, he was a very large man. His broad stomach was the first thing one noticed, matched by substantial legs and thick arms . . . he must weigh seventeen stone or more. The whole was wrapped in an ornate military uniform: red coat dripping with gold braid, tight breeches, and a cocked hat as enormous as the painted Napoleon's. One foot wore a high Hessian boot polished to a mirror sheen; the other was swaddled in a huge soft bandage. The uniform's high collar tried and failed to conceal a fleshy double chin. Yet though his lower lip pouted out like some enormous child's, his eyes showed intelligence, humor, and even compassion.

"Mrs. Singh," said one of the Prince's companions, "may I present to you His Royal Highness the Prince of Wales?"

"Your Royal Highness," she said, dropping a trembling curtsey.

"Oh please, call me Prinny." He gestured her to rise. "Every one of any consequence does."

Arabella felt her jaw drop. She looked around at the encircling crowd, which mingled common people, soldiers, and—those closest to the Prince—men and women whose clothing marked them as people of very high quality indeed. They seemed as astonished as she. "I, sir? I am of no consequence whatsoever!"

The Prince pulled up on one of the levers beside his seat, causing the chair to propel itself toward her. He then brought it to a stop beside her, the engine hissing and clattering, and took up her hand. Stunned, she let him do so. "*Au contraire*, madam. You are, or so I am told, one of the chief architects of our victory over Napoleon. I have been intending for some little time to send a note of gratitude and congratulations to you, and of course your husband the dashing Captain Singh. But that fellow there"—he gestured foppishly with his off hand to a gray-haired gentleman, oddly dressed, who stood with a female Negro companion—"pointed you out to me here, and so I am able to extend my felicitations to you in person."

"I . . . I am honored," Arabella managed. "But . . . really I did only what was necessary. Any loyal subject would have done the same."

"Perhaps. But not any other loyal subject did." He kissed her hand, then released it; it fell limp to her side. "I would be delighted if you and your companions would join me in a drink." And without another word he wheeled his conveyance about and headed off, the engine puttering and spitting out steam and drops of hot water onto the ice.

Still trembling, Arabella found herself swept up in the Prince's coterie. Captain Singh supported her arm—indeed, he practically kept her standing by main force—as they traveled in a group across the ice, the murmuring crowd parting before the Prince's machine and rejoining behind his party like the turbulent air in the wake of a passing ship.

They made their way to a large illuminated pavilion, entering between liveried attendants who bowed deeply as they drew the door-cloth aside. The air within, redolent of wine and snuff, was far warmer than without; the hubbub of the crowd, contained by the fabric walls and roof, still louder; and the quality of the company much more elevated. "Prinny!" called one, and "You must try this sherry!" another.

Some one handed a glass—fine crystal—to Arabella, and she took it, the alternative seeming to be allowing it to smash upon the ice at her feet. It was extremely full, so she took a sip, finding it to be something of deep flavor and considerable strength. It was really very delicious, and she sipped at it to calm herself as the crowd swirled around her like the turbulent winds of the Horn.

So numerous and animated were the company that she felt herself battered by the noise alone, let alone the elbows and shoulders which frequently bumped against her, yet she felt it would be impolite to depart.

Captain Singh, beside her, held a glass of his own, but she noted that he did not appear to have imbibed any of it. His demeanor, always reserved, seemed still more so now; he held himself straight and aloof, looking out at the assemblage from his considerable height as though from the cross-trees of his own mainmast. The assemblage, in turn, looked upon this tall, lean, very dark man in a Mars Company captain's buff jacket as though a Martian had suddenly stepped into the tent. Captain Fox, meanwhile, seemed to be in his element; along with Lady Corey he was already engaged in uproarious conversation.

"You do not seem to be enjoying yourself, madam."

Arabella looked down to the source of the voice, realizing that she had drifted away somewhere inside herself. It was the Prince, who held a glass of his own. "If you please, sir," she said, "I find myself quite discomfited by the noise of the crowd. The contrast with the still of the interplanetary atmosphere is quite . . . quite discomfiting." She chided herself for repetition, and took another sip of her drink.

"Indeed." He drank deeply from his own glass, finishing it, then held it out negligently to one side. A silent attendant immediately appeared and refilled it, even as the Prince continued to converse. "Though this Jubilee is truly extraordinary—the expense would be enough to make even *my* steward blanch—the presence of so many of the common people is really quite tedious." He propelled his chair closer and leaned in, conspiratorially. "I plan a private victory celebration at my home in Brighton next week," he said, his glance taking in both Arabella and Captain Singh. "It would give me pleasure if you would join me."

Arabella, amazed and rather overwhelmed by the offer, looked to her husband for advice. His face remained impassive, though she thought she could detect some hesitation around the eyes. "If you wish, my dear," he said.

Why did every thing in London have to move so *fast*? But still . . . to escape from this jostling crowd was appealing, and to visit the Prince's private home—an architectural marvel, from all she had heard—was an opportunity which might never be repeated. "I am honored to accept your invitation," she replied, bowing deeply—and immediately regretting it, as her head spun quite distressingly.

"Excellent!" the Prince cried, patting his free hand against the one which held his wine in a semblance of applause. He then raised his glass. "To new friends!"

"To new friends," Arabella replied, and drained her glass.

"To new friends," Captain Singh muttered, and sipped.

---

Arabella peered from the Prince's carriage, the wind from the horses' rapid progress chilling her face. She rubbed her hands together beneath the blanket on her lap and clapped them to her frozen nose, not wanting to miss the first sight of Brighton Pavilion.

The Prince's caravan consisted of three luxurious carriages, plus a wagon which carried the Prince's Merlin chair. Arabella and her captain shared the third carriage with Colonel the Honorable G. Dawson Damer, the Honorable Frederick Byng, and Byng's enormous dog, a placid elderly poodle by the name of Buck. For the first hour of the journey the two Honorables had conversed excitedly between each other on the topics of hunting, horses, politics, and wine, including Arabella and Captain Singh only occasionally and reluctantly. Eventually, though, the con-versation had trailed off and the two men, sharing a flask, had eventually drifted off to sleep. Captain Singh too, following a long-standing habit, took advantage of any occasion in which his attentions were not absolutely required to close his eyes and rest. For her part, Arabella had been largely content to admire the passing countryside, whose peculiar trees, farm-houses, and occasional snowdrifts were strange and marvelous to her.

After six uneventful hours of travel the town of Brighton had begun to appear, with sparse farm-houses replaced by more frequent, more substantial dwellings, and the driver had knocked upon the carriage roof to point out the spires of Brighton Pavilion in the distance. Arabella ducked and weaved her head, trying to get a better view of this magnificent structure through the strange trees, black and leafless, which grew on either side of the road. Bright sunlight, sharp and clear as the chill air through which it shone, flickered in the branches.

And then, quite suddenly, they rounded a curve and the whole pavilion hove at once into view. Arabella could barely suppress a gasp.

The enormous building—broader than the eponymous fort of Fort Augusta, though not nearly so high—sprawled across several acres, the bright Mars-red of its stones shining in the sun and contrasting oddly with the brown of the English hills beyond. It was designed, as she had been informed on the journey, in resemblance to Martian architecture, with the typical Martian slant-sided, flat-topped arch visible in profusion, and sweeping curves of shining steel leaping into the sky from every corner. But, due to Earth's higher gravity and the lower quality of English steel, those metal spires were thicker and less elegant than those of the satrap's palace in Sor Khoresh. All in all it seemed like a child's sketch of a Martian palace—a talented child, admittedly, but one who had only ever seen pictures of Martian palaces, never actually visited one.

As the carriage drew nearer, Arabella saw that, like Martian royal palaces, the pavilion's stones were carved with a multitude of figures in bas-relief. But these carvings represented not Martians but human beings—ancient warriors with spears and shields, and women in a shocking state of undress—along with horses and dogs . . . though not a single poodle.

The carriages pulled into the drive, disgorging their passengers with a great creaking of wood and groaning of men. The Prince's carriage, heavily weighted as it was with the corpulent Prince and five of his closest companions, creaked the loudest as they emerged and saw the greatest complaints. "I swear," the Prince remarked to the world as he was helped down from the carriage with the aid of a cane, "that journey grows longer every year." As he reached the ground, one of the coterie of servants that had descended upon the arriving caravan silently handed him a steaming mug. "Still, it is good to be home." He drank deeply.

Arabella herself marveled silently at the soaring structure above her. From this close distance it could easily be seen that, rather than being constructed entirely of red sandstone as the equivalent Martian palaces were, only the lower, structural portions of the pavilion were stone; the upper reaches were actually painted wood, though so cunningly executed that the difference could scarcely be detected. The bas-reliefs also served to disguise expansive windows, where a real Martian palace would be of solid stone, perforated only by arrow-slits and hot-oil sluices. Plainly this was a fantasia—a folly of a palace, which merely aped the stern defensive strength of its models on Mars.

She contemplated, as she passed through the slab-sided entrance gate, to what degree this reflected the personality and priorities of its owner.

The entrance-hall, had she not been warned of its design by the Honorables, would have been an utter shock. Even with this warning, it was still overwhelming. Whereas the pavilion's exterior was Martian in design, the interior was done in a Venusian style, with green brick, black stone, and ceramic tile every where. The ceilings were hung with white Venusian silk, lavishly embroidered, and enameled statues of finned and tentacled Venusian gods glowered from every corner. Illumination was provided by hissing gas flames, contained in lanterns of green glass, which approximated the light of the giant glow-worms employed by the actual Venusians. Arabella had seen gas street-lamps in London, but had never before encountered gas illumination indoors.

Arabella gaped in every direction as servants took the fur cape and muff with which she had been provided for the journey. She was immediately glad of their service, as the room was warmed to a nearly Venusian level of heat by the urn-shaped patent stoves which stood at intervals along the walls.

"So!" cried the Prince, rolling in from the cold upon his puttering, clattering contrivance. "Captain and Mrs. Singh—you have just recently returned from Venus. What do you think of my entrance-hall? My decorator has been hard at work upon it for nearly two years now."

"It is . . . most impressive," the captain said. Arabella reserved judgement—or was perhaps stunned into silence by the hall's extravagant bad taste. "Though I must confess we had little experience of the native Venusian architecture or ornament during our stay on that planet. We were the unwilling guests of Napoleon, as you may know, in a town which had been built by and for the French. And quite hastily assembled as well."

The Prince's face fell, just fractionally, as Captain Singh spoke. Had Arabella not happened to be looking directly at him, she might not have noted his disappointment. "I apologize for your treatment at the Great Ogre's hands. I am assured, however, by other travelers that my humble home does credit to the finest palaces and temples of that distant planet, to which I hope some day to pay a visit." He gestured inward. "Perhaps your stay here will serve to whet your appetite for Venusian art and architecture."

The party moved through a vast curtained archway into a long gallery, which plainly served as the pavilion's central avenue. A rich carpet in green and black bore a pattern of water running over stones; the walls were painted with flowers and vines in fanciful— and, to Arabella's eye, entirely invented—colors and shapes; and from the high ceiling hung a massive iron chandelier, also designed in imitation of vines, dripping with green glass baubles. Ceramic statues of Venusian gods stood here and there, man-sized and larger, though in this vast space they were not so intimidating as they had been in the entrance-hall. This gallery, too, was heated to an unpleasant degree by patent stoves; Arabella daubed at her face with her handkerchief and fanned herself with one hand.

"If you please," murmured a servant, "I will conduct you to your chambers." His clothing was European in style, but made of white Venusian silk with green piping that matched the walls. He led them up a grand staircase—the railings of dark wood were carved to resemble twisted branches—and down the hall to a room where their traveling cases had already been unpacked. The Venusian theme continued here, though thankfully to a much more restrained degree, and though the room was larger than any bedchamber Arabella had ever before experienced it was, at least, neither as inordinately vast nor as drastically overheated as the house's public spaces. "Dinner will be at six o'clock. Do you require anything?"

"I do not believe so," Captain Singh replied.

"The bell-pull is there." He gestured to a tapestry ribbon with a pattern of vines in the corner. "Please feel free to call upon us for any need." Then he bowed himself out.

"You are unhappy," Arabella's husband said to her as soon as the door had closed.

She stared over his shoulder at the painted wall for a time before replying. "If my wicked cousin Simon had nearly drowned," she said at last, "and suffered the loss of half his wits under the water, he might have designed a . . . *monstrosity* like this."

"The Prince's taste is . . . cosmopolitan," he hedged. "He pays homage to the styles of other planets."

"Homage?" Arabella sniffed. "I would call it simple theft! He imitates his betters, no more."

Captain Singh stiffened. "Permit me to remind you that we are discussing the Prince Regent of the entire British Empire! He *has* no betters!" But this argument did not seem very convincing even to him.

For a moment Arabella considered a sharp reply. But then she relented, and allowed her husband to fold her into his strong, warm arms. "I will attempt not to hold his taste in ornament too much against him."

"He has, at least, provided us with a very comfortable private chamber," he murmured into her shoulder.

"He has," she agreed, and after that, for a time, there was no more conversation.

———————————

Later, Arabella and the captain dressed and found their way to the banqueting room. This room, though not nearly so long as the long gallery, was much broader, higher, and even more gaudily appointed. Pillars in the form of gigantic, fanciful trees supported a high domed ceiling, from the center of which was suspended a pair of enormous frogs, crafted of some shining metal with jeweled eyes, seeming frozen in the act of dancing about each other. Below the frogs hung an iron chandelier nearly thirty feet tall; it was illuminated by gas, the bright and hissing light harsh to both eye and ear, and its glass panels were painted with colored scenes of Venusian natives at work and play. It must, Arabella thought, weigh several tons, and she looked skeptically at the chain from which it hung, which seemed barely capable of supporting it.

Beneath this enormous fixture a magnificent table stretched over sixty feet in length. At its center, of course, sat the Prince, his bulk and his Merlin chair occupying what might otherwise have been space for three diners, and ranged to either side in order of precedence were over fifty people, all clearly men and women of importance.

Arabella's table companion was one Robert Dundas, the Right Honorable Viscount Melville. He was a Scotsman, with a light mellifluous accent, and his jacket was of rich black superfine wool. "I am given to understand," he said to her after the first fish course, "that you actually participated in the Battle of Venus as a combatant?"

"I played a small part," she concurred modestly, then proceeded to relate her story of the battle. It was a story she had told many times since arriving on Earth and by now it was nearly routine, though she still took pleasure in the reactions of the hearers.

"Such times we find ourselves in." He shook his head in wonderment. "In my position I have read many a battle report, but a female navigator is a marvel I have never before encountered."

"And what position might that be?"

"First Lord of the Admiralty."

"Heavens!" Arabella glanced down the table to where Captain Singh was conversing with his own dinner companion, an elderly woman with an extraordinarily large bonnet. "My husband, Captain Prakash Singh of the Honorable Mars Company airship *Diana*, would be most honored to speak with you."

"Ah yes, the famous Captain Singh. I am aware of his presence here, though we have not yet had the chance to speak." The waiter delivered the next course—beef with onions and pepper—

and Dundas took a bite before continuing. "If I may ask, how came you to meet him?"

"I served as his cabin boy." Though Dundas was a very disciplined man, she noted that his eyes reflected a very satisfying degree of surprise. "I was compelled to disguise myself as a boy and join his ship's company in order to preserve my family fortune."

He regarded her frankly. "I cannot imagine such an attractive girl as yourself being mistaken for a boy, even for a moment."

She acknowledged the compliment with a bow of her head. "'The apparel oft proclaims the man,' as the Bard said. Replace this dress with an airman's slops, and no one in this company would give me a second glance." She sipped her wine. "I have found that most people rarely see beyond surfaces. Captain Singh is one of the perceptive few who can, and even he took some time to penetrate my disguise."

"Perceptive, is he? And well respected by his men?"

"Very much so. His is a very happy crew."

"But I have heard that he suffered a mutiny some years ago."

"It is true that he did." She felt her ire rising at the recollection. "I was aboard his ship myself at that time, and I will say from personal experience that it was motivated by the mutineers' greed and intolerance rather than by any fault of the captain's. Once the leader was exposed as a martinet and bully, the men's loyalty to their captain reasserted itself and the mutiny rapidly collapsed."

"It is . . . unusual, for a Mussulman to command an English vessel." He took a bite, chewed thoughtfully, then swallowed. "Has this intolerance caused any other difficulties for him?"

Arabella thought of the looks the Prince's coterie had given him in the pavilion at the Jubilee. She thought of how the French had dismissed and belittled him on Venus . . . to their eventual regret. And she thought of Lady Corey's objections to Arabella's marriage to him, and the anguish he himself had shown when he had very nearly turned down her proposal, wanting to spare her the effects of bigotry. But what she said was, "None that he has been unable to overcome through intelligence, discipline, and kindness. Despite all objections to his color and creed, he has risen to the very highest ranks of the Honorable Mars Company, and served admirably under Nelson in the Battle of Venus."

"So he has worked with the Navy?"

"Indeed! And for the last several months he has served as captain of the Admiral's temporary flagship."

Dundas tapped his silver fork against his lower lip, considering. "You have given me much to think about, Mrs. Singh," he said at last. "I will be certain to speak with your husband over the cigars and port."

Eventually, after countless courses of delicious food and much conversation on the weather, the latest advances of science and invention—"you simply must visit the kitchens, the Prince is so proud of the innovative equipment he has caused to be installed there"—and the prospects for prosperity now that decades of war had finally come to an end, the hostess, Lady Hertford, rose from her seat and conducted the ladies to the withdrawing-room, leaving the gentlemen to continue their conversation without the restraint required by female company. Arabella resented this separation, but there was little to be done about it. She nodded to Captain Singh as she passed, to which he replied with a deep bow of his head.

———————

The withdrawing-room, though nearly as large as the banqueting room in plan, had a much lower ceiling and was far more restrained in ornament—apart from the several substantial iron columns that supported the rooms above, which were decorated as vine-wrapped Venusian trees with spreading limbs. Had it not been so very hot, Arabella would have found the space quite agreeable. The ladies seated themselves on the chairs and settees ranged about the carpeted floor and engaged in conversation, cards, and backgammon.

Arabella found herself in a game of whist with three other ladies, including Lady Hertford. Tall, handsome, and elegant, she wore her gray hair and matronly girth with panache. Every one knew her to be the Prince's mistress, but Arabella saw no rancor or opprobrium toward her—indeed, the company seemed to treat her with the greatest respect. Princes and Admirals, she thought, did not seem to be subject to the same rules as the rest of society.

"Mrs. Singh, is it?" Lady Hertford said to Arabella after the game concluded and the two of them had been left alone with tea and biscuits. "An unusual name, and one which keeps coming up in conversation. May I assume the Mussulman is your husband?"

Arabella was growing tired of that word. "My husband is Captain Singh of the Honorable Mars Company, yes."

"Ah." Lady Hertford nodded. "This explains why it was that Mr. Reid mentioned him so favorably."

"Mr. *Thomas* Reid?" Arabella asked, astonished. "Chairman of the Company?"

"The very same." Lady Hertford smiled at Arabella's reaction. "Do not be so amazed, Mrs. Singh. Your husband's actions in the Battle of Venus put him among the greatest heroes the Company has produced in a hundred years. Some mark him as even greater than Lord Clive!" Arabella blinked, startled, at the comparison. Robert Clive—Clive of Mars, as every schoolboy knew him—was the general who had consolidated English rule over Saint George's Land in the last century. "And your own accomplishments are scarcely less famous."

"Oh, I could not possibly!"

"Do not be over-modest, my dear." She leaned in, conspiratorially. "Prinny is extremely fond of you, you know."

Arabella's heart pounded at this revelation. "I am a married woman!" she blurted.

Lady Hertford shrugged. "As am I. But you need have no concerns about untoward advances, my dear. Prinny prefers his women more . . . substantial. No, his sentiments toward you are entirely avuncular. You are nearly the same age as his daughter, you know. As she has recently become engaged to Prince Leopold, and will soon be departing to begin her own independent life, I believe he may be casting about for another young woman to be his protégée."

Arabella was not certain how she felt about this. "My intention is to return to my family plantation on Mars as soon as possible."

"Do not dismiss the favors of a Prince so lightly, Mrs. Singh. His attentions can lead to greatly improved prospects for you and your husband." She set down her tea and looked into Arabella's eyes with great sincerity. "I warn you, he is fickle. But he is also manipulable. If you appeal to his self-importance, if you can convince him that his interests align with yours . . . there is no end to the opportunities he can bring to you."

"Why are you telling me this? I am no one."

Lady Hertford sat back in her chair. "At the moment." She took up her tea-cup and regarded Arabella over its painted rim. "But you have a bit of celebrity, and a certain provincial charm, and your husband is poised for greater things." She sipped her tea. "Consider it a favor from a friend."

"I . . . I see." Arabella raised her own tea, and was discomfited to find the liquid trembling in the cup. She steadied it with the other hand and sipped. "I will give your advice due consideration."

"Please do. Remember, Mrs. Singh . . . a pawn can become a queen, if she reaches the last rank."

---

Eventually the gentlemen finished their port and cigars and joined the ladies in the withdrawing-room. Captain Singh—resplendent in his best Mars Company captain's buff coat, a sight very dear to her eyes—was deep in conversation with Dundas and another gentleman as they entered the room, but as Arabella approached he shook their hands and the three men parted.

"The Right Honorable Mr. Dundas was my dinner companion," Arabella said to her husband as she took his arm, "and he did mention that he would be speaking with you after dinner. But who was the other? He seems vaguely familiar."

"That was Mr. Reid."

She smiled up at her husband. "You are moving in very rarified circles, Captain."

"Indeed." But his mood, always reserved, now seemed even more so.

"You are troubled."

"I have been offered a very great opportunity."

But before he could clarify this statement, the Prince came puttering up, bringing his conveyance to a wheezing, steam-spitting halt before the two of them.

"I am so terribly sorry I was not able to chat with you myself over port," the Prince said to the captain, acknowledging Arabella's presence with a nod. "The Princess's wedding plans have become all-encompassing. But I see that you did manage to talk with Messrs. Dundas and Reid. I do hope you found their conversation enlightening?"

"It was . . . intriguing."

"I must emphasize that this topic is not yet suitable for general conversation. But I am given to understand that you are eminently suited for the task at hand, and I hope to be able to discuss it with you in person later this week-end. Now, if you will excuse me, I see that Lady Hertford requires my attention."

But when the Prince engaged the lever, the little steam engine let out a choking clatter and the chair refused to budge. The Prince immediately called for an engineer, and there was an awkward period of silence while the servants went in search of one. "May I examine the mechanism?" Arabella asked the Prince.

"I imagine so. But be aware—the steam can be frightfully hot."

Arabella knew very little of steam power, but she was familiar with the basic principle. And, as she bent and peered at the engine's shining brass, she saw that the system of wheels and jointed rods that connected it with the chair's wheels was not dissimilar to clockwork movements she had seen before. But the steam cylinder, with its valves and fastenings glistening as though with dew, was more mysterious.

Before she could complete her examination, a frock-coated gentleman with a large leather satchel of tools emerged from the kitchens and none-too-gently directed her aside. After a few brisk adjustments, too rapid for her to follow, the engine resumed its previous rhythmic chug and the Prince, waving a cheery farewell, directed his machine away.

For a moment Arabella and the captain stood alone. "You must explain what that was all about," she said to him.

"It has been a long evening," he said, consulting his watch. Indeed, the hour had grown quite late. "Perhaps we should retire."

This scarcely seemed a response, but the expression on Captain Singh's face did not invite further discussion. Without a word she put her arm through his and they departed the room, saying good night to the company as they passed.

---

As soon as the bedchamber door closed behind them, Arabella turned to Captain Singh, regarding him with an unspoken question upon her face.

"I have been presented with a very substantial opportunity," he repeated, then hesitated. "I was not able to discuss this with you in the withdrawing-room because my role as a government agent is not supposed to be known to you."

Shortly after Napoleon's escape from the far side of the Moon, Captain Singh had been sent to Venus on Mars Company business . . . or so the world had thought. The actuality was that he had been recruited by the Government as a secret agent and sent to Venus to investigate the Great Ogre's plans there. But he had been captured and imprisoned there, and Arabella had traveled thence to aid his escape. Eventually they had discovered, investigated, and defeated Napoleon's secret weapon, the armored airship *Victoire*, and along the way, with great reluctance, the captain had taken Arabella into his confidences. But he had never received authorization to do so.

Eventually Arabella's silence compelled the captain to speak once more. "Messrs. Dundas and Reid, from their lofty positions in the Admiralty and Company respectively, are aware of my dual role as captain and agent, and they told me that they were very favorably impressed by my performance in the Marieville prisoner-of-war camp and in the subsequent Battle of Venus. They say that they are now in search of a man to lead a very significant operation on Mars, and that my combination of navigational expertise, demonstrated leadership ability, and experience of the Mars trade makes me uniquely suited for the position."

"Why, that is *wonderful* news! Why are you so hesitant?" For his countenance and attitude were not at all what she would have expected from a man who had been so lavishly praised by his very highest superiors.

"For one thing, I am only one of several men under consideration . . . though I am the only one of them on Earth at this moment. For another, they . . . they questioned my loyalty to Crown and Company, due to my . . . origins. I assured them that I am entirely devoted to my adopted country and to the Company in whose service I have spent my entire adult life, but they did not seem completely convinced. And . . . and they were not entirely forthcoming about their plans. I gather that the operation will involve both command of multiple airships and negotiations with the Martians, but further details will only be provided to the man selected to lead the operation. Although I understand that confidentiality must be maintained, something in their unspoken demeanor leads me to wonder with some . . . unease, what lies beneath that cloak of secrecy." He shook his head. "I should not even be telling you this much."

"Of course you should not." She embraced him then, and his arms wrapped around her shoulders. "But you know that I am discretion personified."

"I seem to recall that, on Venus, your 'discretion' eventually brought practically the entire crew of *Touchstone* into our confidences."

"And if I had not done so, we would still be there, and Napoleon's armored fleet would certainly have conquered the entire solar system by now."

He sighed, his chest pressing and relaxing against hers. "You are a most vexing young person, boy second class Ashby."

"And you are honorable to a very fault, my maharaja." She held him more tightly. "Do they require an immediate response?"

"I must give them my reply before we all leave Brighton."

"Well, then, that will be no sooner than to-morrow. So let us sleep upon the question."

But sleep did not come, at least not for a while. And even after Captain Singh was gently snoring away, Arabella found herself staring into the bright eye of Earth's enormous moon, wondering what the morrow would bring.

## 2

---

# SNOW

What the morrow brought, as it turned out, was a great storm of snow, which left the grounds and the hills beyond coated in a gleaming blanket of purest white, in places several feet in depth.

Arabella, taking a few steps onto the path beyond the door, found the experience extremely peculiar. The crunch of the substance beneath her foot—the artificial one, alas, did not transmit the sensation well, and in fact she was extremely concerned about her balance—was rather like that of the very dry sand called *torokoshke*, but, unlike any sand, the snow compressed into a solid mass under pressure, forming a firm friable plate in the shape of her boot-sole. Whether compressed or not, the snow was slippery underfoot, and its chill to the touch was quite remarkable—a nearly painful, crystalline sensation, which immediately melted away to water beneath her fingertips. "Is it edible?"

The captain, having grown up in India and spent much of his adult life in the air, was as ignorant as she. But one of the Prince's set—the Duke of Argyll, she thought, though she could not at the moment recall his name—had come out to stand beside her, and laughed at the question. "Of course!" he said, and digging up a handful he popped it into his mouth. "Just be careful," he said, with white crumbs dissolving on his chin, "that it be the pure white stuff."

"I shall keep this in mind," she said. Hesitantly she scooped up a small quantity of snow with two fingers, licked at it delicately, then put it in her mouth. The result was much more a feeling than a flavor; it had a prickly texture, reminiscent of the pins-and-needles sensation she sometimes felt in her extremities upon arising from sleep, which quickly evanesced to pure, cold water.

"Wonderful packing stuff," the Duke remarked, impenetrably, bending down again and taking up a double handful. This he quickly compressed into a ball between his hands, which he then threw with some force against a pillar some five feet away. To Arabella's surprise it exploded into a puff of white, leaving only a few stray flakes where it had struck.

"My goodness!" Arabella cried out, delighted, and immediately followed suit, forming her own ball of snow and throwing it toward the same pillar. But hers was not sufficiently well made, and fell into fragments before reaching its target. Immediately she squatted to form another, this one with more snow and more tightly packed.

Soon the three of them were making and throwing snow balls at the walls, the trees, and each other—Arabella found the impact of the first one to strike her a vast surprise, but hardly painful at all, and retaliated with gusto—laughing and exclaiming "Aha!" with each new attack. Captain Singh, hesitant at first, soon joined in with great enthusiasm, dodging Arabella's missiles with alacrity and flinging his own with great precision. She had rarely seen him so happy.

So great was the hilarity that the Duke was soon compelled to beg off, with hands on knees and the air fogging around his head, until he was recovered enough to stand again. "Haven't had so much fun since I was a boy in Inverness," he gasped when his breath returned. "And now I don't have to shovel it, ha ha!"

Arabella, decades younger and not long removed from work aboard *Touchstone* and *Diana*, was not so exhausted by the exertion, but did find herself breathing heavily. The cold air, she discovered, burned in her breast in a way she had not encountered since her girlhood adventures in the Martian desert, and when combined with Earth's unaccustomed gravity the sensation was surprisingly enervating. Her hands, too, tingled from the cold and wet, and the toes of her natural foot, despite its sturdy Mars-made half-boot, had gone nearly numb from chill. "Shovel it?" she asked, uncomprehending.

The Duke, seemingly baffled at her ignorance, mimed shoveling—an action with which Arabella was achingly familiar, from her time shoveling coal aboard *Diana*. "Shovel the snow. Off of the paths. So one can walk upon them? Pretty, yes, but the stuff can be a frightful nuisance. This deep, even carriages can't get through."

Suddenly a thought struck her—a thing she recalled from her reading—and the chill seemed to penetrate to her heart. "The snow will remain upon the ground until the weather turns warm, will it not?"

"I imagine so," said the Duke, brushing snow from his jacket sleeves.

Arabella gazed off toward the hills, considering the hundreds and thousands—perhaps millions—of cubic feet of snow she could see, and the Lord only knew how much more lay beyond that. "The weather, though, has been most uncommonly cold. What if it does not go away for weeks, or months?"

"A week, perhaps. Two at the most. Any more would be highly unusual."

"The current system of weather *is* highly unusual," observed the captain, his breath coming out in a cloud above the hand which stroked his chin contemplatively. "Due to the volcanic eruption."

"Humph," said the Duke. "Well, if we are compelled to remain in Brighton for a time, as guests of the Prince, that is not such a terrible fate."

Arabella and the captain exchanged an anxious glance, then— he was, no doubt, concerned about *Diana* and her crew—but, as there was nothing to be done about the situation, they brushed themselves off and returned inside.

---

Compelled to remain they were; the roads to London, all agreed, were completely impassable. But the pavilion was well stocked with foodstuffs, well equipped with entertainments, and fully occupied with the Prince's guests, so no one feared either starvation or boredom.

No one save Arabella. For her, this extended party was a return visit to the heavy, overheated, enervating, tedious Hades of her unwilling sojourn at Marlowe Hall, the family residence in England—not so very many years ago, but it felt like a lifetime. Here she found herself surrounded by her betters—or so they considered themselves—whose interests extended no further than billiards, gambling, horses, and gossip. The Prince's fascination with the latest developments of science and engineering was promising, but she soon learned that his attitude was that of a patron rather than an active participant; he cared only for the results which could be attained and not the means by which they were achieved. And very few of the Prince's entourage shared even that level of interest—except to a shallow, fawning degree.

The pavilion, despite its grandiosity, soon became oppressive to her. Heated to a near Venusian degree, brilliantly lit by searing gas flames, and every where decorated with pretended branches and leaves, it seemed to press in upon her from every side. But going out of doors proved impractical. Though she managed to equip herself with a fur wrap and gloves—a sad approximation to her long-lost, beloved *thukhong*—the cold, wet air chilled her bones in a way that the crisp dry cold of even the deepest Martian winter never had. And her artificial foot, satisfactory though it was upon carpet or even upon rough ground, frequently betrayed her upon the snow and ice, bringing her many blows to her dignity and some serious bruises. She worked with the captain upon improvements, but though they did equip their shoes with cleats to enhance traction, no change they made to the foot itself with the limited resources available seemed to improve its overall stability.

One good thing that came out of Arabella's imprisonment was an acquaintance with Kiernan, the Prince's chief coach-maker, to whom she had been directed while seeking materials to enhance her artificial foot. Because of the Prince's enthusiasms, the coachmaker's usual duties—which already united the skills of carpenter, tailor, and shoemaker—had been extended to many other conveyances and devices, such as the Prince's Merlin chair. To Arabella's disappointment Kiernan had no personal experience of steam power himself—the steam engine was the responsibility of a Scottish engineer, who held its secrets tight to his chest—but he and his workmen had fashioned the chair's frame, wheels, and steering mechanism, and his workshop was to Arabella a wonderland of tools and materials, inhabited by bright, energetic minds of a mechanical bent. Kiernan himself, a heavyset man with thick gray hair and hands as hard as a *huresh* shell, had a ready wit and a tendency to rough humor, which Arabella found refreshing.

Kiernan's workshop was but a small part of the Royal Stables, a vast building in some ways even more lavish than the pavilion which it served. Surmounted by an enormous segmented glass dome, eighty feet in diameter and sixty-five feet high, the structure held stalls for sixty-one horses. The grand circular space beneath the dome, floored with sawdust and smelling, not unpleasantly, of horses and hay, was amazingly light at all hours of the day, and though it was heated, even the Prince's patent stoves could not raise it to the same near-Venusian unpleasantness as the house itself. A second level of galleries, above the stables themselves, gave a splendid view onto the arena, and was luxuriously equipped for the viewing of riding exhibitions and the display of prize animals.

Perhaps most importantly to Arabella, the stables were connected to the pavilion by a long underground passage, which meant that she could visit this blessed space—so cool and so uninhabited by the Prince's set—without risking bruises or chills from the slippery snow outside. According to Kiernan, the widely-known rumor that the passage had been built so that the Prince could have secret rendezvouses with a former mistress was false. It had, instead, been constructed so that the Prince could enjoy riding his horses while avoiding the ridicule of his subjects, his girth at that time having already grown to a quite outrageous extent.

Of course, that had been ten years ago, and the Prince was now even larger and goutier. Kiernan had worked out an apparatus—a sort of platform, raised by screws—which enabled the Prince to be lifted from his Merlin chair and lowered gently into the saddle. In this way he could be seated upon a horse in motion, but it could scarcely be called riding, and though the Prince had been suitably grateful for Kiernan's work and every one had applauded his ingenuity, the public reaction to the invention had been scorn and hilarity, and the experiment had not been repeated.

---

"Here, let me show you a thing," Kiernan said to Arabella one day. She had just escaped the billiards-room, where a tedious billiards tournament among the more enthusiastic gentlemen threatened to extend all day and well into the night. "It had just arrived from Germany when the snows came down," he said as he led her to the arena, "and it strikes me as just the sort of thing you might appreciate."

The item was a peculiar contrivance, a sort of half-carriage— it had a wooden frame and two iron-shod wheels, but unlike any gig or curricle she had ever seen the wheels were set in tandem, one behind the other, with a padded leather saddle for a single rider between them. It also lacked pole, yoke, traces, or any other visible means to attach a horse or other animal. "How is it drawn?" she asked.

"It is not drawn at all!" Kiernan replied with a laugh. "It is *pushed*, with the driver's feet!" He demonstrated by swinging his leg over the saddle—once seated, his toes barely touched the ground—and pushing himself forward with a sort of extended walking motion. Amazingly, the two-wheeled device did not immediately tumble over on its side, but remained upright, albeit in an extremely precarious fashion, as Kiernan drove it in a great circle around the arena.

"How does it not fall over?" she marveled aloud as Kiernan returned to his starting place.

"I do not entirely understand it myself," Kiernan confessed, "but it has to do with the angle of the front wheel." He moved the tiller which controlled the wheel to one side and then the other. "It requires considerable practice to keep the thing upright, a skill which I have as yet barely begun to acquire. But, once the knack is acquired, a skilled operator can stride with the speed of a trotting horse!"

Arabella inspected the machine carefully, noting that the wheels rode on brass bushings to reduce friction. The device was called a *Laufmaschine,* German for "running machine," by its inventor, one Baron von Drais; in his honor—and preferring to avoid the harsh German consonants—the English called it a *Draisine.* "May I try it?"

"By all means. I will walk along with you until you catch the trick."

Arabella's dress proved rather an impediment to her mounting the device properly, but she soon abandoned decency and tied up the excess fabric with leather laces, girding her loins like an ancient Philistine. Kiernan, an older gentleman with much experience of the world's vagaries, took this impropriety in stride. Once mounted, though, her first few attempts at driving the machine ended quickly and awkwardly, with Kiernan catching her as she began to tumble over. But after a little practice, she reached the point that she could wobble along for a few feet by herself. The sensation was exhilarating and a bit frightening, the lightness and smooth rapidity of the motion—not to mention the roiling of her stomach—reminding her in some ways of her first experience of free descent. "My goodness!" she gasped after her longest voyage, a distance of some fifteen feet, during which Kiernan was compelled to jog to keep up with her. "I believe that is quite enough for one day. But I hope to repeat the experience before departing Brighton, if I may."

"You are always welcome in my workshop, ma'am," he replied with a bow. "I am grateful to find in you an appreciative audience for my enthusiasms."

Arabella rearranged her clothing—her dress had become rather badly wrinkled and soiled, but she considered the experience well worth the cost—and took her leave. But as she walked the long tunnel back to the pavilion, her mind whirled with practices, methods, and possible improvements to the device.

Upon returning to the main pavilion—its surfeit of counterfeit *Vénuserie,* its glaring gas lamps, and its suffocating heat even more oppressive to her after her clean exhilarating flight on the Draisine—before she could ascend the stairs to her bedchamber she was met by none other than the Prince. "Ah, there you are," he said as his conveyance chugged up to her. "I was told you had gone to the stables, and was just going thence to meet with you." Unusually, he was alone, lacking the crowd of sycophants and hangers-on which generally accompanied him.

"I am in no fit state to meet with a Prince, Your Royal Highness," she said, managing to gesture to her soiled dress and execute a tolerable curtsey at the same time.

"Pish pish," he replied, gesturing negligently. "We are all friends here. Come, I must have a word with you." He puttered off down the long gallery, forcing Arabella to walk at a brisk pace to keep up. Her thighs immediately reminded her that they had just recently undergone an unusual exertion, and did not enjoy being called upon for this additional task so soon.

The Prince led her to an anteroom she had not visited before, and shut the door behind her. Her heart hammered at the sudden isolation—not so much because she feared impropriety as because she had no idea what the Prince Regent might ask of her and, as he was her acting sovereign, she knew that she could not deny him any request.

"Pray take a seat," the Prince said. Arabella did so, recognizing even as she did that this was not only a generous offer of comfort but also brought her down to the Prince's level, removing her advantage of height. "This regards your husband, as well as yourself." He paused, tapping his fingertips together. "How old are you, if I may ask?"

"Twenty, Your Royal Highness."

Again he waved away the honorific. "As I thought, exactly the same age as my dear daughter, the Princess Caroline. You remind me of her in many ways. She, too, is headstrong and irrepressible . . . though at least, unlike you, she has never run away to Mars, ha ha!"

"Indeed she has not," Arabella temporized.

"It is perhaps because of this resemblance," the Prince continued, "in addition to your heroism and great service to the Empire, that I feel very kindly toward you. And so I wish to grant you and your husband a great boon."

"A boon, sir?" Arabella's heart pounded still harder.

The Prince sat back in his chair, looking down his nose and across his steepled fingertips with what she imagined he thought was a benevolent expression. "Now that Bonaparte has been definitively defeated, England finds herself the sole decisive power in the entire solar system. But other nations—and not only human nations!—will soon attempt to fill the spaces vacated by the Great Tyrant, like rats moving in after the dog has chased the cat away. I have been approached by a coalition of men from the Admiralty and the Honorable Mars Company, who intend to take the battle to these rats before they can attain a foot-hold!"

"What has this to do with me?"

"Mars!" the Prince shouted, striking the arm of his chair with his closed fist. "Mars will be one of the chief battle-fields in this coming war. Did you know that Saint George's Land covers less than seven per cent of its surface area? *Seven per cent!* The entire remainder of the planet belongs to those filthy Martians."

Arabella pressed her lips together, rather than angrily correcting His Royal Highness on the topic of Martians as was her first impulse. It was their planet, after all, and the English colony merely a guest thereon. But if Lady Corey were here, she would certainly advise Arabella that to contradict the Prince Regent in his own home on a topic clearly dear to his heart would be both impolite and impolitic.

"Mars is the only source of the special wood of which our

aerial ships are constructed," he continued, lecturing her upon a topic with which she was intimately familiar, "and Martian steel is the finest in the solar system. England *must* control Mars, for the sake of her future!"

"But surely, with Napoleon's defeat, England no longer has any significant rivals in this?"

"The Martians themselves, my dear," he said as though addressing an ignorant child. "*They* are our rivals. You may think them primitives"—she did not, not by any means—"but they are warlike and ambitious, and some of them are most exceedingly shrewd! And now that we have dealt with Bonaparte, we can devote our full energies to bringing them to heel."

"But *why*, Your Highness? We have traded with the Martians quite amicably for generations. Surely there is no need for this to change?"

"They have been content to leave the defense of their planet from Napoleon and suchlike warlords to us, and now that that threat has been removed they may feel free to move against us! It is only by dint of treaties, and lack of expertise, that they lack aerial ships of their own . . . and we cannot rely upon this situation to continue if we do not take measures to enforce it."

"Your argument makes no—no difference, Your Highness." She had been about to say *no sense*. "The Martians have no ambitions to empire!"

"Nor have I, child, nor have I. But I am assured—I am assured by both the Admiralty and the Honorable Mars Company— that the possibility, indeed the likelihood, exists. Furthermore, the profits to be realized from English dominance of Mars are well-nigh incalculable."

The Prince Regent delivered that last sentence in an offhand manner, but the expression on his face as he uttered the word "profits" showed that it was more significant to him than he let on. The effect was subtle, but suddenly she suspected she understood the real purpose of the Prince, the Mars Company, and perhaps even the Admiralty in this scheme. And she was horrified.

Her first impulse was to rise, spit in his face, and stride from the room. But she must confirm her suspicions. Recalling the words of Lady Hertford, regarding the Prince's sense of self-importance, she leaned forward and smeared a smile across her face. "Oh, but Prinny, you have so much money already! Surely mere profit is of no significance to you."

"Ah, that is where you are wrong, my dear," he replied with a matching smile—causing her to wonder just how sincere any of his previous smiles had been. "I am, in fact, most grievously constrained by Parliament—grievously! My position, my responsibilities . . . they require, absolutely require, me to furnish myself and my household in accordance with my station. But given the paltry pittance provided me by my father, with the collusion of Parliament, I have been forced to borrow the necessary funds, to such an extent that I am now burdened with a truly mountainous debt. But with the assistance of my friends in the Mars Company, who in exchange for my help in this matter are prepared to share with me a portion of the funds realized, I will be able to discharge this debt and return my full attentions to the grandeur and glorification of England!"

"But what of the Admiralty? Surely they care nothing for mere capital?"

"Indeed they do not. But a soldier, or an airman, deprived of the opportunity for glory—cast ashore on half-pay, as the Navy men say—is an unhappy creature indeed. With Napoleon's defeat, they find themselves staring idleness in the face. A new campaign, such as one to pacify the Martians, would give them reason to live." And, Arabella reflected, continued income, and authority within the government. "Which brings me to my original point," the Prince continued. "This scheme requires, absolutely requires, a man to lead it—a very particular kind of man. And with your Captain Singh's long experience in the Mars Company, and with his demonstrated and quite innovative military mind, he is the very man for the job. But, for some reason, he seems reluctant to accept the position, despite the many emoluments we have offered."

Arabella's sense of love and pride in her captain swelled at this evidence of his strength of character in the face of considerable persuasion from above. "It is, of course, his decision to make," she said in a neutral tone.

"So it is. Ah, but no man is immune to a woman's charms." He raised one finger. "Especially a lovely young woman such as yourself. And so I approach *you* with an additional enticement: if your husband agrees to participate in this scheme, and if it is successful, I shall create him the First Duke of Mars, and you his Duchess." He smiled benevolently. "You have your Prince Regent's word on this."

The offer was breathtaking in its magnanimity—it promised land, riches, and influence for herself and her posterity, forevermore—and yet Arabella found her heart shrinking to a cold hard lump in her chest. "I thank you for your generosity, Your Royal Highness," she said, bowing her head in deep respect—and to conceal the expression on her face. "I shall convey this offer to my husband."

"Pray encourage him to give it the most serious consideration. But we must move quickly. If he does not accede before we return to London, we will be forced to approach the next most satisfactory candidate." He shook his head in anticipatory disappointment. "I do hope he will agree."

------

"A generous offer indeed," Captain Singh said, turning away from her to regard the three-quarter moon shining upon the snowy drifts outside their bedchamber window. "I have asked for more time to consider this opportunity, but apparently he felt that he must apply additional pressure on me, through you."

She stepped up behind him, wrapping her arms around his waist and leaning her cheek upon the warm buff fabric of his jacket. "He seems to place great faith in the persuasive abilities of women upon their men."

He turned and embraced her in return. For a time they breathed together, each with their own thoughts.

"The ambition of the Prince's scheme is breathtaking," he said after a time. "The consequences, should it succeed, are enormous; those if it should fail are beyond prediction. I must confess that it frightens me." Arabella looked up into her captain's face and saw no sign of fear, but his usual calm self-assurance was marred by a crease of worry between his brows. "My intuition is that this scheme is wrongheaded, misguided, or worse. But if the Directors of the Mars Company, the Lords of the Admiralty, and His Royal Highness command it, I cannot shirk my responsibility. When I received my Letter of Denization, I swore an oath of allegiance"—he straightened in her arms and spoke as though declaiming from memory—"to be faithful and bear true allegiance to His Majesty King George the Third, his heirs and successors, according to law, so help me God." He relaxed then, though only slightly. "And the Prince Regent, whatever his other qualities, *is* the King's heir and successor; the allegiance I owe to him, *personally,* is required by my most solemn oath."

Arabella felt the weight of the responsibility upon her husband's shoulders as though it had settled upon her own. "You owe him nothing more than consideration. He has only requested your assistance, not commanded it."

"That is true. But still—it is clearly his strong desire." He sighed. "On a previous occasion in my life, as you know, I defied my sovereign father. Though I cannot regret that choice—it brought me together with you, after all, among many other wonderful things—it also carried with it so much pain . . . I do not know that I have the strength to do so again."

"But you *must*! For England to impose its will upon the entire planet would be . . . unconscionable! We are *guests* of the Martians, no more!"

"I cannot disagree. Yet if I decline this opportunity, the undertaking will surely continue, with some other man at the helm. Through my participation I may be able to prevent the worst excesses."

Arabella's heart ached at his dilemma, surely only a pale echo of the pain her husband must be facing, but she felt she must stand up for the Martians. "This scheme is so abhorrent that no amelioration is sufficient. It must be nipped in the bud! And for you to take a principled stand against it, now, while you have the Prince's ear, is our best—perhaps our last—opportunity to do so." She embraced him tightly. "I have every confidence that you will make the right decision, despite all influences."

"I am not at all certain what the right decision is."

---

At dinner that night, Arabella's table companion was Lord Foley, whose youth and vigor—he had acceded to Parliament at the age of twenty-one—belied his staunchly Whiggish opinions. "Surely," he said to Arabella after swallowing a mouthful of *filet de boeuf en croûte*, "your constant exposure to Martians, from such a young age, must have convinced you of their inferiority!"

"Quite the opposite, sir," she replied frostily.

"But they are *savages*!" he insisted, pounding the butt of his silver fork upon the damask. "They have no literature, no art or science, and no proper religion at all!"

"They have many religions, each as properly constituted and

regulated as any of our own, and can any mere mortal ever be certain which is the most valid, until we depart this life for the next? Their literature, I am assured, is extensive and profound, though my command of their written languages is insufficient to testify from personal experience. And their arts and sciences, especially the decorative and architectural, are beyond question. Are we not at this very moment dining in a pavilion built in imitation of their model?"

"Imitation? Inspiration, at most. I am certain that it is far superior to any thing on Mars, in quality of construction as well as in beauty. I have seen colored plates of the best Mars has to offer, and this pavilion is far lighter and airier than those heaps of stone."

"Those *heaps of stone*, as you would have them, are evidence of the superiority of Martian architecture! Despite their beauty . . . and they *are* beautiful, sir,"—for her interlocutor's face betrayed his incredulity at this statement—"they are built to withstand any assault, and many have stood unconquered for centuries!"

"Against spears and stones, perhaps," he sniffed. "Which are, of course, the best Mars has to offer. Against English cannon they would stand not a chance."

"I have myself faced both stones and cannonballs, and I assure you that Martian catapults are every bit as deadly as English cannon. In any case, the only reason the Martians are restricted to spears and stones—not to mention their lack of aerial ships—is the treaties we have imposed upon them. I am certain that, absent these restrictions, they would develop machineries of warfare equal to, or perhaps even superior to, our own!"

"All the more reason they must be subjugated!" he cried, and the lady beside him glared at the eruption. "For their own good as well as ours. For if they are allowed to put these warlike ambitions into practice, they might be tempted to invade England!

And should that catastrophe come to pass, they would inevitably be eradicated by our superior forces."

"The Martians," she replied evenly, "are not so stupid as to attempt such a thing. Unlike some I could name."

---

After that disastrous conversation—which had, at least, ended in stony silence rather than fisticuffs—Arabella insisted upon an after-dinner walk in the snow with her husband. "They have no idea what they are on about!" she cried, clutching his bicep as they walked side by side. "Foolhardy English ambition will be the ruination of England as well as Mars."

"I must remind you that, in the absence of English ambition as regards Mars, your family fortune, and indeed your own sweet self, might never have existed."

"But both England and Mars might be better off." She sighed. "I cannot deny that my family and I have been the beneficiaries of a . . . questionable history. If I were somehow to become Queen of Mars, I would certainly wish to restore the ownership of the *khoresh*-plantations to the Martians in some fashion. But the rights of the English owners, many of whom have held and diligently managed the property for generations, cannot be ignored either." Again she sighed. "It is a difficult question."

"All of the most interesting questions are difficult." And then he lapsed into silence.

"I know that you face a difficult question of your own," she put in after a time. The silence continued, relieved only by the crunch of snow underfoot. "You know my opinions on the topic."

"Indeed. As does every one at table to-night."

She paused, turned, and took both of his hands in hers. "I *cannot* play the silent, supportive wife in this. The lives of thousands, perhaps millions, both Martians and humans, will be ir-revocably changed by your decision."

"That is true no matter which alternative I choose." His dark eyes glistened in the gas-light reflected from the snow at their feet. "Responsibility to those millions, and further millions yet unborn, as well as loyalty to crown and country, may demand that I accept command of this scheme . . . even though I reject its premises."

"But you may be the only person who can bring it to a halt! The Prince Regent respects you. Lodge your objections with him, in the most strenuous terms, and saner heads may yet prevail."

"Perhaps. Yet I fear the hour has grown too late."

And with that ambiguous statement, he directed their steps back to the house.

# 3

## DIFFICULT DECISIONS

Days passed, endless days of cards and billiards and constant, tedious gossip. The snow outside grew crystalline, changing in character day by day as the Sun warmed it each day and the night froze it anew. Paths were trampled through the snow by the more adventurous, and a few brave carriages came through from town with letters and supplies, but by all accounts the roads to London were still impassible. Captain Singh spent his days in earnest discussion with Reid, Dundas, and the other projectors of the scheme, but continued to withhold judgement upon his own participation in it.

Arabella spent as much time as she could in the Royal Stables, away from the sweltering heat and incessant prattle of the pavilion. She grew proficient in propelling the Draisine about the arena—remaining upright for as long as she wished, driving in figures-of-eight, achieving quite breathtaking speeds, and bringing herself to a stop exactly where she desired—and spent the time between these exercises with Kiernan, discussing possible improvements to the machine.

"Aboard ship," she told him, "we use a system of pedals and belts, powered by the muscles of the crew's legs, to turn the propulsive sails which drive the ship forward in the absence of a favorable wind. Surely you have noted the mighty calves and thighs which mark an airman?"

"I have," he said, gazing off into the distance—in clear avoidance of a glance at her own lower limbs, which displayed some of the same development. She wore a borrowed pair of workmen's breeches for her work with the Draisine, a habit which would surely have driven her mother to apoplexy but which the elderly coachmaker took well in stride.

"I was thinking," she went on as though she had not noticed Kiernan's reaction, "that a similar set of pedals could be fitted to the Draisine, possibly producing even greater speed and efficiency . . . and also sparing the operator's footwear." She had worn the toes of her favorite Mars-made half-boots entirely through in her first day's work with the machine. Though the royal bootmaker had already repaired them, the damage was still painful to her.

"A capital idea! I shall have my workmen look into it immediately." He held the machine upright while Arabella dismounted. "It will provide a relief from this infernal, enforced idleness."

--------

At last there came a day when the Sun beat down upon the snow with such force that it began to retreat, laying bare the brown and sodden ground upon which it had lain for so long. A coach arrived from London, the horses mud-spattered and weary, with news that Nelson's body was now lying in state in the Painted

Hall at the Greenwich Hospital, with a grand funeral procession scheduled for two days hence. "We must attend," the Prince proclaimed at dinner that evening . . . a simple statement of fact, which was nonetheless greeted by toasts and resounding hurrahs.

Conversation over dinner and afterward was almost entirely devoted to the forthcoming funeral. A Grand River Procession on the Thames from Greenwich to London was planned, with Nelson's coffin borne by one of the royal barges, followed by a flotilla of the nobility and all the City Livery Companies. The coffin would then be transferred to an ornate funeral car—built to resemble Nelson's flagship *Bucephalus* and hung with all of his trophies—and carried through the streets with a military escort, finally to be delivered at St. Paul's for a triumphant state funeral. The whole procession and funeral would take three days. All the world would be in attendance, including every member of the English nobility and heads of state from all over Europe, and tickets to the ceremony were a treasure greater than rubies.

But Arabella, though she did her best to participate in the conversation, sharing again and again the story of her personal encounter with the late Admiral, found her mind occupied with other thoughts. The return to London, she knew, marked the end of their idyll in Brighton, a return to crowds, the renewed pressure of society . . . and the requirement for Captain Singh's decision upon participation on the Prince Regent's scheme for the subjugation of Mars.

Though she and her husband had talked of nearly no other thing in the past few days, she was still not certain what his decision should be—nor, she felt, was he. His hesitation showed that he knew the enormity of the Prince's scheme was too vast to contemplate, yet duty, that shining beacon which had guided him throughout his career, drew him ever forth.

During a lull in the dinner conversation, Arabella looked down the table to Captain Singh, who, along with Dundas,

Reid, and the other projectors, was now seated much closer to the Prince Regent. As the conversation on Nelson's funeral prattled about him like aerial cross-currents around an asteroid, he stared down at his plate . . . silent, morose, preoccupied.

She did not envy him in this conundrum. Yet she trusted that he would eventually come to the right decision . . . the only possible humane decision.

"You simply must try the venison," her table companion prompted her, "before it grows cold."

Arabella raised a forkful, chewed, swallowed. "It is delicious," she said.

It might as well have been sand in her mouth.

———————————

After dinner that night, when the gentlemen returned to the withdrawing-room after their port and cigars, Captain Singh was not among them . . . nor was the Prince. Thus it was that, after all the other gentlemen had collected their companions and retired, Arabella found herself alone with Lady Hertford.

"I expect that Prinny is pressing your husband for a decision regarding his offer," the great lady said, dismissing the servants with a wave of her hand and conducting Arabella to a private corner. "His hesitation in this matter has been most vexing."

"I imagine you are correct." Arabella bit her lip, wishing for a cup of tea or hand of cards to distract her worried mind. If only there were some *action* she could take!

"You do not wish him to accede." It was not a question. Arabella's opinions on the matter were far from secret.

"I am a child of Mars, my lady."

"You are also a subject of His Majesty."

She acknowledged this truth with a nod. "Yet in this instance I feel there is more at stake than simple loyalty."

"Loyalty is never simple, my dear." She sat, patting the settee beside her, and Arabella sat as indicated, drawn as though by a sudden increase in gravity. "And you are not the only one with multiple loyalties here."

"Oh?"

Lady Hertford leaned forward just fractionally, lowering her voice so that Arabella was compelled to pay close attention. "I fear that Prinny is being used, as much as your husband."

"What?" Arabella gasped.

"Hush, child. This is women's work, and women's work must be conducted quietly." She leaned forward still further. "I have just this evening learned from Lady Reid that Lord Reid, contrary to his public statements, privately resents your husband's success and fame. The term 'uppish darkie' may have been used."

"B-but why . . . ?" Arabella stammered. She had seen no sign of such sentiments from Reid . . . though this revelation made her consider certain attitudes and statements of his in a new light.

"Why does he support him so firmly in public? An excellent question. I suspect—and this is only a suspicion, mind—that his intent is to raise Captain Singh up, and then by some intrigue to cause him to fail, and thus be brought low."

"But how could he possibly . . . ? If Captain Singh fails, the Company fails!"

"Multiple loyalties, madam. The Company is a beast with many heads. It may be that a failure in one area can open opportunities in others." She shrugged. "Or perhaps not. Do not underestimate the importance of personal resentment in even the largest decisions. In any event, this new intelligence causes me to suspect the entire scheme. If Lord Reid does indeed intend Captain Singh to fail, that implies that the true aim of his plan is something other than what he has presented to Prinny and the

Admiralty. . . . which implies, in turn, that the scheme is in the Company's, or at least his own, best interest and not in England's."

"W—why have you not brought your suspicions to the Prince yourself?"

"This information has just reached my ears this evening." Lady Hertford sighed. "But my influence upon him is not as great as most people suppose. When his mind is firmly fixed upon some goal he is not easily dissuaded, especially by what he would certainly dismiss as mere gossip." She shook her head. "I am afraid that the scheme itself cannot be stopped. But you may be able to rescue your husband from it."

"I . . . I thank you for this intelligence."

"You are most welcome. But I am afraid I must ask that you not disclose where you learned it . . . to *any one*. Do I make myself clear?"

"Perfectly." Arabella rose. "Now I must beg your ladyship's leave."

"Of course." She held out a hand, and Arabella clasped it. "Brave heart, dear."

---

It was well past midnight when Captain Singh returned to their bedchamber. The door creaked open quietly—clearly he expected her to already be asleep—but instead she stood at the foot of the bed, fully clothed and trembling with anxiety. She had not even sat down since speaking to Lady Hertford, instead pacing endlessly in the narrow space beside the bed.

"I have received some vital intelligence," Arabella said, before he could even close the door. "Lord Reid's heart is secretly set against you."

Captain Singh's head jerked backward at this revelation. "What?"

"He despises your color and creed, and resents your accomplishments. This implies that his public support of you is false, and that he secretly intends you to fail. His mendacity upon this topic makes the entire scheme suspect."

He blinked, turned, gently closed the door, turned back. His frown was thunderous.

"Well?" she prompted, when he did not speak.

"I cannot believe this." His gaze was directed to the floor, but his attention was elsewhere. "Reid is a man of impeccable honor, who has . . ." He paused, considering. ". . . who has hardly ever displayed any disapproval of my background." He thought a bit longer, then shook his head and looked to Arabella. "No. I *cannot* believe this. What is your source for this information?"

"I may not say."

To his credit, he accepted this with a slight nod. "Very well. But are you certain of it? Is there any possibility that your source could have some ulterior motive?"

"I . . ." She knew herself to be naive in the ways of court gossip. Could she herself be a pawn in some scheme of Lady Hertford's? "I must confess I cannot be absolutely certain. But, even so . . . this new intelligence is only one more stain upon an already filthy scheme. Even if you do not accept its veracity, you *must* decline the Prince's offer. For your own safety—for the sake of Mars—for the sake of simple human dignity—you *cannot* participate in this horrific scheme of subjugation!"

He turned away from her, facing the half-open wardrobe door. "I do not doubt your sincerity," he replied. His voice echoed in the empty wardrobe; most of their clothing had already been packed away by the Prince's servants for the morrow's journey to London. "However, after discussions with the Prince Regent and representatives of the Company and the Navy, I have come to the conclusion that, if properly supervised, this plan can be put into action with minimal loss of life and property, both English and Martian."

The implication of his carefully chosen words was distressingly clear. "And *you* are to be the one to properly supervise it?"

He hung his head, still facing the wardrobe. "Yes. I have informed His Royal Highness that I will accept the position he has offered me. I am to be Fleet Commander for the Royal Navy's Mars Expeditionary Force, and thereafter First Duke of Mars. The announcement is to be made at Nelson's funeral ceremony."

Command. Responsibility. Authority.

Land. Riches. Peerage.

Yet the emotion in his voice was like that she would have expected if the news were that he had been diagnosed with some fatal disease.

Arabella's own sentiments were even more desolate, for not only must she contemplate his service and its consequences, but she must consider his betrayal of the principles she thought they had held in common. "How *could* you?" she burst out.

"I had no choice," he replied, and now he did turn back to her. His face was hard, unmoving—a death-mask of his usual imperturbable self. "I swore an oath."

"You *cannot* participate in the subjugation of the Martian people!" she said, feeling tears forming at the bottoms of her eyes. She blinked hard, willing them back to the well from which they came. "You know how important they are to me! Consider Khema, who saved your life!"

"I did consider your sentiments, my love. But the scheme will certainly go forward whether or not I accept this appointment. By taking command myself, I will at least be in a position to prevent the worst errors and excesses. And I hope that you will help me in this, with your superior knowledge of the Martian culture and language."

"You say 'culture' and 'language' as though there were only one!" she spat. "This . . . this *enormity* you contemplate will affect the entire planet—hundreds of cultures and dozens of languages! I cannot—I *will* not!—assist you in this madness. It is a fool's errand, and will bring nothing but bloodshed and ruin!"

"I . . ." He paused, then allowed his gaze to fall to Arabella's feet. "I am truly sorry. I have no alternative."

"Please!" she cried. She covered the distance between them in a single step, placed her hands upon his shoulders, and squeezed hard. "You *cannot* do this despicable thing. It is not too late! We can leave here this instant—take a coach to London—take *Diana* to Mars—and warn the Martians of the invasion that is coming their way! Even a few months' warning could make all the difference!"

He did not look up. He did not meet her eyes. He ignored the pressure upon his shoulders, which must be painful. "Mars is in conjunction," he said without emotion. Meaning, of course, that the two planets were on opposite sides of the Sun—the worst possible situation for a rapid, easy passage from one to the other.

"All the more reason to depart immediately!" A white fleck of her spittle landed on the dark brown skin of his cheek. He did not reach to wipe it off. "It will be a long journey and we must begin *now!*"

Gently—oh, so gently—he reached up and removed first one, then the other of her hands from his shoulders. Still not meeting her eyes, he held both of her hands in his and said, "I cannot. I am His Royal Highness's subject and I must do as he commands."

Arabella snatched her hands from her husband's and stamped her foot. It was the artificial foot, and the shock ran up its rigid brass and wood to jar painfully against her stump. She accepted the pain—practically reveled in it, as it echoed and amplified the pain in her heart. "Very well!" she cried. "If you will not take me to Mars, then perhaps Fox will!"

Pausing only to snatch up her fur wrap, bonnet, and gloves, she dashed from the room.

"Mrs. Singh!" came the captain's call from behind her. "Do not do this."

She paused, breathing hard, looking down the hall and toward the stairs. The heat was intolerable, the ceramic Venusian gods ludicrous. "You may refer to me as Ashby," she said without turning, then continued on her way.

# 4

---

## TREASON

Arabella wiped her eyes as she hurried down the stairs, propelled by grim determination. She had no plan, no course of action in mind—she knew only that she could not bear to remain here, trapped in this farcical burlesque of a Martian-Venusian palace with the grotesque Prince, his simpering coterie, and her faithless husband.

But even as Arabella's feet carried her unconsciously down-ward, the soles of her boots tapping rapidly upon the stair treads, a plan began to form in her mind. And so, as she reached the base of the stairs, she did not proceed down the long gallery toward the entrance-hall, but doubled back . . . heading for the underground passage to the Royal Stables.

The passage itself was chill and plain, uncluttered with either the Prince's patent stoves or his execrable taste in *Vénuserie*, and as she clopped along its hard stone floor her tears dried in the wind of her motion, replaced by a cold hard anger and a will to action.

She paused at the end of the passage, just before the door to the Royal Stables, and hiked up her skirts. Removing a brass winding-key from its recess by her artificial right ankle, she inserted it into its hole and wound the foot's mainspring to its maximum torsion. She might not have another opportunity any time soon to pause and wind her foot, and it would not do to have it run down unexpectedly in the midst of her escape.

Removing the key from its hole, she turned it over in her fingers, feeling its smooth brass and recalling how she and Captain Singh had selected it—of all the available keys, it had been the one with the smoothest finish, most suited in size and shape to the task at hand. But before the tears could start anew, she gripped the key in her fist, jammed it roughly back into its recess, straightened, and swept her skirts back into position. Then she seized the door handle, took a breath, let it out, and stepped into the Royal Stables.

The arena stood dark and still, the air cold and a bright full moon shining down through the glass panes above. As she stepped briskly across the sawdust of the arena floor—the mechanism of her artificial foot just audible in the silence—one of the horses stabled near the arena raised its head, whickering a question. But she passed the stables without pause, heading for Kiernan's workshop.

The workshop stood empty at this hour, but the Draisine was exactly where she had last seen it—its brass fittings gleaming in the moonlight, the modifications they had discussed now complete. She bent and inspected the work, finding it satisfactory. The machine awaited only a test ride, to see how well the modifications worked.

The test ride would be to-night. She hoped there would be no serious problems.

The breeches she had been using also hung in their accustomed place, not far away. Heedless of possible observation, she hiked her skirts up to her waist and slipped the breeches on, tying the skirts in place with leather thongs. Another thong served to fix her bonnet to her head. The fur wrap she fastened about her shoulders as best she could, and her fine fur-lined gloves—a gift from the Port-Admiral—she pulled on and adjusted carefully, to avoid any wrinkles on the palms. She knew she could not afford blisters.

She also could not afford the Draisine itself, of course, but its theft weighed lightly on her conscience. For the Prince could easily bear the expense, and furthermore he was in no position to make use of the stolen item himself. Not to mention that the pedals were Arabella's own invention, and she no longer had any desire to share her innovation with him.

Arabella walked the machine across the workshop to the door that led outside. A cold wind blew against it, making it rattle on its hinges and blowing sawdust around her feet. Grimly she adjusted her gloves, her wrap, and her bonnet, then eased the door open.

A blast of frigid air struck her in the face, making her eyes tear up. Squinting against the cold, she quickly walked the machine outside and shut the door behind herself.

Then she mounted the modified Draisine and rode off into the darkness.

---

The first half-hour of the ride was a tricky, juddering, slippery near-panic, as she learned how to work the pedals, manage the steering, and avoid running into trees all at the same time. Not only was the pedal mechanism entirely new—within the first mile she had already made mental notes of a half-dozen changes which would improve it substantially—but this was the first time she had ever driven the Draisine under the open sky, at night, *or* on rough ground, never mind all three at once. But the night, though cold and windy, was clear—Earth's enormous moon shone down full and bright, illuminating her path most satisfactorily—and she soon learned the trick of keeping herself upright with the machine's new configuration.

As she had expected, the pedals allowed her to make even better speed than the machine's original design, and with less effort. The motion was strange—traveling swiftly down the road with a smooth rotary motion of the legs, her head not going up and down as it usually did while walking, running, or riding, but rolling along at a constant height. It was also unlike riding in a curricle, for no horse or *huresh* clopped along before her; she, herself, was the vehicle's only motive power. The experience was, all in all, very nearly like flying . . . except for the harsh vibration of the road's rough surface, transmitted through the iron rims and wooden spokes of the Draisine's wheels. Only the machine's leather seat, and the natural padding of her own fundament, provided any relief from the continual jarring shocks. This, she thought, was another area where improvements would be necessary.

The wind in her face was brutally cold—from it she estimated her speed at between six and eight miles per hour, even more down hill—but the rest of her soon grew overheated from the exertion. She tried loosening her fur wrap at the throat, but the chill air upon her perspiring skin was even more uncomfortable and she soon tightened it again.

On and on she pedaled, mile upon mile, hour upon hour—her feelings of anger and betrayal propelling her forward through snow, ice, slush, and growing fatigue like a great propulsive sail at her back. Again and again she wobbled and slid on a rock or a patch of ice; sometimes she was able to recover, but other times she and her machine fell heavily to the hard, icy ground. Her clothing soon grew ragged and torn, and filthy with mud and blood, but, fortunately, despite the high gravity neither she nor the Draisine was ever seriously injured.

Many another person, she thought, would be unable to keep

up the effort so long, but aboard *Diana* she had frequently pedaled for an entire watch—four hours—without the slightest pause, and on the long chase while fleeing the French aboard *Touchstone* she had pedaled for ten hours or more at a stretch.

But unlike pedaling a ship, where the air belowdecks was still, hot, dark, clamorous, and rank from the breath of dozens of airmen, here she pedaled in chill silence—save for the rush of the wind in her ears—with a constantly changing vista under the clear pale light of the moon.

It was very nearly pleasant.

Or so she told herself.

She pressed onward.

———————————

As Arabella pedaled and pedaled, the full moon crept downward to her left, marking the passage of the hours from midnight toward dawn. Though the effort of pedaling kept her warm—or warmer, at any rate, than she would otherwise have been—the evening's chill grew still deeper as the night advanced and her hands, face, and foot became first icy, then painful, then alarmingly numb. Her stump, too, began to ache dreadfully from the cold and from the repeated, unaccustomed motion and pressure. She continued pedaling.

Her palms blistered, despite her gloves. The blisters broke open. She continued pedaling.

She lost count of the number of times she fell. In one such fall she received a nasty abrasion on her cheek, which stung and persisted in bleeding despite the numbing cold. She continued pedaling.

She met no one and encountered nothing other than endless roads and icy trees and fields crusted with patchy snow. She continued pedaling.

Until she came upon a road sign which brought her to a shuddering halt.

CROYDON, it said, with an arrow pointing to the right.

Suddenly her eyes, already moist from the cold wind of her passage, became so flooded with tears that her vision was completely obliterated and her cheeks crackled with freezing salt water.

Croydon. The nearest sizable town to Marlowe Hall, the Ashby family home in England. She had noted it in passing as the Prince's caravan had passed through on its way to Brighton, and had considered that she ought to visit her sisters as long as she was in the vicinity. But the very thought of facing her mother was intimidating, and at the time there had seemed no urgency to the idea, so she had allowed it to languish.

But now she was cold, exhausted, and despondent, and only four-fifths of the way from Brighton to Greenwich, where *Diana* and *Touchstone* were docked.

A very small detour—less than half an hour, at the Draisine's speed—and she could have a bed, a hot bath, a change of clothes.

She would also have to confront her mother, whom she had not seen since her sudden and unexpected departure from her cousin's home in Oxfordshire three years earlier. The very prospect was nearly as chilling as the wind in her face.

But after a long, long pause she pushed the tiller to the left, directing her machine to the right—toward Croydon, and Marlowe Hall, and her sisters . . . and her mother.

---

It was Cole, the butler, who met her at the door. He wore a dressing-gown and slippers, and his nightcap sat askew upon his head. "Miss Ashby!" he cried, astonished. From the expression on his face in the light of the lantern he carried, she must look a dreadful fright.

"It is Mrs. Singh now," she said with as much dignity as she could muster. Her voice creaked from cold and disuse. "May I come in?"

"Of course, of course!"

Arabella did her very best to maintain decorum and composure as she entered. She would *not* show weakness in front of her mother. But as soon as she had crossed the threshold, something— the warmth of the air within, or the familiarity of the surroundings, or perhaps some quality of the Ashby house's timbers—sapped the strength from her limbs and she collapsed in Cole's arms.

"Help!" he cried, struggling under the unexpected weight. "Oh, help!"

"The Draisine . . ." she muttered, as the cook and stable-boy hurried to his aid. "Bring it into the stable . . ."

And then, quite against her will, she fell asleep.

———————————

Arabella woke in her own bed, warm and safe and nestled between crisp cotton sheets, and for a moment she marveled at the implausibility of the long, strange, complex dream in which she had been ensnared. And then she woke fully, and realized that the dream had, in fact, been nothing more than reality . . . and that it was, indeed, still continuing. Her eyes snapped open and she sat upright with a gasp.

"Arabella!" her mother cried, sitting up in the chair which stood near the head of the bed. She, too, had apparently been asleep. In a sudden and uncharacteristically uninhibited moment she embraced Arabella with firm and tender affection, and Arabella gripped her mother's shoulders with equal warmth.

There were tears.

Eventually the moment passed, and Arabella sat back against her pillow, wiping her eyes and nose with the corner of her duvet cover—her very familiar duvet cover, with the Ashby monogram she had herself embroidered on its hem. Her mother leaned close, laying one finger gently upon her daughter's abraded cheek. "We will have to have Dr. Freitag look into this. It may require stitches." She shook her head and tut-tutted. "More stitches. What on Earth have you done to yourself this time?"

What on Earth indeed, Arabella thought. Were it not for the accursed gravity of this wretched planet, she might not have fallen so hard. "I am sorry I was not able to visit sooner," she said.

"I do wish that you had," her mother chided. "I would not even have known of your return to Earth, save that I read it in the *Chronicle*! I sent a letter to you at Greenwich, but it was returned."

"We had most likely left there by the time your letter arrived. We were very busy with the victory celebrations at first, and then we went to Brighton, where we were trapped by the snow."

"Oh yes, this beastly weather. But what took you to Brighton?"

"A personal invitation from the Prince Regent." Arabella felt a bitter satisfaction at the astonished, barely-contained envy on her mother's face. But this emotion lasted only a moment, replaced by distress at the memory of the reasons for her sudden departure from Brighton.

"You do not seem very happy at this state of affairs."

Arabella looked into her mother's eyes—her loving, disapproving, concerned, judgemental eyes—and immediately burst into tears. Arabella embraced her mother and sobbed into the soft, warm flannel of her night-dress shoulder, while her mother patted her back and comforted her.

Eventually Arabella recovered her composure sufficiently to give an account of the past week's events—a confused and rambling account, to be sure—while her mother held her hands, alternating reassuring sounds with tut-tuts of disapproval.

"I might have expected such a shambles," her mother summarized eventually, "from marrying a Mussulman. Oh, if only I had been there to advise you against such a heedless course of action!"

"My husband's religion has nothing to do with the case!" she snapped. But then she pushed her anger down, took her mother's hand, and looked deeply into her eyes. "What is done," she said, "is done. But now I have no choice; I must proceed at once to Greenwich, in hopes of persuading Fox to carry me to Mars and warn every one there of the invasion which is to come."

"Impossible!" her mother burst out. "You are in no fit condition to travel even as far as the Claret and Ale"—it was a public house in the town of Croydon—"never mind Greenwich! And a voyage to Mars is absolutely out of the question." She stood, crossed her arms upon her breast, and nodded decisively. "You will remain here until we can have your marriage to that beast annulled and a proper husband found for you."

"Annulled!" Arabella gasped.

"Certainly. For a girl of nineteen to marry outside of her religion, under such trying circumstances, and without her mother's permission? A plea of incompetence would meet with no opposition whatsoever."

"Incompetence!"

"Legally unqualified to enter into the marriage," her mother explained, unnecessarily. Arabella was well aware of the legal meaning of the word—it was the implication she resented.

Arabella sat up, shoving the duvet aside and intending to leap from the bed. But her artificial foot, she discovered, had been removed while she slept. Instead she rose to her knees upon the bed, glaring down at her mother from the height thus achieved. "I am *not* incompetent in any sense of the word, Mother. I married Captain Singh of my own accord, with full consideration of the consequences, and with the permission of my brother *in loco parentis*."

"Sit down immediately, child! You are in my household now, you are under twenty-one, and in my house you will obey my rules."

"I am a married woman, and any regrets I may have at the moment regarding that situation are entirely my own affair." She crossed her arms on her chest, realizing as she did that she was matching her mother's posture almost exactly. "I thank you very much for your hospitality. But now I must ask that you return my artificial foot to me, and I will be on my way."

"I will not. You are a callous, headstrong child and you require discipline."

"You would keep me here against my will?"

"If I must!"

Arabella surged forward, landing on her hands and knees upon the bed and causing her mother to recoil most satisfactorily. "The last person who attempted to do so," she snarled, "was cousin Simon. Despite the fact that he and his wife threatened me with pistols, I escaped that very night. And in the end he met his death."

"Are you threatening me?"

"If I must," Arabella replied, spitting her mother's own words back in her face.

The two women glared at each other across the rumpled bed-clothes. Arabella recognized that her position was by far the weaker of the two; her mother held her foot, her Draisine, and her clothing, and any protestations of independence by reason of marriage would fall upon deaf ears within this house. Yet she stood her ground, though she did so upon her knees.

And then, suddenly, her mother's face softened. "Oh, my dear child," she said. "You have so much of your father in you."

"I do?" Arabella replied, taken aback. This was not a sentiment her mother had ever before expressed.

"You do." A small, sad smile crept upon her mother's face, and her eyes grew distant. "You should have seen him when we were courting. Such a handsome lad, and so full of fire! He *would* have me, he said, and he would take me to his family plantation on Mars, and there we would build an empire of Marswood." She sighed. "We faced many obstacles in those days, not least of which was his own father, who disapproved of me. Nevertheless, he persisted, and in the end we were married, and raised four lovely children."

"Oh, Mother . . . I am so very sorry for the pain I have caused you."

"You have always and ever done what you thought was right, no matter the cost. Do you recall the time Mopsy escaped her pen?"

"Mopsy!" Arabella had not thought of her old pet *skorosh* in years. "She was so cold and hungry when I found her."

"We absolutely forbade you to run off in search of her. You were only eight, and it was the dead of winter!"

"Yet if I had not, she would surely have died."

"She would surely have died," her mother acknowledged.

Again the two women gazed at each other across the duvet, but now their gazes held sympathy and understanding as well as disagreement.

"My dear child," Arabella's mother said at last, taking Arabella's hand. "My dear, willful, troublesome, terribly vexatious child. You know I cannot approve of your intended course of action. This is . . . this is *treason* you are contemplating."

"I understand," Arabella replied—though, in fact, this was the first she had truly realized that she was, in fact, contemplating treason—preparing to defy the sovereign lord whom law and God had placed in authority over her and all her countrymen. The great consequences of this realization weighed heavily upon her heart . . . but she paused, swallowed, and steeled her resolve.

"Nonetheless, I am determined in my course, and you cannot prevent me."

Arabella's mother glared at her for that . . . but she did not deny it. She drew in a breath then, and let it out slowly—not quite a sigh, more a gathering of energy for what must come. "Very well. What do you require?"

"The return of my foot, and of my machine. I do not suppose you would allow Cole to convey me to Greenwich in the carriage?"

She hesitated, then shook her head. "My benevolence cannot extend so far. For the household to offer such visible support . . ." She did not say *to a traitor* but the words were clearly in her mind. ". . . would jeopardize our standing. I must think of your sisters."

Arabella's heart fell, but she nodded acknowledgement. "A bite to eat, then. A change of clothing. And also a set of men's clothing. Do you still have any of Michael's old things?"

"I believe so." The expression on her mother's face clearly showed her disapproval . . . and her resignation to her fate.

"And one more thing . . . though time presses upon me most severely, I must visit with my sisters before I depart."

"Of course."

They embraced then, and there were more tears, on both sides.

---

"Arabella!" Chloë shrieked, rushing to embrace her the moment she entered the sisters' bedchamber. She leapt into Arabella's arms, driving Arabella back onto her heels. Mother remained in the corridor, the light from her lamp drawing a bright line across the sisters' beds.

"How you've grown!" Arabella noted with a laugh. Indeed, when last they had seen each other Chloë had been a mere slip of a thing, and would have climbed Arabella like a *tukurush* without either of them noticing the weight. She was still every bit as energetic and keen, but was turning into quite a substantial girl.

Fanny, the elder of Arabella's two younger siblings, had always been more shy than her sister, more slender, and less physical. Nonetheless she too gave a high-pitched shriek of joy, and as soon as Chloë had descended from Arabella she embraced her in turn, albeit less strenuously. Arabella could not fail to notice that she was maturing into a young woman.

"I am so very happy to see the both of you," Arabella said, and felt considerable emotion welling up in her breast even as she uttered the sentiment. Indeed, she had not realized how much she had missed her dear, dear sisters.

"Have you come back?" Fanny asked, her light high voice so familiar and dear to Arabella's ears. "Will you be staying for ever?"

Arabella bit her lip. "I regret this immensely, but I may not remain even one more day. It is very pressing business that has brought me here, and I must continue to Greenwich without delay."

"Oh!" both the sisters cried miserably, and both embraced Arabella.

"I love you both so very dearly," Arabella murmured into Fanny's slim flannel-clad shoulder. And then she looked up and saw her mother, still standing with her lamp in the corridor. "And I love you too," she said, feeling the sting of tears in her eyes, and disentangled one hand to reach out to her.

Arabella's mother set the lamp upon a table and joined her daughters then, the four of them forming a warm familial knot wrapped in flannel and love.

# 5

## THE SWENSON CURRENT

The Sun, now well up, glinted off the snow as Arabella pedaled into the outskirts of Greenwich—cold, hungry, aching, exhausted, and dispirited, but not nearly so much so as she would have been without her few hours' respite at Marlowe Hall.

Soon after leaving Croydon she had begun to encounter people on the road—bakers and milkmen at first, later farmers and servants heading to market—who had been so astonished by her peculiar machine that they had taken no notice whatsoever of the fact that she was a woman in men's clothing. Despite their amazed entreaties, she had sped past them with a cheery wave, not giving them the opportunity for further inspection of her disguise.

Soon the masts of the dockyard hove into view, gently nodding and waving in the breeze. This visible indication of the nearness of her long journey's end at first gave new energy to Arabella's pedaling legs, like the rush of a homeward-bound *huresh* upon sighting the paddock. But as her destination drew still closer she found herself flagging, perhaps from awareness not only of how very far she had come from Brighton but how many tens of thousands of miles still lay before her, and the last half-hour turned into a dreadful, weary slog. But eventually—weary, gasping, shivering, and filthy—she presented herself at the dockyard gate to an astonished pair of Marines, who offered her tea and biscuits in their guard-house while word of her arrival was sent to *Touchstone*.

It was Brindle, Captain Fox's steward, who came to the guard-house to convey her to the ship. "I am so very pleased to find you here," she told him after they had taken their leave of the Marines. "I was afraid you would all be in London already, for Nelson's funeral."

"Oh no, Mrs. Singh," Brindle replied. "None of us was invited."

"None? Not even Captain Fox?"

"No, ma'am. Only Navy people. Even Greenwich pensioners going to march in the funeral procession, but not *privateers*." He sneered the word, with a tolerable imitation of the pinched London accent. "We get to watch the parade from the pavement, like common folk."

"That seems terribly unfair."

"It do."

Finally she was handed up *Touchstone*'s side, to be met by Captain Fox and his officers, arranged on the deck with nearly Naval precision. "Welcome back, Mrs. Singh," Fox said, bowing. "We had not known to expect you." Despite his formality, she could not fail to note the expression of cheeky bemusement upon his face, nor the studied disdain on that of Lady Corey, who stood just behind him. Both, she realized, were directed at her scandalously clad lower limbs.

"I must apologize for my dress," Arabella said. "Skirts are not suitable for the machine upon which I have been traveling." She gestured to the Draisine, which had just been handed up from the lighter to the deck.

"A most unusual conveyance indeed," Fox acknowledged. But she sensed that his interest in the machine was only polite . . . quite unlike the reaction she would have expected from Captain Singh, whose fascination with all things mechanical was equal to her own.

The thought of which, unfortunately, brought the bleak despair of her situation heavily to mind. Having achieved her immediate goal of making contact with Fox, she must now persuade him to take her to Mars . . . and away from her Judas of a husband. Tears stung the corners of her eyes, but she swallowed to force them back.

"May I beg the use of your cabin," she asked Fox, "to change into proper clothing? And once I have done so . . . I have a request to make of you." This last was directed to Fox, but with her eyes she included Lady Corey, the officers, and the men. "A most serious request, which may have grave consequences for every one aboard."

Fox's expression immediately changed from amusement to concern. "Of course," he said, bowing and gesturing to the cabin . . . but his troubled gaze never left her face.

For a moment Arabella hesitated, desperate to tell him every thing that had happened since they had last seen each other—and hoping against all hope that he would agree to assist her. But then she closed her eyes, shook her head, and hurried past him. Before she presented her case she must compose herself, and changing her clothing would give her the opportunity to do so.

———————————

". . . and that is why I must ask that you carry me to Mars at once, to warn them of the coming invasion. I recognize that this is an extraordinary, indeed extravagantly audacious, request, but immediate action is the only way to prevent a grievous, interplanetary wrong from being committed."

Arabella looked around at the crowd in *Touchstone*'s great cabin—which was, despite its name, much smaller than Arabella's bedchamber at Marlowe Hall, with a far lower ceiling. The shutters over the broad paned window at the cabin's stern were closed, for privacy, but a lantern on the captain's navigational table illuminated their faces evenly. Most of the officers she held as familiar acquaintances—she had dined often with them on her voyage from Mars to Venus, and then they had all been held prisoner together by Napoleon—but among them she counted only Liddon, Fox's chief mate, as a true friend. Their reactions to Arabella's plea varied from skepticism to sympathy, but every one plainly looked to their captain, Fox, for his decision.

Fox himself gazed levelly at Arabella, his expression revealing little. He was, she knew, fiercely independent, and the opportunity to tweak the Prince Regent's nose would surely make this rebellious action more appealing than otherwise. But he was also an intelligent, practical man, and very much aware that England, now indisputably the greatest power in the solar system, was not a force to be trifled with. Behind those hooded eyes he was certainly weighing his options with future profit in mind.

To Arabella's surprise Fox turned to his left, where Lady Corey had been listening to Arabella's appeal with one pale forefinger resting on her chin. "Mrs. Fox," he said to her, "what is your opinion on this matter?"

The forefinger tapped once, twice, three times, then descended to Lady Corey's lap. "As a loyal subject of His Majesty," she said, "I am, of course, inclined to support the Prince Regent in whatever course of action he chooses. Yet I am also a denizen of Mars. Though I was not born there, my late husband was, and I have spent nearly my entire adult life upon that planet; as such, my sympathies lie with the brave men and women who have wrested their livelihoods from its dry, unforgiving sand. I must consider whether the Prince's scheme will benefit them or harm them."

"I implore you to consider the plight of the Martians!" Arabella entreated. "What the Prince contemplates is nothing less than slavery!"

But at this declaration Lady Corey's expression chilled. "The same Martians who killed my husband and reduced our family home to a pile of broken stones?"

Aghast at her own insensitivity, Arabella's gaze dropped to her lap. "I beg your forgiveness, Lady Corey. You know that I am passionate about maintaining peace between the English on Mars and the Martians, whom even you must acknowledge vastly outnumber us." She looked up, confidence returning. "As well you know, they are a proud and resourceful people. I am certain that when the Prince attempts to subjugate them, English people and English property will suffer just as greatly as the Martians. The bloodshed on both sides will be horrific."

"Unless your oh-so-clever husband can find a way to avoid it," Lady Corey countered.

Arabella's feelings on this point were extremely mixed, but she strove to stick to facts. "Consider the Martians' numbers," she said. "Consider the vast spaces of the Martian desert. Consider the determination and organization they showed during the recent rebellion. And consider Khema, who was renowned among her people as a brilliant tactician even before she became an *akhmok*. In the rebellion she remained neutral, defending the property and humans of Woodthrush Woods, rather than joining the mobs that burned so much of Fort Augusta. But in the coming war—and, I assure you, it *will* be war—the consequences of defeat for her people would be so high that I am certain she will put all of her considerable abilities at their service. In a game of chess between Khema and Captain Singh . . . I do not know who would emerge victorious, but there is no doubt that many, many pawns would fall before the game was done."

Again Lady Corey's finger tapped against her chin. "Your

argument is persuasive, child. But to take arms against the Prince Regent . . ."

"Oh *tush,* my dear!" Fox burst out. "How can you profess such loyalty to the man when you have been treated so shabbily by the *ton* of which he is the very head and symbol?"

Lady Corey's lips pursed tightly. "I wish you would not mention this personal issue in company. It is irrelevant, in any event."

"It is *far* from irrelevant!" Fox replied. Addressing the company, he said, "You all know as well as I how fine and elegant a lady my wife is—a far better person than I, to be sure—and yet the *ton,* the cream of London society, considers her a mere provincial, a parvenu! I have, with these very ears, heard it said of her, 'Her husband, alas, is dead, and even worse a Martian!' Which is an even greater insult to her than it is to myself!"

Though Lady Corey's self-control was excellent, Arabella noted that a slight smile crept onto her lips at Fox's fervent defense of her.

"Surely," Fox continued, "if these London rogues—who have the gall to call themselves 'polite' society—consider even my dear and noble wife so unworthy of respect, what treatment can the common Englishman on Mars expect from their leader? Even leaving aside the damage done to the native Martians." He shook his head theatrically. "I may be an Englishman, but I sail under the flag of Sor Khoresh, not England . . . and I have ever sided with David over Goliath." He turned to Arabella and gazed into her eyes with deep sincerity. "As you well know, I am a rogue of a privateer—a man for whom mere riches count more than king or country. Yet my respect for my dear wife, and for *you,* my dear Mrs. Singh—you who have done me so many valuable services in the past year that I could never hope to repay them all—compels me to throw in my lot with the Martians!" He looked around at his officers. "Are you with me, lads?"

"Aye aye!" the men chorused, and Arabella's heart swelled with emotion.

As for Lady Corey, though she gazed at her husband with frank admiration, her face was troubled. Fox saw this too, for he turned to her and said quite tenderly, "I know that you do not enjoy interplanetary travel." This was true, Arabella knew; the older woman had never learned to handle herself properly in a state of free descent, and was much better suited to the salon and the tea-room than to the raging currents of the interplanetary atmosphere. "And this voyage may prove even more hazardous than the last. But I have an idea how you may serve the cause without exposing yourself to any discomfort or danger."

"How so?"

"I propose . . . espionage." He waggled his eyebrows suggestively.

Lady Corey tilted her head at him, amused. "I am intrigued, sir."

"Your ability to thread the needle of polite society is legendary. If you would consent to remain in London, I am certain you could discern many particulars that would be useful to the Martian cause."

She considered the idea. "I can do better than that," she said. "I believe I may be able to not only acquire intelligence, but throw sand in the works." Her eyes fell half-closed and her mouth curved into a dangerous, cat-like grin. "That would, I believe, provide adequate revenge upon those termagants of the London *ton*."

"Excellent!" Fox cried, and rubbed his hands together. "Gentlemen . . . we have much to do before we may depart. Let us begin immediately!"

"Sir . . ." Liddon put in, hesitantly. "I feel I must point out that Mars is very near conjunction." As, of course, it was, which Arabella should have mentioned before even proposing her scheme.

Her spirits immediately fell, and the expression on Fox's face showed that he was equally dismayed.

"Forgive me," Lady Corey said, "but what does this mean?"

"Suppose," Arabella explained, "that you are the Earth, I am Mars, and the lantern between us is the Sun. The two planets are on opposite sides of the Sun, as you and I are now."

"But how can 'conjunction' mean that the two planets are as far from each other as they can be? I would expect the opposite."

"During conjunction, Mars and the Sun are conjoined, or very close together, in Earth's sky." Arabella ducked her head down until Lady Corey's face was obscured behind the lantern's wavering flame. "Do you see?"

"So it is impossible to travel to Mars at this time without being burnt up by the Sun's flames? Oh, dear."

"Interplanetary navigation is rather more complicated than that," Fox clarified gently. "The tides and currents of the interplanetary atmosphere, not to mention orbital mechanics, mean that one almost never travels in a straight line. But, indeed, travel from Earth to Mars at this time would be exceedingly difficult." He frowned. "I suppose we must wait until much closer to opposition."

"But that is exactly when the Prince's fleet will launch!" Arabella cried. "If we wait until then, the Martians will have no warning at all!"

Fox spread his hands helplessly. "What choice do we have? We could not possibly carry sufficient weight of food and water for the long passage at this season."

Arabella paused, considering the flickering lantern on the table between them, her mind superimposing aerial currents and orbital paths upon the scene. "I do not yet know," she admitted. "But there may be an alternative. Do you have the greenwood box?"

The "greenwood box" was a clockwork device Arabella had

constructed during *Touchstone*'s passage from Mars to Venus. Although not nearly as sophisticated as *Diana*'s automaton navigator Aadim, it worked upon the same principles, and made possible many navigational calculations which would be unreasonably complex or time-consuming with pen and paper. It had been captured, along with *Touchstone*, by the French, but with any luck it would still have been aboard when Fox reclaimed the ship after the Battle of Venus.

"It is in the hold," Fox said. "Have it brought up forthwith." This last was directed to Liddon, who touched his forehead with a knuckle and dashed out of the cabin.

"Thank you," Arabella said. "But even if I can work out a feasible course, it will certainly be a long and difficult journey. We will need to lay in as many supplies as we can carry."

Fox turned to his quartermaster. "Do as the lady says. Smartly, now! But also as quietly as you may . . . when we go, I should like it to be a surprise." The quartermaster nodded acknowledgement.

The next half-hour was taken up with a rush of muttered plans, calculations, and speculations. "Will you encounter windwhales?" Lady Corey asked Fox. A close meeting with a pod of whales on their previous voyage had nearly scuttled the whole expedition.

"It is not unlikely, once we pass within the orbit of Venus." Fox met his wife's eye levelly. "And in the hot depths near Mercury, there may be even worse things. Things that *eat* wind-whales. Or so I have heard."

"Airmen are a credulous lot," Arabella countered, dismissively. "I, too, have heard legends and tales, but we are now in an age of enlightenment . . . and natural philosophy has found no actual evidence of any such monsters."

"'There are more things in heaven and earth, Horatio,'" Fox quoted.

Arabella had no response to that. But, just then, the greenwood box appeared, and she busied herself with setting it up.

There was no time to be lost. Arabella's use of the Draisine had permitted her to reach Greenwich before the Prince and his party, but *Touchstone* would have to be away before they caught her up.

———————

Fox and his officers busied themselves with readying the ship and crew for a long voyage as quickly as possible without making too much noise about it. Airmen were called in from shore leave; replacements were recruited for those who refused to return; and load after load of victuals and water made their way aboard.

For her part, Arabella labored ceaselessly with the greenwood box. It had been constructed hastily, from whatever materials were available at the time, and was frequently recalcitrant, but even so working with it was rather like chatting with an old friend. Time spent with the box was even more welcome in that it was entirely her own creation, and carried few associations with Captain Singh—contemplation of whom was nearly guaranteed to bring tears to her eyes.

"How goes the battle?" Fox asked on the afternoon following Arabella's arrival, entering the cabin with a cup of tea.

"It is a struggle," she confessed, gratefully accepting the proffered cup. She gestured to the heaps of scribbled notes piled upon the navigational desk and drifting down to the deck below. "It almost seems as though there were some good reason not to journey between planets in conjunction."

"I have put some queries about," Fox said, seating himself upon a sea-chest, "and I hear that the Muller Current has been running particularly fast in recent months." He moved some papers off of a large chart of the interplanetary wind currents, tapping the Muller. "Could we perhaps make use of this?"

"I have heard the same, but it runs too far from the Sun at this season. The diversion would cost more time than it gains."

"If only the Swenson were in the plane of the ecliptic," Fox commented.

The two of them sat shoulder-to-shoulder, both looking at the chart. Most of the named currents flowed westward—counter-clockwise on the chart, following the rotation of the planets around the Sun—in the plane of the ecliptic, where all the known planets orbited. But the vast majority of the interplanetary atmosphere's currents—the powerful but unnamed flows not normally used for navigation—ran perpendicular to that plane, rising with the heat from the Sun's poles and, cooling, falling back down to the plane of the ecliptic somewhere well beyond Jupiter. The Swenson Current, discovered and named only ten years earlier, was one of these, but it was particularly swift, and unique in that it rose from within the orbit of Mercury and fell near Mars. For a time there had been speculation that it might be usable to provide a rapid passage from Venus to Mars, but several expeditions had failed to transform this speculation into reality.

But still . . . might there be something here that she could use?

Arabella's hours of work with the greenwood box had served to embed a thorough understanding of the planets' motion into her mind. As she gazed at the chart, she could not only visualize but *feel* Mercury, Venus, Earth, and Mars whirling about the roiling Sun, sweeping the currents along as they went. To this understanding she now added the Swenson Current—a power-ful loop of air that rose from the Sun perpendicular to the table-top, then fell back toward Mars, only to return to its starting point and rise again. If it were only in the plane of the ecliptic, as

Fox had suggested, it would provide a rapid channel for the latter part of the journey from Earth to Mars, at the proper season.

In theory, the current could be used in this way even though it was at right angles to the usual course. The difficulty was in making the transition from the plane of the ecliptic to the plane of the current. The change in velocity required was far, far beyond what was possible using pedal-driven propulsive sails, and all attempts to perform the transfer using cross-currents had failed. Failed spectacularly in one case, resulting in the loss of all hands.

But then there was Mercury. At this season, that rocky and uninhabitable planet sat right at the root of the Swenson, on the opposite side of the Sun from Earth. If only, she thought, it were possible to *start* there. A ship inbound from Earth would necessarily have a substantial orbital velocity in the plane of the ecliptic, making the shift to the Swenson Current difficult or impossible. But with a standing start on Mercury, one could launch straight northward, directly into the current, and sail along with it for a rapid delivery to Mars.

Arabella's heart began to beat faster. Breaking the problem in two—Earth to Mercury, Mercury to Mars—might take a knife to the Gordian knot.

"Oh, thank you!" she cried, and planted an impulsive kiss upon Fox's cheek.

"You are more than welcome," he replied, rubbing the spot. "For what?"

Orbits and currents whirled in Arabella's head. "I will explain later," she said, pulling the greenwood box toward herself.

---

"I call it 'planetary circumduction,'" Arabella said . . . or tried to, as the last word was obscured by a prodigious yawn. "Circumduction," she repeated, enunciating carefully.

"Have you slept at *all*?" Fox asked.

Arabella considered the question, rubbing her burning eyes. The light of the freshly risen sun, glinting off the snow outside, slanted in across the navigational desk and made the greenwood box's exposed brass gears gleam like gold. The device had broken down so frequently from heavy use that she had stopped bothering to replace its casing after each repair. "I do not believe so, no. But, nonetheless, I have great confidence in this course. I have run the calculations time and again."

"Explain it again," said Liddon, tapping the bead representing Mercury. The bead was pinned to the desk upon the chart at Mercury's present position. Rising above it was a curl of wire, representing the Swenson Current, ending at another bead representing the current position of Mars. Collins, Fox's sailing-master, gazed dubiously at the improvised assemblage.

"Mercury orbits the Sun thus," she said, tracing her finger along the planet's orbit in a counter-clockwise direction. "We will come upon it from behind, thus, traveling in the same direction, and as we approach the planet, its gravity will increase our velocity. If one were to ignore orbital effects, this course would result in an impact upon the surface." Her moving finger touched the bead. "But according to my calculations"—she patted the greenwood box with her other hand—"with the additional speed derived from our fall toward the moving planet, we will have just enough orbital velocity to whip around Mercury from south to north, departing on a northerly course at nearly a right angle to our original approach. This will put us in exactly the right place to catch the Swenson Current." Her finger rose upward from the table-top, tracing along the wire. "We emerge from Mercury's gravitational field like a stone from David's slingshot, aimed toward the Goliath of Mars."

"But as we rise from Mercury," Liddon asked, "do we not lose every bit of speed we gained as we fell toward it?"

"Very nearly," Arabella acknowledged. "But because of the direction of our approach, we steal a bit of the planet's orbital velocity, so we actually come away faster than we went in. In exchange, the planet slows imperceptibly in its orbit."

Fox crossed his arms upon his chest. "Has any one ever attempted such a maneuver before?" he asked.

"Not so far as I know," Arabella admitted. "But the same could be said of the maneuver that won the battle against *Victoire*. Which was, may I remind you, also calculated with this instrument."

"I seem to recall that all of us nearly lost our lives in that battle. And you lost your foot."

"That was only because of the quantity and velocity of *Victoire*'s wreckage after we destroyed her. The maneuver itself worked exactly as—" Again she interrupted herself with a tremendous yawn.

Fox, still skeptical, turned his attention to Liddon and Collins. "What do you think of this . . . circumlocution? Circumspection?"

"Circumduction," Arabella corrected.

"Whatever it is called, I have certainly never encountered the like," Collins said, removing his glasses and polishing them on his sleeve. He was a small, round man, looking very like a banker or accountant, whose presence upon a privateer vessel had always struck Arabella as incongruous. "But I have seen Mrs. Singh pull many a seemingly impossible trick from this greenwood box. I certainly cannot say with certainty that it would *not* work."

"I agree," said Liddon. "Though I cannot follow the mathematics, I am prepared to accept that they are correct."

"Would you stake your life upon it?" Fox demanded. "All of our lives? And the fate of Mars?"

Liddon and Collins conferred on the question, then both turned back to Fox. "Yes," said Liddon, simply.

Collins concurred with a nod. "It is not without risk. But I do not believe that any other course can get us to Mars in time. This is an extraordinary situation, which requires an extraordinary course."

"Very well," said Fox, looking sternly at both of his officers and at Arabella. He opened a cabinet, bringing out a bottle of fine port and four glasses. "To the circumduction of Mercury."

"To the circumduction of Mercury!" they all chorused, and drank.

---

Victualing and watering the ship required most of another day, during which Arabella became increasingly anxious on a variety of points. Would the course she had worked out—a novel, risky, even insane maneuver never before attempted—actually work as expected? Would their plan to warn Mars of the coming invasion be detected and halted before they even departed? And what of the hazards of the unseasonable, exceptionally long, and nearly unprecedented journey itself? No one aboard *Touchstone* had sailed within the orbit of Venus before, and even the explorers of the Royal Society had rarely visited lifeless, broiling-hot Mercury. To distract herself, she assisted Fox in stocking the ship's larders, but *Touchstone*'s crew was a well-oiled machine and her attempts to help more often proved a hindrance.

Despite her exhaustion, she found herself unable to sleep, staring at the deck above her hammock. She felt constantly exhausted and on edge. She was not hungry, and when she did remember to eat she craved only sweet pastries and coffee.

Just after noon Arabella sat half-dozing on the forecastle when a cry from the masthead of "Boat ahoy!" roused her.

"*Touchstone!*" came the reply, indicating that the lighter was bringing Captain Fox back from one of his provisioning expeditions across the Thames to London. But the boat, when it arrived, proved to contain not only Fox and some hundredweight of casks, but two additional visitors: the American engineer Fulton, and Nelson's surgeon Dr. Barry.

"I encountered them in a public house at the Mars Docks," Fox explained to Arabella, "and they absolutely demanded to come aboard for a visit." He then lowered his voice and added, "And possibly more."

"Oh?"

"Come with us to the cabin," he said, cryptically, and also requested Brindle to pass the word for Liddon and for Lady Corey.

---

"Our meeting at the Mars Docks was not a coincidence," Fox explained to Liddon, Arabella, and Lady Corey once the cabin door was shut behind them. "I had sent word to Fulton requesting a meeting, and he brought Dr. Barry along, for reasons which I believe I should leave to the good doctor to explain."

"Captain Fox has been very forthright with me," Fulton said, his diction educated but his American accent grating to Arabella's ear. "I greatly admire and respect the trust with which I have been treated, and I promise you I will return it in kind. He has explained to me the horrific scheme of the Prince Regent's to dominate and enslave Mars, and requested my assistance in resisting it. As an American, I could not refuse. I offered my services as an engineer to the United States in resisting the depredations of his father George the Third—services which they declined, for which reason I eventually found myself in Napoleon's employ. I now offer my services to Mars, likewise, and hope that they will be accepted." He cast an adoring glance at Lady Corey, who smiled in return . . . but as soon as his eyes left her face it relaxed into a disgusted frown.

Fulton had plainly set his cap for Lady Corey on Venus, an affection she had exploited in their plan to escape from the prison camp but had never truly returned. She thought of him as a vulgar arriviste whose selfish ambition led him to sell his services to the highest bidder. Arabella shared this opinion, though she found his company more tolerable than did Lady Corey, and neither of them could deny that his talents in invention and engineering were unparalleled.

"As for myself," Dr. Barry said, "I desire nothing more than to escape the unwanted attention which has come my way since my return to Earth." Barry, a slight and soft-spoken young man of only about twenty, was nonetheless an extremely capable surgeon, and had certainly saved the lives of both Arabella and Captain Fox with his expert care after the Battle of Venus. But he was an extremely shy and modest man, and the fame which his role in the death of Nelson had brought him was plainly quite distressing. Arabella was not surprised to find that he was willing to travel to Mars in order to escape it. "I would be happy to serve as *Touchstone*'s surgeon in exchange for my passage off-planet."

"And you would be very welcome, sir," said Fox, "for we have no surgeon of our own, and the coming voyage is likely to prove exceptionally hazardous. However, as a former Navy man myself, I must warn you that if you join us you may find yourself in conflict with the oath you swore to the King upon joining the service."

"I thank you for your concern, sir," Barry replied with a bow. "However, I find myself so uncomfortable with the gaze of the public eye that I have already considered resigning my commission and retiring to private practice. It will be no great hardship to file the necessary papers before departure."

The two men retired from the cabin while Arabella, Fox, Liddon, and Lady Corey conferred on whether to accept them into the crew. "My main concern," said Liddon, "is that the addition of two more mouths to feed will strain our already slim rations to the breaking point. If the voyage were to take even one week more than we expect . . . well, there are no chandlers in the Swenson Current. Nor even asteroids, so far as we know. It may prove a very hungry and thirsty voyage."

Fox stroked his chin contemplatively. "I understand," he said, "but in such a situation Dr. Barry's medical expertise could make the difference in our survival. And as for Mr. Fulton, though I find him personally repugnant"—he looked to his wife, whose expression showed her agreement—"I believe that his military ingenuity would be invaluable in the defense of Mars from the Prince's navies." He firmed his chin and nodded decisively. "Have the purser muster them both aboard. We can shift some stores from Mr. Fairchild's old cabin to make room for them."

"Aye aye," said Liddon.

"Apart from that, how goes the provisioning?"

"Assuming you were able to obtain every thing on the list on this most recent trip, and that we can find a place to stow it, we are nearly ready to depart."

"Could we raise ship at high tide to-morrow?"

Liddon's mouth quirked as he considered the question, then he nodded. "I believe so, sir."

Fox looked around. "Then let us prepare to depart. And may God have mercy on us all."

# 2

## IN TRANSIT, 1816

# 6

## CROSSING VENUS

In the darkness, a hesitant knock sounded on Arabella's cabin door. "Come in," she said at once. She had not been asleep.

It was Brindle, his dark face half-illuminated by a lantern. "Last lighter's just going ashore, ma'am," he said.

"Oh! Thank you." Arabella rose from her hammock—fully dressed, as she had lain atop the covers, merely napping, if that, for the last several hours—and from the tiny writing-desk affixed to the wall she drew two folded letters. "Here you are."

Brindle accepted the letters. "Any thing else, ma'am?"

"Just those."

One of the letters was addressed to her mother in Croydon. It thanked her for her recent hospitality and begged her forgiveness for any disappointments she had offered as a daughter.

The other was addressed to Captain Singh, in care of the Honorable Mars Company—though she had hesitated at the use of the first word in that title. This one, too, begged forgiveness, but only for her sudden and untoward departure from Brighton.

Primarily it listed the reasons for her disappointment in him, and offered her hopes that he change his mind about accepting the position offered him by the Prince Regent.

She did not expect to receive a reply to either letter.

Contemplating the future, she could foresee any number of possible outcomes to the voyage about to begin. Far too many of those ended with her dead, in prison, exiled, or disgraced. But she had no choice. She owed it to her home planet, to her friends and family there, and to her own sense of honor—*okhaya*, as Khema's people called it. To rest in comfort as the people of Mars, Englishmen as well as native Martians, suffered would be intolerable.

All about her, *Touchstone*'s timbers creaked as the ship rocked in the water, muttered conversations and gentle footsteps punctuating the ship's rhythm as the crew roused themselves for departure. She slipped on her shoes, put her fur wrap about her shoulders, and went out on deck.

---

Earth's enormous moon glared down from a clear black sky as Arabella came out on deck. Nearly full, it outlined *Touchstone*'s spars and lines with a frost of icy white light and turned the golden *khoresh*-wood planks of the deck to silver. Silhouettes of airmen clambered in the rigging, managing the balloon envelope as it filled with hot air from the Navy furnace-house on shore close by.

Arabella requested and received permission to ascend to the quarterdeck, where Fox and Liddon conferred in hushed tones. "Morning, ma'am," said Liddon, for it was well after midnight.

"Good morning," she replied. "How much longer?"

Fox turned his face skyward, inspecting the swelling envelope and the moon above it. "Less than an hour." He pointed to one of the airmen and raised his voice, but only enough to be heard. "Mind the ratlines, there!"

"Aye, sir," came drifting down from above.

From the other ships close by, all Navy vessels, came very little sound. Only a light watch stood on any deck, with a few lanterns here and there. "Will we encounter any opposition when we launch, do you think?" Arabella asked Fox.

"I do not expect that we will." Despite his confident words, his eyes scanned the dark water in every direction. "For the Prince to oppose us in public would tip his hand. He might attempt to prevent our departure through some administrative action or subterfuge, to be sure, but I do not anticipate any overt action. The fewer people who know about this Mars scheme before it is set in motion, the more likely it is to succeed."

"But stopping us would prevent people from finding out about it."

"I said that opposing us *in public* would tip his hand. If there is to be opposition, it will find us somewhere above the falling-line—out of sight and out of mind."

"And what will you do if that should occur?"

"I have a few tricks in mind." He winked. "Have no fear, this old privateer knows how to get his ship out of port in one piece. But after that it will be up to you to get us to Mercury, and then to Mars."

"I will do my very best."

"I expect nothing less."

Fox excused himself then, and Arabella fell back to the quarterdeck rail, where she could observe the launch while remaining out of the way.

Fox's management of his crew, she noted, was remarkably different from Captain Singh's. Although Captain Singh's darting brown eyes seemed to take in every detail, he trusted his men's discipline entirely, offering only the occasional word of direction or correction. Most commands issued aboard his ship came from the mates or the captains of divisions, based upon the captain's stated or implied wishes. But Captain Fox took a far more active part in the operation of his ship. Even given the unusual noise-lessness of this moon-lit launch, he was constantly flitting about, commanding individual airmen directly and sometimes even hauling on a line himself. None of his officers or men took any offense at this—they were, if nothing else, used to their captain's behavior. Furthermore, they understood that he knew all of their jobs as well as his own, and though he seemed omnipresent his actions and advice never interfered with their work.

Soon the envelope had swollen to its maximum extent, and with the very minimum of shouting the furnace-gut was detached and the furnace-men rowed away. *Touchstone* now rode high in the water, swaying uneasily in the light breeze with most of her weight carried by the balloon.

"Easy now," Fox said, just loud enough to be heard, "ballast away."

On every other launch she had observed, the command *ballast away* had been immediately followed by a great roar and rush as the water, or sand on Mars, was rapidly released from the lowest level of the hold. But now the ballast-ports creaked open slowly, and the ship simply floated higher and higher until her keel rose dripping from the water's surface.

Gently, gently, *Touchstone* eased herself into the sky. A few pale faces turned up curiously from the Navy men on the other ships close by, but no halloos nor hurrahs greeted her departure. It was as surreptitious a launch as Arabella could imagine, nearly eerie in its silence.

But even as *Touchstone* began her ascent, a lighter set out from the quays toward her, its oars splashing with fevered haste. "Flag *Queen Charlotte*!" came a cry from the lighter's coxswain.

At this call, incomprehensible to Arabella, Fox's eyes widened in shock, then narrowed in calculation. "Did you hear something just then, Mister Liddon?" he remarked to his chief mate, delivering the seemingly casual question with a very serious gaze.

Liddon looked back with a matching expression of surprise followed by understanding. "I do not believe I did, sir."

"Carry on, then."

"Flag *Queen Charlotte*!" repeated the lighter's coxswain, more urgently, as *Touchstone* continued her ascent. "Flag *Queen Charlotte*, d—n it!" But Fox and Liddon only exchanged looks—Liddon's concerned and questioning, Fox's firm and insistent—and spoke no words, nor took any action. The crew, following their commander's lead, continued raising ship, ignoring the lighter completely save for the occasional worried downward glance. Soon the splashing and continued shouts had drifted into inaudibility.

"Just out of idle curiosity," Arabella said to Fox with studied nonchalance, "have you ever heard of a Flag *Queen Charlotte*?"

"*Queen Charlotte* is the largest ship in the dockyard," he replied in a matching tone. To Arabella's blank expression, he clarified, "The largest ship in dock is considered the dockyard's flagship, and is thus the nominal command of the Port-Admiral in charge. If a boat, or perhaps a lighter, should happen to pull alongside a ship with the hail 'Flag *Queen Charlotte*,' that would indicate that the Port-Admiral himself is aboard the boat. Perhaps bearing some important papers, such as an order that under no circumstances is the ship to depart the dock." He raised one eyebrow. "Why do you ask?"

"No particular reason."

Higher and higher the ship drifted. Moonlight sparkled on the surface of the black Thames and glinted from the snowdrifts that still heaped its banks; a few cawing seabirds sculled past below. Soon the ship had floated so high that the whole of London could be seen—a jumble of dark gray and black buildings contrasting with snowy parks and alleys, illuminated only by the occasional street-lamp: white gas flames on the main streets, yellow whale-oil elsewhere. A few carriages clopped along the streets, their tiny lanterns shimmering like summer stars, but the overall impression was of stillness—the city lying cold and sleeping beneath a tattered blanket of snow. No other ships rose from the dock; all remained still.

In remarkably short order the city became vague and indistinct, merely a dirty patch at a bend in the river. The countryside around it spread out beneath the moon, sparkling snowy fields and gray forests laid out in a gigantic checkerboard. The wind freshened then, striking at Arabella's face with a cold crisp bite, and she pulled her wrap and her bonnet more tightly about herself.

"Set main-course and main-tops'l," Fox remarked casually to Liddon.

*What?* Arabella thought, and her surprise was echoed by the expression on Liddon's face, but nonetheless he immediately conveyed Fox's command to the captains of divisions. The crew immediately set to, raising the two lower sails on the mainmast and sheeting them home. But Arabella knew that it was pointless to set sails before reaching the interplanetary atmosphere; the balloon itself was essentially one giant sail, and additional sails could not direct the ship any where other than with the wind. What was Fox doing?

"I mean to catch every tiniest particle of this breeze," Fox explained to Arabella's unspoken question, "to get as far away from London as I can before reaching the falling-line. If any one should await us above the Horn . . . I intend to miss that rendezvous."

Several other surprising commands followed, not the least of which was to sway out the side and lower masts—though not yet to set their sails—far earlier than usual. This was certainly more dangerous, but *Touchstone*'s experienced crew were up to the challenge, and it would let the ship set sail and take up the wild winds of the Horn immediately once the falling-line was crossed— far sooner than any pursuing ship would anticipate.

Fox's trickery continued after they entered the Horn. Using every ounce of his skill and experience, Fox sought out, caught, and rode the fastest, wildest winds of that perpetual storm, re- sulting in an exceptionally rapid passage . . . and a horrifically turbulent ride. No sane captain would deliberately seek out such a rough road, of course, but *Touchstone* and her crew took the jolts in stride—in fact, most of the crew's faces, illuminated by the nearly constant lightning, bore broad excited smiles at the chal- lenge. Arabella was very glad for Lady Corey that the great lady had stayed back on Earth—she would have been absolutely miserable.

So turbulent, though, was *Touchstone*'s journey through the Horn that Arabella became violently ill, spewing her breakfast over the larboard rail and into the lashing rain beyond. Nor was she the only one to do so—even Liddon, whose scarred face and world-weary demeanor bespoke his decades of airfaring experi- ence, "sacrificed to Uranus," as the airmen said. But Fox, cling- ing to a backstay with one hand and one foot, merely laughed uproariously at their discomfort, the wild rain washing his bared teeth and the wind whipping the brim of the hat tied upon his head.

Arabella glared at him and retired to her cabin, where— despite feeling as though she were a pair of dice being rattled in a dice-cup—somehow she managed to fall asleep.

———————————

When Arabella awoke, the ship had ceased to lurch and the sun— the ever-present sun of the interplanetary atmosphere—shone through the prism in the deck above. She pushed herself up out of her hammock, drifting freely until she collided gently with the deck above.

It was good to be back in a state of free descent. She stretched languidly, extending her limbs as far as possible in the tiny cabin and enjoying the relief from the constant pull of Earth's oppressive gravity. Pulling her arms in suddenly, she spun herself on her long axis, whirling like a top in midair and grinning at the sensations. She then extended her arms, slowing her spin, ending with a light touch of one finger upon the wall that stopped her motion altogether.

She had not forgotten. She had not forgotten a thing.

Still grinning, she opened the door and pushed herself into the ward-room outside with her natural foot. The space was crammed with boxes, crates, and casks, an unavoidable trade-off between maneuvering room now and survival later. But at least now, in a state of free descent, the narrow path on the floor between the stacked supplies was no longer the only route. She sailed with ease over the top of them.

Up on deck, the chaos and havoc of the Horn had been replaced by the peace of the interplanetary atmosphere. Only a few puffy clouds marked the clear blue of the sky all around, and though the ship was no doubt racing sunward at a speed of some thousands of knots, she was unmoving relative to the current in which she was embedded and the air on deck seemed perfectly still. A few airmen, whistling negligently, floated above the deck, engaged in coiling cables; the ship's balloon envelope had already been deflated and stowed. Earth floated in the blue sky abaft, a gleaming sphere as big as a dinner plate, her visible face fully illuminated by the Sun toward which *Touchstone* now sailed.

"Good morning!" called Fox, emerging from the great cabin with a sandwich of ham and cress in his hand. "I trust you slept well?"

"No thanks to you," she replied, accepting his offer of half the sandwich, "and that wretched passage." The sandwich was delicious, and she determined to enjoy it thoroughly; unsalted pork, soft bread, and especially fresh greens would very soon be nothing more than a happy memory, and would remain so for all the months of their long and unconventional voyage.

"It is thanks to me, and that wretched passage, that your slumber was uninterrupted by cannon-fire! When we emerged from the Horn, we spotted a flotilla of Navy vessels in the distance, but our velocity was sufficient that we easily evaded them. I am certain that they were lying in wait for us, and that our turbulent passage was the reason we did not come out right in the middle of them."

"I thank you for that, then, my dear sir," she replied with exaggerated politeness, and gave him an elaborate midair curtsey.

He smiled at that, and bowed. "Your skirt is riding up in back," he commented mildly.

"Oh dear! Thank you." Feeling a blush rise in her cheeks, she reached behind herself and pushed the offending garment back down. In her cabin she had a sort of large garter to hold it in place, which she had forgotten to slip on before coming out on deck. But though that device was effective at preserving her modesty, she found it interfered greatly with her maneuverability. "I suppose," she remarked, "with Lady Corey not here, that I may be able to get away with wearing my brother's trousers on deck. Would that be too scandalous?"

"With Lady Corey not here," Fox replied, "there is no telling what you might get away with."

"Sir!" she replied, genuinely shocked at the implication. "I *am* still a married woman . . . as are you." At his obvious amusement she immediately corrected herself. "Married, I mean." Again she felt herself blushing. It was far easier to blush in free descent, she reminded herself, due to the absence of gravity drawing the blood downward from the head.

"Of course," he said, inclining his head and barely suppressing laughter. "I meant no impropriety."

"I am certain you did not." She was not certain at all.

Their eyes met then, and something was communicated in that gaze. But she was not entirely sure what that something was . . . and definitely did not know what she wanted it to be.

"Excuse me," she said, and before the blush could appear in her cheeks again, she pushed off the rail and descended the ladder to the deck below.

---

Back in her cabin, Arabella considered the garter and the trousers for a long time.

A skirt, with the garter, was the more feminine garment. The trousers would give her a more masculine, serious air, and would free her limbs for action . . . but it could not be denied that the limbs thus exposed could be considered an enticement to inappropriate gazes and inappropriate comments.

Really, neither choice could completely spare her from unwanted attention. But the skirt was ordinary, conventional, and expected . . . and as such it was nearly invisible. It made no statement either way regarding availability or attraction, and did not call any more attention to her sex than did her voice and figure, neither of which could be completely disguised.

With some regret, then, she removed the garter from its bag and fitted it about her ankles. For now. But she would hold the trousers in reserve . . . they might be needed in case of battle.

She sincerely hoped it would not come to that. And yet she could not deny that some part of her desired it.

Days passed. Soon the days became weeks, and the weeks months.

Arabella spent quite a bit of her time in her cabin, reading upon topics of navigation and aerial battle from Fox's considerable collection of books, and took most of her meals in the wardroom with the officers, Fulton, and Dr. Barry. Occasionally she was invited to the captain's cabin for dinner, but she made sure that she and the captain were never left alone together.

Sometimes the captain's remarks verged upon indelicacy, or occasionally even indecency. Sometimes, she had to admit, her own remarks ventured into that same territory. But though she was now thousands of miles away from her husband, and—she was certain—even further from him in his emotions, she was still married to him.

And though he had betrayed the principles she had thought they held in common . . . though he had chosen loyalty to crown and country over love, honor, and decency . . . though he was now, of his own free will, fully embroiled in a horrific scheme which would, if unchecked, end in war, bloodshed, and terror for millions . . . despite all that, she still loved him. It was against her will, her principles, and her intellect, but the pull of her heart toward him could no more be denied than the force of gravity which held the planets in orbit around the Sun.

She could not deny, though, that Fox held a bit of gravitational attraction for her heart as well.

She pedaled against that attraction. Oh, how she pedaled.

But sometimes she grew weary of pedaling.

They crossed the orbit of Venus—a milestone for which, as no one aboard had ever crossed before, they had no particular ceremony in mind. So, perforce, they celebrated with an improvised observance involving costume, music, and wild gyrations in free descent. While raucous and hilarious, the affair lacked even a semblance of solemnity and was thus, at least to Arabella, somewhat disappointing. But she tried to mask her disenchantment.

In any case, the crossing of Venus was significant in that it marked the approximate midpoint of their journey to Mercury and, if Arabella's calculations were correct and the speed of the Swenson Current had been properly estimated by the Royal Society, nearly one-third of the entire voyage. Arabella and the quartermaster inventoried the stores, sampling some casks for spoilage—fortunately they found very little—and determined that, if all went well, they would neither starve nor perish of thirst before reaching Mars. But it would be a near thing, and would require careful apportionment of their supplies.

The heat grew intense, as she had known it would—a parching dry heat, which seemed at first more tolerable than the steamy suffocating dampness of the air near Venus, but soon grew debilitating in its own way. Most of the crew went about near-naked, and Arabella wore only a very light dress. In her cabin, she sometimes soaked it with water for the slight relief it gave. Lady Corey would have been completely scandalized.

Every once in a great while they came upon another ship, which inevitably proved to be a wind-whaler. Most of these were Americans, and as such their meetings were extremely strained, but as a state of war no longer existed between their two countries there was no need for actual hostilities. Once they met a Russian, and the mutual incomprehension of language and culture proved rather entertaining. And on two occasions the whalers were English, which provided a welcome respite from the inevitable isolation of the airlanes. One of the two, homeward bound after a very successful expedition, hosted a celebratory feast for

*Touchstone*'s officers, which raised Arabella's spirits greatly . . . until they departed, and she realized how very many more months the voyage would last.

The sky turned pale and cloudless, and shimmered with heat in every direction. The Sun grew gigantic, and pounded his rays upon the ship and crew like red-hot iron hammers. Not an asteroid, nor a whale, nor even a bird relieved the endless featureless brightness in which the ship seemed trapped and unmoving.

And Mercury was still weeks away.

# 7

## ROUNDING MERCURY'S HORN

Arabella floated in the dubious shade of a sail which the crew had stretched across the ship's waist to offer a bit of a respite from the Sun's endless pummeling brilliance. But even the heavy, double-strength canvas proved permeable to his rays, and she still saw red through her closed eyelids. Her outward breath blew hot on her lips, her inward breath nearly as much so. But at least here, unlike her cabin, the air moved a bit.

The time when she was too abashed to go out on deck with her dress soaked in water was long past . . . but so was the water. The crew's consumption of the irreplaceable stuff was so much greater than anticipated in this dry, unending heat that they had been required to limit its use to drinking and cooking alone. So Arabella's dress was wetted only with her own perspiration, and its hems were stiff with salt. Every other washable thing on the ship was equally filthy. This slovenly situation would no doubt have incensed Captain Fox . . . if he had had the energy to stir from his cabin more than once per watch.

Suddenly Arabella's indolent misery was interrupted by a cry from the quarterdeck: "Sail ho!"

She cracked open first one eye and then the other, squinting against the unending brightness. Following the gazes of the men floating in the yards, she peered into the distance abaft . . . away from the burning Sun, at least.

The air shimmered like a pot on the boil, making seeing difficult. Here and there an eddy or a vortex swirled, looking momentarily like a thing alive . . . "strange phenomena of the near-solar atmosphere," Collins had called them. But finally Arabella saw it.

Sail ho, indeed. A white fleck swimming in the pale, roiling blue of the overheated sky.

And something about that fleck, a half-glimpsed detail, made the hot breath catch in Arabella's throat. "May I borrow your glass?" she asked Collins, who floated near her. His broad exposed belly, once milk-white, was now brown as strong tea.

The telescope's brass nearly burnt her fingers. She pulled her sleeve down to protect her hand, and held the glass carefully away from her eye. Even so, the detail the device revealed was more than sufficient to confirm her suspicion.

Three masts. A triangle of sail, proudly set to catch the current, and heading directly toward them.

Whalers were all four-masters, like *Touchstone* herself. Navy ships-of-the-line generally bore six masts, three fore and three aft forming a hexagonal "snowflake" when seen head-on.

Three masts . . . might be a Yankee clipper, or a Navy frigate.

Or might be a Marsman—a ship of the Honorable Mars Company.

Arabella made her way aft, where she encountered Fox as he emerged, shirtless, from his cabin. "Have you seen . . . ?"

"I have," he said. His voice was dry and cracked from disuse, and he swallowed several times before continuing. "Three masts, ship-rigged. But she might not be a Marsman."

"There is no good reason for a Marsman to be on this course," Arabella said, trying to convince herself.

"There is no good reason for *us* to be on this course." He shrugged. "Might be a ship of the Royal Society, on a scientific expedition. Or a courier, bound for . . ." But he could not come up with a single plausible destination, and the sentence died unfinished. He took out his glass and peered aft at the interloper.

How, Arabella wondered, could *Diana*—assuming it were indeed she—possibly have followed them? *Touchstone*'s course was so unprecedented that Arabella herself could scarcely have imagined it even a week before they had taken the air, and despite Captain Singh's brilliance and the assistance of Aadim she doubted that he could have reproduced it. But he had other skills than navigation. Through interrogation of ships they had encountered in their course, inspection of cast-off barrels and other aerial flotsam, observation of the air currents, and knowledge of Arabella's navigational proclivities—many of which he himself had inculcated in her—he might have been able to follow in *Touchstone*'s wake even without knowing her intended course.

The Navy flotilla which had awaited them above Greenwich showed that he had informed the Prince immediately of her departure and likely course of action, and when *Touchstone* had evaded that trap he must have set out in pursuit as soon as *Diana* could be provisioned. Even so, it was a testament to his skills, and Aadim's, that he had been able to catch *Touchstone* up at all, never mind as quickly as he had.

"Whoever she is," Fox said, interrupting Arabella's uncomfortable musings, "our courses may merely be parallel." He handed his glass to Arabella. "Note the sails. With her sails set like that, she is traveling with the breeze, as we are. Now, if she were to strike the square sails and set spankers and jibs . . . we'd know she's pedaling. And in mid-current, as we both are, the only reason for her to pedal is to catch us up."

Arabella raised the glass to her eye—it was better than Collins's, and cooler to the touch as well—and noted the other ship's sails. They were, indeed, all square to the ship's course, a wide spread of canvas shining bright white in the devastating sun. But even as she watched, they folded themselves up, diminishing with crisp precision. The men performing the operation were too distant to be seen, but in her mind's ear Arabella heard the commands, the disciplined rhythms of an experienced captain and crew.

The sails vanished exactly as rapidly as she expected. She had performed those actions so many times herself. And the next step in that oft-rehearsed dance . . .

Yes. There it was. Spankers and jibs, flashing out on all three masts in perfect unison. The fore-and-aft sails that would prevent the ship from rotating counter to the spinning propulsive sails, driven by the crew at the pedals.

Wordlessly, she handed the glass back to Fox. He looked through it and grunted, then lowered it from his eye. "Well," he said.

"Well," she agreed.

"I suppose we must prepare for visitors."

---

Arabella, Fox, Liddon, and Collins conferred in the sweltering dark of the great cabin. "Hard to tell for sure with the air so lively," Liddon said, "but I'd say she's some two hundred miles behind us. If they pedal watch on watch at six knots, she'll catch us up in two days."

"*Diana* can do seven or eight knots, pedaling," Arabella said. She told herself she was merely offering information on the capabilities of a typical Marsman.

"Day and a half, then," Fox said. "Or a bit less. Not much difference."

Arabella tried to think strategically. "If we pedal watch on watch as well, we can maintain the distance between us indefinitely."

Fox snorted. "Until we collapse from the heat. And if she is a Marsman, she'll have a bigger crew, and likely better fed and watered than ours. That's a race we can't win." He shook his head, just slightly. "No. We'll need to save our strength for the circumduction of Mercury. Which is . . . ?"

Collins glanced down at the chart laid out on Fox's desk. "Three days off. At least."

The four of them stared at each other across the chart. Liddon rubbed the scar that marred his cheek. "So . . . we turn and fight?"

Fox considered the question for a long moment, then grimaced. "No, d—n it. We're too weak from heat and thirst. Even if we win the battle, we'd lose in the end."

"So what remains?" asked Arabella, despairing. "Surrender?"

"Might not be any need for that. She might just be coming by for a friendly chat. Perhaps bringing tea and crumpets." But his eyes showed he knew better. "Still . . . let us keep our dance card clear and our powder dry. We will await our visitors, conserve our strength . . . and if they prove hostile, hit 'em with a double-shotted broadside before they know what's what."

"Scarcely sporting," said Collins.

"We are filthy privateers," Fox replied, spreading his hands. "And, so far from civilization as we are, there's none to keep track of the score."

Arabella, aghast at Fox's callous brutality, felt her breath catch in her throat . . . but nonetheless held her tongue.

She had made her bed, and if murder were the price for lying in it, she would have to pay it. The tears would come afterward.

---

They shifted all stores and empty crates from the gun-deck, freeing the eight eight-pound guns for action. They cleared the path from the gun-deck to the magazine, and filled bags with powder and with shot. They rehearsed firing the great guns, running them in and out in dumb show . . . not wanting to reveal their intentions with live fire. Cannon-balls were chipped to perfect roundness; slow-match tubs laid out clean and ready; rammers, sponges, and worms racked at each gun for immediate use. Every man cleaned and loaded his pistols, if he had them, or practiced with his cutlass if not.

Aboard *Diana*, Arabella knew—she was forced to admit the three-master, whose every maneuver was as familiar to her as her own face in the glass, could be none other—they would be doing exactly the same. Her crew, largely composed of Venusians, had proved themselves remarkably adept gunners in the Battle of Venus. And though a Marsman usually carried only three four-pound guns, *Diana* had been refitted as a ship of war by the French and now was armed with twelve eight-pounders—throwing half again *Touchstone*'s weight of metal. *Touchstone* might be a privateer, a vicious predator of the air, but if it came to a battle between her and *Diana* . . .

Arabella hoped it would not.

She floated at the quarterdeck rail, staring aft. *Diana* had grown as large from masthead to masthead as a spread hand held at arm's length, and her crew could be seen with the naked eye as moving specks. Yet she had not signaled, which was worrisome.

Perhaps she merely had nothing to say.

Arabella touched the rail, turning herself in the air on her long axis, and looked down the length of the ship. There, beyond the bow-sprit—barely visible against the pale shimmering sky—stood Mercury, big as a clenched fist. The planet, pocked with craters and lifeless as a sun-baked rock, shone half-full as they approached it from behind in its orbit about the Sun. It seemed to grow as she watched, but she knew that was only wishful thinking. The pale, boiling sky shimmered all around it.

Mercury was smaller in the sky, but much bigger and further away than the other ship. *Diana* looked bigger, but was smaller and closer. And the two ships, drawing ever closer together by dint of *Diana*'s constantly whirling pulsers, were both falling toward Mercury at a speed thousands of times faster.

Would the two ships meet before they both encountered the planet? So long as *Diana* kept pedaling at the same speed, they would. And what would happen then was any one's guess.

Arabella had worked out the details of the planetary circumduction again and again, refining and adjusting every detail as they drew closer to Mercury and gained more information about the planet, the currents in its vicinity, and the ship and crew's capabilities in the heat. She was as certain as she could be that the maneuver, however novel, would succeed . . . but it would be conducted at unreasonably high speed and with exceptionally tight tolerances. There was no room whatsoever for error, and if *Touchstone* were distracted by battle, or even an uncertain rendezvous, during the maneuver or in the critical hours beforehand, she might find herself shooting away from Mercury into the trackless void between planets, or directly into the Sun, rather than into the welcoming arms of the Swenson Current.

"Aha!" It was a shout of surprise and triumph. Arabella turned to see Fox, on the other side of the quarterdeck, peering aft through his telescope and grinning like a fiend.

"What is it?"

"See for yourself!" He shot across the deck, bringing himself to a neat halt with one foot on the quarterdeck rail, and handed her the glass.

At first *Diana* seemed the same as before, if a bit closer. But then Arabella saw a wisp of white curling away behind her like a stray bit of *sukureth* peel. "What am I seeing?" she asked.

"One of her pulsers has torn loose!" he crowed. "I knew he was pushing them too hard, too long. This heat does terrible things to the grommets and clews."

Arabella raised Fox's glass to her eye again. Tiny crewmen were already moving to retrieve the wayward sail. If Captain Fox had considered this sort of damage a possibility, she knew that Captain Singh would have done so as well, and would surely have laid plans to recover from it. "How long will it take to repair?"

"Some hours, at least. Perhaps as much as a day, if the torn sail fouled the hub." He rubbed his hands together. "At this rate we may very well beat her to Mercury. And, as she lacks the aid of your greenwood box, we will surely lose her there."

"Surely," Arabella agreed, but without conviction. For if the pursuing ship were indeed *Diana*, she carried Aadim, by comparison with whose capabilities the greenwood box was little more than a toy.

Even with this injury to their opponent, she knew, the race was not yet won.

---

Hours passed. Ahead, Mercury swelled rapidly . . . not quite so fast that its growth could be detected with the unaided eye, but quickly enough that the difference was easily noticeable from one hour to the next. Abaft, *Diana* maintained her same distance.

Arabella inspected her frequently, using Fox's glass, but the progress or lack thereof of the repairs to her damaged pulser was undetectable at this distance.

But, still, every hour *Diana*'s pulsers did not turn increased the chances *Touchstone* would reach Mercury before the two ships came within cannon range of each other. And if that should occur . . . one of two things would happen.

Arabella was confident in her projected course around Mercury, and had studied the Swenson Current specifically before leaving London. Captain Singh, in pursuit, would not have known the specifics of Arabella's course, and could perforce have made only a general plan. He might, by observation of *Touchstone*'s course and with the help of Aadim, be able to match her planetary circumduction maneuver, but even so might not come out of it in a position to catch the Swenson. So if *Touchstone* reached Mercury before *Diana* caught *Touchstone* up, they might very well leave her behind, as Fox had asserted . . . indeed, might leave her stranded and becalmed, or hurtling uncontrollably toward the Sun. Alternatively, *Diana* might perform the maneuver perfectly, perhaps by following in *Touchstone*'s wake, and the pursuit would continue in the Swenson Current. With *Diana*'s more numerous crew, the outcome of that pursuit was not in doubt.

So to lose her husband forever, or to be chased by him until he caught her . . . these seemed to be her alternatives. Neither was very attractive.

Captain Singh had made a very serious gamble in pursuing her, she knew, and to a certain degree this flattered her. Yet by doing so, he had declared himself her enemy, and for this she could only condemn him.

Of course, there were many other possibilities. If *Diana* caught *Touchstone* before Mercury, Captain Singh would be in a position to seize her, board her, or disable her, and Arabella's expedition would end right there. Or, if Arabella had erred in her calculations or *Touchstone* failed to perform the circumduction correctly, the ship might be lost without *Diana*'s help.

Arabella bit her lip and raised Fox's glass to her eye again. And swore.

*Diana*'s pulsers were turning. Turning fast.

She turned in the air and shot down the ladder from the quarterdeck to Fox's cabin. There she consulted the chronometer and the charts . . . and swore again.

*Diana* would catch them up just as they reached Mercury.

And there was nothing at all to be done about it. For if *Touchstone* began to pedal now, in an attempt to outdistance her pursuer, she would round Mercury with too much speed and would miss the Swenson completely.

----

Mercury now loomed above like a giant's face, peering down at *Touchstone* as though the ship were a tiny *skorosh* scuttling about on a table-top. Now only quarter-full, as the ship whipped around toward its dark side, the planet was plainly a sphere rather than a disc, its heavily cratered surface turning visibly overhead as *Touchstone* shot past its south pole at a speed of over twenty thousand knots.

Arabella lowered her sextant, adjusted one of the greenwood box's dials minutely, and pressed the lever to activate its clockwork mechanism. She, Fox, and Liddon all stood upon the quarterdeck, with leather belts about their waists fastened by straps to cleats in the deck; the greenwood box, too, was firmly pegged to the deck. All of this was necessary to ensure a safe circumduction of Mercury.

They were, in fact, already in the midst of the maneuver, skating the upper reaches of Mercury's Horn. Careful touches of the sails and pedals had been needed to compensate for those turbulent winds, and Arabella had been thoroughly occupied with the sextant and greenwood box even as Fox utilized all his skills in ship-handling to keep them on the course she laid out.

*Diana,* too, had grown, now wider in the sky than Arabella's spread hands held thumb to thumb. But though the two ships had closed to within cannon range, she had not fired. Arabella suspected that Captain Singh and Aadim were as busy as she and Fox were, if not more so due to their lack of knowledge about *Touchstone*'s intended course, and had no attention to spare for battle.

The box's bell rang, announcing the end of calculations with a sound that came to Arabella through her feet as much as through the hot, noisy, storm-shot air. "Half a point to larboard," she told Fox after inspecting the dials.

"Aye aye," Fox replied, giving the ship's wheel a slight nudge to the left.

"Sir?" said Liddon, addressing Fox. He seemed uncharacteristically uncertain.

Arabella pulled her attention from the planet rolling so enormous overhead to Liddon, who was extending a trembling finger ahead and a few points up.

*Something* shimmered there. It looked like a whorl in the roiling, overheated air, only tighter and much better defined than any air current she had ever seen before. And then, a moment later, it was gone.

"Did you see . . . ?" asked Liddon, and Arabella acknowledged that she had. But Fox had not.

"Strange phenomena," Fox said, and left it at that. It was time for another course correction, and they had no time or attention for any thing else.

Arabella took a moment to look upward. Mercury was now

directly overhead, and its illuminated face had shrunken to a narrow, brilliant crescent with the gigantic Sun just about to vanish behind it. The sight was spectacular and beautiful, and she had no time or attention to appreciate it. "We will be in shadow in less than a minute!" she told Fox and Liddon.

She had no idea what would happen when they crossed from perpetual broiling day into Mercury's shadow. But there would almost certainly be a precipitous drop in temperature, and that might be accompanied by an unpredictable change in the wind.

The enormous Sun dove toward Mercury's horizon with astonishing speed. The illuminated crescent narrowed like a closing eye. The two met in a flare of light, and then . . . sudden darkness, and chill.

Arabella gasped aloud at the shock, which struck her like a dive into cold water. Fox, too, gasped "Oh!" in surprise.

And then the planet's shadow swept across the sky . . . and the stars came out.

So many stars! They peppered the cloudless sky in vast profusion—a sight she had not seen since that endless night of pedaling the Draisine from Brighton to Greenwich.

And more! In the sudden darkness the cratered dark side of Mercury leapt from impenetrable black to mottled gray—a bleak and pock-marked face which, nonetheless, inspired awe as it rolled overhead like a stone about to crush them all.

Then Liddon cried out "*Aaah!*"—a shriek of terror like nothing she had ever before heard from him, not even in the most desperate moments of battle. Following his gaping eyes, Arabella turned and looked to starboard.

She could not help but cry out herself.

An enormous, glowing, twisted shape stood out from the cratered surface above. It looked like a curl of fire—a whole nest of such curls—carved with a knife from the glowing sky and spread out across the planet's face. But it was not actually upon the planet; it was plainly much closer, and *huge*. A gigantic form, a physical thing, and much bigger than *Touchstone*.

Even as they watched, the glow faded, dimming so that the monstrous thing was plainly visible as a living creature rather than as a ragged patch of glowing sky. Illuminated by sky-glow like the gray craters beyond it, it resembled nothing so much as a gigantic squid!

Squids on Earth, Arabella knew, changed their colors to disguise themselves from their prey. This creature—this aerial kraken—plainly took on the brightness of the sky behind itself for a similar purpose.

She could not imagine why so huge a creature might need to disguise itself. But then she noted the double rows of scars that marked the length of its body . . . marks like those that might be left by the toothy jaw of a great bull wind-whale.

All of this ran through Arabella's mind in an instant as the creature became visible. But then Fox cried, "Forward pulsers! Smartly! Smartly! Put your backs into it!" A moment later the ship jerked beneath her feet, nearly knocking her over despite the stout leather straps that held her to the deck. She clung to the greenwood box, not certain whether it was saving her or she was saving it.

But though *Touchstone* surged forward with vigor, the kraken had resources of its own, and jetted toward them with even greater rapidity. Its many tentacles—eight? ten? more?—whipped through the air, seeking to envelop and crush the ship, which was nearly the size of a wind-whale but far stiffer and more fragile. Arabella found herself looking up into a vast black eye, big as a hogshead, which gleamed with intelligence in the light of the stars beyond.

Tentacles closed in from every direction, blotting out stars and planet and every other thing. A gigantic beak, like a pair of toothy ship's prows, gaped above the deck, preparing to bite and crush.

And then came a tremendous rattling *b-b-ba-bang*, accompanied by a lancing flash of flame that drove away the darkness for a moment, only to leave Arabella blind. When sight returned, she saw the kraken coiling away from *Touchstone*, tentacles writhing against the craters beyond. A minute later came a second *ba-ba-bang*. This time, not quite so surprised, Arabella understood what she was hearing and seeing.

It was *Diana*—brightly illuminated abaft, as she had not yet entered the planet's shadow. She was firing her twelve eight-pounders at the kraken. Arabella let out a cheer, which was barely audible even to her own gunshot-deafened ears.

"All hands to the guns!" Fox shouted through the scuttle to the airmen belowdecks. "Fire as the creature bears!" He spun the wheel, simultaneously calling commands to the topmen, to bring the ship about so that her great guns faced the kraken. *Touchstone*'s chasers and rifles were already being discharged in its direction, but the little wounds they made seemed to discomfit the great creature not at all.

Soon both ships' guns were firing at the creature, vast noise tearing the air and gouts of flame lancing out to pierce its scaly hide again and again. It jerked and spasmed in response, flares of light and color flashing across its body and tentacles lashing in every direction. One flailing appendage whooshed through the air just a few feet from Arabella and smashed the starboard mast to flinders. Topmen tumbled shrieking through the air in the tentacle's wake.

But despite the damage to both ships, their guns gave them the advantage. Minutes later the battle was over—the kraken was reduced to a twitching mass of dying flesh, black blood leaking into the air—but the peril was not. Gasping, reeling, half-faint with shock, Arabella found her sextant and took a sighting on Jupiter. "Ten points starboard!" she shouted in Fox's face. "Now! *Ten* points!"

"Aye aye!" Fox replied, and turned the wheel to the right.

It was a good thing she had gone over the maneuver so frequently and so thoroughly in the last few months. She knew exactly what she needed and exactly how to set the greenwood box to get it. Again and again she adjusted their course, sometimes by vast and desperate degree, in a frantic attempt to return the ship to her proper heading.

The planet rolled on by above.

The kraken's ruined corpse was left behind.

The ship emerged from Mercury's shadow, returning to blinding light and sweltering heat.

And suddenly the deck surged beneath Arabella's feet like a *huresh* that had sighted the barn.

Was this another strange phenomenon of the near-solar atmosphere? Or had something else—another kraken, or a whole pod of enraged wind-whales—attacked them?

But no. This surge went on and on, pressing *Touchstone* forward like the rush of a mighty river. Raising the sextant with trembling hands, she took a sighting on Jupiter, and on Mars.

The readings were unambiguous. "It's the Swenson!" Arabella cried. "The Swenson Current! We've found it!"

"Huzzah for the Swenson!" cried Liddon, and soon the rest of the crew took up the cheer as well. "*Huzzah for the Swenson!*" they cried. "*Huzzah! Huzzah! Huzzah!*"

But Arabella did not join in the cheer. She was searching, instead . . . searching the sky for any sign of *Diana*. Of her beloved, faithless, brilliant Judas of a husband.

Nothing abaft or ahead.

Nothing to starboard or larboard.

Nothing above or below.

Nothing. Nothing. Nothing.

But then, rising from below the horizon of the quarterdeck rail . . . veiled in gunpowder smoke, her bow-sprit shattered by a flailing tentacle . . . there came *Diana*. At this short distance it was unquestionably she, with the figurehead of proud Diana herself plainly visible beyond the torn sprit-sail, and the tattered ensign of the Honorable Mars Company fluttering behind her whirling and undamaged pulsers. And there, on the quarterdeck . . .

The lean, upright, dark-skinned figure of Captain Singh.

The pursuit might continue. But at least her captain yet lived.

"*Huzzah!*" Arabella cried. "*Huzzah! Huzzah! Huzzah!*"

# 8

REUNITED

Further observations confirmed Arabella's initial impression: despite the kraken's intervention, they had managed a successful planetary circumduction and were now fully embedded in the Swenson Current, speeding toward Mars at a speed of over seventeen thousand knots. But as damage reports filtered in to the quarterdeck, the full consequences of the battle rapidly became clear. *Touchstone* had lost her starboard mast and half the mizzen to the creature's thrashing tentacles, while *Diana*, sailing along with them in the same current only a few hundred yards away, had only suffered some damage to her bow-sprit. Any attempt to run or to fight would be doomed before it began.

"Well, we gave it a good try," Fox said as they watched Captain Singh's gig push off from *Diana*'s deck. The light aerial boat was pedaled by two crewmen and carried only the captain; this was no boarding-party. But the gun-ports in *Diana*'s bow remained open, her twelve guns run out and pointed directly at *Touchstone*, and shining Venusian eyes blinked from behind the cannons' gaping maws. Clearly this would be a negotiation from a position of strength.

Despite the obviousness of the situation to all concerned, the formalities must be observed. The lookout at the mainmast head called "Boat ahoy!" and the gig's coxswain replied *"Diana!"* The gig drew alongside then, and Captain Singh's strong distinctive voice called clearly across the short distance, "Permission to come aboard?"

It was the first time Arabella had heard that voice in months. The last time he had been begging her to return to his side, having just horribly disappointed her, but she had continued with chill determination down the stairs. She had spent every minute since then doing all she could to distance herself from him, in terms of her sentiments as well as her physical body, but now it was clear that she had failed in every respect. He had found her, he had captured her, and from the breath that caught at the back of her throat there was no doubt that she had never, despite her best efforts, escaped her love for him.

Captain Singh stepped with regal dignity down from the gig onto the deck, propelling himself in free descent with light touches of fingers and toes such that he gave the appearance of moving in gravity. Unlike Captain Fox, who often lounged horizontally in the air, Captain Singh always kept his feet pointed to the deck, and she could not fail to note that, even in this horrific heat, he was fully attired in the formal dress uniform of a captain of the Honorable Mars Company, down to the white Venusian silk gloves.

"Welcome to *Touchstone,* Captain Singh," said Captain Fox, bowing in the air. "First, I would like to offer you my personal thanks for your assistance with that despicable creature. Furthermore, I commend your restraint in not blowing us out of the sky even when you held the upper hand. I believe I speak for the entire crew when I say that, although we disagree most fervently with the Prince Regent's plans for Mars, we acknowledge that we have been bested fairly and will accept the consequences for our actions."

"I thank you for your congenial reception, Captain Fox," Captain Singh replied with reserved formality, "and for your gratitude. However, your understanding of the situation is incorrect."

"I see," said Fox, straightening in the air. His face showed that he was trying to prepare himself for the worst.

"You have not been bested," Captain Singh continued. "Not in the least. Indeed, it is you who have bested me. Your navigation, and your handling of your ship, through that unprecedented maneuver were astonishing. I had thought that I knew what you were about, and that with Aadim's help I would easily catch you up as you entered Mercury's Horn. But I understand now that you had a completely different aim in mind, one which I had not anticipated and could not duplicate. Had I not simply followed your lead around the planet, *Diana* would now be nothing more than a heap of shattered timbers upon the planet's surface."

Captain Fox blinked in surprise and incomprehension. "I am honored," he said after regaining his composure a bit, "but your compliments are, in fact, due to *Mrs.* Singh." He inclined his head to Arabella. "It was her greenwood box which made our course possible, and her navigation after the creature's attack which made it successful."

"Ah yes, the greenwood box." Captain Singh bowed deeply and respectfully to Arabella. "An excellent device. But, of course, it is the operator's knowledge and skill which make the difference between success and failure."

Now it was Arabella's turn to blink in incomprehension. "You say you have not bested us," she said, "but you also said that you planned to catch us up in Mercury's Horn . . . and you have, indeed, now caught us. Is your intent not to return us to Earth to stand trial for treason?"

Captain Singh's expression, constrained as always, did not alter. "Not in the least," he said. "I am here to join forces with you, to aid in the defense of Mars against the Prince Regent's scheme." His gaze dropped from Arabella's eyes to her feet, and his voice, though still reserved, took on a tone of contrition. "Even though we are no longer man and wife, I have become persuaded as to the validity of your concerns and the rightness of your cause. I intend to assist you to the very best of my ability." He looked up again, his brown eyes softer than she had ever seen before. "If you will have me."

Without thought Arabella suddenly found herself in her captain's arms. "Of course I will have you," she said. "I greatly respect your abilities, as you know; I admire your sense of honor, even when we disagree . . . and I love you with all my heart." She kissed him then, upon the lips . . . right there on deck, in every one's view, heedless of propriety.

"*Really*, Mrs. Singh," called a familiar voice from some distance away. "That is *quite* enough."

Arabella disengaged herself from her husband and looked over his shoulder to *Diana*, which had drawn even nearer during their conversation. There, upon the quarterdeck, floated Lady Corey!

"Mrs. Fox!" cried Fox. Immediately he shoved off from the deck, sailing unerringly between the two ships and ending neatly at her side. "What a pleasant surprise!"

"I trust you have comported yourself properly in my absence?"

Even across the several fathoms of air that separated them, Arabella noted Fox's eyes flick briefly to her. "I have been a perfect gentleman," he said, returning his gaze to his wife and bowing over her hand.

"He has," Arabella called to Lady Corey. Though, in truth, she had to acknowledge some imperfections on his part . . . as well as her own. Still, under the circumstances, she felt that both of them had behaved acceptably.

Captain Singh pressed Arabella tightly, then released her and held her at arm's length, gazing admiringly into her eyes. "Well, my dear," he said after a time, "we have much to discuss. May I invite you to breakfast?" He glanced to Captain Fox. "You and your officers are invited as well."

"It is closer to supper time, for us," Fox replied, "but I am happy to accept your invitation."

———————————

The party was so numerous that they were compelled to dine in *Diana*'s ward-room rather than in her captain's great cabin. For Arabella, after so many months in the constrained and rather shabby confines of *Touchstone*, it felt as grand as a palace. And the presence of her husband, now reunited with her in spirit as well as body, by her side made it grander still. Despite the unremitting heat, it took all her will to keep her hand from stroking his leg.

"I must begin with an apology," he said after the syllabub. "To my dear wife, who saw more clearly than I the inexcusable inhumanity of the Prince's scheme of conquest." He bowed his head to Arabella. "I had thought—I had the arrogance to presume—that such a scheme could be . . . ameliorated, with proper direction. But it cannot. The rot goes all the way to the root. Evil such as this cannot be managed, it can only be resisted."

"What was it that changed your mind?" asked Fox, not unreasonably.

"Have you ever heard of *ulka*?"

The faces of the Dianas present showed that they were familiar with the word, and that they did not like it. But Arabella was not, and plainly neither were most of the rest of the Touchstones. Fox, however, frowned. "It is a Venusian word, from the sound of it," he said. "I believe I may have heard it mentioned from time to time in the gambling-hells of Marieville. I do not recall ever having learned its meaning, but its associations are . . . not salubrious."

"Insalubrious indeed, Captain Fox. It is a drug, one refined from a plant native to Venus. The refined version renders the user indolent, suggestible, feeble, and highly dependent upon further doses. Once habituated—and, depending upon circumstances, a single dose can be sufficient—the user suffers terribly if the drug is withheld, and will do nearly any thing to obtain more. And humans and Martians are as vulnerable to these horrific effects as Venusians." He shook his head. "By the good graces of Lady Corey, I learned that it was Reid's plan to import *ulka* from Venus to Mars."

"Lord Reid did not inform the Prince of his plan to profit personally from English domination of Mars," Lady Corey explained. "But he did share that information with his mistress. And that mistress, when properly lubricated, could be persuaded to confide in a dear friend." She laid two fingers upon her bosom.

"The profits to be realized from the sale of a drug so powerfully habituating," Captain Singh continued, "are, of course, effectively unlimited."

"Why did you not immediately bear this news to the Prince?" Arabella asked.

Captain Singh sighed. "That was my first thought as well. But Lady Corey, fortunately, stayed my hand."

"Lord Reid, as you yourself discovered," Lady Corey said with a nod to Arabella, "detests your husband. So he has prepared a considerable volume of false evidence—forged papers, suborned witnesses, and the like—implicating Captain Singh as the scheme's author. If the plan is discovered, the drug is prohibited, or the whole scheme collapses of its own weight, your husband takes the blame and Reid walks away free. And if, at any time before that point, Reid desires your husband's destruction, a few words in the right ears will accomplish that goal in short order."

"If it came to my word against the Chairman of the Honorable Mars Company," Captain Singh said, "I do not doubt who would be believed, and who dismissed as a Godless Saracen."

"But now that you have departed," Captain Fox observed, "Reid must surely have pulled the lanyard on that trap-door."

"I am certain that he has. So now I have no choice but to throw in my lot with the Martians." He closed his eyes and blew out a breath through his nose. "In any case, as I said, the rot goes all the way to the root. Once I became aware of Reid's horrific scheme, I began to understand that, whether or not the Prince was party to it, it is part and parcel of his plan. Domination of Mars—imposition of the English will upon the Martian people— implies, indeed requires, domination of individual Martians by individual Englishmen. Even if Reid's drug scheme could be prevented, some other scheme, equally foul, would surely spring up in its place.

"Once my eyes were thoroughly opened to the horror of the Prince's scheme," the captain continued, "I had no choice but to turn in my resignation at once. But I was fortunate in that I was able to leave my letter of resignation on the Prince's desk shortly after his departure for Princess Charlotte's engagement dinner in Brighton. Knowing he would not receive it for some days, I could take the time to recall my crew and equip *Diana* for a long voyage. I was also very fortunate to know your destination and general course"—he nodded to Lady Corey—"though not the astonishing details of your maneuver around Mercury."

"I call it a planetary circumduction."

"By whatever name, it is an extraordinary feat of interplanetary navigation." He wiped his lips, folded his napkin, and tucked it under the clip which held it secure in free descent. "Now . . . we have the advantage of privileged information, and can expect to arrive at Mars some months in advance of the English. How can we best thwart the Prince's scheme, with minimal loss of life and property?"

---

The Prince's scheme, Captain Singh explained, was to take control of Mars in two stages.

The first stage of the invasion was a small advance fleet of some sixteen ships-of-the-line, each with a full contingent of Marines. "Their mission is to reinforce the existing Mars Company troops, perform reconnaissance, and prevent an effective resistance from forming. These ships lack Fulton's improvements, and their captains are men of no particular distinction. However, they will arrive quite soon—perhaps even within the year—and among their number are several experienced with the Mars trade."

"Within the year?" Collins gasped. "How can they possibly arrive so quickly?"

Captain Singh's eyes grew distant. "Immediately after accepting the Prince's commission," he confessed, "I dispatched a fast clipper to the Ceres fleet with orders to send a detachment at once to Mars. The winds were favorable, and a fast, unladen ship with an experienced navigator can move far faster than a fleet." His gaze dropped to the table between them. "I selected the very best navigator, and I also equipped him with Aadim's most rapid course. And with the short distance from Ceres to Mars at this season, they will arrive within months after receiving their orders."

Arabella was both impressed by her husband's perspicacity and disturbed by the rapid pace of events. "But because they were dispatched before your . . . departure," she said, "they will not be expecting an *informed* resistance."

He hesitated briefly before replying. "We can hope so," he said. "In any case, we must spend the time before the advance fleet's arrival organizing a resistance. We will require as many allies as possible, Martian as well as English, and will need to establish stocks of materiel and train men for an extended siege. But our largest concern is the second stage: the arrival of the Prince's fleet, which for reasons of planetary proximity can be expected in approximately twenty-six months."

This fleet, he explained, made Napoleon's planned fleet of armored men-of-war seem a mere flotilla by comparison. Though it had just begun construction when Captain Singh had left Earth, when complete it would consist of several dozen armored ships, the first-rates being larger and more heavily armed than Napoleon's flagship *Victoire,* and based on a design improved by Fulton after that ship's destruction. "The weakness at the stern," he explained, "which permitted *Diana* to defeat *Victoire,* has been corrected in this new draught."

*Victoire,* a single armored airship fresh from the ship-yard, had come close to defeating Lord Nelson's entire fleet by herself. The thought of a fleet of dozens of *Victoires*—no, even worse, dozens of ships *better* than *Victoire,* all fully shaken-down and manned by the cream of England's aerial Navy—descending upon Arabella's home planet filled her mind with horrific visions.

"The one area," Captain Singh continued, "in which the Prince's fleet is inferior to *Victoire* is its source of hydrogen: the Venusians used animals, larger versions of our own beloved Isambard, to produce that gas, whereas the Prince is dependent upon chemical processes, requiring a large and expensive manufactory. By the time they reach Mars, inevitable hydrogen leakage may reduce the ships' lift capacity to the point that some will be unable to descend safely to the surface." Again he glanced downward.

"I instructed the shipbuilders to spare no effort nor expense in finding a way to address this concern, and I have little doubt they will find a solution to the problem."

"Do not berate yourself for doing your best," Arabella said, placing her hand upon her captain's beneath the table, "for the cause to which you had committed yourself at the time. Although we disagreed then, we are both on the side of Mars now, and I am certain you will do even better for us."

"I thank you for your confidence," he said, inverting his hand to hold hers. "I wish I could be as certain." He closed his eyes. "I find myself contemplating a chess game in which, after a strong opening, I am compelled to change sides and defend a weaker position against my own very best strategies. I fear that even knowledge of those strategies may not be sufficient to carry the day." He opened his eyes again, and they were filled with care. "The Prince's Mars fleet will be the most powerful ever seen, and the most technically advanced. Even if we are able to interdict the drug and prevent the advance force from gaining a foot-hold, all Mars's resources may not be sufficient to withstand his assault."

"We can but make the attempt," Arabella said. Beneath the table-top, she squeezed her husband's hand in reassurance.

His hand pressed hers in return, but he did not meet her eyes. "Now . . . let us discuss our plans for resistance."

# 3

MARS, 1817–1819

# 9

## MARS

Arabella gazed forward at Mars, whose northern polar cap gleamed white against the red and orange of the deserts which covered most of the rest of the planet. From this unusual vantage, approaching via the Swenson Current from above the plane of the ecliptic, it presented the appearance of a disturbingly colored eye, with white pupil and red sclera glowing beneath the dark upper lid of the planet's night side. And from this distance—the planet's disc was merely the size of a dinner plate, and showed no visible curvature—the ruler-straight silver threads of the canals which carried polar melt water southward to the cities were completely invisible even in Captain Singh's best glass. But Arabella knew they were there, as she knew so many other things about the planet of her birth.

Saint George's Land, the English-controlled territory in which she had spent nearly her entire life, spanned only seven per cent of the planet's surface. Much of the rest was divided among hundreds of satrapies, princessipalities, and lesser fiefdoms, with the

balance being uncontrolled territory roamed by uncivilized no-
mads. But now they faced a common enemy. They would have to
join together against the Prince, or all would suffer domination
together.

With a sigh, she turned away from Mars and regarded *Touchstone*, which sailed in convoy a few hundred yards away. With all
sails spread to catch the current, guns run out, and airmen
bustling about the decks and masts, she presented a handsome
face to the world . . . but Arabella's keen eye saw that she was an
old ship, and tired. Her *khoresh*-wood planks were a mosaic in
shades of gold, showing decades of repairs and replacements, and
the copper of her hull was patched in many places. Her starboard
and mizzen-masts, smashed by the kraken, were fished and jury-
rigged, little more than splinters held together with cordage; her
sails bore the scars of the kraken attack and many others before
that. Her people, too, Arabella knew, were hungry, thirsty, and
weary, still half-baked from their close passage to the Sun and
parched by short allowances of water and grog. Even the usually
joyous ceremony of crossing Earth's orbit had been muted and
perfunctory, not least because the ship's position high above
the plane of the ecliptic made the exact date of that crossing
uncertain.

*Diana* and her crew were in somewhat better condition, largely
because Captain Singh's greater personal fortune had bought
them more in the way of supplies before leaving Earth. But even
though *Diana* was larger, newer, and better-appointed than
*Touchstone*, she had still been sorely taxed by the difficult passage,
and her officers and crew were looking forward with great eagerness to landfall on Mars—and to the return of full allowances of
fresh water, meat, and vegetables.

Arabella, too, would be greatly relieved to stand once more
upon the red sands of her home world. But she knew that
any rest they would gain there would be transitory—perhaps

even illusory. For the Prince and his men were already on their way and the struggle for the freedom of Mars must begin immediately.

Two ships, no matter how stalwart their men or brilliant their commanders, seemed no more than straws against the tide. But, as the Martians themselves were prevented by treaty from building their own, two ships were what they had.

For now, she reminded herself. They would find confederates and build alliances. Surely the inhumanity of the Prince's scheme would compel ships of other nations, and hopefully at least a few Englishmen, to join in the defense of Mars.

Surely.

---

Days later, Mars had grown from a disc to a globe, a butterscotch-colored sphere which turned lazily below the ships' keels as they approached the turbulent winds of Mars's Horn. Though the dryness of the atmosphere near Mars prevented his Horn from developing the roiling storm clouds seen at Earth, and the planet's smaller size made the winds less severe, the Horn still presented a tricky navigational exercise, one which must be solved precisely if one wished to land at one's destination rather than in the trackless desert some miles away.

Fortunately, Aadim had been built with just this exercise in mind, and Arabella had very little difficulty setting his dials and levers appropriately to request a course for the coming approach. But when it came to designating the final coordinate, she encountered an unexpected obstacle. As she moved his hand toward Fort Augusta, she seemed to feel some resistance, indeed a veritable pull to the north.

Arabella looked with surprise into the automaton's face—the green glass eyes peered neutrally forward, as always—and said aloud, "What is the matter? We *must* land at Fort Augusta. All our friends and allies are there."

Aadim's mechanisms ticked and whirred beneath his desk-top as always, but he made no reply—as, indeed, he had never done in all the time she had known him, save for one memorable occasion which had, almost certainly, been nothing but a dream.

But though Aadim hardly ever offered up advice of his own volition, he did seem to provide reactions to, or even criticism of, the courses with which he assisted. She looked down at the chart spread out upon his desk, which showed the Martian landscape beneath them . . . then closed her eyes and allowed Aadim's hand to seek its own path across the map. After a motion of a foot or so, the moving hand stopped with a slight click.

She opened her eyes. Aadim's finger was pointing to a spot in the desert north of Khoresh Tukath—a desolate area far from any settlement, canal, or overland trade route, and lacking in any notable feature. But there were a few small symbols in its vicinity, crosses and triangles and other marks with which she was not familiar.

Consulting the chart's legend, she discovered that those symbols represented mineral resources—tin, iron, and limestone, among other things. Further, notations at the chart's foot indicated that these deposits, just a small part of Sor Khoresh's vast mineral wealth, were not currently being actively mined, no doubt due to their great distance from civilization.

"We cannot possibly land there," she said. "Whatever do you have in mind?"

Then the panes of the broad stern window rattled, accompanied by a clatter of the sheets and braces against the sails, and the deck shifted perceptibly beneath Arabella's floating feet. The ship was beginning to enter the Horn's turbulent winds, and there was no more time for abstractions. With a whispered apology Arabella gently moved Aadim's hand to Fort Augusta—it offered only token resistance—and pressed his finger to initiate the calculation.

While Aadim's gears ground away, Arabella stared at the isolated spot he had indicated. Plainly he thought it was significant, but to what end? She tore a sheet from her note-book, drew a quick sketch-map of the area, and noted the indicated spot with an X, tucking the paper into her reticule for later study. And then the bell rang, indicating a completed course.

Arabella wrote out two copies of the course, one of which would be conveyed to *Touchstone* by the captain's gig. But she gazed one more time into Aadim's unseeing eyes before returning abovedecks. "What *are* you on about, you exasperating machine?"

The automaton, of course, was as reticent as ever.

———————

Arabella came out on deck, where she requested and received permission to ascend to the quarterdeck. There she found Captain Singh already belted in for the passage through the Horn; a broad leather belt attached by straps to cleats on the deck held him down as though he were standing in gravity. A similar belt awaited Arabella, and after handing the sailing orders over to Stross, *Diana's* sailing-master, she buckled herself into it.

"Is all well with Aadim?" the captain asked in a conversational tone, his eyes scanning the sky. "I was beginning to wonder what had become of you."

"All is well, I believe. But you know how . . . opinionated he can be, sometimes."

He gave her a brief thoughtful glance before returning his attention to the currents ahead. "We will discuss this later, but our immediate concern is descent to Fort Augusta. The proximity of Phobos"—he pointed ahead—"causes great volatility in the winds."

Phobos, the closer and larger of Mars's two moons, loomed beyond the bow-sprit a few points to starboard. So great was its orbital velocity that it grew visibly nearer even as they watched—but its angle was changing, indicating that no collision need be feared. Though the moon was a gray, barren, and lifeless rock, a few lights nonetheless glimmered on its dark side; it had a small permanent population, and served as a trading post and free-descent ship-yard for traders and privateers.

"Phobos moves so rapidly through the air," the captain continued, "that it creates a substantial vortex—very nearly a second Horn within Mars's own. I have attempted several times to incorporate this turbulence into Aadim's calculations, but its small scale and great complexity make this a very thorny problem. Captain Fox," he remarked conversationally, "told me that he was required to hire a pilot from Sor Khoresh for approach to Phobos. Apparently they have unique expertise, without which a ship risks being dashed upon the moon's surface by the unpredictable winds."

The existence of experienced khoreshte pilots was new intelligence to Arabella, and raised numerous questions in her mind. "Mills once provided the same service to the Portuguese," she said, "piloting small boats through the choppy waves off Gambia."

"I hope that some day automata may be able to serve this purpose, freeing men—and Martians too, I suppose—for higher pursuits."

At that moment the deck lurched beneath their feet, as the winds of the Horn suddenly took hold of the ship. Their conversation was perforce curtailed, replaced by a more utilitarian exchange of observations, course corrections, and commands to guide the ship through those ever-changing winds, now made even more capricious by the passage of Phobos.

Arabella watched that moon hurtle past the starboard beam,

then gave it no further thought. Even with Aadim's help, the descent to Fort Augusta would be tricky enough.

———————————

After many hours of capricious, jarring, and sometimes even nauseating turbulence, *Diana* and *Touchstone* passed below the Horn's fickle winds and into the calmer—though still variable— breezes of the upper planetary atmosphere. The planet below had turned from a globe to a landscape, curving away from them in all directions to a hazy horizon, and was echoed by the three great balloons, now filled with hydrogen, above. *Touchstone* too had deployed her balloon, a single envelope filled with coal-heated air.

The balloons were necessary now because, with their proximity to Mars, the force of gravity had begun to return; Arabella's feet now pressed against the deck with her own weight as well as the force of her leather straps. With relief she unbuckled herself and handed the belt to an airman, though she kept a steadying hand upon the rail. Her weight at this altitude, still well above the falling-line, was as yet quite slight, and there was still some risk of being tumbled overboard by an unexpected gust. But the freedom to move about as she wished was delicious, and she desired to re-accustom herself to walking in gravity as quickly as she could. There would be much work to be done as soon as they alighted.

———————————

Khema's home was an imposing structure in the Martian quarter of Fort Augusta town, which also housed the *akhmok* of several other tribes. Three stories tall and formed of smooth fused sand, it rose like a great swelling gourd above the smaller buildings around it. From its peak fluttered the colorful banners of the many tribes and clans of Saint George's Land, all of whom were represented here either directly or indirectly.

Arabella and Captain Singh took tea with Khema in the council chamber, a large oval room which filled the house's highest story. Rounded windows overlooked the town, providing an inspiring view of Fort Augusta itself on one side and the vastness of the desert on the other. The silvery thread of the great Khef Shulash canal cut through the red sand, straight as a cannonball's flight.

Khema sipped her tea, her lightly faceted eyes spread gently in contemplation. The delicate tea-cup, imported from China via England like the tea itself, might have seemed ludicrous in her massive fingers but for the assured dexterity with which she handled it.

"I thank you for the intelligence which you have brought," she said, setting down her cup. And that was all.

"I do not believe you understand the severity of the situation," Arabella said, after waiting a moment longer. "This is, perhaps, the greatest threat that Mars has ever faced! The Prince's fleet of armored first-rates will make short work of your every defense if you do not take steps immediately! Now, what I have in mind is—"

But Khema raised one thick and stony finger, silencing Arabella immediately. "I do *not* underestimate the severity of the situation. This is, indeed, a very serious threat, and I assure you that we will take very serious steps to counteract it. However, this is far from the greatest threat that Mars has ever faced."

"Do tell," said Captain Singh, leaning forward over his own tea-cup.

"The greatest threat Mars has ever faced," Khema continued mildly, "began with a single ship. The *Mars Adventure*, commanded by one Captain William Kidd."

"I scarcely think—!" Arabella began to protest. But Captain Singh, she noted, nodded slowly in dawning comprehension, and she swallowed her objection.

"I do believe that Mars eventually adapted to that threat," Captain Singh remarked. "However, the English *are* still here. And may I humbly suggest that this new threat, while not as completely without precedent as that one was, is perhaps of greater magnitude."

"I take your point. However, with the warning you have very kindly provided, I believe we have sufficient time to prepare a defense."

"But you have no aerial ships!" Arabella blurted out. "No cannon! No firearms! And no ability to produce them, certainly not in time!"

Khema rose from her seat then—an imposing figure indeed, eight feet tall and nearly half as broad, with prongs and spines extending from every joint—but her voice continued gentle. "I feel I must remind you," she said to Arabella, "that the only reason we lack ships and firearms is the treaties imposed upon us by the English."

It was the same voice of tender rebuke she had used when, as a small child, Arabella had broken the mainspring of her father's automaton dancer and tried to hide the evidence, and Khema had explained to her the Martian concept of *okhaya*, or personal responsibility. And Arabella felt now the same shame she had felt then.

"And the reason we have no ability to produce them," Khema continued, "may be found in our schools, also imposed upon us by the English, which for some reason give greater weight to the skills needed by servants and majordomos"—here she gestured to herself, reminding Arabella that, even when Khema had taken charge of the Ashby household during the rebellion some years earlier, she had done so in a subordinate role to the absent

owners—"than to those of artisans, engineers, and natural phi-
losophers."

"I . . . I see," Arabella said, bowing her head. "But what can
be done about those limitations now?"

"Treaties can be . . . quietly contravened. Perhaps they already
have been. And schools . . . well, that is perhaps an area where
you can assist us."

Arabella blinked. "I?"

"Your talents with automata, navigation, and manufacture are
well known. And, as I recall from your youth, you showed little
hesitation, and some skill, in explaining your latest discovery to
any one who would listen . . . and even a few who did not wish
to." At this Arabella could not suppress a small smile. "If you
were to turn these impulses to the education of Martians in
science and engineering, who can say what might be possible in
a year?" For it was, indeed, approximately one Martian year until
the Prince's fleet was expected to arrive.

"I . . . I would be honored to serve the cause of resistance in
any way I can," Arabella said, chastened.

"And you are very welcome to assist. But this is the Martians'
struggle, never forget this."

"I shall endeavor to keep this in mind," said Arabella, quite
sincerely.

"As for myself," Captain Singh put in, "I am privy to some of
the Prince's plans of conquest, and I may be able to offer some
strategic assistance."

"Thank you," Khema replied, inclining her head. "Do you
have any specific suggestions at this time?"

"We do," Captain Singh said, nodding to Arabella. The two
of them, along with Lady Corey and Fulton, had discussed strategy for many long hours in *Diana*'s great cabin on the voyage
from Mercury to Mars. "We propose the construction of an entire
fleet of armored ships, sufficient to match or better the Prince's

fleet. But in order to produce this fleet, an iron refinery and ship-yard must first be built. The American inventor Fulton, who is with us, designed and built a similar facility for Napoleon, which was entirely successful."

"The location must have iron, coal, limestone, and *khoresh*-wood in close proximity," Arabella continued, "and a sufficient population of workers. Saint George's Land is well supplied with *khoresh*-plantations, of course, and I know of several coal mines. But are you aware of any limestone quarries in the vicinity? The reference materials we had aboard *Diana* were silent on this matter."

Khema thought for a moment before replying. "I am, myself, ignorant of this issue, but I believe there are more important considerations. Saint George's Land is not large, and all of it is very much under the English eye. I cannot imagine any place in the territory where such a large operation—and I gather from what I have read of your adventures on Venus that it would be very large indeed—could possibly escape English attention."

"The facility would be several acres in extent, at least," Captain Singh admitted.

Khema thought still further, her eye-stalks downcast in concentration and concern. "Sor Khoresh . . ." she began, then paused.

"Why do you hesitate?" Arabella asked. "Tura would make an excellent ally, and we did her a very great service not long ago."

Sor Khoresh, a powerful Martian satrapy which bordered Saint George's Land to the north, was well known to Arabella. Rich in iron, coal, and other minerals, it was ruled by Tura, an intelligent and aggressive potentate. No other satrap in the hemisphere controlled so much territory, or carried so much influence with her peers, and the proximity of Khoresh Tukath, her capital city, to Fort Augusta would make it an excellent headquarters for operations against the invasion.

Tura's strategic and diplomatic expertise were, admittedly,

equaled by her mercurial temper. After a recent conspiracy against Sor Khoresh by one of her neighboring states had been revealed, Tura had gone so far as to execute her own daughter—who had, to be fair, been one of those involved in the plot. But Arabella herself, along with Captain Singh, had been key to the exposure of that scheme. "I am certain," she continued, "that Tura would at least be willing to entertain an entreaty."

"I agree," said Captain Singh. "And we would be happy to convey you to her upon *Diana*."

Khema still seemed unconvinced. "Relations between the Martians of Saint George's Land and those of Sor Khoresh have varied in cordiality over the years," she replied rather darkly, "and Tura and I have not always seen eye-stalk to eye-stalk." She considered a moment more. "Still, I suppose we must make the attempt. I will be happy to accept your offer of conveyance"—she politely inclined her massive head to Captain Singh, who replied with a nod of his own—"as soon as certain obligations have been discharged here. Please return to-morrow afternoon."

After a few more details had been worked out, Arabella and Captain Singh took their leave. "Before we meet with Tura," she said to him as they descended the steps to the street, "I must call upon my brother. We could arrive at Woodthrush Woods by coach in time for dinner."

---

Michael came out from the manor house as they descended from the coach which had carried them from Fort Augusta. "Dear sister!" he cried as he stumped toward them.

"Michael!" she said as he embraced her, his crutch falling to the ground. "It has been too long."

She could not help but notice how heavily he leaned upon her, even two years after the loss of his leg. She would love to fit him out with a clockwork limb like her own, but she could not do so without committing to perform the constant maintenance and adjustments the sometimes-temperamental device required. Perhaps some day it would be possible to manufacture these limbs in quantity, she thought, and make them as simple and dependable as a spring-wound lantern.

Michael released Arabella, retrieved his crutch, and shook her husband's hand. "Captain Singh," he said with a cordiality just a bit shy of brotherly. He had never quite reconciled himself to his sister's choice of husband, she knew. "I trust you are well?"

"Very well, sir," the captain replied with genuine warmth. "Unfortunately, we are not able to remain here long."

Michael hesitated momentarily, then said, "Will you join me for luncheon, sir?" It was plain his heart was not in the invitation.

Arabella looked to her husband, attempting to indicate with her eyes the sentiment *at least he is trying*. He caught her gaze, bowed, and said to Michael, "I am happy to accept your hospitality, sir."

Michael offered his elbow to Arabella. "May I?" he said . . . looking to Captain Singh, not Arabella.

"That choice belongs to the lady, sir," Captain Singh said with cold civility.

Arabella accepted Michael's proffered elbow before her brother could form any reply. "The pleasure is mine, dear brother."

To argue with him now risked souring him on the request she intended to make of him. But she would call him to account later for his presumption.

———————

The luncheon Michael's staff laid out was every thing Arabella could have hoped for, with *khula* and *gethown* for dessert—both among her favorite dishes of her childhood, and delicacies she had not tasted for years—and the conversation was joyous at first, with Arabella bearing the news of the final defeat of Napoleon, the victory celebrations in England, and the good health of their mother and sisters. Michael, too, had done well since Arabella had last seen him, having acquired several hundred prime acres from a neighbor and built several more drying-sheds, increasing the plantation's production of kiln-dried *khoresh*-wood by nearly fifty per cent.

But as the dessert dishes were being cleared, and before Michael could take Captain Singh away for port and cigars in the drawing-room, Arabella finally raised the issue which had brought her back to the family plantation.

"The Prince Regent," she explained, "intends nothing less than the utter and complete conquest of Mars. As a child of Mars, I must oppose this, and I hope that I may depend upon you to do so as well."

"But he is our lord and sovereign!" Michael protested. "Born on Mars we may be, but we are still English subjects! If you should happen to have been born in a boat upon the sea, would you swear fealty to Neptune above your own King?"

A boat upon the sea, Arabella reflected, was a thing Michael had never in his life even beheld; unlike Arabella and her sisters, he had not been transported back to Earth by their mother. How curious—and very English—it was that he, a denizen of the sand for his entire life, should choose a watery metaphor. "This is not merely an accident of birth," she protested. "It is a matter of simple humanity. Can you not see how unfair—how cruel—it would be for England to seize control of an entire planet, merely because the Prince has more and better ships?"

"I cannot agree at all! Surely it is not 'unfair' for a more civilized, more advanced nation to offer guidance to a less developed one, even if that nation should happen to span an entire planet. And as for cruelty . . . England's civilizing influence upon Mars might cause some pain, yes, but it is not in the least cruel! It is the same sort of pain that a loving parent may inflict upon a dis-obedient child: proportional, deliberate, and entirely justified. And the child will, as it grows to maturity, understand this, and indeed come to appreciate the lesson learned."

Arabella held her voice level by an effort of will. "Comparing Mars, whose history is some thousands of years longer than our own, to a child does nothing more than display your own igno-rance." Captain Singh, she noted, sat rigidly, allowing Arabella to take the lead in argument with her brother, though his senti-ments were plain from the scowl that creased his brow. Seeing this, she realized that her own brow was furrowed with anger—which, knowing Michael, would surely not help her cause. She took a deep breath and strove to relax her features. "Be that as it may . . . we may disagree, but as even Mother eventually real-ized, you cannot prevent me from doing what is right. And as your sister—and, I must point out, as the one who rescued the family fortune from our dear cousin Simon—I hope that I may impose upon you, out of family loyalty if nothing else, to support the cause of Mars with a share of that same fortune."

"You have ever and always done what you thought was right," Michael acknowledged. "And, whatever our current differences, I know that we have always supported each other in our . . . unconventional adventures." He smiled slightly then, obviously recalling some happy memory, and Arabella's heart lightened. But then his smile collapsed, and with it Arabella's hopes. "But I *cannot* support you in this. I will grant you an allowance of . . . let us say two hundred pounds per year, so long as you are on Mars. But I will not open the family purse any further than that."

Two hundred pounds was exceedingly generous for an allowance—she must give him that—especially for a married sibling not living under the same roof. But it was a mere pittance by comparison with the vast sums that would be required to fund

any sort of organized resistance, and far less than she had hoped
for. "Is that your final decision?"

"No," he replied coldly. "If your behavior requires . . . I may
reduce it."

---

Two days later, Arabella peered ahead from *Diana*'s forward rail,
where she soon recognized the distinctive silhouette of Khoresh
Tukath, the capital city of Sor Khoresh.

Even at this distance, it was clear that the inner city alone,
ringed by a substantial wall, was larger than the entire town of
Fort Augusta, the largest human settlement on Mars. With the
outskirts included, Khoresh Tukath was more than five times Fort
Augusta's size, and that larger area was thickly clustered with tall
towers, dense blocks of habitations, and the magnificent munici-
pal buildings fitting the capital of a major nation. But still more
impressive than the city itself was the palace that rose above it.

Tura's palace stood atop a vertiginous, craggy hill at the center
of the inner city. The hill itself, a single massive block of deep red
Martian stone, loomed high above the city; the palace mounted
still higher above its peak, a soaring arrogant gesture of steel
and stone. Every corner was anchored by a gleaming curve of
steel, rising like an upthrust sword from the red rock at its base;
the walls between those shining steel arcs were of stone, carefully formed and artfully fitted. Even from very close, she knew,
the gaps between those stones could barely be discerned; from
this distance they seemed a single mass, solid and impenetrable.

As *Diana* and *Touchstone* drew nearer the palace, more details
came into view: pinnacles, minarets, balconies, and monumental
sculptures of khoreshte warriors loomed above those massive
walls like a forest of upthrust spears. Yet for all their elegant

splendor these features were not fanciful at all—instead, like the ornately carved figureheads of English and French men-of-war, they projected a power so confident that no amount of ornamentation could reduce their effectiveness.

By now they had approached so near the city that the port—a vast expanse of flat, smooth sand densely forested with masts—was plainly their destination, and indeed within the hour they would be above it. "Ease off pulsers!" came the command from behind Arabella, and the constant drumbeat from belowdecks slowed to half its previous pace. Curious as to why the command had been given so much sooner than she had expected, she looked about . . . and saw several balloons rising toward them from a fortress below. Beneath each balloon hung a small ship, or rather a boat, of a design she had never before encountered. Flat-bottomed and angular in construction, they were exceptionally lightly built and carried but two masts, extending horizontally to larboard and starboard. Three-sail pulsers drove them toward the English ships.

"What are those vessels?" she asked Edmonds, the chief mate, as the captain was occupied. Khema, who might also know, had retired below; for all her size and strength she was possessed of a remarkably delicate stomach, and the motion of the ship through even quite gentle breezes made her rather air-sick.

"Never seen the like, exactly," Edmonds said, "but they're Martian-made for sure."

"I thought the Martians were not allowed aerial ships?"

"Not interplanetary ships, ma'am. But some of 'em worked out the building of inshore vessels"—he gestured to the Martian boats—"before the treaties, and they were allowed to keep 'em." He peered more closely. "They're armed."

Indeed, Arabella saw that each boat carried two large cross-bows, each manned by an alert crew of Martians. Each bow—as long as a tall man's height—was drawn back in a taut curve, with a massive arrow, or bolt, laid in the groove ready for firing. A flame flickered at the head of each bolt.

"Those are fire-bolts!" Arabella cried, alarmed. This type of weapon, she knew from her reading, was ineffective in interplanetary aerial combat; in free descent, flames tended to suffocate unless deliberately fanned. But in gravity, with the flames fed by rising air, a burning crossbow bolt could set a balloon envelope afire, sending the ship plummeting to the ground below. Even worse, as *Diana*'s balloons were filled with hydrogen, a single bolt could easily cause a tremendous explosion.

Immediately Edmonds reported this intelligence to the captain, who at once ordered "Back pulsers!" The ship slowed to a stop, still some distance from the port.

In the sudden silence that fell after the drums belowdeck ceased, Arabella made out a harsh sound from the nearest boat. It was a call from a Martian throat, she felt certain, but its meaning eluded her. She moved closer to Captain Singh.

"What is he saying?" he asked her.

"I do not know," she confessed. "It must be khoreshte dialect. Khema would have a better idea."

Captain Singh turned to Watson, one of *Diana*'s midshipmen. "Pray convey to Miss Khema my very best regards, and request her presence upon the quarterdeck." Even as Watson scurried off, the Martian hailed *Diana* again, repeating her previous request with greater urgency.

"Khema was in a very bad way when last I saw her," Captain Singh said. "She may not be in any position to assist us. Can you ask the Martian what he wants?" He handed her a speaking-trumpet.

"She," Arabella corrected, taking the device. "I will try." She paused a moment, trying to bring Martian language, unused in some years, back to the forefront of her mind, then formulated a reasonably polite request in Khema's tribal dialect. Drawing in a lungful of the cool, fresh, dry air, she bellowed the request as loudly as she could . . . then bent over, coughing, from the unexpected effort. Martian language was not easily shouted by the human throat.

The boat replied almost immediately, and to Arabella's relief it was in the same language. "They desire to come aboard and inspect our ship before we land," she translated.

"Highly unusual," Captain Singh muttered. "But I suppose a Company ship is unusual in this port."

"I suppose they would be more used to privateers, and independent traders."

"Tell them they must extinguish their fire-bolts before approaching."

Arabella considered her grammar, then raised the speaking-trumpet to her lips to make the request, adding an explanation that the ship carried highly inflammable cargo. It was not exactly a lie.

The Martians did not reply immediately, debating amongst themselves. "If we were lifted by coal," Captain Singh said quietly, "we would be running low on fuel at this point. Surely their strategy depends upon our desperation to land quickly."

"Perhaps we should not yet reveal our advantage in this area."

The captain's expression soured. "With the fire-bolts in play, that advantage is also a disadvantage."

Arabella glanced around, trying to imagine what her captain was seeing with his strategic eye. They were now completely surrounded by khoreshte air-boats, above and below as well as to all sides, though only the boat directly ahead lay close enough to be worrisome. The ground directly beneath was rocky and inhospitable—if they were forced down, it would be a rough landing indeed.

A rasping call from the lead khoreshte boat roused Arabella

from her reverie. "They refuse," she translated, even as the boat moved closer. Smoke rose from the flames of its crossbow bolts, and drips of flaming fuel fell toward the jagged rocks below.

Not taking his eyes from the advancing boat, Captain Singh took a step back to stand beside Edmonds. "Quietly, now," he muttered. "Pass the word to the sharpshooters in the tops: target the Martians' gunners. But do not fire unless and until I give the command."

Arabella's heart hammered in her breast. They were surrounded by eight or nine khoreshte boats, each bearing two crossbows with several Martians on each. Even if *Diana*'s sharpshooters fired rapidly and accurately they would not be able to take all the Martians out of action before they fired. And if even a single flaming crossbow bolt struck a hydrogen-filled balloon the result would be disastrous.

The gun crews in the lead boat readied their weapons, cranking the bows to their maximum tension. Captain Singh drew in a breath.

And then a call—a brief, loud utterance in the same rattling language the aerial boat's commander had used—interrupted the proceedings, and Arabella looked over the quarterdeck's forward rail to the source of the sound. It was Khema, who had just emerged from belowdecks. Her knees wavered, her fingers clutched the gunwale, and even her eye-stalks waved uneasily, but she was nonetheless vertical and capable of speech.

In the silence after Khema's cry, nothing moved. The Martian crossbows and *Diana*'s rifles remained fixed upon their targets. Even the wind seemed to have fallen silent.

"What did you say?" Captain Singh asked Khema.

"I invoked *akhmok*-right." Khema made her way carefully to the base of the quarterdeck ladder, creeping along the gunwale hand-over-hand. She was too large to comfortably ascend to the quarterdeck itself. "Our authority crosses boundaries of tribe and nation."

Captain Singh blinked, but he said nothing, nor did his gaze stray from the gun crew in the nearest khoreshte boat. The Martian gunners, in turn, stared right back at him, their faceted eyes glinting in the summer sun. No one moved or spoke.

"Under most circumstances *akhmok*-right is accepted without hesitation," Khema said uneasily. "Carts and canal-boats carrying *akhmok* are not subject to inspection, and it seems obvious to me that this privilege should extend to ships of the air as well."

"The commander of this flotilla," Captain Singh said, "may not agree."

The silent impasse went on and on. Then the lead boat's commander, who stood upon a small platform in the boat's waist, called a question. Khema called back in the same language. This received what seemed to Arabella a very brusque reply.

"She asks why an *akhmok* travels upon an English airship," Khema translated. "I told her that I have come from Fort Augusta with a matter of import to all Martians. She does not seem impressed."

Finally, the commander waved a hand in a gesture of disgusted resignation. "Very well," she called in Khema's dialect. "You may proceed. Let Tura deal with you!"

None of the Martians on that boat or any of the others seemed entirely pleased with this outcome. But they backed away, pulsers whirling, and allowed *Diana* to proceed toward the port.

"Thank you for your assistance," Captain Singh said to Khema. "I hope to have you on solid ground shortly."

"I look forward to that moment with great pleasure. But I fear that even greater challenges may await us after we land." Her eye-stalks drew together in concern.

On the one previous occasion that Arabella had encountered Tura, it had been in her audience chamber, a lofty and grandiose space designed to impress with costly materials, architectural magnificence, and the simple intimidation of a raised dais. But this time she, Khema, and Captain Singh were ushered into Tura's private study—a smaller, closer, and yet somehow even more intimidating space. For here Tura was plainly at home, and every curve of wall, every smallest item of furnishing, indeed every breath of the cinnamon-scented air, proclaimed this to be a Martian space, a space into which humans were rarely, if ever, even tolerated to enter.

Before this moment Arabella had not realized the degree to which the audience chamber, as awe-inspiring as it was, had been designed to welcome visitors as well as impress them . . . but this room granted no concessions to any one other than the ruling elite of Sor Khoresh, and Tura in particular.

As Arabella and her companions entered, Tura did not rise from the desk behind which she worked, her busy pen scratching. Though Martian books were inscribed upon coils of thin steel ribbon, many Martians had adopted pen and paper from the English for less permanent communication.

After allowing her visitors to stand for some minutes before her desk, with two armed warriors standing sentry behind them and no chairs for them to rest upon, Tura finally stopped writing and regarded them, turning the pen over and over between the hard and sharpened points of her fingers. "You claim to have come on a matter of import to all Martians," she said. "Why have you come here on an English ship, and why do you bring these *humans* with you?" She spoke in Khema's tribal dialect, but the word "human" was English, and in Tura's mouth it was an imprecation.

"I bring them," Khema replied, "because they have personal

knowledge of the issue, which involves the Prince Regent." This term, too, was English, and though to Khema it plainly lacked the rancid flavor that "human" held for Tura it was nonetheless apparently somewhat distasteful. Arabella suspected that this was, to some extent, a pretense for Tura's benefit . . . but to what extent exactly, she could not be certain.

"These people have come directly from Earth," Khema continued, "on a mission of the greatest urgency—indeed, they took an unprecedented and quite dangerous course to arrive as quickly as possible. As soon as they presented their information to me, I requested them to bear me here from Fort Augusta, because only Your Highness can save the entire Martian people from this threat."

But Tura did not take Khema's flattering bait. "Your story makes no sense," she said. "It is unheard-of to take an aerial vessel for such a short journey." Khema translated this to Captain Singh, and he began to reply, but Tura pointed one sharpened fingertip at him and snapped, "Silence, male."

To his credit, Captain Singh correctly divined the intent of the Martian words and fell silent.

But Arabella realized that Khema did not know the answer, and so she took it upon herself to reply. "Our ship is lifted by a special gas rather than by hot air," she said, and Khema translated her words. To this, at least, Tura did not object. "We can ascend and descend at will, without the requirement of a launch-furnace for ascent or coal for descent, making short journeys far more feasible. And the urgency of our mission required this unusual step."

"Another triumph of human ingenuity," Tura said, but she tapped the butt end of the pen impatiently upon her desk.

"Do you not," Khema asked, plainly trying to gain the offensive, "desire to know of the threat which faces all of Mars?"

Tura sat back, now drumming the pen negligently upon the

carapace of her abdomen. "You may attempt to convince me," she allowed after a time. "Come to the point quickly, and do not attempt to distract me with unverifiable details." Arabella found her hand clutching her captain's. She had not even noticed herself reaching for it.

"The Prince Regent of England," Khema explained, "having defeated the emperor Napoleon, has become the most powerful human in the solar system. Emboldened by this, he now intends to seize complete control of Mars." She gestured to Arabella. "This human, my former ward, is well known to me and bears my every trust. She has more information on the situation."

Tura leaned forward, setting the pen down and fixing her full and terrible attention on Arabella. "Speak."

Arabella did speak. She spoke in some detail. Tura asked many questions, and Arabella replied to the best of her ability, frequently turning to Khema for translations and to Captain Singh for his particular knowledge of the Prince's strategy—which Tura, thankfully, permitted.

"Even supposing I accept your story," Tura said at last, sitting back in her chair, "I fail to see why I should be concerned. Not even the Martians have ever conquered all of Mars, and in three hundred years the English have occupied less than one-fourteenth of it—and that only with our forbearance. Even if these supposed armored ships can fly at all, I cannot imagine that the English will do any better with them than they already have."

"It is not merely the ships," Khema insisted. "Though the ships themselves, with their guns and aerial bombs, are threat enough, they will also bear troops, and cannon, and most disturbingly the drug *ulka*. Its deleterious effects are difficult to imagine." In truth, Arabella herself had some difficulty envisioning them, but the terror that Ulungugga and the other Venusians in *Diana*'s crew held for the drug was clear.

"But the invasion," Tura replied, "and the drug, will begin in

Fort Augusta, and it is the feeble, English-dominated Martians of Saint George's Land"—here she directed her eye-stalks significantly to Khema, who stared back with cold formality—"who will bear the brunt of it. The weakening of a neighboring state does me no ill at all, and I see no reason to oppose it."

Arabella, Khema, and Captain Singh had anticipated this objection and prepared a response. "The English of Saint George's Land will eagerly participate in the invasion," Khema said. "And those Martians who cooperate—sadly, I expect they will be in the majority, at least at first—will not suffer from it. Saint George's Land will rapidly form a base of operations for the invasion of the rest of the planet—with Sor Khoresh being first on the list. But Sor Khoresh, with its great wealth of raw materials, is also in a unique position to lead the resistance. To this end we have prepared a specific proposal." She nodded significantly to Arabella.

Arabella gulped. They had originally intended the ship-yard and refinery plan to be described by Captain Singh, but now it seemed that Arabella must present it. She did so to the best of her ability. "But the fleet can only be completed in time," she concluded, "if we begin work on the refinery immediately."

"Where do you propose this . . . monstrosity to be constructed?" Tura replied.

"We had thought that Khoresh Tukath—"

"Here in my capital city?" Tura roared upon hearing the name, before Khema had even translated Arabella's reply. "Impossible! Not only would it be a hideous stain upon my beautiful city, but it would make Khoresh Tukath an obvious and immediate target when the English fleet arrives." She slammed her hand down upon her desk, scattering papers every where. "You have thrown in your lot with the English," she told Khema, "and it has made you like them—pale, weak, and vacillating. *Akhmok* or no, I should have you cast from my presence immediately!"

One of Tura's flying papers landed atop Arabella's foot. Arabella, flustered beyond words by Tura's outburst, bent automatically to pick it up.

As she did so she felt a crinkling at her waist.

It was the sketch-map tucked in her reticule.

*Thank you, Aadim,* she thought, finally understanding his purpose in pointing the spot out. For he had been present at all the discussions between Arabella, Lady Corey, Captain Singh, and Fulton, and was very much aware of the needs of the iron refinery and ship-yard.

Acting before fear or doubt could stay her hand, she drew the paper from her reticule and spread it on Tura's desk. "Here is an alternative site, Your Highness," she said, to the silent bafflement of both Khema and Captain Singh. "A location rich in minerals, and far from any center of population . . . the perfect site for a clandestine ship-yard. All it lacks is lumber and laborers."

Tura's eye-stalks bent downward, inspecting the map. "This wasteland is of little use to me," she acknowledged, without ceding any more.

"Sor Khoresh is rich in *khoresh*-wood, proud warriors, and skilled laborers," Khema said, attempting to regain her composure. "If you could commit a very small portion of that wealth, we will build you an aerial navy which can stymie the Prince Regent and keep Mars free forevermore. And *you* will be for ever hailed as the satrap who made it possible."

Khema gazed levelly at Tura. Tura stared back. Captain Singh looked on with a tense anxiety that, had she not known him so well, might have been mistaken for mere formality. Arabella, for her own part, merely held her breath.

Then Tura sat back in her chair, interlacing her fingers with a small clattering sound. "You have my permission to use that worthless scrap of desert and any thing you can scratch from the ground there. I will keep the project secret—so long as it benefits me to do so—and I will provide a detachment of forty warriors to help secure the site. The rest is up to you."

Tura's skimpy offer plainly took Khema aback. "May we perhaps request a loan for our initial expenses?"

"No. You are such a friend to the English . . . ask *them* for funding."

Arabella found her breath running short and fast. This was far, far less than they had hoped for, but certainly better than nothing . . . and most likely better than they would get from any satrap to whom they were not already known. And time was very much of the essence. She glanced to Captain Singh, whose worried expression matched her own.

Khema hesitated a moment more . . . then gave Tura a deep respectful bow. "Thank you, Your Highness. We are happy to accept your generous offer."

# 10

## TEKHMET

"You must seal the bearings more tightly," Arabella said, taking up a pair of pliers and demonstrating the technique. "If you do not, the sand will get in. Do you understand?"

Gonekh, the youngest student in Arabella's grandly-named Institute of Martian Arts and Sciences—which was, in fact, little more than a drafty shed equipped with a few work-tables and an entirely inadequate collection of tools—nodded her assent. Though Gonekh's comprehension of English was quite good, she did not speak the language very much. Arabella suspected she remained silent because she was more embarrassed by her lapses than proud of her ability, when the opposite should really be the case. For herself, Arabella was keenly aware of her own limitations in khoreshte dialect, but she nonetheless persisted in mutilating the language as necessary until she got her point across.

Arabella smiled, patted the hard carapace of Gonekh's shoulder, and moved on to the next student. There were nineteen of them at the moment. More were always arriving, mostly from

Sor Khoresh but a few from the northernmost parts of Saint George's Land, enticed in by Khema's recruiters. But some were always drifting away as well, unfortunately . . . life at Tekhmet was hard and isolated, and many young Martians soon found a conventional life with their own family and tribe far more preferable.

They were building Draisines. Pedaled Draisines, to be specific.

"I cannot imagine," Fulton had said when she had proposed this course of study, "that this absurd contrivance could possibly benefit our efforts in any way whatsoever. It is nothing more than a toy . . . a plaything for gentlemen with more money than sense!"

"I would beg you recall," Arabella had replied, "that if it were not for the pedaled Draisine, we would none of us be here now. For it was the pedaled Draisine which bore me from Brighton to Greenwich to deliver the news of the Prince's horrid scheme."

"I often wonder," he had replied, "if we would all be happier if it had not."

Although sometimes Arabella agreed with this sentiment, if only to herself, she still felt fondly toward the Draisine and continued to defend its place in her curriculum. Despite its novelty, it was comparatively simple—far less complex than an automaton or a steam engine—and required no specialized tools and a fairly small amount of material for its construction. This meant that each student could build her own Draisine, from beginning to end, which exposed her to all stages of the process of production, from drafting through construction, and on to testing, maintenance, and repair. Some of the students, including Gonekh, had actually refined the design, to Arabella's enormous satisfaction.

The completed machines, too, had a role to play in the resistance, and upon successful completion of Arabella's course of study many of the students continued building Draisines as well as participating in the work of the iron refinery and building the ship-yard. For although the Draisine was not nearly so suited to travel across soft sand as the *huresh,* much of the desert consisted of stone, clay, and hard-packed dirt. Furthermore the Draisine, with its two wheels in line, could make use of an extremely narrow track, far narrower than any cart or carriage. With an experienced and robust operator, a Draisine could carry a message or small package nearly as far and as fast as a *huresh,* and by comparison with that beast it required barely any care at all.

"Carry on, now," she told her students once she had inspected all their work. "I have a luncheon to attend, but I shall return in the afternoon."

———————

Arabella carefully closed the Institute's door behind herself, making certain that the leather seal at the sill was properly seated. The dust of the deep desert, fine and corrosive, got into everything, and if not kept out of the workshop it would play havoc with the gears. Then she turned around, leaned heavily against the door, and let out a deep sigh of fatigue and frustration.

In many ways, she thought as she gazed out across the bustling yard, the town of Tekhmet was similar to Marieville—a rough and hastily-constructed town in the trackless wastes far from civilization, dedicated to the production of armored airships.

But though Marieville had been a town on Venus, built and populated largely by Venusians, it had been fundamentally European in character. Established by Frenchmen, laid out by Frenchmen, ruled by Frenchmen, and managed by Frenchmen for the purpose of French victory, it stood aloof from its planet. Had it not been for the constant heat and damp, it might almost have been possible to look down a street lined with white-washed wood buildings, with signs all in French and even some of the

Venusians dressed in the French style, and forget upon which planet one stood.

Tekhmet, by contrast, was very much a Martian native settlement. Nearly all of the inhabitants in Arabella's sight were Martians in native costume, and most of the buildings were constructed of fused sand in the Martian fashion. The streets were laid out radially, rather than at right angles as in English settlements. And the sand . . . the sand blew unimpeded across every street and square, treated by the populace as something like air—omnipresent, unavoidable, but easily ignored—rather than as the filthy, destructive invader the English considered it to be.

But still, she reminded herself, this was *her* town too. Unlike Marieville, if she did not leave this place, it was by *her* choice, not Napoleon's . . . nor the Prince Regent's.

---

*Tekhmet* meant "resolution" in Khema's tribal dialect and several other Martian languages. Resolution was a quality that the resistance required in abundance, but fortunately it was also a quality with which they were already well equipped.

"You must understand," Khema had said to Arabella as they had first looked out over the sere and forbidding spot which was to be their home and headquarters for the foreseeable future, "that, as I hinted at our first meeting in Fort Augusta, resistance to the English has been in progress ever since the arrival of Captain Kidd. It is true that this resistance has at times been sporadic, disorganized, and ineffectual, but we have found that when it becomes organized and overt—as with the violent uprising following the theft of the Queen's egg—the end result is a significant step backward in Martian rights, freedoms, and respect. For this reason I, and many other prominent Martians in Saint George's Land, have advocated against hostility and aggression."

Her eye-stalks spread downward. "For this we have been derided as weak by Tura and those of like mind. Nonetheless, we retain *tekhmet*—resolution—and we believe that as long as we work resolutely toward our goals we will, eventually, achieve them."

"I had never known," Arabella admitted . . . and wondered what else she had not known. What other significant facts of Khema's life, and the lives of the other Martians with whom she had been surrounded in her early years, had slipped her notice?

She had considered those Martians nearly family. Only now did she come to wonder what they had thought of her.

---

The town of Tekhmet was small, isolated, spartan, and—at least as of yet—ill-equipped for the coming conflict. One of the few advantages they had was that hardly any one outside of Tekhmet knew that every one who had come to Mars aboard *Diana* and *Touchstone* would be considered a traitor by the English government. But as soon as the first fast packet-ship from London arrived—which could be as soon as next month—the latter advantage would evaporate. Once that occurred they would be forced to conceal themselves completely from the English, but until that day they were able to move freely among the populace, making recruitment of people, acquisition of materials, and appeals for funds much easier.

But even with the wholehearted efforts of the Leadership Council of the Martian Resistance—headed by Khema and her fellow *akhmok*, with the participation of several other prominent Martians—back in Fort Augusta, and the very tepid assistance of Tura from Khoresh Tukath, they had fewer than two hundred Martians and a handful of Englishmen, plus the crews of *Diana* and *Touchstone*. This company was sufficient for their current needs, barely, but for the production of a full fleet of ships they would require several times as many.

Money was a still greater concern. Captains Singh and Fox and Lady Corey had all pledged their personal fortunes to the cause, but Fulton, for all his success in numerous fields, had not managed to hold on to any of the proceeds for long—he kept reinvesting his income in new projects—and Arabella's family fortune was controlled by Michael. But even if Fulton and Arabella were as rich as Captains Singh and Fox, it would not be sufficient in the long run—a project of this magnitude would need far more than that before it was done.

---

"I have received a note from Lady Corey," Captain Singh said, seating himself with a steaming plate of *kokore*. "She reports that her attempts to inculcate resistance to the idea of quartering troops in private homes have not met with much success. The women of Fort Augusta, both the young ladies and their mothers, have a great admiration for men in uniform, and the imposition of such quartering is perceived as less significant than the possible advantages arising therefrom." He shook his head, examining his *kokore* dubiously. He did not care for the sautéed crustacean, but at the moment it was the only dish on offer.

Arabella, Captain Singh, and Fulton were the only ones at the luncheon table this day. Fox, aboard *Touchstone*, was patrolling the skies above the port of Khulesh in hopes of interdicting one of Reid's *ulka*-smuggling ships, and Lady Corey was making the rounds of high society in Fort Augusta, seeking information, sowing dissent, and surreptitiously soliciting donations from those few Englishmen who supported an independent Mars. Ever since the completion of Common Hall, the first permanent structure in the infant town of Tekhmet, some months ago, these five humans had made a habit of gathering there for luncheon each Monday. At these meetings they would discuss the progress of the resistance, celebrate victories, and commiserate over their losses, setbacks, and disappointments.

Of late, there had been much more of the latter than the former.

"I cannot believe," Fulton said, piling *kokore* upon his own plate, "that they can be so foolish and short-sighted as to trade their future freedom for a chance at marrying well."

"For most English women," Arabella countered, "to marry well *is* their only chance at any thing resembling future freedom, on a personal level."

Fulton sat beside her. "That they cannot see beyond that limited horizon is the fault of society." His American accent, Arabella noted, was more pronounced when he was denouncing some habit of the English.

"You said last week," Arabella asked Fulton in an attempt to change the subject, "that you hoped for a first trial run at the hydrogen manufactory. How did that fare?"

"Not well, I'm afraid." He peeled off a *kokore* shell and popped the meat into his mouth. "All the parts of the process"—he chewed as he spoke, a disgusting habit—"seem to be working, but the gas actually produced was negligible in quantity and horrifically impure." He washed the bite down with a big swallow of *lureth*-water. "It may be that the acid is not so strong as we require, or the iron contaminated with some alkaline substance."

The ships that Fulton had designed for the projected Aerial Navy of the Martian Resistance were based upon the Martian *khebek*—the same type of small, light, flat-bottomed aerial boats which had met *Diana* on her arrival at Khoresh Tukath—but adapted to interplanetary service. This design was easy to build, economical of materials, and particularly suitable to Martian conditions, and would be familiar to the Martians who would form the bulk of their crew. To this basic design he had added several improvements of his own, including a limited amount of armor plating for the protection of the crew, swivel-guns instead of crossbows as weapons, and the use of hydrogen rather than hot air for lift.

It was the hydrogen that was the most problematic part of the design. The gas was absolutely required, Fulton said, both to compensate for the weight of the armor and cannon and to avoid the necessity of constructing massive launch-furnaces at Tekhmet's ship-yard. But where Napoleon's ship-yard on Venus had made use of native creatures—larger relatives of *Diana*'s pet Isambard—to produce its hydrogen, on Mars they were required to use a chemical process of dissolving iron filings in acid. Mars, fortunately, was rich in iron, and the acid could be produced by distillation from compounds present in the soil. But Fulton was less experienced in chemistry than he was in mining, refining, mechanics, and ship-building, and progress at the hydrogen manufactory had not been nearly as rapid or straightforward as desired.

"As for the rest," Fulton continued, "operations at the mines and foundry continue apace, and the rope-walk should be ready for use within the week. We have ordered all the Venusian silk we will require for the sails and envelopes, and eighteen graving docks are ready for keels to be laid." He glanced to Arabella. "We lack only a source of *khoresh*-wood."

Arabella glanced down at her plate, which suddenly seemed far less appetizing. "Michael has still not responded to my letters," she admitted. "But perhaps he has not received them—I do not trust the khoreshte post in the slightest. I intend to pay a call upon him this week."

Captain Singh wiped his mouth, pushing his half-finished plate away. "*Diana* is to take over blockade duty from *Touchstone* this week. I will carry you to Woodthrush Woods by ship, and you may return to Tekhmet by coach with Fox after he lands." *Touchstone,* being dependent upon a launch-furnace for ascent, was still using Fort Augusta as her home port. Once their treason was exposed, she would have to shift to Khoresh Tukath.

Two days later, Captain Singh joined Arabella and Michael for dinner at Woodthrush Woods. "I was disappointed," Arabella said to Michael, "not to receive any response to my letters in the last three months. Did you not receive them?"

"I . . . I do not recall the date of the last letter I had from you," Michael hedged. "What did they treat upon?"

"I requested you to consider donating a portion of the plantation's production to a personal project." More detail than that she preferred not to provide, for here in the dining-room there were always servants close by, but she put a very slight stress on the word "production" to point out that she meant actual *khoresh-*wood, not merely a charitable donation of funds.

"Ah, that," Michael said, as though it had merely slipped his mind—though they both knew it had not. "Perhaps we should return to this question in the morning."

"I would prefer to discuss it now." She met his eye levelly.

Michael looked to Captain Singh, perhaps hoping that the captain would rescue him with an urgent request for port and cigars, but he merely matched Arabella's forthright gaze. "I . . . ah . . . oh, very well. Come with me to the office."

As they departed the dining-room, Michael requested of one of the servants that a bottle of port be brought to his office.

Michael settled himself down behind the grand desk which had been his father's, leaving Arabella and Captain Singh to take the guest chairs. Arabella noted that, while her father's collection of small automata remained on the shelves above the desk, they had plainly not been touched or even dusted in months; this observation lowered her already-diminished spirits considerably.

"You are as aware as I, dear sister," Michael said as the servant departed, leaving a bottle of port on the desk and closing the doors behind him, "how negligible are the profits in this business. You know that I cannot simply *give* you any kind of *khoresh*-wood, never mind the prime stuff, in the quantities you have requested without driving the enterprise into debt." He poured himself a glass of port and took a generous sip before continuing. "My failure to respond to your letters, although inexcusable, can perhaps be explained by the difficulty of forming a reasonable response to such an *un*reasonable request."

"I am thoroughly aware of the consequences of such a large request, dear brother," Arabella countered, "but—as I said quite clearly in my letters—this is a matter of life and death not only for Mars and the Martians, but for Woodthrush Woods. We depend upon our Martian neighbors for so much . . . labor, food, and water are the least of it! If the Prince Regent has his way, and subjugates the planet completely, do you imagine they will continue to provide these goods and services so willingly?"

"If he has his way, they will provide those goods and services whether they will or no! And more cheaply at that."

"If you truly believe that, you are naive." She reached across the desk and took her brother's hand. "Can you imagine Khema—even the Khema of our youth, never mind the powerful *akhmok* she has become—acquiescing with any grace to the loss of her freedom and independence?"

"You have spent too much time under Napoleon's heel," Michael scoffed, taking his hand back. "I cannot imagine that an *English* monarch, or even a regent, would behave so intolerably toward his subjects, whether human or Martian."

"The Prince Regent does not consider the Martians at all," Captain Singh argued. "He cares only for the money that can be extracted from Mars for his personal profit, and gives not a fig for how it is done. But to his underlings, the men who lead the Navy and the *Honorable* Mars Company"—he pronounced the adjective as though it had turned to vinegar in the bottle—"the Martians are little more than cattle, or perhaps something a bit more clever, like dogs. And they mean to use English cannon and Venusian drugs to bring them to heel."

Michael's face showed that the self-evident truth of the captain's words warred with his unwillingness to believe ill of his betters. "Nonetheless," he said at last, "I cannot possibly provide the quantities of wood you request. Most of the timber, as you know, is already committed—has, indeed, been committed for years—and an Englishman's word is his bond!"

"I am asking you," Arabella said, though she was nearly certain she knew what the response would be, "to consider a higher cause." She leaned forward, her hands clasped before herself. "War is coming, Michael. There will be violence, and bloodshed, and death . . . a broken business contract is the least of our worries. We cannot prevent this war; once the Martians realize what the Prince intends, they *will* resist. Our only choice now is to side with the Prince Regent, or to side with Mars." She sat back in her chair, though her back remained rigidly upright. "I have made my choice—to resist the Prince's predations upon the planet of my birth—and I can only hope that you join me in it."

Michael toyed with his near-empty glass, not looking at Arabella. "I could end this farcical resistance of yours with a word, you know," he said. "Your letters betray your aims, your schemes, your location . . . and I have made powerful friends in the years I have sat in this chair." He rapped his glass upon the arm of the chair—the chair which had been his father's, and his grand-father's before that—and his eyes rose to meet Arabella's. "Out of love for you, dear sister, I will not. But neither will I bankrupt this family for the sake of a scheme which, however noble its aims, cannot succeed." He inspected the glass, raised it to his mouth, and tipped it back, draining it of its final drop of port. Then he set it down with careful finality. "I will, if you cannot be dissuaded, *sell* you a quantity of *khoresh*-wood, at a fair price. But I will not renege on my existing agreements, and if I can-not supply your entire needs, you must inquire elsewhere for the rest."

Arabella looked to Captain Singh, whose expression matched her own feelings of disappointment, anger, and determination. "Very well," she told her brother. "I shall take all you can spare." She stood then, and as a matter of course the two men immediately rose as well. "However, I find I am no longer interested in spending the next few days in your company." She curtseyed to Michael—quite perfunctorily, without allowing her gaze to de-part his face—then turned to Captain Singh. "Let us depart. I shall spend the night with Lady Corey."

She did not begin to cry until the door had closed behind them.

---

"Whatever shall we do?" Arabella sobbed as they walked back to *Diana,* arm in arm. "Our funds will quickly be exhausted if we must pay the going rate for the quantities of *khoresh*-lumber we require . . . even assuming we can find it! Every other plantation in Saint George's Land will also have committed most or all of their production to existing customers."

"We will purchase what we can," Captain Singh assured her, patting her arm, "and seek other sources for the rest. Khema's *storek* can be very persuasive."

"Only to Martians! And, though the tree itself is a Martian native species, the cutting and drying of *khoresh*-wood for aerial ships is almost purely an English practice."

"We will consult with Fulton. Perhaps some alternative can be discovered."

Arabella wiped her eyes and nose with her handkerchief. "You are very good," she said, "but I fear you may be overly confident."

"Recall what I have said about the necessity for the *appearance* of confidence, whether justified or not, in achieving one's aims." They reached *Diana* and ascended the gangplank, while airmen bustled about, making the ship ready for an immediate departure. "Proceeding *as though* one is assured of success can often lead to opportunities, and at the very least permits progress toward one's goals."

Arabella sighed and inclined her head, acknowledging the truth of his words even though she was not very reassured. "Will you be departing immediately?" she asked.

"Very nearly. I have no further business here. I shall, of course, convey you and your trunk to Lady Corey's apartments in Fort Augusta first." *Diana* was to rendezvous with *Touchstone* midair, to provide a continuous blockade against the incoming *ulka* smuggler; *Touchstone* would then land at Fort Augusta, from which Fox and Arabella would return to Tekhmet by coach.

Arabella paused, and perforce Captain Singh, his arm linked in hers, paused as well. She turned to him and took his hands. "There is no need for you to make a detour to Fort Augusta for me. I shall simply remain on board *Diana* with you, for the duration of your blockade duty."

Captain Singh looked askance at that. "Are you certain? If we go into action against the smuggler, I cannot guarantee your safety."

"I understand that. But the events of this day have instilled in me a strong desire for *action*. I could not bear to bide my time in Lady Corey's sitting-room, exchanging gossip with Fort Augusta society, nor to sit isolated at Tekhmet, assisting Mr. Fulton with his account-books. I wish to do *something* to forward the cause of the resistance, and at the moment that thing seems to me to be my work in aerial navigation." Arabella had continued her work with the greenwood box in every spare moment since the circumduction of Mercury, and her current undertaking was to improve its abilities regarding navigation within the turbulent winds of a planet's Horn. She felt that a better understanding of this complex topic might aid them in the defense of Mars against the Prince Regent's fleet, and intended that any improvements would eventually be incorporated into Aadim's design. "To spend the next few weeks of blockade aboard *Diana,* in the very midst of the Horn, would be invaluable to my researches."

"What of your work at the Institute?"

"The more experienced students are fully capable of training the newer ones for a few weeks."

The captain's proud, impassive face relaxed slightly into a small smile. "Be careful, my dear. If you train them too well, you are in danger of making yourself unnecessary."

Arabella found her own lips drawing themselves into a matching smile, but as her mind continued to work she felt her expression go serious. Suddenly she reached for her husband, grasped him about the waist, and pressed his broad, warm chest against her own. "I could not bear to let you go and face the smuggler without me," she said, her voice muffled against the wool of his uniform jacket. "Every time we part, whether by my initiative or yours or some other's, it seems that some awful thing happens to one or another of us."

Captain Singh's long, strong hand stroked Arabella's shoulder. "Very well," he said. "But you will be required to fill and wind my lamps, boy second class Ashby."

"Of course, my maharaja."

# 11

---

## BLOCKADE

All around Arabella the great cabin rocked and shuddered as the whole ship was shaken by the chaotic winds of Mars's Horn, and the needle of the wind-speed dial on the side of Aadim's desk twitched and jerked like a nervous *shareth*'s tail. Although this agitation was unpleasant, it was far from unusual, and Arabella strove to ignore it and concentrate her attention upon her calculations. But then a sudden jolt dislodged her pen from Fuller's Patent Free-Descent Inkwell, sending it spinning across the cabin trailing drops of shimmering ink. With a disgusted sound she unstrapped herself from her seat and pursued the stray instrument across the cabin, mopping up the drops from the air with her pen-wiper.

Once she had retrieved her pen and cleared the ink from the air, she found herself by the cabin's broad window, holding herself steady against its jamb with one hand. The inconstant, unpredictable winds pushed the ship this way and that, making her

sway and drift in the air. But the sky without the window was as
pale and blue and clear as ever, for the air near Mars was generally
too dry to form clouds no matter how tempestuous it became.
This lack of cloud, of course, made the currents invisible—except
to the very most practiced eye, and even then not all the time—
which made navigation difficult. Finding some way around this
conundrum was the entire point of her presence here.

But despite days of effort, embedded in the very midst of the
winds she studied and equipped with the finest instruments available, she was no closer to finding a solution than she had been on
the ground. In fact, loath though she was to admit error, she was
beginning to come to the conclusion that hers was a fool's errand—
that the winds of the Horn were simply too fickle and arbitrary to
be predicted by observation and mathematics.

But, in the spirit of *tekhmet*, she refused—she simply refused—
to admit defeat. So she continued her studies, and helped out
where she could, and worried along with every man aboard that
the smuggler would simply pass them by. For though they knew
his destination and the approximate date of his arrival, the sky
was very large and *Diana* was but one ship.

For a moment longer she stared upward through the window,
hoping but not expecting to be the first to spot the smuggler as a
tiny white spot against the sunward sky's untroubled blue. But
there was nothing there—nothing save Phobos, sailing serenely
above them on its eastward path. So rapidly did that tiny moon
travel in its orbit that it rose in the west and set in the east, catching
up and passing the Sun every seven and a half hours.

In her mind's eye the invisible air around Phobos swirled with
waves and eddies, the already-turbulent air of the Horn further
disturbed by the moon's rapid passage, like the froth behind a
hand drawn through a rushing stream. Those eddies had, so
far, resisted all the efforts of better mathematicians than she to

describe and predict their capricious motions. Yet, somehow, the khoreshte pilots could navigate those tumultuous currents, guiding ships to a safe berth on Phobos many times each day.

How did they do it? She had not yet had the opportunity to question one—they were constantly occupied, and not numerous—but she had discussed with Mills his occupation as a *grumete* for the Portuguese slavers in West Africa, navigating small boats through the treacherous surf. "No rules," he had said. "No path, no plan. You must *feel* the wave."

*Feel* the wave, he had said. It reminded her of a conversation she had had with Captain Singh some months ago, over dinner on the long passage from Mercury. "I may understand the currents, and the sails, to a greater degree than you," he had said. "But my knowledge is entirely intellectual, whereas your navigation is more . . . intuitive. It is as though you can *feel* the ship, whereas I must *think* of her motions." This had led to an interesting discussion on the differences between men's and women's mentality, and consideration of the degree to which their different approaches were determined by their sex as opposed to their individual constitution and upbringing, but she had given it no further thought until this moment.

But now, as she hung in the air, feeling the changing tensions in the muscles and tendons of her arm as the ship was pushed this way and that by the Horn's mercurial winds, she realized that this might point the way to a solution.

The apparatus alone would be difficult to build. To combine its measurements with the navigational calculations would be thornier still. And to extrapolate from the conditions of the air in the vicinity to predict the winds ahead . . . at the moment, she had no idea how that might be done. But still, it was a start.

Pushing herself away from the shuddering window jamb, she sailed across the cabin to the navigational table. There she strapped herself in, drew out a clean sheet of paper, and began to sketch a new mechanism.

The ship's continued motions made her lines irregular. But she smiled at this, and sought to incorporate the irregularities into her work.

———————

For days Arabella labored endlessly, often forgetting to sleep or to eat, as was her habit when engaged in a difficult intellectual exercise. Much of her work was entirely theoretical, and Captain Singh grew accustomed—or so he said—to creeping about the cabin so as not to disturb her as she gazed sightlessly at the wall or out the window, deep in thought. At other times she could be found performing such peculiar actions as tying a string around a cannon-ball as though it were a Christmas package, pushing it gently through the air of the cabin, then bringing it to a halt with a careful tug on the string. Sketches of gears, levers, and cams crowded the navigational table and drifted in the air like gently-falling snow.

Her days became disordered, unconnected with the bells that governed the crew's lives. She slept only when she could not keep her eyes open any longer, and often found herself working while Captain Singh slept or vice versa. He was remarkably indulgent of her in this. "I am glad," he said, "that you have found a productive task to occupy your mind during the endless boredom of blockade. I wish that I could do the same."

It was easy to work for ten or twelve hours at one stretch, as the Sun did not rise and set as he did for those who dwelt upon a planet's face. But, unlike in the spaces between planets, here in the Horn above Fort Augusta the planet Mars did sometimes interpose himself between *Diana* and the Sun, and the ship was plunged into night for a time. Thus it was that, one day, she opened her eyes after one of her forced, unwilling naps to find herself in unaccustomed darkness.

For a moment she blinked, disoriented, thinking herself caught in a dream of Mars or Earth. But the floating sensation of her limbs and the tension of the band which kept her in her hammock reminded her that she was still in free descent, still aboard *Diana*. At once her mind began to spin, returning to the problems which had occupied her attention for so many days.

And then the Sun returned, rapidly and in full force as was his recent habit, as *Diana* moved in her orbit from the cone of Mars's shadow to the eternal day of the interplanetary atmosphere. Arabella grunted, shutting her eyes tight against the sudden glare and pulling her coverlet up over her face.

But a moment later the annoyance of the light was joined by another, more significant interruption—a sudden cry of "Sail ho! Sail f——g ho!"

"Where away?" came Captain Singh's voice in reply, from the quarterdeck just the other side of the planks above her hammock.

"Below! F——g below! Two points off dead sunward!"

A moment later Captain Singh cursed as well—a highly unusual occurrence—followed by a series of commands, of which the most urgent was, "Idlers and waisters to the pedals! Smartly now!"

Shouts and cries came from above, accompanied by the slaps of feet upon the deck and the hissing rattle of lines being hauled upon. The ship spun dizzyingly on her axis for a moment as the men at the pedals began their labors before the stays'ls and spankers were fully set, but after further shouting the situation was corrected and the ship surged forward, driven by the pulsers which creaked and rushed outside the cabin's stern window. All during this time Arabella was disentangling herself from her suddenly-recalcitrant hammock and struggling into her dress.

---

Arabella came out on deck into a scene of controlled chaos, with topmen leaping from mast to yard while Venusian waisters dashed hither and yon, all fully engaged in pressing the ship forward at her best speed toward a prey determined to escape them. A rumble from below the forecastle told Arabella the guns were being run out, even as powder monkeys dashed across the deck bringing gunpowder to them. At the center of all this activity stood Captain Singh, the calm eye of the storm, braced to the deck in his leather harness and peering forward through his glass. "Starboard half a point," he said to Edmonds at the wheel.

"Aye aye, sir," Edmonds replied.

Arabella, following her captain's gaze, looked ahead and down to where their quarry—a distant fleck of white, brilliant against Mars's night side—was descending rapidly and just inflating her single large balloon envelope. Requesting and receiving permission to ascend to the quarterdeck, she held tight to the forward rail—there was no harness here for her—and asked her captain, "Are you certain that is the smuggler?"

"No one but a smuggler would use a course like that," he muttered, still with one eye to the telescope. His expression was thunderous. "Approaching from skyward."

It was certainly an unusual course, Arabella thought. A ship from Earth nearly always approached Mars from its sunward side. But this ship must have gone well past Mars, then looped back to approach the planet from its skyward side, hiding in its shadow the whole way. It must have taken considerable skill and effort to remain in Mars's cone of darkness for so many days, avoiding the easier curving path dictated by orbital mechanics.

Only at the last moment, as they neared their destination on the planet's surface, were they forced out into the light.

"Can we catch them?"

"He's a cocky one, I'll give him that," Captain Singh said, "waiting to fill his envelope so far below the falling-line. He risks a very hard landing indeed . . . but he also stole a march on us." He collapsed his glass with a brusque, disgusted gesture. "Avast pulsers!" he called. "We could dive after him with pulsers full ahead, I suppose," he commented to Arabella as the ship slowed. "But to pull out at the bottom of such a dive is a maneuver I have never practiced . . . unlike that fellow there." He gestured with the closed telescope toward the descending smuggler. "I should have known we could not beat an experienced player at his own habitual game."

Belowdecks, Arabella knew, the men at the pedals would be collapsing against the handlebars, gasping from the effort just ended. "So what shall we do now?"

"We return to Fort Augusta, to report the sad news of our failure to the Council," he replied. "Then I suppose we must make an attempt to interdict the drug on the ground." His expression became pensive then. "It is unfortunate that we will have at most two more weeks to move about town freely. Once the news of our treason arrives from England, we will be required to recruit agents to act on our behalf while we remain out of sight."

Arabella, not knowing what to say, took her captain's hand then. But though he accepted her touch, his gaze did not budge, remaining fixed on the planet below.

---

They met with the Council in a store-room at the back of a chandler's shop in Fort Augusta, one of several rendezvouses used by the Council. There they found Khema; another *akhmok*, named

Thekhla; and half a dozen other Martians of various tribes. One of the latter had a very bad crack on the carapace of her arm, bound up with steel wire and oozing a clear fluid. All seemed far more downcast than they had been at their last meeting, which had not itself been particularly cheerful.

"We are sorry to hear that the drug-smuggler was not stopped," Khema said after receiving Captain Singh's report, "but, given that the Ceres fleet may arrive soon, our immediate concern is the production of aerial vessels. How many ships do you have ready to launch?"

Arabella and her captain exchanged a concerned glance. "As of our last visit to Tekhmet," Arabella said, "we had six complete *khebek*, with more under construction, and the hydrogen manufactory was finally producing at full capacity. But recruitment and training of the crews has been difficult, particularly in the areas of command and navigation. Martians with aerial experience tend to be loyal to the Company."

Khema and the other *akhmok* spoke briefly in some Martian tongue with which Arabella was not familiar. Working with Mills, she had made considerable progress in khoreshte dialect, but Mars was home to hundreds of languages and no one could learn them all. "My colleague here says that she knows several members of her tribe who work the docks and ship-yards and are extremely unhappy with the Company. Perhaps some among these could be recruited to our cause."

"Ship-yard skills do not always translate to airmanship," Captain Singh explained gently. "But still, even a landsman can eventually be educated, and a stevedore knows larboard from starboard at least. We will accept any Martian willing to be trained."

"And any ship-yard worker," said Arabella, "of any skill whatsoever, who might remove to Tekhmet would be welcome." After Khema had translated their words to the other *akhmok*, Arabella turned to another item of concern. "On the topic of the ship-yard, have you made any progress in obtaining the *khoresh*-wood we require? Were the names I provided at our last meeting helpful to you?"

"The negotiations have been . . . delicate." Khema contemplated her steepled fingertips. "The plantation owners you suggested are all landed gentlemen, and hence extremely conservative. So we must work through jobbers and dealers . . . and even with many of those we must use agents to hide our interest."

Arabella's spirits fell at this reminder of her brother, with whom she had not even exchanged letters in months. But from what she had heard via other friends, he was siding more and more with the Company as the plantation became more prosperous, and in fact was becoming quite a prominent Tory.

"We have, nonetheless," Khema continued, "managed to secure contracts for six hundred loads of prime *khoresh*-wood, for delivery in the next three months." This was, Arabella knew, enough wood to construct three or four *khebek* . . . and less than one-quarter of what they had hoped to obtain by this time. "Payment, however, remains uncertain. We have funds on hand for only the first shipment, of three."

Captain Singh's expression, already grave, became still grimmer. His capital, she knew, was already heavily committed to the cause, but his purse was not yet completely depleted. "How much do you require for the other two shipments?" he asked.

"Twenty-four hundred pounds."

Arabella was dismayed, though not at all surprised, by the figure. It was, though a very substantial sum, not an unreasonable price for such a quantity of timber under the circumstances. "I believe I can write you a bank draft for twelve hundred pounds," Captain Singh said after consulting his pocket-book. "That will cover the second shipment. The third . . . will be paid for somehow."

Khema's eyes spread in acknowledgement and thanks. "Some months yet remain to find a solution to that problem."

The conversation paused then, a pause which Arabella finally broke with a question which had been in the back of her mind for weeks. "You mentioned the Ceres fleet. Has there been any news while we were on blockade?"

"Not a word," Khema said. "Which is curious and distressing."

"Indeed," said Arabella. Usually the movements of an entire fleet of Naval vessels, even a smallish one, could not be obscured. Yet, though commerce from Ceres had not been completely cut off, it had greatly diminished, and no information on the fleet's position or progress had reached Mars for months. They might be months away yet, or weeks, or even days. Captain Singh felt that, given the winds and the positions of the planets and asteroids, they were unlikely to arrive in less than two months . . . but this could not be guaranteed, and the lack of any information to the contrary was not reassuring. Quite the opposite.

"We will keep our feet firmly in the sand," Khema said, using a Martian expression meaning that they would remain vigilant, "and send a Draisine courier to you immediately if the merest rumor should reach us of the fleet's whereabouts."

"Thank you." Still, Arabella worried. But before she could voice her concerns, a cry came from without—a human voice calling in English, "Captain Singh! Captain Singh!"

Immediately the captain excused himself from the meeting and dashed outside, with Arabella and Khema right behind him. It was Watson, one of *Diana*'s midshipmen, panting hard with his hands on his knees. Plainly he had come from the ship at a dead run. "What news?" the captain asked.

"It's *Excelsior*, sir!" Watson gasped back. "She's just descending now!"

Arabella and Captain Singh looked at each other. This was

the fast packet-ship which they expected to bear the news of their treason to Mars. "Return to *Diana*," the captain told Watson, "and tell Edmonds to prepare to raise ship at once. We will join you as soon as we may."

"Aye aye, sir," Watson piped, and ran off.

"Can we be away before the news is abroad?" Arabella asked him, winding her artificial foot.

"It will depend on exactly where *Excelsior* docks." He dashed out through the chandler's front office toward the street.

"Oh, Khema . . ." Arabella said, taking her former *itkhalya*'s hard and massive hand. "I do not know when I shall see you again."

"I shall visit you in Tekhmet as often as I am able." She touched her other hand to her mouth-parts, then touched Arabella's fore-head. "This *storek* will encourage any Martians you meet to assist you. Now go."

Arabella went. But as she exited the chandler's office, a sudden metallic *twang* sounded from her foot and she fell sprawling in the dust of the street.

Captain Singh, though he was already well down the street, heard her cries and immediately doubled back. "What has happened to your foot?"

"The mainspring snapped!" Arabella diagnosed, rubbing at the abraded heel of her hand. "I must have over-tightened it in my haste."

But on inspection, the situation proved to be even worse than she had feared. Not only had the mainspring broken, but in the resulting fall she had snapped the foot's shank. The device was certainly too badly broken to be mended with the time and materials available here, and might be completely beyond repair.

"I will carry you," Captain Singh said, and despite her strident objections he did exactly that.

Immediately upon their landing at Tekhmet, they gathered the most prominent citizens at Common Hall to give an account of their last few disastrous days. "I doubt we shall be able to return to Fort Augusta again," Captain Singh admitted, "even in disguise." He gestured to his distinctive brown face and Arabella's missing foot. She was walking with a crutch; the broken artificial foot remained in *Diana*'s great cabin.

"But the wood!" Fulton fumed. "I must have more *khoresh*-wood! And you were supposed to negotiate for it!"

"Khema is doing the best she can," Arabella replied. "My own . . . contacts, are of less use now than I had hoped." Her spirits, already low, sank still further at this reminder of her brother. "In any case, finances are currently our chief constraint . . . we have obtained contracts for more wood than we can actually pay for."

The company fell silent then, as every one considered the resistance's fiscal situation and their own personal role within it. Every one present, Arabella knew, had already pledged all they could, and several of them were enduring substantial financial hardship because of it.

Captain Fox broke the impasse by delicately clearing his throat. "I continue my correspondence with Lady Wilde," he said. "She is, I believe, working her way toward open support of our cause, and it is my hope that she may bring her husband—and his ten thousand a year—with her." But they all knew that process could take months, and the silence returned.

"I have written Khema a draft for twelve hundred pounds," Captain Singh said at last. "That is the very last that I can spare, but I hope that it will be sufficient to secure the current contract."

"And what of the future?" Fulton demanded, barely mollified. "The ships, once constructed, must still be fitted out!"

"We will find a way," Captain Singh replied levelly. "Do not despair. Remember, *tekhmet* means resolution."

No one had any thing to say to that.

————————

Later, back in their bedchamber, Arabella and Captain Singh discussed the replacement of her artificial foot, which was indeed entirely beyond repair. "We still have the draughts," he said as he massaged liniment into the abraded skin of her stump. "And some of your students at the Institute are extremely skilled. It will not take nearly as long to build a second one as it did the first." He paused, considering the idea. "We might, indeed, build two at the same time, so as to have one in reserve in case of further loss."

This statement brought to mind an idea which had been nibbling at the back of Arabella's mind for some months. "When last I met my brother," she said, "I wished that we could somehow produce these clockwork limbs in quantity, so that every one who lacked a leg might receive the same benefits as I. If we were to turn our attention to this now, especially with Fulton's assistance . . ."

Though Arabella was becoming more and more intrigued by the idea the more she considered it, Captain Singh shook his head. "It is a very . . . promising notion," he acknowledged, "but we have neither the time nor the facilities for such speculative efforts—not when the Ceres fleet could arrive at any time. We must concentrate our energies upon undertakings which directly aid the resistance."

"I do not disagree. I was thinking of the many who may lose

limbs in the battles to come." Her brain continued to churn. Once one had worked out how to craft a complex part, such as a gear or cam, from raw metal, making ten or twenty more, just the same, would be ever so much simpler than the first.

"We would do better to try to prevent those losses in the first place. And for that we need money, guns, and experienced officers." He sighed. "Ships we can build, and landsmen—lands-Martians—we have in plenty. Given time they can be trained up to ordinary airmen. But what I would not give for ten skilled pilots."

At that statement something seemed to *click* in Arabella's mind. "We can *build* them."

"Pardon?" Captain Singh was genuinely astonished.

"You know that I have been working upon improvements to the greenwood box—giving it the means to assist in navigation within the Horn—and have seen some success. If these improvements could be added to Aadim . . . a moderately-trained steersman could navigate the Horn without requiring a pilot at all!"

Captain Singh's eyes widened fractionally, and Arabella recognized instantly that his active brain had seized upon the idea. "The *khebek* is a smaller, simpler ship than any Marsman," he said. "With only two sails, the calculations are more straightforward. And I have felt for some years that Aadim's workings could be greatly simplified. I understand the geometries so much better now than I did when I first began his construction." His eyes grew distant as his excitement increased. "A much less complicated mechanism . . . fewer moving parts . . . and yet more capable."

Arabella felt exhilaration rising in her own breast. "And if we could build one for each *khebek* . . ."

"Which would be ever so much easier if we build it in as the ship is constructed, rather than to add it after the ship's completion as I was required to do with *Diana* . . ."

"We could have a whole fleet of ships as brilliant as Aadim!"

"And armored!"

Arabella seized her captain then and kissed him passionately.

Then they got out pen and paper, and sketched plans and notes long into the night.

# 12

## EVACUATION

Arabella threw down her file in disgust. "It is no good at all!" she cried. "We must absolutely start over from the beginning."

The ruined gear lay upon her work-bench, seeming to stare back at her like an accusing eye. The idea of casting gears from brass had seemed so promising, but the hand-work required to file the teeth into their final shape was so great that the expected improvement in efficiency had become a net loss.

Still, several of the other innovations she had developed for the rapid construction of automaton pilots, with the help of Captain Singh and the graduates of the Institute, had borne fruit. Fifteen of the devices had already been completed and installed in *khebek*, and seven more lay in various states of assembly on the benches around her, each being diligently shepherded toward completion by a team of Martian technicians. But many more would be needed, and Arabella and Captain Singh were constantly in search of ways to produce them more rapidly and with higher quality.

The automaton pilot, despite the anthropomorphic implications of its name, was more closely related to Arabella's greenwood box than to Aadim. It was in appearance a simple affair, a trapezoidal brass frame filled with clockworks and having no semblance whatsoever of humanity. Also, relative to Aadim, every bit of extraneous mechanism had been pared away, including all functions of interplanetary navigation . . . all the device's components were concentrated upon navigating near Mars, in particular in the winds of the Horn. And flexibility had been discarded in favor of ease of operation, to permit successful use by a Martian with minimal training.

But despite its simplicity, in some ways the automaton's capabilities rivaled Aadim's. At the heart of the machine lay a block of lead, suspended in a steel cage by wires from its six faces. These wires led to mechanisms that used the block's motion relative to the ship—which, by Newton's inexorable laws of inertia, reflected in reverse the ship's motions relative to the fixed stars—to calculate from the general course laid in by the operator a sail-plan which compensated for the winds in the ship's immediate vicinity.

The design was full of compromises. The mechanism sometimes jammed, sometimes produced impossible results, and sometimes refused perfectly good settings. At times Arabella felt that the clockworks, however well she understood them, were deliberately resisting her desires, like a willful adolescent. But still she did not truly believe the device was self-aware as Aadim was.

"I am going for a walk," she declared to Gonekh, "to clear my head."

Gonekh, although still one of the youngest of the Martian technicians, had proven herself so invaluable that she was now Arabella's chief assistant. She was already a skilled machinist and would some day, Arabella was certain, become the first Martian inventor. But she still spoke very little, preferring to communicate via precisely-rendered diagrams and through the elegance of her manufactured items.

She strode off along the dusty street, allowing her feet—the natural one and the new artifical one—to follow their habitual path while her mind worried at the technical problem of gear manufacture. If casting would not work, perhaps the raw discs could be ganged together, so that several accurate gears could be machined simultaneously . . .

"Ahem."

At the sound Arabella looked up and stopped short, inches from crashing into Fox, who stood in her path with a bemused expression. "Oh!" she cried.

"You really should watch where you are going, ma'am," he said, tipping his hat.

"I beg forgiveness," she said, genuinely flustered at her own inattention but nonetheless pleased to see Fox, who had been away from town for several weeks on a scouting cruise. She took his arm and they continued walking together. "When did you return?"

"Just now. We landed in Khoresh Tukath day before yesterday, but before returning here I wanted to make sure dear *Touchstone* was properly victualed and watered." His expression fell serious. "And well provided with shot and powder."

"Did you learn any thing on your cruise?"

He shook his head. "There is barely any traffic from any of the asteroids any more." His gaze drew inward. "I never would have thought the English could keep a whole fleet secret, but I suppose that if one is willing to give up commerce for a time . . ."

"That is worrisome. But Captain Singh calculates that they are still unlikely to arrive for some weeks."

"I know; I have just come from discussing this with him. But the skyward breezes have been quite brisk of late." He paused, and Arabella paused with him. "I am concerned," he said.

"Oh?"

"I believe that we are in more danger here than Captain Singh acknowledges, and I suggest that you consider removing to Khoresh Tukath."

"Impossible! The Institute shares too much—people and materials—with the hydrogen manufactory, and that absolutely cannot be moved."

"I did not mean the Institute. I meant yourself. For safety's sake." He took her hands and looked into her eyes with deep sincerity. "I will be shifting Lady Corey and our household thence later to-day, and I strongly advise you to accompany her."

"I will *not*!" She pulled her hands from his grip. "Our work on the automaton pilots is too important. Even if—*especially* if—the arrival of the Ceres fleet is imminent, we must concentrate all our attentions upon that until the last possible moment."

"Your devotion to the cause is admirable." He inclined his head in respect. "But I fear the last possible moment may be too late."

"I thank you for your concern, sir, and I shall give your suggestion due consideration." But she stepped back from him as she said it, and both of them knew her mind was made up.

For a moment Fox seemed about to follow her . . . but then he, too, took a half-step backward. "Very well. But I am certain you would be welcome *chez nous*."

"I thank you for your most generous offer, but please do not be too worried. In case of danger we are prepared to evacuate to Tekh Shetekta." Tekh Shetekta, an uninhabited but defensible canyon in the deep khoreshte desert, was the place they had chosen as a fallback position in case Tekhmet was exposed. Arabella curtseyed. "Good day, sir."

He lifted his hat. "Good day to you, ma'am." But as she turned away, he called out, "If you wish to accompany Lady Corey, I expect that she will depart from Common Hall no sooner than three o'clock. We can have your things sent along later."

She almost turned back to him. But instead she straightened her back and returned to the Institute.

———

Back at her bench, Arabella stared down at the gears before her—the prototype and the several failed copies—but did not truly see them. Instead, she considered Captain Fox's warning.

Every thing she had said to Fox was true, she was certain. But every thing he had said to her, she knew, was equally true, at least in his estimation. And for all his faults, Fox was neither an unintelligent nor an unobservant man . . .

"Gonekh," she called. "I should like you to make a list, ordered by importance, of what we would take with us if we were required to evacuate the Institute to Tekh Shetekta."

"Ma'am?" the Martian inquired, eye-stalks rising in alarm.

"There is no danger at the present time," she said, putting more confidence into her voice than she actually felt, "but it would be foolish not to plan for every eventuality."

"Ma'am." Gonekh curtseyed and turned to her assigned task.

Arabella, for her part, looked about and gave her own consideration to the question. They were fortunate in that they knew the fleet's orders, which had been transmitted to Ceres by Captain Singh before his departure. The fleet would land at Fort Augusta for resupply and to coordinate with Company forces already in place. Even if the Company already knew Tekhmet's location—which she fervently hoped they did not; the resistance had taken every possible step to keep the town's location secret—the earliest an attack could occur would be several days after the fleet's arrival, so they would have some time for an orderly evacuation. The draughts and the tools, she thought, would have to be the first priority, then the complete and near-complete automata, then the more complex and precise sub-assemblies.

But *where* would they go? Tekh Shetekta was no more than a fallback position; it was not a place they could stay for long. And surely if Tekhmet were exposed, Khoresh Tukath would be equally vulnerable to attack.

Should she have accepted Fox's offer?

Arabella glanced at the clock. It was a little past two in the afternoon.

She should, at least, give Lady Corey her best wishes before her departure for Khoresh Tukath.

---

Arabella found Lady Corey and Captain Fox in the midst of instructing their servants in the loading of her cases atop a coach. Gowse, Arabella's old messmate, was managing the *huresh*. "Oh!" Lady Corey said as Arabella approached. "Are you coming along after all?"

"I am not, unfortunately. I merely came to bid you farewell."

"I *do* wish you would accompany me," Lady Corey said, taking Arabella's hand and walking a few steps away. Captain Fox continued supervising the loading of the coach. "We have engaged quite spacious rooms in Khoresh Tukath, and it is ever so much more civilized there than here. You would be far more comfortable, and I would so welcome your company."

"I do regret the necessity, Lady Corey. But my place is here."

"Oh yes, the automata, I completely understand. But . . . but Captain Fox is concerned that we are so very *exposed* here."

"Do not be anxious on my behalf," Arabella said, pretending more confidence than she felt. "All will be well here."

At that moment one of the servants came up, touching his hat brim. "All is in readiness for departure, ma'am."

"Thank you," Lady Corey said, then turned back to Arabella. "Well, if you are determined to remain, I suppose this is *adieu*."

"*Au revoir*," Arabella corrected with a smile. "Until we meet again."

"Until we meet again," Lady Corey replied with a matching smile. But then something caught her attention and she looked upward . . . and her smile faded, quickly replaced by an expression of alarm. Arabella, seeing Lady Corey's face, turned to follow her gaze.

A fleet of ships—a dozen at least, under a full spread of silk—was descending toward them from the zenith. The early-afternoon sun, shining directly behind them, must have hidden their approach until the last moment. Even now Arabella, shading her eyes with a hand, could not see them clearly and certainly could not count them all. But she did spot the English ensign fluttering from the stern of one of the nearer vessels. "Raise the alarm!" she cried in her best airgoing voice. But she was not the first to do so, and already shouts, rattles, and bells were sounding from all around, Martians and humans running in every direction.

It was the Ceres fleet. Somehow they had come directly to Tekhmet . . . a town whose very existence, not to mention its location, was the resistance's greatest secret.

How had they found it?

"Michael," Arabella said aloud, and her lips drew back from her teeth in a grimace.

Lady Corey's servants—they had come with her from Fort Augusta and were not in the least military—were staring all about, wondering what to do. "Get her to Khoresh Tukath!" Captain Fox called to them, rushing to Lady Corey and propelling her toward the coach. The servants hastened to comply, though their actions were disorganized. Gowse tried to marshal the coach-*huresh* into some kind of order.

And then something black and round dropped from the sky,

landing between the coach and Common Hall with a deafening explosion.

Arabella was thrown to the ground by the blast. A moment later she shrieked and covered her head with her arms, as clots of dirt and bits of metal and wood rained down upon her, striking with fierce impacts upon her back and legs. But the rain of debris did not last long, and as soon as she could gather her wits she raised her head, ears ringing, coughing from the dusty air.

Common Hall was burning. A huge hole had been smashed in the near side, shattered timbers spreading from the point of impact like some harsh, dangerous flower, and at the heart of that flower a fierce orange flame was spreading, sending black smoke billowing upward. The coach, between Arabella and the hall, was also smoldering. Though not so badly damaged as the hall, it had been knocked askew, and the *huresh* hitched to it were squealing and thrashing in their traces. Whether they were injured or merely panicked Arabella could not tell.

"Lady Corey!" she shouted into the chaos.

"Here, child!" came a reply from the vicinity of the coach. Arabella could barely hear the voice over the ringing in her ears, but she followed it as best she could, finding Lady Corey half-pinned under a pile of cases which had fallen from the top of the coach. Captain Fox, his clothing filthy with dirt and ash, was already trying to unearth her. Servants rushed about in confusion, like *thurok* whose nest had been kicked over.

Arabella and Fox together managed to get the cases off of Lady Corey. "Are you hurt?" Arabella asked, helping her to her feet.

"I do not think so. But the coach—!"

The coach, indeed, was in no condition to go any where. It looked as though both its axles were broken, and the traces were all in a tangle. Lady Corey's cases and possessions were scattered all about, some smoldering or in flames.

Then a second explosion sounded from quite close at hand, causing every one to cry out and duck, shielding their heads from the rain of fragments.

Fox looked upward and cursed, and Arabella followed his gaze. The English ships were much closer now, appearing to descend still more rapidly, and many black dots fell from them . . . more aerial bombs. Tiny glimmers of light and puffs of smoke in their rigging showed rifle fire as well. At this range the bullets were unlikely to find their targets, but that distance was closing quickly . . . and soon the fleet would be low enough that their great guns could be brought into play as well.

"I must get to *Touchstone!*" Fox shouted in Arabella's face. Explosions were now bursting all about them, far and near, accompanied by cries of pain and panic from Martians, humans, and *huresh*. *Touchstone,* requiring a launch-furnace as she did, was berthed at Khoresh Tukath, an hour away for a fast rider.

But the coach was smashed, and Fox, raised on Earth, was no *huresh*-rider at all. Nor could he ride a Draisine.

"Gowse!" Arabella shouted.

Gowse—who had served for over a year as Arabella's *huresh*-groom—turned from where he was assisting Lady Corey's servants in getting the panicked animals under control. "Aye, ma'am?"

"Take one of these *huresh* and get Captain Fox to *Touchstone* as fast as you possibly can!"

"Aye aye!" Gowse immediately moved to the lead beast, leaving the others to the rest of the servants, and began unhitching him from the coach. He was a fine specimen, a lean fast runner called Hardy.

"I will get Lady Corey to safety," Arabella told Fox.

Without a word Fox nodded to Arabella, then took Lady Corey's hand and kissed it. "Be safe, my love," he told her.

"And you," Lady Corey replied, the second word ending in a choking sound as tears clogged her throat.

Fox then ran to Gowse, who had already unhitched Hardy and leapt up upon his back. "Have ye ridden bareback before?" Gowse said to Fox, extending a hand.

"On a horse . . ." Fox replied, taking Gowse's hand and pulling himself up behind.

Gowse shook his head. "This might be a bit different, sir. Hang on tight." Then he clucked his tongue at Hardy, digging his heels in at the soft spot behind the beast's thorax, and the *huresh* surged forward. Fox whooped and clamped his hat onto his head with one hand, clinging with the other to Gowse's waist as they vanished into the smoke.

"Come with me!" Arabella said to Lady Corey, putting an arm around the older woman's waist and urging her forward.

---

"Where are you taking me, child?" Lady Corey asked after a time.

The two women were running through chaos. Explosions and rifle fire sounded at irregular intervals from all around. Black smoke smudged the sky, rising from the fires that burned uncontrolled here and there, and panicked people and beasts of every description dashed about without visible method or organization.

"To *Diana!*" Arabella said.

As they ran they gathered up others, humans and Martians alike. Those with experience flying *khebek* she encouraged to get to their ships—or, indeed, any they could reach—and take them into the air as quickly as possible, for on the ground they were immobile and nearly defenseless. The rest they brought along with them toward *Diana*, though some were panicked or injured and had to be helped along or even carried. Arabella soon forgot her own cares and concerns, concentrating all her attentions upon helping as many others as she could.

But when they rounded the corner of the rope-walk and saw *Diana* standing tall in her berth—seemingly undamaged, with her three great balloon envelopes already fully inflated and straining at the network of cables which tethered them to the ship's hull— her heart leapt into her mouth from simultaneous exaltation at the ship's safety and fear for her captain. "Hurry!" she called to Lady Corey and the others who accompanied her, just as though they were not already all pushing themselves to their utmost pace . . . and, somehow, they did manage to eke out a bit more speed, racing toward *Diana* as bombs continued to burst on the ground and in the air all around.

*Diana*, though not yet airborne, was already defending herself, with the swivel-mounted chasers on the forecastle and quarterdeck firing as rapidly as they could. This fire accounted for her as yet undamaged condition, as it discouraged the English ships with their aerial bombs from approaching too closely. Yet *Diana* was still quite vulnerable . . . if a single bomb or shell should strike her balloons, it would make a rapid end of her as well as every thing around her.

Up the gangplank Arabella and her companions ran, tumbling exhausted into the waist. The situation they found aboard ship was nearly as much of a bedlam as on the ground, but this pandemonium was at least more organized, with airmen rushing to defend the ship and simultaneously prepare her for an immediate ascent. With relief Arabella handed Lady Corey and some of the others—those injured, exhausted, or otherwise incapable— to the surgeon, Dr. Barry, who shepherded them below. The rest of her people she sent to Faunt, the captain of the waist, to offer whatever assistance they could. Plainly not all of *Diana*'s usual crew had managed to return to the ship in the chaos of the attack, and every hand would be welcome.

Having discharged her immediate responsibilities, Arabella did not even pause for breath before hastening to the quarterdeck . . . where she immediately spied Captain Singh, safe and in command!

Requesting and receiving permission to ascend the ladder, she rushed to her husband's side. The expression of panicked relief on his face matched her own sentiments, but they had no time for more than a brief embrace before he pulled away. "Thank Heaven you are here! Now get below and have Aadim plot us a low-altitude course for Tekh Shetekta."

But though Arabella longed to be away, she could not do so without one assurance. "Has Gonekh come aboard with the automata?"

"Not to my knowledge."

Arabella held her breath, peering over the rail at her Institute, which lay between *Diana*'s berth and the hydrogen manufactory. It seemed as yet undamaged, and if the automaton pilots could be rescued they might make all the difference in the fighting to come.

But every minute *Diana* remained on land was another opportunity for the English to destroy her.

"I will send some one to collect them," Captain Singh said, seeing her hesitation.

But contemplating this alternative made Arabella realize just how important the automata were to her and to their cause . . . and how much she had come to depend upon Gonekh. "I must do this myself! I will return as quickly as I can." She kissed him on the cheek and ran.

---

She found Gonekh and the other technicians scrambling about the Institute, gathering papers and tools and piling them upon an already overloaded cart. Plainly it would not even cross the threshold without spilling its contents. "This will not do!" she cried.

"Chekta, I saw another cart on my way here, near the water-trough. Go and bring it back. Torkei, Gonekh . . . you two and I will shift some of this onto the second cart. The rest of you . . . each take one of the completed automata and run to *Diana* immediately!"

As the technicians leapt to comply, Arabella looked about. Gonekh had done a good job of locating the most important items . . . except that she had missed the set of metal files, which Arabella had been using in her work on the cast gears and now lay on the shelf beneath her work-bench. Arabella snatched the set up and crammed it into a gap near the bottom of the pile upon the cart, even as Chekta returned with the second cart. "Hurry!" Arabella cried.

Quickly they moved materials from the first cart to the second, until Arabella judged that neither cart was in danger of over-turning. Then the four of them shoved the two carts to the door. As Gonekh and Torkei pulled the heavy double doors open, Arabella looked around the Institute one last time.

In the last months the Institute—this filthy shed—had become something like her home. She had certainly spent more time here than in her bed, and it was a place that, in some ways, she had built with her own two hands. Every thing here had been brought to this place and put where it was because she had needed it for the sake of her home planet. And now she was abandoning it . . . driven from her home by force of arms.

By the Prince Regent. By her own sovereign lord.

No! He was not her sovereign. Perhaps he never had been.

She was a *Martian*.

Arabella was a Martian born and bred, and she would not let any King or Prince, no matter how powerful, do to her people what he was doing to her right now.

Not if it was within her power to prevent it.

The pandemonium without had grown still more chaotic during the few minutes Arabella had been inside the Institute. Flames roared on every side, filling the air with choking black smoke, and explosions sounded at irregular intervals . . . the continuing barrage of English bombs now accompanied by detonations of gunpowder and hydrogen from the ship-yard as the fires spread. *Diana* added to the noise with the reports of her guns, and shouts and commands in a variety of languages came to Arabella's ears through the murk.

Coughing, eyes running, Arabella put her shoulder to the cart and helped Chekta propel it across the irregular ground. The distance to *Diana* was not great, no more than two hundred yards, but the sand was littered with debris and even the body of a fallen *huresh*, around which they were compelled to detour.

Even as she struggled forward, Arabella kept an eye turned upward, where English ships floated like malevolent copper-bottomed clouds. They were now being joined in the sky by *khebek*, the light small vessels rising swiftly from the ship-yard beneath their single balloons, and some of the Royal Navy vessels were turning to bring their great guns to bear upon these new targets. But the Martian ships, though their crews were not yet fully trained and some of them lacked guns and even complete hulls, were so small and nimble that the ponderous English first-rates could not target them effectively. Even the English frigates, smaller and more maneuverable, were unused to such agile adversaries, and though they fired again and again, most of their shots went wide.

But not all. First one of the rising *khebek* was smashed to flinders by a well-timed English broadside, and then another's balloon was pierced—the cannon-balls' hot metal causing the hydrogen within to explode with a tremendous *bang*. A wave of heat rushed out from the falling ship, so intense that Arabella felt its flush upon her face even half a mile away.

Fortunately she could not hear the crew's screams over the many other sounds of the attack.

Grimly Arabella returned her gaze to *Diana,* now just one hundred yards away, and her heavy heart lightened as she saw a mixed crowd of people—waisters, topmen, Venusians, and some of the Martians she had gathered on her run from Common Hall—rushing down the gangplank to assist her and her technicians in unloading the carts. With renewed vigor she pushed her cart the last few yards.

Within minutes all the precious automata, plans, tools, parts, and assemblies had been brought aboard. But as Arabella checked to make sure that every bit of material had been collected, she noticed one significant absence. "Has any one seen Gonekh?" she shouted.

"She went back for something that fell off the cart!" came the reply.

Casting her eye back along the cart-tracks that wobbled across the sand, Arabella soon located her assistant, struggling to drag a heavy metal lathe across the wreckage-strewn ground. "Gonekh!" she cried, and rushed toward her.

But then Gonekh jerked, fell over, and lay still, red stains spreading across her clothing.

Arabella shrieked and looked upward, soon finding the English first-rate from which the fatal shots must have come. Red-coated Marines hung in its rigging like evil, overripe fruit, aiming their rifles down toward the running figures below.

Another wordless cry of anger and indignation was wrenched from Arabella's throat as she ran to Gonekh's aid. But before she could move more than a few steps, something struck her from behind. She fell to the filthy sand, with a moist and heavy weight landing on top of her and driving the breath from her lungs.

A moment later the sand before her eyes fountained up from the impact of several bullets. If she had continued running, those bullets would have struck her instead.

The weight that had knocked her over was Ulungugga, the Venusian waister. "You cannot help her," he croaked as he hauled her to her feet. "We leave now."

Stunned from exhaustion and grief, Arabella did not protest as Ulungugga half-carried her up the gangplank, which was immediately drawn up behind them. Every one else was already aboard, or lay unmoving on the sand below.

---

Moments after Arabella and Ulungugga came aboard, she heard the cry "Dump all ballast!" from the quarterdeck. Immediately a shuddering, rushing hiss sounded from belowdecks and the ship shot skyward. The sand-anchors and other moorings must already have been taken up.

The ship's precipitous rise was accompanied by shrieks and whoops from all aboard, along with cries and thuds as some people, unprepared for the sudden lurch of her departure from the ground, fell to the deck . . . Arabella among them. She hoped as she struggled to her feet that no one had fallen very far.

Shooting upward as rapidly as she was, *Diana* quickly rose above the level of the English ships; Arabella found herself looking right into the eyes of an astonished airman for a moment as she swept past him. So swift, in fact, was *Diana*'s rise that not a single cannon shot was fired during the brief period when she was within their firing angle. The great guns on English aerial men-of-war were designed for use in free descent, not near a planetary surface, and relied upon turning the entire ship for aiming. The individual cannon had only a few degrees of upward and downward motion within their gun-ports, so beneath the falling-line the great guns were useless on any target substantially higher or lower.

But the English ships were also equipped with swivel-guns on their decks and snipers in the tops. The *crack* and flash of gunfire burst out from the ships all around, and shot large and small whined past above Arabella's head. Several of these connected with masts or the hull, sending splinters flying, and Arabella quickly ducked down beneath the gunwale, covering her head with her hands. But she could not bear not knowing what was happening. Keeping low, she scuttled aft until she could peer through the scupper.

The sight that met Arabella's eyes was truly astonishing. Dozens of balloons loomed above, below, and in all directions, filling the murky sky like pickled eggs in a bottle of vinegar. The smaller single ones, rising rapidly, were Martian *khebek*; the larger ones, in groups of eight and ten, were those of the English fleet. By contrast with the *khebek*, these hung steady in the air or were sinking slowly, and the ships beneath them were magnificent specimens of the shipbuilder's art, with spectacular carved figureheads and gleaming copper bottoms. And beneath those . . .

The town of Tekhmet, which Arabella had beheld from above so frequently in the past months, was scarcely recognizable as itself. The pleasant curving streets of Martian buildings, now devastated by bombs, resembled a vegetable patch that had been trampled by giant beasts. The ship-yard, formerly an organized bustling hive of activity, was now nothing more than a collection of cavities—some empty of ships recently departed, others filled with smoldering wreckage. Fires burned every where, spreading like spilled acid, eating up every thing they touched and blackening the air above with smoke. The sight was devastating.

But worse was yet to come. For the flames were already licking at the hydrogen manufactory, and even as Arabella watched the thing she feared most was beginning to occur. With a tremendous boom, loud even at this distance, the nearest corner of the manufactory to the fire exploded, sending visible pressure waves washing through the filthy air and fragments of roof and beam spinning upward. A moment later came a second explosion, and then a third—each one more devastating than the last, as each damaged the structure more severely, causing yet more hydrogen to spill into the air, feeding the fire, and leading to yet more and larger explosions. Soon the entire manufactory had burst into bits in a paroxysm of explosions, reducing one of Fulton's most amazing engineering achievements to a smoking, shattered ruin in less than a minute.

Arabella could only hope that Fulton and his manufactory workers had escaped before the disaster.

"Idlers and waisters to the pulsers!" came the command from the quarterdeck, and for a moment Arabella's old habits came to the fore, compelling her to rush below with the other waisters. But she immediately corrected herself, and reversed her course for the great cabin where Aadim awaited her.

Shaken and unnerved she might be, but she had her orders, and she would not fail her captain as she had failed Gonekh.

---

Aadim sat, imperturbable as always, facing away from the great curved window at the cabin's stern. He was, she reflected as she unrolled the chart of Sor Khoresh upon his table, somewhat the worse for wear from when she had first met him. The callous treatment he had received in the hands of the French had left the painted wood of his face and hands scarred and chipped, and the hurried modifications she and Captain Singh had made to him since their arrival on Mars had added significantly to his bulk with little attention to aesthetics. A large box of gears and levers, close kin to the automaton pilot, had been crudely bolted to one side of the desk which formed his lower body; it spoiled his symmetry and hid some fine inlay work, but added considerably to his navigational capabilities within Mars's Horn.

They would likely need every one of those new capabilities before this day was out.

Quickly she laid in the course Captain Singh had requested, a low-altitude path to Tekh Shetekta. But before she could press down Aadim's finger upon the chart a second time to begin the calculations, the ship was jolted hard by a sudden impact, throwing her across the cabin. Bruised and shaken, she ignored the shouts, cries, and thundering footsteps that followed the blow and hauled herself back to Aadim's desk. But when she pressed on the finger, a dull click was the only response she received.

Cursing, Arabella threw open the access panel on Aadim's desk and inspected the clockworks therein. Feverishly she worked to find the problem, swinging hinged brass assemblies aside and inspecting the gleaming works thus revealed with a lamp and a practiced eye. There were so *many* moving parts within, and nearly any one of them could have been jarred loose by a blow like the one the ship had just received. Or even worse . . . Aadim's mechanisms extended throughout the ship, and if the damage were elsewhere there would be little she could do to repair it in the midst of battle.

Outside the window the pulsers whirled, the great triangular sails rushing past more than once per second as the men and Venusians belowdecks literally pedaled for their lives. Beyond the spinning pulsers lay the English ships, their own pulsers whirling as they rose in pursuit. Lifted by hot air as they were, rather than the more buoyant hydrogen used by *Diana*, they could not match her speed of ascent . . . but their crews were far more numerous, and battle-hardened by years of war with Napoleon. By dint of vigorous pedaling they would quickly overcome *Diana*'s advantages in maneuverability, and once they matched her altitude their great guns would come into play. Each one of the English first-rates threw twice or more *Diana*'s weight of metal.

Watson burst in the cabin door. "The captain asks, have you the course?" he half-shouted.

"Hold this" was all the reply Arabella offered, handing him the lamp and putting her head entirely inside Aadim's desk. Was that a sliver of wood jammed in the mechanism?

It was! And, with the aid of a pair of fine needle-nose pliers, Arabella was able to prise it free. It must have been knocked loose by the impact from the inside of Aadim's case.

Quickly she put every thing back in place. Then, holding her breath, she pressed down upon Aadim's wooden finger . . . and with a satisfying whir his gears began to turn.

"Tell the captain I shall return momentarily with his requested course," she told Watson as she closed and latched the access panel. Watson knuckled his forehead and hurried off.

A moment later a bell sounded and Arabella copied down the sail-plan from the dials on the front of Aadim's desk. This course would not have been possible a year ago, she reflected as she hurried up the companion ladder with the paper clutched between her teeth. It was, in fact, only within the past few months that they had completely incorporated the capabilities of *Diana*'s hydrogen balloons into Aadim's calculations.

---

"Here is the course, sir," Arabella said as she presented the paper—slightly damp and tooth-marked—to her husband.

"Thank you, Ashby," he replied absently, taking the paper and reading it over. Immediately he translated the sailing-plan into instructions to Edmonds, who relayed them to the captains of divisions and thence to the crew.

Edmonds spun the wheel hard as the larboard stuns'ls flashed out, sending the ship into a steep, diving turn propelled by the still-whirling pulsers. Arabella clung to a backstay as the deck tilted precipitously beneath her feet, the world seeming to spin around as the ship turned through twelve points—more than a third of a circle—while rapidly losing altitude.

For a moment they seemed to be driving directly toward the pursuing English fleet, and even as the enemy ships came into view ahead they began firing, gouts of flame and smoke reaching out toward *Diana*. But Diana could descend far more swiftly than they, by drawing hydrogen from her balloons back into her tanks, whereas the English were forced to either rely upon the slower cooling of their hot air or take the risky choice of venting it. She quickly dropped below their range, leaving their shots to whine overhead and damage only a few sails and lines.

"It will take them a little while to match our altitude change," Captain Singh remarked to Edmonds, nearly conversationally. "We should take this opportunity to chastise them."

"Aye aye, sir!" Edmonds replied with enthusiasm, then cried, "All hands rig for pitch!" Arabella had never heard this command before, and grasped her backstay more tightly, wondering what might follow. Her answer came a moment later, as he called out, "Set main-royals and t'gallants! Haul up on the for'ard balloon-stays! Idlers and waisters aft!"

This unprecedented and perilous series of directives had the effect of tilting the ship back upon her heel by a good twenty degrees, leaving every one holding tight for their lives to whatever they had happened to be closest to when the order "rig for pitch" had come. For, unlike the usual circumstances of aerial battle, they were still well below the falling-line, and a fall overboard would be rapidly fatal.

But the maneuver brought *Diana*'s great guns, located in her bow and facing strictly forward, up to target the nearest ship of the English fleet. "Fire!" cried Edmonds, and at once the cannon spoke, deafening Arabella even as the ship jerked beneath her from the force of the discharge. Flames lanced toward the English fleet, and a moment later the lead ship's bow shattered under the impact of *Diana*'s twelve eight-pound balls, to resounding cheers from *Diana*'s people. "Fire!" cried Edmonds again, and a second English ship suffered the same fate.

But two such salvos were all they had time for, as *Diana* continued to drift forward and down, passing below the English fleet and taking them above the range of her guns. Soon *Diana* had settled back to her original attitude, and the pulsers began to spin again—the idlers and waisters returning to the pedals from the after end, whence they had crowded to help tilt the ship backward with their combined weight—driving the ship forward toward Tekh Shetekta.

But though *Diana* and her English adversaries were no longer able to harry each other with their great guns, their chasers and rifles were still in play, and many a ball pinged and whined through the air in both directions. As the distance between them grew— *Diana* again descending more rapidly than the English—Arabella's confidence grew as well. They were still badly outnumbered, and though the English were struggling to turn and give chase to the rapidly-receding *Diana*, they would soon get themselves in order. "Do you think," she asked Captain Singh, "that, having seen how we pitched the ship to attack them, they will do the same to us?"

"They may attempt it," he replied, examining the damaged ships through his telescope. "But I doubt they have practiced the maneuver as we have." He lowered the glass. "I devised it last month, while you were occupied with the automaton pilots."

Arabella considered this as she watched the English forming up on their leader. They did not appear to be attempting to duplicate *Diana*'s maneuver, but with the greater number of men they could put to the pedals they were no longer falling behind, and indeed were already beginning to catch *Diana* up. But not all of them, she realized, were attempting to do so. "Some of the English fleet are separating from the main force," she observed to her captain.

He grunted and raised his telescope again. "They are pursuing our *khebek*," he muttered darkly. Even an unaided eye could see that the greater part of the fleet was now rising upward in pursuit of the ascending *khebek*, while the three most heavily-armed first-rates were continuing to drive toward *Diana* with all the force of their rapidly-spinning pulsers. "I had hoped to distract them with a larger prize, but Admiral Thornbrough is apparently too wily for that stratagem to succeed."

"So what can we do?"

Captain Singh's expression was as grim and determined as she had ever seen upon his face. "We must turn and attack."

Arabella was astonished. "One ship against three?"

"One frigate-class ex-Marsman against three first-rates, to be specific. But we do have a few advantages." He turned to Edmonds. "Fox and hounds, Mr. Edmonds."

"Aye aye, sir. Fox and hounds." He then bellowed to the men at the pedals to put their f——g backs into it, and offered similar friendly encouragement to the gunners and topmen. Abandoning the course Arabella and Aadim had just worked out, *Diana* immediately turned about and drove upward, heading directly toward the three English ships. They were still well above her altitude, but descending rapidly.

"What shall I do?" Arabella asked, still clinging tightly to her backstay.

"Once we dispatch these adversaries, we will immediately ascend to the winds of the Horn. I will require Aadim's assistance then . . . and no one understands his new mechanisms as well as you. You will remain on the quarterdeck to appraise the currents until your services are required below."

"Aye aye, sir," she replied.

Shortly an airman appeared with the leather belts and straps which would hold the officers in place on the deck in free descent; these were not yet needed but would soon be. Arabella quickly strapped herself in place, but deliberately did not fasten the second set of safety buckles, for she anticipated that a rapid departure might be required.

*Diana* became a riot of noise as she and the English rapidly drew nearer each other. Belowdecks, men chanted and grunted rhythmically at the pedals and powder monkeys dashed back and forth to the gun-deck. Aloft, topmen called back and forth as they positioned themselves for rapid action with the balloons and sails. In the waist, men and Venusians—and a few of the brave, inexperienced Martians whom Arabella had brought with her from the ship-yard—rigged fearnought screens: lengths of dampened burlap stretched across the hatches, to prevent splinters and sparks from getting below. All the while Chips the carpenter and his crew hammered and sawed away in the forecastle, making hasty repairs to a great gash in the hull there. This must be the result of the impact that had temporarily disabled Aadim. Despite the rushing air of their rapid ascent, powerful scents of powder, sawdust, and sweat assaulted Arabella's nose.

Distant *bang*s and flashes of flame were coming from the English now, but the shots howled far overhead. Captain Singh, more sparing of his shot and powder, held his fire.

And then, suddenly, some invisible line was crossed and they were in the midst of battle.

All three English ships let fly at once, their simultaneous broadsides forming a continuous wall of flame and smoke and noise that momentarily obscured the ships themselves. "Get down!" some one shouted, and Arabella ducked down where she stood, covering her head with her hands. A moment later came the rising screams of incoming cannon-balls—many of which diminished as quickly, falling in pitch as they flew past, but some ended in shattering crashes that shook the deck beneath Arabella's foot and rattled her stump in its straps.

"Return fire!" cried Captain Singh, and the deck jerked again, accompanied by the thunderous roar of *Diana*'s twelve eight-pound guns. As Arabella raised her head, she heard the cries of injured men—none appeared to have been struck by shot directly, but flying splinters could be just as deadly—and the shouts of carpenters and captains of divisions struggling to repair the damage to ship and course. Then a second command to "Fire!" obliterated those sounds as well.

The sky all about was a mass of smoke and flame and destruction, with howling shots and spinning fragments of *khoresh*-wood flying at unpredictable intervals out of the murk. The noise and confusion were far greater even than in the midst of the Battle of Venus—the number of ships had been greater there, but the quarters here were far closer, and the influence of Mars's gravity added the fear of falling to all the other perils of aerial battle.

Arabella's duty was to monitor the winds, the better to direct Aadim when his navigation would be required, but in this madness—the ship turning, diving, and lurching upward seemingly at random, with Edmonds calling out commands faster than she could follow and the sky an impenetrable murk—she barely knew which direction was skyward.

But then she realized the howl and crash of incoming shot had been replaced by howls alone—the English cannon were no longer finding their target. How was this possible? Even with her hydrogen balloons, *Diana* could not have risen so rapidly through the deadly stratum of English fire, and the English were too experienced to simply miss their target due to the smoke.

Then a stray breeze blew a momentary hole in the smoke and the answer became clear: the English were not below, but above! *Diana* had ascended to their level only briefly, then descended again—hidden by the fog of war. "Fox and hounds," muttered Arabella to herself.

"Pulsers double time!" shouted Edmonds, and the drumbeats from belowdecks increased their pace. *Diana* surged forward, leaving the English ships above and behind. But the English reacted quickly, turning and descending still more rapidly in pursuit. *Diana*'s lead was not large and they would soon catch her up.

"Five hundred feet, sir," Edmonds muttered to Captain Singh—referring, Arabella inferred, to the difference in altitude between *Diana* and the pursuing first-rates.

"A moment longer, Mr. Edmonds." Captain Singh raised his glass and carefully inspected the oncoming English ships. "Davies . . ." he muttered to himself, "Mason . . . and Scott."

"Three hundred feet," Edmonds said, visibly growing nervous.

"Maintain course. Those three captains will not be easily fooled."

"Two hundred feet, sir!"

"Steady."

Indeed, Arabella now found herself barely raising her gaze at all to take in the looming English ships, which were falling swiftly toward her, closing the distance both horizontally and vertically with distressing rapidity. In just a few moments she would be looking directly down the barrels of their large and very numerous cannon. Already the *crack* of small arms fire could be heard, so close had they drawn.

"One hundred feet!"

But even in the face of the rapidly-approaching English men-of-war and Edmonds's near-panic Captain Singh remained imperturbable. "Now, Mr. Edmonds," he said in a quite normal voice.

"Start the water!" Edmonds howled. "And ease off on the hydrogen!" The unanticipated command startled Arabella nearly as much as the sudden upward thrust of the deck below her.

With a rumbling rush, a fountain of clear water burst from the hull below Arabella, arcing off in an elegant stream to disperse on the desert below. Three more such streams of water appeared at the same moment . . . jettisoning the drinking water *Diana*'s people would need to survive a long journey, but also lightening the ship suddenly and substantially. At the same time, at Edmonds's command the Venusians belowdecks were working the hydrogen pumps, slightly reducing the pressure in the balloons. This operation would only increase the ship's buoyancy if they had been run at a slight overpressure for the entire battle up until now . . . which meant that Captain Singh had been holding that additional lift in reserve for just such an occasion as this. The overall effect of the two commands was to send *Diana* flying upward still more precipitously than her original departure from the surface.

The English, meanwhile, remained committed to their swift descent toward *Diana* . . . the inescapable facts of physics and their construction preventing them from matching her rapid reversal in altitude. They fired upon *Diana* as soon as they noted her maneuver, but nearly every ball passed harmlessly below her. One shot did strike her hull with a splintering *crack* that made the whole ship jerk, but damage to the lower hull or keel would cause little problem unless and until they next landed upon a planet. Within minutes Arabella found herself looking down upon the English ships, their hulls eclipsed by the numerous white moons of their balloons.

"They will have to shovel coal for a long time to match our rise," Captain Singh remarked to Arabella. "They may be compelled to call off the pursuit, due to lack of coal. But even if they do not, by the time they catch us up we shall be well embedded in the Horn." He peered upward, and Arabella matched his gaze.

The first *khebek* to escape had already reached the falling-line and were collapsing their envelopes, drawing the precious hydrogen—irreplaceable now, with the loss of the manufactory—back into the tanks in their hulls and relying on the winds of the Horn to carry them further upward. "Where are they bound?" Arabella asked.

"Phobos," he replied, returning to inspecting the English through his telescope.

"Phobos!" Arabella gasped. "But it lies in plain sight!" She gestured upward, to where the moon did, indeed, stand visible to all of the sky and half the planet. "We cannot hide there!"

"We cannot hide there," he acknowledged, "but we can fight there. And your work on the automaton pilot may prove critical to this effort." He collapsed the glass and tucked it into his tail-coat pocket. "Phobos's winds make it very difficult to approach safely. But with the help of the automaton pilots, I believe our *khebek* can overcome this natural barrier, take Phobos, and hold it. Once we have done this, the moon's natural defenses will become an advantage rather than an obstacle for us. Therefore, before departing Tekhmet I signaled the *khebek* fleet to make their way there by any means possible, relying on *Diana* to draw the English away to Tekh Shetekta."

"But that subterfuge failed, and now the English are in pursuit."

"Exactly. Our work this day is not yet done."

# 13

## IN THE HORN

As the smoke of the battle began to dissipate, Arabella assessed the situation. The *khebek*, being smaller, lighter, and lifted by hydrogen, had a substantial advantage in maneuverability and ascent speed over the English, and furthermore they were more numerous—she counted over twenty, versus nine English ships of various sizes—and had nearly an hour's lead in their escape. But not all of them had their cannon mounted, and most of their crews lacked any experience in gunnery; furthermore, the English with their much larger complements of able airmen could easily out-pedal them. All in all, she thought, the English held the decidedly-stronger position.

But within the Horn's unpredictable winds . . . who could say?

In all of Arabella's studies of aerial combat she had never read of a battle taking place within a planet's Horn. The tempestuous winds were challenge enough to navigation that engaging an enemy at the same time was a thing no sane captain would attempt. But aerial battle in the midst of ascent was also nearly unheard-of, and *Diana* had just performed that feat admirably.

Of course, that had been against three ships, not nine, and the men at the pulsers were growing more weary by the minute.

She stepped forward to share her observations with the captain, who stood at the rail peering forward through his glass. "I agree with your concerns," he replied, "but with our automaton pilots we may yet be able to carry the day. How many of the *khebek* are thus equipped?"

"Sixteen, out of about thirty capable of ascent."

He considered this intelligence for a moment. "I anticipate that the English will attempt to drive the *khebek* into the comparative calm of the interplanetary atmosphere, where with their superior ship-handling skills they can make short work of them. Once we are within signal range, I will instruct the *khebek* that those whose cannon and automaton pilots are installed and in operation are to harry the English within the Horn, engaging them closely and keeping them mired therein, while those less fortunate escape to Phobos. We will assist as soon as we are able."

"This strategy places our most valuable ships at the gravest risk."

Captain Singh nodded grimly. "It does. But they are also the most capable, and the most likely to survive the encounter."

A distressing thought occurred to Arabella then. "But how are those *khebek* lacking automaton pilots to land safely upon Phobos?"

"They will have to do their best with their native skills." The captain's expression, already dour, darkened still further. "Though Phobos may be deadly, it is less so than the English."

Arabella looked out upon the rising ships, Martian and English, and the pale rocky moon sailing rapidly by above them . . . and left her misgivings unspoken.

Arabella was on the lower deck, assisting Lady Corey in carrying skins of precious water to the men laboring at the pedals—and worrying how long the few gallons remaining on board would last—when the sound of distant cannon reached her ears, followed by shouts from abovedecks. Immediately she excused herself and ran up the companion ladder, her steps high and floating in the reduced gravity.

The sight she beheld was splendid, chaotic, and deadly. Nearly every ship in view had risen above the falling-line and collapsed her balloons. The English had all swayed-out their lower masts for navigation within the Horn, or were in the process of doing so; the *khebek* they pursued lacked any requirement to do so, their two horizontal masts being no different above the falling-line than below. Now beyond the influence of Mars's gravity, they tumbled this way and that in the chaotic winds of the Horn, with only a slight preference among them as to which direction was "up."

Cannon fired frequently and at unpredictable intervals, but the winds were so strong and erratic that the sound of each shot was often far dimmer and more tardy than would ordinarily be expected given the distance, and sometimes lost completely. Furthermore, the cloud of smoke produced by each broadside was quickly shredded by the capricious winds, sending dense black tendrils streaming across the battle in every direction and rendering the scene extremely difficult to comprehend.

Arabella wondered whether there were any point at all to a ship firing her great guns in such a shambles of air—both ships moving rapidly and erratically, the target barely visible, and the winds so fierce that not even cannon-balls could be depended upon to fly straight. But then she saw one of the *khebek* struck by a full English broadside at close range. The little ship flew completely into splinters, and a moment later even the splinters were burnt up and scattered by a rapidly expanding globe of pale hydrogen flame.

But the *khebek* were not completely outmatched. Here she saw two of them assaulting an English frigate, their tiny guns harassing the officers on the quarterdeck like a pair of spirited *tokoleth* scratching at the eyes of a much larger and fiercer *shorosh*; there she saw another ducking and dodging, seemingly bending the wild winds of the Horn to her will, while an English second-rate blundered ineffectually in pursuit. This agility, she knew, was the work of the ship's automaton pilot, and for a moment her spirits rose. But then the *khebek* and her pursuer dashed through a cloud of smoke and debris, and Arabella realized that cloud was all that remained of another destroyed Martian vessel. Indeed, the number of such ragged clouds of wreckage was dispiritingly large, while all nine English vessels were still largely intact.

Dismayed, Arabella looked to *Diana*'s quarterdeck, where she saw Captain Singh spinning a gold sovereign in the air. Carefully his eyes followed it as it rose, glinting in the filthy sunlight, and then fell ever so slowly toward the deck. He snatched it from the air at waist level, returned it to his pocket, and spoke firmly to Edmonds, who immediately called, "All hands prepare to sway out!"

Clearly there would be no falling-line ceremony on *this* voyage.

The men leapt into action, experienced hands moving with swift precision while those who had just joined—including, Arabella noted, all of her Martian technicians from the Institute—made their best efforts to assist, despite the exhaustion many of them must be feeling after hours at the pedals. Arabella herself longed to haul on a line, the better to bring *Diana* into battle swiftly, but she knew her skills were better employed elsewhere. Pausing to let a gang of men rush by on their way to sway out the larboard mast, she ascended to the quarterdeck.

Captain Singh was fully engaged in the swaying-out, but during a brief lull he addressed her, though his gaze remained fixed on the rising main-sail. "If you please, Mrs. Singh," he said—she was surprised he had not called her Ashby—"ask Aadim for a course to intercept *Marlborough,* there." He pointed to the largest and least damaged of the English fleet, which lay in the very midst of the roiling chaos of battle.

"Permission to remain on deck until we enter the Horn?" she requested in return. "I wish to observe the winds."

"Granted." Still not looking at her, he drew his telescope from a pocket. "You may use my glass." Once she had taken it from his hand, she plainly ceased to exist to him, as he devoted his full attention to the fitting-out of the lower masts and stowing of the balloon envelopes.

As the topmen scuttled about, leaping from mast to mast with lines in their teeth, Arabella fastened herself into her restraining belt and trained Captain Singh's telescope upon the distant battle. *Marlborough* was beset by *khebek,* four or five of them harassing her from every side, and though fire and smoke lanced at intervals from her great guns they repeatedly evaded destruction. But the *khebek,* in turn, were too lightly armed to do *Marlborough* any great damage, leading to a near-stalemate . . . a stalemate in which the larger vessel, due to the stamina of her more numerous crew and the great destructive power of her cannon, must eventually prevail. But if that one English ship could be taken out of action, freeing the *khebek* harrying her to attack other ships, the tide of the overall battle might turn.

Next Arabella turned her attention to the winds. Between the smoke and detritus of the battle and the many ships involved therein, they were very clearly visible, and she swiftly wrote down the major currents in a note-book drawn from her reticule. But the winds between here and there would determine *Diana*'s critical initial course, and those were less easily discernible. Here she wished she had her husband's experienced eye—it seemed that he could make out a current from a mere shimmer of distortion or fleck of dust. Alternating naked-eye observation with close examination through the telescope, she soon managed to pick out a substantial and, she hoped, durable breeze which might bear them swiftly toward the battle. This, too, she noted down.

Once, she thought, this little note-book had been intended to record her dance partners at some ball at Marlowe Hall. How her life had changed since those days!

But there was one last bit of information she required, which only contact with the Horn itself could provide. So she waited, continuing to observe the ever-changing breezes and watching with considerable trepidation the progress of the battle. *Diana* must join soon or the battle would surely be lost. Even as she watched, another *khebek* was dismasted by English cannon, spiraling away in an uncontrolled tumble. A moment later, the faint victorious cheers of the English airmen reached her ears, and she cursed beneath her breath. She looked to Captain Singh for some reassurance, but his attentions were entirely devoted to the running of the ship.

And then the deck surged beneath her, bending her knees and bringing a faint metallic ping from the mechanisms of her artificial foot. *Diana* had entered the winds of the Horn.

Swiftly Arabella noted the direction and force of the initial thrust, then unbuckled herself and hurried below. Mars's attraction was now so faint that she barely touched the deck, skipping lightly across the *khoresh*-wood planks and sliding down the ladder without touching its treads. Soon she entered the great cabin, where Aadim waited, ticking rhythmically. "We need you as we have never needed you before," she said, gazing into his sightless green glass eyes, then set to work.

The chart of Mars's northern sunward Horn was already spread out on Aadim's desk, though of course no chart of any

Horn could be any thing more than a general suggestion. Quickly she bent and added to this her observations from the deck, placing special emphasis upon the last—the most recent and most directly relevant—before positioning Aadim's finger upon the destination: *Marlborough*'s projected position. Finally she swung the large, crude wooden lever which released the catches on the lead weight at the center of the box now bolted to the side of his desk. The weight floated free, the wires which held it in place creaking gently as the Horn's winds pushed the ship this way and that.

She paused a moment, carefully inspecting the settings of all Aadim's levers and dials. Many of these were worn from years of use. Several others, the most critical to-day, were fresh and new, and generally carved from *khoresh*-wood rather than machined from English brass and steel. None of these had ever before been tested in battle.

"Make us proud," she said, and depressed Aadim's finger on the chart.

The whirr and chatter of Aadim's gears sounded different now, louder and more insistent, the new mechanisms being mounted externally to his wooden desk. The wires and levers which detected the motions of the lead block had their own distinctive sounds, as well, which echoed the creaks and moans of *Diana*'s timbers as the tempests of the Horn began to take hold in earnest.

A moment later came a click, and the bell announcing a result. But unlike Aadim's previous configuration, after this the gears continued to turn . . . navigation within the Horn was a continuing process. Arabella bent and studied the dials on the side of Aadim's desk. "Two points a-starboard," she called up through the open scuttle to the quarterdeck above. Aboard the *khebek*, the automaton pilot was mounted on the quarterdeck and controlled the sails directly, but Aadim's mechanisms were so deeply embedded in *Diana*'s structure that he could not be moved from the great cabin.

"Two points a-starboard," came the acknowledgement from Edmonds. The ship veered gently to the left—the motion was nearly lost in the greater tumult of the Horn's winds—but before Arabella could wonder whether it was enough the bell sounded again.

Occupied though she was with navigation, Arabella could not fail to notice that the sounds of cannon were growing from a distant *bang* to a close roar, and the sky behind the ship, visible through the cabin's broad stern window, was changing from the eternal clear blue of the dry air near Mars to a mottled gray streaked with smoke and spotted with drifting hunks of wreckage . . . and occasional Martian corpses. And the winds of the Horn, growing ever stronger as the ship drew deeper into that realm of eternal storm, now shoved *Diana* brutally and with cruel caprice in every direction and at every angle. Aadim's course changes kept pace with the growing winds, though, becoming more frequent and of greater degree, and from what she could hear through the scuttle above her head the ship was driving through the Horn's gales with unprecedented, indeed nearly supernatural, speed and directness.

Arabella was kept busy adjusting Aadim's settings as *Diana* moved into new and unpredictable currents. The force of Mars's gravity diminished as well, forcing Arabella to cling to Aadim's desk and once, embarrassingly, his nose, lest she be thrown against a wall by an unexpected gust. Aadim, for his part, accommodated these indignities with his usual silent aplomb.

But then another blow—much louder, sharper, and more sudden than any previous—drove the ship upward, striking hard at Arabella's floating feet and making her teeth meet with a painful click. The shouting and screams of pain that followed left little doubt that the impact had been that of a cannon-ball. But where had it struck? How much damage had it done? How many good men had been injured or killed? And then came another such impact, just as forceful.

Arabella was petrified. *Diana* was under attack! Part of her ached to take her place on the gun-deck, running powder to the guns and helping to aim, load, and fire them. Part of her longed to run to her captain and make certain he was safe. A shameful part of her wanted nothing but to find the deepest, most protected corner of the hold and cower there in fear. But she knew her place was here, and as Aadim's gears ground and whined in response to each new impact she did her part and relayed the necessary course changes to the quarterdeck.

In some ways Arabella found herself in the very center of the action—her speed and precision in setting and reading Aadim's dials could make the difference between victory and death for every one aboard. But she was also nearly completely detached from the battle raging all around. She floated in a wooden box, rattled like a dice-cup by the winds of the Horn and the blows of English cannon; all she could see through the stern window was the fog of war and the wreckage left behind the ship in her passage, and all she could hear was a bedlam of explosions, shouts, hammering, and the occasional thump of bare feet striking the deck above her head.

But though her perception of the world beyond the great cabin was limited, Arabella became increasingly aware that the battle was not going well. Again and again, louder and closer than the noise of the battle itself, she heard screams, shouts of dismay, and the crash of shattering timbers. She did her best to ignore these disturbing sounds and concentrate her attention upon Aadim's controls and Edmonds's voice through the scuttle.

Then, without warning, the bulkhead beside the stern window erupted with a splintering crash.

Arabella's right side was jolted by a hundred sharp impacts. Shrieking from surprise as well as the pain, she curled into a ball in midair, instinctively protecting her face from the pelting hail of debris. But the storm passed quickly, and when she uncurled, ears ringing, she was amazed to find herself alive and not seriously injured.

The cabin was not nearly so fortunate. A tremendous ragged hole had appeared in the upper aft larboard corner of the cabin, with wind and noise coming through it from the battle without. The cannon-ball had apparently merely clipped the corner, but the wall and window were both smashed to bits; the cabin's air was filled with deadly fragments of wood and glass, clattering and colliding in a dangerous dance. Heedless of propriety, she pulled up her blood-spotted skirt to breathe through it—to inhale those glittering particles would surely bring a slow, painful, hacking death—and pushed off the wall behind her with the other hand. Aadim!

The automaton seemed undamaged, but his green glass eyes stared forward in fixed surprise, not animated by the constant slight motions of his ever-turning clockworks. Panicked, Arabella reversed herself in the air, batting splinters away from her face, and inspected his dials . . . where she found, indeed, that nothing moved. Jammed.

Any of a thousand things, she knew, could be the cause. But to open his access panels to assess and repair the problem now, with the cabin filled with flying debris, would surely only make matters worse. And every moment she remained here risked injury to her person.

"I must leave you!" she shouted to him, though her words were muffled by the continued ringing in her ears as well as by the fabric held across her mouth. "I shall return as soon as I may!" And then she pushed off Aadim's desk with her flesh and blood foot, propelling herself through the clattering air to the cabin door. A moment later she was through it, closing and dogging it behind her, coughing from exertion and from the smoke and tiny particles she not been able to avoid inhaling.

Faunt was there, and Ulungugga. "Are ye injured?" Faunt yelled in her face.

"Not badly," Arabella gasped, wiping debris from her face. Glittering bits of glass sparkled with dangerous beauty in the air around her, and she noted with a curious calm that blood was seeping from a gash on her hand. "But Aadim is hopelessly jammed."

Faunt's expression immediately darkened. "Tell the cap'n," he said to Ulungugga. "I'll get her to the surgeon."

"Aye aye," Ulungugga croaked, and sprang away.

---

The infirmary was a riot of noise and stink, with men whimpering or screaming all around and the smell of blood and powder thick in the air. "You have been extremely fortunate," Dr. Barry said, cleaning her eyes with a soft cloth soaked in alcohol. It was cold, and stung terribly.

"Agh!" Arabella said, batting the cloth away and blinking the painful stuff from her eyes. "Must you? I am right enough. These other men require your attention far more than I."

He looked dubiously at her, the cloth still poised for further action, but then shrugged and lowered it. "Very well. But if you feel any thing in your eye, you must *not* rub at it. If this should occur, come back to me at once."

"Aye aye, sir," she replied. Naturally her eye immediately began to itch, but though her hand began to rise, she held it back with a strong effort of will. "Am I discharged?"

He still seemed unconvinced, but after a further moment's

consideration he shook his head and gestured her brusquely away. "Go," he said, and turned back to a man who was white, trembling, and clutching his blood-soaked leg with both hands. Behind his back, Lady Corey cleaned blood from a saw; meeting Arabella's eyes, she shook her head fractionally.

Arabella swallowed hard and departed.

---

Arabella came out on deck to find a situation yet more chaotic and charnel than the infirmary. The tumultuous air was choked with smoke, and she could see barely a hundred yards in any direction; within that short distance, the only things visible were bits of floating wreckage, some of them flickering with fire. A man's body, missing one arm, drifted just off the bow-sprit; a long thread of blood trailed from the ragged shoulder. But beyond the range of view, the battle continued, betrayed by sounds of violent action and flashes of orange flame.

Moving cautiously across a deck heaving from the Horn's storms and cluttered with broken spars and tangled cables, she worked her way to the quarterdeck, where, coughing, she called up for permission to ascend.

No voice replied . . . at least, none that she could hear over the screams and explosions. Nevertheless, she ascended, heart in her mouth.

But her very worst fears, at least, had not come to pass, for there stood Captain Singh, still alive and active and in possession of all his limbs—though his jacket was badly torn and stained with blood. He stood tall in his leather straps, booted feet firmly planted upon the deck, as he called commands in every direction. Of Edmonds there was no sign; the wheel was manned by little Watson.

"Captain Singh!" Arabella called into a momentary lull, and the expression of relief on his face at the sight of her briefly lightened her heavy heart. But his mien immediately returned to weary determination.

"I thank Heaven you are well," he shouted back at her—the distance between them was no more than a few yards, but between the tumult of the battle all about and the ringing in her ears she could barely make out his words. "What of Aadim?"

"Jammed!" she called back, making her way to him. "Not beyond repair, I think, but we must clear the cabin first."

He nodded grimly. "I feared as much. I have pulled back from the battle for now, but we must return soon . . . the *khebek* are being slaughtered." He gave her a stern assessing glance. "Can you navigate the Horn without Aadim's assistance? You have made a great study of the winds—at this point I dare say you may understand them better than I."

She swallowed. "I will do my best."

"We can ask nothing more." And without another word he turned to Watson and said, "Take us back to *Marlborough*'s last known position."

"Aye aye, sir," Watson replied, his young voice cracking, and called out, "Set jibs and spankers! Pulsers ahead! Cheerly, now!"

Surely it was only Arabella's own weariness that made the grunts of the men at the pedals seem so tired and dispirited. But she could not deny that the ship moved sluggishly, what with her sails torn, yards all askew, and rigging clogged with wreckage.

And it was in this condition that they were moving to intercept a fully-armed man-of-war?

"One point aloft," Arabella said to Watson, noting a curdling whorl forming in the filthy air ahead.

"Aye aye, ma'am," he replied, and nudged the wheel up a bit.

The dark, curdled air of the battle, Arabella found, actually made immediate navigation easier, as the winds of the Horn could plainly be seen in the drifting smoke and wreckage. But navigation in the broader sense was nearly impossible, and she and the captain were forced to rely upon their intuition and interpretation of vague clues. Was that distant boom an English broadside? Should they divert toward it, or remain upon their current course? And with the winds as capricious as they were, could the direction of the sound even be relied upon? The solar compass, never the most reliable instrument, was useless this close to Mars, so they could not even be certain which direction was north. At least sunward and skyward were plain, as there was no question in which direction the murk was brightest.

And then a stray current blew a momentary hole in the fog, and Arabella realized the situation was even more desperate than she had thought.

There lay *Marlborough*, her copper pocked with the wounds of many tiny *khebek* cannon-balls but otherwise quite hale and whole. And beyond her lay the rest of the fleet, nine ships all told, running close-hauled and in tight formation. They stood with their sterns together, their great guns facing out, and though the storms of the Horn battered their formation the English Navy had the skill and discipline to hold it. Against this deadly ball of *khoresh*-wood and iron the swarming *khebek* were nothing but an annoyance; though they persisted valiantly, and dodged most of the broadsides aimed at them, it was a game they could never win. They were simply too badly outnumbered.

"Move to engage *Marlborough*," Captain Singh barked to Watson. "Ready the guns!"

"Aye aye, sir!" he replied. "Pulsers ahead! Smartly now!"

The fog of war closed in around them again, but Arabella now had a firm grasp on the English fleet's location, and the frequent hammer blows of their broadsides provided all the information she needed to navigate directly toward them. But *Diana,* too, had been seen, and the sound of those fusillades changed noticeably . . . the howl of cannon-balls after each *bang* no longer diminished to one side or the other, but rose steadily in loudness, dropping suddenly in pitch as the balls passed by. The range was as yet too great, and the visibility too poor, for those balls to strike except by chance, but that chance could not be dismissed and was growing greater by the minute. "Evasive maneuvers!" Captain Singh commanded Watson, and Arabella did her best to assist, trying to keep the ship on general course toward the English even as she jigged and dodged and the Horn's mercurial winds seemed determined to send her tumbling away completely.

Then came a boom of English cannon that was starkly different from those before. It was accompanied by an orange flash in the smoke directly ahead; the sound was distinctly multiple, a *b-b-b-bang* of eight guns or more; and the shriek of cannon-balls rose steadily and did not budge from its position in the sky ahead. "Get down!" came the cry from the lookout at the bow-sprit head, and Arabella hauled desperately on her straps with both hands, laying her body flat on the deck as quickly as she could. A moment later came a shivering, tearing crash from above, as a full flight of hot metal tore through the main-topsail, reducing half its yard to splinters.

"They have our bearing now," Captain Singh said. He was, Arabella noted, still standing tall in his straps. "But we have theirs! Fire!"

"Fire!" repeated Watson immediately. A moment later *Diana's* great guns spoke, a fearsome blow upon Arabella's ears and body—her leather belt wrenched her waist as the deck jerked beneath her, sending the breath from her lungs with a painful gasp.

So fierce was the sound of the battle, so dense the murk ahead, that the effect of the shot—if any—was imperceptible. Nonetheless, Captain Singh followed that broadside with a second, and then a third, while continuing to drive forward. So battered was Arabella by the tumult and agitation of the many forces converged upon *Diana* that she was barely able to assist at all, but she did what she could, keeping a sharp eye on the swirling smoke ahead and advising Watson to nudge the wheel one way or the other.

And then one of those swirls was suddenly parted by the bowsprit, jib, and sprit-sail of an English man-of-war, thrusting directly toward them out of the fog at extremely close range.

Arabella could not help but scream.

"Fire!" cried Captain Singh, and, "Back pulsers!"

Immediately *Diana's* cannon boomed, and Arabella would have sworn she felt the deck twist beneath her as the men below strove to reverse the spinning pulsers' motion. The sails, yards, and masts ahead—still all that could be seen of the English vessel—flew into flinders, a sudden storm of deadly fragments that threatened the Dianas as much as the English airmen.

And then the two ships collided with a sickening, lurching *crunch*.

Arabella was hurled forward into her straps, again driving the breath from her lungs in a painful gasp. Men flew across the deck, well-secured casks wrenched from their places, and yards tore from their masts at the sudden impact. All about her bedlam ruled, the already-tumultuous noise of the battle now joined by continued tearing and wrenching sounds as the two ships ground into each other, screams of injured or enraged airmen, and frantic shouts from officers and men on both ships as they attempted to manage this new, surprising situation.

"Back pulsers, double time!" reiterated Captain Singh. "Get us free of that ship! And prepare to repel boarders!"

Venusian waisters, grim airmen of the afterguard, and even some courageous Martian technicians took up axes and moved forward, where Chips and his men were already hacking at the tangled morass of splintered wood, raveled rope, and torn silk where the two ships could barely be distinguished one from the other.

And then there came another crash and another lurch—a series of crashes and lurches, indeed—and yet more shouts, curses, and cries of pain from the murk ahead. But before Arabella could make sense of this new and inexplicable development, a cry of *"Marlborough! Marlborough!"* came from beyond the wreckage, followed by a chilling war-cry from a hundred throats as the English airmen swarmed aboard—clambering over the tangled timbers with cutlasses in their teeth, flinging grappling-irons and hauling themselves hand-over-hand along the cables, or simply leaping fearlessly from one ship to the other through the murk. Rifles cracked and flashed in the rigging of both ships.

Two Dianas came out on deck then, bearing armloads of cutlasses and pistols from the arms locker below; waisters and topmen immediately converged upon them, taking up arms and charging forward with war-cries of their own.

"Victory or death!" cried one of the Marlboroughs, clinging to a yard aloft and waving his cutlass left-handed. *Victory or death indeed*, Arabella thought, and without further consideration she unbuckled herself and leapt down to join them.

"Ma'am?" cried the man with the cutlasses as she took one from his nerveless fingers. She did not bother to reply; instead she took the sword and slashed away her encumbering skirts, then jumped forward into the melee.

*Victory or death*, she thought. She could cower on the quarter-deck or join her shipmates in battle, but either way she would not likely survive—her entire *planet* would not likely survive—if *Diana* were lost. She had no choice but to give her utmost.

Others were as surprised by her sudden appearance and her attire as the man with the cutlasses had been. One English airman, all eyes and teeth in a face smeared with blood and soot, gaped stupidly when she came into view, giving an opportunity for the Venusian with whom he was grappling to slit his belly open. Another, clinging to a top-shroud above the deck and taking careful aim at the quarterdeck with his pistol, actually shrieked when she leapt up to his level, catching herself upon a ratline directly in front of him. So disconcerted was he by her unexpected advent that he did not even seek to defend himself as she smacked the pistol from his hand with the flat of her cutlass, then struck him hard on the head with the sword's heel on the return stroke. He lost his grip and floated away then, stunned or unconscious . . . she neither knew nor cared which. She reversed herself in the air and, pushing off on the main-yard, propelled herself back down to the deck where the fighting was thickest.

She was not as strong or as tireless or as skilled with the sword as most of the Dianas or any of the Marlboroughs, she knew. But she was quick and agile and had a sharp eye, and few of the English considered her a threat until it was too late. She hung back, mostly, looking for a chance to strike a man from behind or cut a line upon which he depended, giving aid to those Dianas most pressed and, where no other opportunity presented, hacking away at the tangled cordage and grappling-lines that held the two ships together. She was, she thought wildly in one such moment of desperate chopping, like unto a frigate in this battle—a light ship, nimble and maneuverable, offering assistance and communication and not likely to be attacked unless she attacked first.

But she lacked a frigate's true immunity, and when a fiercely grimacing English airman, stripped to the waist and bulging with muscles, saw her tugging at a grappling-iron, he did not hesitate to swing at her with his boarding-axe. It was only through sheer luck that she was not instantly killed: the grapnel on which she was pulling came free of the deck, sending her tumbling backward, a moment before the axe swished through the space where her head had been. Realizing her peril almost too late, she could do little but raise the grapnel in both hands to block the axe's second strike. The blow of the long axe on the grapnel's shaft sent a jar down her arms, forcing her down to the deck and nearly driving the grappling-iron from her stunned hands.

Again the Englishman raised his weapon, hooking a foot in a scupper for leverage as he brought the axe down for a killing blow. From her position on the deck she could do nothing to resist it . . . but she shoved hard on the heavy grapnel with her still-vibrating arms, pushing it toward her assailant and sending herself sailing away. The axe bit heavily into the deck where she had just been, even as the grapnel struck the English airman's feet, knocking him into the air. He recovered quickly, hauling himself down the axe handle, but its blade was embedded in the deck, giving Arabella a moment to fetch up against the mainmast base and recover her wits. Leaping straight up, paralleling the mast in her course, she lost herself from his view in the litter of shredded sails, cordage, and broken yards above the deck.

She hung, gasping, in that drifting wreckage for a moment, clinging with both hands to a backstay. Her whole body thrummed with frenzied agitation, but beneath that surface she could feel a weariness that ran to the bone . . . she knew she lacked the stamina to sustain this level of activity for much longer, and if she tried to do so she would surely make a fatal mistake. Still seeking to avoid the airman below, though she knew not whether he pursued her, she pushed herself upward toward the main-top. Soon she reached an area where the detritus was sparser, and took the opportunity to look around.

The air had cleared considerably during the hand-to-hand battle—indeed, she realized, she had not heard the sound of cannon in some time—and from this vantage Arabella could see the cause of the series of crashes and lurches that had followed the collision. *Diana's* momentum had driven *Marlborough* backward into the sterns of the other English vessels, and now their pulsers were all entangled together, preventing any of them from moving. The surrounding *khebek* had taken the opportunity to redouble their attack upon the English forces, bedeviling them with their little cannon, but though they had managed to do some damage most of the English fleet were still in fighting trim. Once they managed to free their pulsers from each other the battle would surely turn in their favor.

Looking down upon *Diana*'s deck, Arabella could see that Chips's men and a gang of Venusian waisters had made some progress in freeing her from *Marlborough*. The battle on the deck had moved aft—toward the quarterdeck, where Captain Singh and the other officers were defending their position with pistols—but no new Marlboroughs were swarming across; the men still aboard that ship were now fully engaged in disentangling her pulsers. And *Diana*'s pulsers, alone of all the entangled ships, still turned, pulling her away and drawing taut the lines that still connected her to the English ship.

In fact, just one line—a heavy grappling-line on *Diana*'s starboard bow—seemed to be the crux of the matter. It lay below the view of Chips's gang, vibrating with tension; if that one line could be cut, the loose web of tangled sail and cable on the larboard side might tear free. But Arabella had left her cutlass behind on the deck.

Desperately she looked around, hoping to find a cutlass, or a boarding-axe, or even a simple knife amongst the detritus of the battle. And there one was! A fine long gully-knife floated between her and the deck, perhaps thirty feet away, turning slowly in the filthy air. But it was drifting away . . . if she leapt directly toward it, her momentum would inevitably carry her into the empty space between ships. With nothing at all to catch herself upon, she would drift helplessly until some one was able to rescue her . . . or an English sniper ended her life.

Nothing at all? Or might there be something?

The winds of the Horn still blew, strong and capricious as ever, jostling the entangled ships against each other like garments in a wash-tub. There was, indeed, a strong current below the drifting knife, plainly visible from the bits of floating debris embedded within it. If she could but catch that stream after snagging the knife, it would blow her back toward *Diana*. But the flow changed even as she watched . . . there was no telling how long it would persist.

Without allowing herself to hesitate, she braced her legs against the main-topgallant-yard and sprang toward the floating knife.

Time seemed to distend. The knife rotated before her, drifting slowly as she neared, hands outstretched to snag it from the air. But she had misjudged her leap, or perhaps the currents had changed, and she was not moving directly toward it . . . in fact, she would pass well beyond arm's reach of it.

Heedless of propriety, she pulled up the remains of her dress, stretching its ragged lower edge between her hands as she extended her arms above her head. The action of this feeble improvised sail upon the air through which the force of her leap carried her was slight, but it was sufficient to send her into a slight tumble . . . and provided just enough of a diversion of her course that she could barely reach the knife, plucking it from the air as she passed!

But that brief moment of triumph would gain her nothing if she could not catch the current below . . . and now she was tumbling, disoriented, and diverted from her original course. Again she pulled up her dress, feeling the unaccustomed breeze upon her back and breasts as she waved it above her head, fighting to maneuver herself into a more stable attitude. But in the disordered winds of the Horn she managed only to add a longitudinal spin to her head-over-heels tumble.

She was still tumbling, completely beyond control, when she

drifted into a strong current, which seized her and redirected her onto a new tack. But which way was she going now? Helplessly she floated, with Mars and sky and ships and bodies and drifting clouds of smoke and flotsam turning all about her in a dizzying whirl, wondering whether this was the end . . . whether an English bullet or a stray cannon-ball or a long lingering death of thirst was to be her fate.

And then, with a *crack* that sent bright flashes of light across her vision, the back of her head slammed into something hard.

The impact sent her into still more complex gyrations, and she flailed her arms and legs wildly, completely disoriented, trying to keep hold of the knife. And it was that knife, indeed, which saved her, as its tip struck and stuck into something made of *khoresh*-wood . . . she could tell by the distinctive sound and feeling. Using that as a point of leverage, she managed to moderate her dizzying spin, and though that action pulled the knife from the wooden object, whatever it was, she was still close enough to it to reach out with her hand and pull herself to it.

She found herself face to face with the goddess Diana.

The ship *Diana*'s figurehead, to be precise, three times life size and shining with gold leaf, holding out her bow and arrows before herself with one extended arm. She was all askew, pointing hard a-starboard from a nest of smashed and tangled timbers. And Arabella's knife and hand had found her exposed breast.

"Forgive me!" Arabella gasped, but she did not release that gilded wooden curve until she had completely stilled her tumble and her hammering heart had returned to something resembling its previous, merely rapid, beat.

Arabella looked around. Chips and his men were working away on the far side of the figurehead, and the *Marlborough*'s crew were doing the same to their ship not ten feet the other side of her, but at the moment no one was looking in her direction . . .

though one of *Marlborough*'s cannon, lying askew in the wreckage, was aimed directly at her, its black mouth still shimmering with heat.

The grappling-line she had seen from above still held firm, taut as a harpsichord string, with no one paying it the least attention. With a firm yet polite push against Diana's breast, Arabella propelled herself toward the line, catching it easily with her left hand. Then, making sure to cut between herself and *Marlborough*, she began sawing at the line with her knife.

The line was under so much tension that it seemed hard as iron at first. Yet, by the same token, once its fibers began to give way they parted eagerly, the line seeming to tear itself apart beneath her blade as the two ships strove to pull the cord in two. The cable's twist had an effect as well, causing the line to spiral as it parted; Arabella hooked her good leg around the line to prevent its rotation from flinging her away, and kept cutting. Then, when she was only halfway through, the cable's core suddenly snapped, flinging Arabella backward like the crack of a whip.

Arabella whooped and flailed anew, losing the knife. But she was not so disoriented as before, and soon caught herself on one of the drifting sails which had formerly been attached to *Diana*'s shattered bow-sprit. Dragging herself hand-over-hand across the billowing silk toward *Diana*'s forecastle, she felt through the fabric the tearing tug of the ship, now freed from the imprisoning grappling-line, pulling herself away from *Marlborough*. Shouts and the sounds of rending wood and fabric also came from the far side of the figurehead, as the disorganized tangle of wreckage there also gave way.

"*Marlborough!*" came a cry from the shattered gun-deck of the other ship as it drew rapidly away. It was a Naval officer, the sleeve of his blue coat soaked black with blood but his voice still stentorian. "Marlboroughs! Marlboroughs! To me! To me!"

Ignoring the officer, Arabella reached *Diana*—it was the

stinking outer bulkhead of the head, but no matter—and clung there panting for a moment before scrambling across the planks to the forecastle rail. There she beheld several dozen English air-men leaping and darting through the blood-stained wreckage . . . directly toward her! Their eyes, though, were fixed upon *Marl-borough*, the English ship swiftly falling away behind her as *Diana*'s unflagging pulsers drew her ever more rapidly back-ward. They were in full retreat.

Arabella shrieked and ducked behind the gunwale; a moment later a half-dozen English bodies hurtled through the air above her head. The *crack* of rifle fire sounded from both sides, snipers in both ships' tops striving to aid or prevent the boarders' retreat, and the shrieking war-cries of *"Diana! Diana!"* came nearer, the victorious Dianas seeking to do as much damage as possible to the English airmen as they departed.

Arabella clung trembling to the gunwale as the sounds of fighting drew nearer. A body struck the rail next to her and spun away, flinging drops of blood in an aerial spiral of gore; grunts and thuds and cries of pain marked the ends of other contests. But the larger battle was clearly drawing to a close, as the demoral-ized Marlboroughs abandoned all other goals in favor of escape.

Finally there came a victorious cry of "Heave . . . *ho!*" and a shrieking English airman went sailing over the rail, propelled in the general direction of *Marlborough*. His anguished cries as he spun helplessly in the air—his velocity was clearly such that he would never reach his ship without assistance—were met only by mocking laughter from the Dianas on deck. Arabella was simul-taneously heartened by this clear sign of victory and dismayed by her shipmates' callousness, but under the circumstances she could not bring herself to condemn them.

Arabella pulled herself over the gunwale and onto the fore-castle, assisted by two wild-eyed, grinning waisters. The sight that met her eyes there was barely recognizable as the deck of a proud

Marsman; it was now a shambles of smashed timbers, broken cables, and drifting sailcloth, splashed with blood, and grimly strewn with bodies, some writhing in pain and others unmoving. One of the latter, not far from Arabella's position, was that of Torkei, one of the Martian technicians from the Institute. Though inexperienced, she had been a tireless worker and had shown promise of developing into a full-fledged engineer.

"Damage report!" came a cry from abaft. Arabella looked to the source of the sound—it was Watson's voice, loud enough but cracking adolescently—and was immensely relieved to see her Captain Singh still standing proud and hale behind him.

Her first instinct was to leap to her husband, but Watson's cry made her look around first, to see if there were any thing she might notice that others had missed—much like the cable she had cut. But she saw only wreckage, all of it plain enough to the least experienced eye. The bow-sprit, figurehead, and gun-deck were smashed to flinders; many yards and sails floated free, jarred or torn from their moorings in the collision and the fighting that followed; and the waist was a sea of tangled cordage and drifting belaying pins. It would take days to put right.

Days they did not have, nor even hours. For another cry, this one from much closer, caught her attention: "Sail ho!" cried a man clinging to the larboard mast. "Sail ho! Eight sail of ship!"

Eight sail indeed. For though *Marlborough* was clearly in even worse shape than *Diana,* the other eight members of the English fleet were not nearly so badly hurt. In fact, when *Diana* had pulled free of *Marlborough,* she had actually assisted them, by dragging the disabled English ship away from their entangled pulsers. All eight pulsers now spun freely, driving the English fleet in furious pursuit of the Marsman who had so grievously damaged their sister.

And *Diana,* with so many masts and sails deranged, was in no position to fight back or even to escape. Indeed, though her pulsers still turned valiantly, her bow-sprit was a ruin, its attached jibs and stay-sails now fluttering free. Absent the air resistance of those fore-and-aft sails, the ship was beginning to rotate on her axis in the opposite direction from the turning pulsers, reducing their effectiveness and making navigation difficult. And, of course, the gun-deck was completely out of commission, and even the bow-chasers were unusable.

"Rig up a jury-jib!" came a cry from close at hand. It was Faunt—dear Faunt, the captain of the waist, Arabella's first friend aboard. His ever-present knit cap was soaked with blood, and one eye was red-purple and swollen shut, but he was still lively and urging the waisters into action.

Duty and habit leapt to the fore in Arabella's breast and she immediately joined in, helping the waisters stretch a cable from the mainmast head to the ruins of the prow and fix the largest scrap of jib-sail to it. Busy needles immediately set to, mending the great rents in the sail, while Arabella and others tied the many gaskets necessary to fasten the sail to its cable. It was a crude solution, of little use in steering, but it would help to control the ship's unwanted rotation.

But before the work on the jury-jib was complete, a thunderous rolling *bang* sounded from ahead—far too close—and several voices called out, "Get down!" Arabella and the other waisters flung themselves to the deck as a flight of hot iron shrieked overhead, ending in a hideous shattering crash somewhere abaft. Terrified, Arabella put her head up and looked to the quarter-deck, but Captain Singh and the other officers were safe . . . the English broadside had flown through *Diana*'s rigging and obliterated a wrecked *khebek* floating beyond her stern. Other *khebek* were moving in to help defend *Diana*, but they seemed so few and frail by comparison with the English fleet.

Arabella turned her gaze ahead. The English fleet was in heated pursuit now, pulsers whirling, jibs and stays in taut fine fettle. And as they neared they turned, their cannon coming to bear upon the limping, fleeing *Diana*. The one in the lead, which had just fired upon them, was plainly preparing a second broadside . . . they were so close that Arabella could see and hear the busy gun crews as they readied their deadly charges. And behind that ship lay seven more, all with the same end in mind . . . the destruction of *Diana*, and with her the entire Martian cause.

Arabella could see no possible escape. But Captain Singh continued calling commands, and every man aboard was doing his best to put their damaged ship to rights. Lame, weak, and injured *Diana* might be, but she would fight to the last. "Ready stern-chasers!" cried Captain Singh, and those two small cannon on the quarterdeck—the ship's only remaining defense—turned to face the onrushing English.

But the next sound Arabella heard—a sharp octuple *ba-ba-ba-bang*—came neither from *Diana*'s chasers nor the English, but from far a-larboard. When she sought and found the source of that sound, a cheer was pulled from her throat, with matching cheers echoing all around. For the new arrival, just now emerging from the drifting cloud of the previous battle, was a proud four-master well known to them all . . . *Touchstone*! Dear, dear *Touchstone*!

Two ships—well, to be frank, one and a half—against eight was still very poor odds for the Martians. But those odds were still more than twice as good as they had been, and Arabella huzzahed along with the other waisters as *Touchstone*'s broadside smashed into the lead English ship's bow, utterly obliterating her figurehead and gun-ports. A second broadside soon followed— Captain Fox was fierce in the exercise of his gun crews, and prided himself upon their rapidity of fire—and this targeted the pulsers of the second, and largest, ship of the English fleet. It was not a clean kill—the cannon-balls did not destroy the pulsers' hub—but they did smash several of the propulsive sails, impairing the target considerably. And *Touchstone*'s swivel-guns were not idle, banging away irregularly and harrying the other English vessels. Tiny flashes in her rigging showed her rifle-men were active as well, though the range was as yet too great for them to have much effect.

The English seemed confounded by this unexpected arrival, with every one of the undamaged ships losing precious time by turning to face her. The disabled *Marlborough*, Arabella realized, must have been the flag of the fleet, and with her out of action the order of command had become muddled. *Touchstone* took advantage of the delay by firing upon yet another ship—a solid strike amidships—while *Diana* continued to limp away and the *khebek* moved in, sniping with their little cannon like birds pecking at the English ships' eyes.

But the English confusion did not last long, and with a volley of signal-guns and a flash of colored flags they soon divided themselves, with most turning to face *Touchstone* while three resumed pursuit of *Diana*. Soon they began firing in earnest, with lances of flame flashing across the sky and gouts of smoke fouling the Horn's turbulent air. "About ship!" came the command from *Diana*'s quarterdeck, and "Forward pulsers!" Somehow the badly damaged Marsman's valiant crew managed the feat, bringing her broken head into line with the most prominent current and slightly increasing her speed toward Phobos.

Arabella, for her part, made her way back to the quarterdeck, taking up a dropped cutlass as she went. Her husband gave her only a nod of acknowledgement when she arrived—there was no time for any more—but she immediately strapped herself in place, scanning the roiling, filthy sky ahead for currents which might aid or hinder them in their flight. These she reported to Watson, who nudged the wheel as required with little more than a grunt of acknowledgement—his cheery "aye aye" had been left somewhere in the wreckage abaft.

Phobos, their destination, now lay not far above and ahead, speeding along in its orbit with a churning invisible sea of even greater turbulence—a Horn of its own within Mars's greater Horn—in the air ahead and behind. This little Horn, Arabella thought, was at once their greatest danger and greatest opportunity. Danger because, despite Arabella's study of these winds in recent months, they were still beyond her full understanding—beyond the comprehension of mathematics at all, she feared—and one of those unpredictable gusts could easily smash *Diana* against the moon's surface or fling her away in an uncontrollable tumble. The automaton pilots carried by *Touchstone* and some of the *khebek* would be of great help to them in this, but with Aadim out of action *Diana* would be forced to rely upon Arabella's brain . . . and, of course, Captain Singh's considerable experience in general navigation. But there was opportunity here as well, for the English were even less prepared than any of the Martians to face the winds of Phobos.

But first they must reach that moon's little Horn, and the chances of that seemed slimmer by the minute. For though *Diana* had long been the swiftest of the Honorable Mars Company's ships, she was now a ruined remnant of her former self and the three nearly-undamaged English ships pursuing her were gaining rapidly. Again and again guns boomed abaft and cannon-balls howled toward them, far too many of those broadsides ending in a juddering crash as the shots found *Diana*'s hull or spars. As the range closed, it was only the capricious winds of the Horn, spoiling the English aim, that prevented every single broadside from having full and deadly effect. *Diana* fired back with her chasers to the extent possible, and the *khebek* did what they could to assist, but even without her sextant Arabella could tell that, if current trends persisted, the English would catch them up and board them well before they entered Phobos's trailing Horn.

"Can you possibly make any more speed?" she asked her captain.

"The men at the pedals are half-dead from exhaustion," he replied, not surprising her at all. "We must save as much as we can for the final approach." But he did what he could, sending the topmen into a frenzy of activity as he attempted to catch any transient breeze that might help and avoid any cross-current that might hinder their progress.

Again and again the cannon boomed, fouling the air and blurring Arabella's vision—at least, she hoped the tears that stung in her eyes were caused by smoke and not sheer despair—but Phobos still lay visible ahead . . . nearing, ever nearing, but not perhaps quite near enough.

Then came a savage war-cry from the curdled air abaft, and a grappling-iron came flying out of the murk and caught upon the taffrail. "Prepare to repel boarders!" cried Captain Singh, coughing and waving smoke and floating ash from his face.

One of the afterguard cut the grappling-line with a boarding-axe. But a second and a third followed quickly, then yet more, far too many to prevent, and their lines drew taut, a sound of rhythmic grunting coming from the ship now becoming sketchily visible behind them as her crew pulled the two ships together. The quarterdeck became crowded with Dianas—all propriety abandoned in this desperate hour—breathing heavily and clutching cutlasses and pistols as they awaited the English boarding-party.

Captain Singh put a hand on Arabella's shoulder. "Do you have a knife," he murmured, "if that should prove necessary?" Any one who had not known him as well as she did might have mistaken the desperate steel in his voice for perfect calm.

"I have a cutlass," she replied, deliberately mistaking his meaning, and taking it up she turned with the others to face aft. All might be lost, but she would not meet her fate with silence or deference.

And then came a familiar *ba-ba-ba-bang*—*Touchstone*'s eight guns—followed by the howl and crash of an incoming broadside;

the grunting in the fog abaft changed to shouts and shrieks of pain and rage, and the grappling-lines fell suddenly slack.

"Cut those lines!" cried Captain Singh, and Dianas leapt to comply, Arabella among them. "Pulsers ahead, double time! Stern-chasers, fire!"

The pulsers below the taffrail stepped up their pace, whirling past with a rapid *whoosh–whoosh–whoosh* that pressed Arabella's stomach against the rail even as she continued to saw away at a grappling-line with her cutlass. Meanwhile, men leapt to the stern-chasers, aiming and firing as fast as they could. The two small cannon threw very little weight of metal, but their proximity made the noise deafening.

A stray wind shoved *Diana* hard a-larboard then, momentarily clearing the air. There, falling abaft, lay the English ship which had just attempted boarding, her forecastle a ruined mess of wood and silk and blood. And above lay dear *Touchstone*— battered, wounded, with a huge ragged hole in her lower hull where the mizzen-mast had once been rooted, but still fighting, even as the two undamaged English ships turned to attack her. And they were not alone in doing so . . . three more of the English fleet had followed *Touchstone* and were closing fast from the other side. Captain Fox might have saved *Diana*, but in doing so he had put his own ship in grave danger.

"Make course for Phobos!" Captain Singh called.

"But we must do something to help Captain Fox!" Arabella cried to him.

"We cannot," he replied, the expression on his face as grave as ever she had seen. "Weak as we are, if we make the attempt I fear *both* ships will be lost." He shook his head. "We can at best seize the opportunity for escape he has offered us."

"Aye aye," Arabella replied miserably, and resolutely turned her gaze to the breezes ahead. "Ten points a-larboard," she said to Watson.

"Ten points a-larboard," he acknowledged, turning the wheel.

Even as *Diana* limped away, the English men-of-war closed in and englobed *Touchstone*, hammering her with a horrific series of broadsides from every direction simultaneously. The plucky little bantam of a ship fought back as best she could, but it was plainly a losing battle.

Suddenly *Touchstone* broke free of the surrounding English ships, her ragged pulsers whirling as she dove toward the surface of Mars in a desperate bid for freedom! But the English followed, continuing to pound her with broadside after broadside, and a fortunate shot severed the port mast.

With two masts gone, *Touchstone* became almost completely unmanageable, and her downward course rapidly decayed into an uncontrolled fall. The English pursued for a time, but soon broke off the chase, lest they too be caught below the falling-line with deflated envelopes.

When Arabella lost sight of *Touchstone* she was still spinning rapidly downward, smoke and fragments of wreckage spiraling behind her as she fell ever faster.

# 14

## PHOBOS

Darkness fell, again.

Arabella floated in the doorway of the small, crude shack she shared with her husband, looking up at Mars as the Sun was eclipsed behind the planet's limb, vanishing with a rapidity that still astonished her despite the many times she had witnessed it since landing here. How many would that be? Three eclipses a day, approximately, so nearly a hundred . . . in addition to a hundred conventional nightfalls, with the Sun setting below the moon's horizon.

With darkness came a sudden chill, and she drew her shawl more closely around her shoulders. Phobos, she thought, might be their salvation, but it was still a small, cold, miserable place.

Between herself and the horizon—so close as to barely be deserving of the name, looking more like the edge of a deck save that it curved gently away with no rail nor gunwale in sight—lay nothing but barren gray rock, relieved only by hardy mosses and lichens and the rough, scattered structures that clung to the rock like the lichens' larger, artificial cousins.

Many of these hovels, including Arabella's own shack, had been built from the wreckage of ships which had failed to make safe rendezvous with Phobos due to the treacherous winds which surrounded it—a wreckage which littered the moon's surface in sad profusion. *Diana* herself, with Aadim out of commission, her sails and yards devastated, and her crew weary and disheartened, had barely escaped that fate; had not one of the *khebek* thrown her a line, pedaling fiercely to pull her safely into port, she would surely have careened uncontrolled into the rocks.

Once the resistance had landed safely on Phobos, they had been astonished to find the khoreshte satrap Tura there ahead of them . . . and welcoming them with open arms! "Phobos has been a possession of Sor Khoresh since time immemorial," she had explained. "Why do you think we have our *khebek,* and our famous khoreshte pilots, and why do you think we refused to give them up for any treaty? And now that the accursed English fleet has in fact arrived—I must confess I doubted your tale— and attacked khoreshte territory, I am happy to offer you the temporary loan of this small piece of my property for the purpose of harassing them." And so they had taken the moon without out a fight, along with its small population, its ballistas, and its other engines of aerial defense.

The darkness deepened as even the air-glow which followed the Sun vanished, leaving Arabella peering up at the vast black globe of Mars which blocked so many of the stars. At least this darkness made the concepts of "up" and "down" seem less arbitrary; Phobos lacked gravity almost completely, having less than one per cent that of Mars, and when the planet shone brightly in the sky, rolling huge and red overhead like an ominous storm cloud, it was easy to feel as though one were suspended head-down.

But during an eclipse, if one ignored the sensations of free descent one could imagine oneself upon a planet's surface.

As Arabella's eyes adjusted to the dark, glimmers of light came into view on the planet overhead. Most likely these were Martian settlements of one sort or another; the English occupied only seven per cent of the surface, and Arabella had no idea over which portion of the planet they were passing at the moment. But she had confidence that soon Aadim would be able to answer that question with definitive precision. And when he did . . .

In the darkness she felt her lips draw back from her clenched teeth in a fierce grimace. For once Aadim's mechanisms could determine Phobos's orbital position and calculate a reliable ballistic path through the winds between the moon and the planet's surface—and she was working every day upon that very problem—the massive ballistas which so effectively defended the moon from English ships would become weapons of offense as well. Boulders the size of carriages would rain down upon Company House, Government House, armories, ship-yards, ports, and . . .

. . . and Woodthrush Woods?

Perhaps. For though she loved her family plantation, if Michael had betrayed the resistance he must be punished. Punished most severely.

The Ceres fleet had plainly received intelligence regarding the resistance's activities before their arrival at Mars. They had not reported to Fort Augusta first, as Captain Singh had originally ordered; instead they had struck directly at Tekhmet, a facility which was meant to be a most confidential secret. Very few outside the resistance had known even of Tekhmet's existence, to say nothing of its location in the deep anonymous desert; of those who had known, Michael was one of the few having both desire and opportunity to reveal that information to the Navy. "I could end this farcical resistance of yours with a word, you know," he had said to her once, and though she had known that the threat was meant seriously she had felt—had *hoped*, to be honest—that he would never follow through.

Arabella had exchanged no letters with Michael since before the catastrophic rout which had been dignified in retrospect with the name "Battle of Tekhmet." In part this was due to the practicalities of the situation—since the resistance had shifted its headquarters to Phobos, no ships went to or from Fort Augusta except under the most exigent of circumstances. But this, she knew, was only an excuse . . . she knew that she was highly regarded in the resistance, and if she had truly wished communication with her brother, some means would have been found to bring it about. She was forced to confess, if only to herself, that she had not written to him because she did not wish her suspicions— her very strong suspicions—regarding him to be irrevocably confirmed. And he had not written to her because . . . well, to be honest, she did not know. But he had not, or at least had not succeeded in doing so.

Dawn came then, as swiftly as night had fallen, and Arabella hung blinking in the sudden light. The starry sky cleared to blue; the black globe of Mars changed to mottled gray, with an orange-red crescent growing from the planet's eastern limb; and the little birds called *pooteeweet* began to chitter from their nests among the lichens. They were unique to Phobos, so far as Arabella knew, and to them this sudden dawn, coming every seven and a half hours, was entirely normal. She took a breath, let it out, and returned to her toilette, which had been momentarily interrupted by the fall of night. It was nearly time for the Council meeting.

---

The Council met daily now, as after the disastrous Battle of Tekhmet nearly every Martian in the leadership had moved to

Phobos for safety's sake. Arabella and Captain Singh joined in these meetings, as did Fulton—who had survived the destruction of his hydrogen manufactory and ship-yard, and was now even more determined to prove the value of his inventions. Lady Corey, too, was present at most Council meetings . . . clad all in black and speaking infrequently, but nonetheless determined to support the resistance in any way she could, in honor of the late Captain Fox.

Despite Khema's air-sickness, which afflicted her constantly in Phobos's state of near free descent, she remained the Council's head; however, her many duties often kept her from the daily meeting. In her absence, as to-day, her lieutenant, the khoreshte *akhmok* Thekhla, led the meetings. But the meetings were conducted in English—that being the only language that all the Martian nations had in common—and, as Thekhla's English was limited, Arabella found herself perforce deeply involved in most of her conversations.

"The English made another attempt upon us last night," Thekhla said, and Arabella translated. "Three ships this time. The attack was repulsed by ballista fire, as usual, but all three ships escaped. We suffered no casualties. More stones are being brought from the quarry even now."

"Has there been any new word from the surface of Mars?" Captain Singh asked.

"With the nights being so short," Arabella translated from Thekhla, "there has been little opportunity for an exchange of letters." What little communication there was between Phobos and the Martian surface was provided by khoreshte pilot-boats, which ascended and descended under cover of darkness. "But questioning of the most recent ship-load of refugees continues." She paused, listening intently to an exchange between Thekhla and one of the other Martians which incorporated some unfamiliar vocabulary. "There has apparently been open fighting with the Ceres fleet in some of the southern princessipalities."

"If only we could support them from the air," Captain Singh muttered to Fulton. Fulton humphed, frowning, and stroked his chin contemplatively.

*Diana*, still under repair from the Battle of Tekhmet, was not yet available for missions to Mars's surface. The light unarmed pilot-boats which provided the thin thread of communication that still existed between Phobos and the Martian surface were little more than two-person hot-air balloons with a small three-sail pulser, entirely incapable of combat. And the *khebek* fleet, though the damage they had sustained in the battle had been largely repaired, were trapped upon Phobos by a shortage of hydrogen. For though that invaluable gas was not nearly so perishable as hot air, it did tend to leak away over time—Arabella understood from Fulton that this had something to do with the small size of the hydrogen molecule, which was also responsible for its great lifting power—and with the hydrogen manufactory destroyed they had no way to replace it. *Diana* had Isambard, but his capacity to produce hydrogen was little greater than *Diana*'s needs; Fulton had been attempting to engineer some means of making hydrogen with the facilities available upon Phobos, but to no avail so far. They had even considered refitting the *khebek* to use hot air rather than hydrogen, but even if such a feat were technically possible—Fulton was doubtful—the quantities of coal required made the idea completely unworthy of consideration.

"Word has also reached us," Thekhla continued, interrupting Arabella's melancholy contemplations, "that another Venusian drug-smuggling ship has arrived, carrying still more supplies of the drug and further means of production."

Suddenly an idea occurred to Arabella. "Have these smugglers come directly from Venus?" she asked Thekhla in khoreshte dialect.

Thekhla considered the question. "I believe they must have," she said, "as many of the materials are found only there."

"Is the ship of Venusian make?" Arabella continued, quite seriously.

Thekhla's eye-stalks drew together in puzzlement. "To the best of my knowledge, yes."

"Do you know how much longer the smuggler will remain on Mars?"

"They tend to come and go quite rapidly and fly by night. They will almost certainly have departed by dawn to-morrow."

Arabella looked to Fulton, Captain Singh, and Lady Corey, who were looking on with puzzlement. None of them spoke khoreshte dialect, not a word.

Here was an opportunity for Arabella to do something about the resistance's most pressing problem. But if she translated what Thekhla had just said, and told them what she had in mind to do about it, they would certainly never allow it.

"What are you on about, child?" Lady Corey asked.

"It is a matter of Martian reproduction," Arabella lied. "When the females go into *huthksh*, or heat, the males react by—"

"That is quite enough," Lady Corey interrupted, as Arabella had known she would.

"Let us proceed to the urgent question of finances," Thekhla said, impatiently, and this Arabella translated without hesitation or prevarication.

But despite the desperate urgency of the financial problem, Arabella translated it with only half her mind. The other half was engaged in planning a foolish and dangerous operation—an operation that might save the resistance, but only if she acted within hours.

She had confidence in her own abilities—perhaps too much

so—and she knew that if she opened the question to debate the Council would argue until it was too late. So she would do it herself—alone, without permission, and against all common sense.

She would steal another Isambard.

---

Arabella's plan, as such plans were wont to do, did not proceed exactly as she had at first anticipated. For one thing, her intent to proceed alone, with only a khoreshte pilot to take her to the surface in a pilot-boat, foundered upon the fact that even a half-grown member of Isambard's species would be far too large for such a light vehicle to lift.

Fortunately, she had many friends in the resistance . . . friends who were willing to support her even in a most unsupportable enterprise. Mills, whose command of several languages was superior to her own, and her old messmate Taylor, a lean fair-haired veteran of the seagoing Navy who had engaged in many a turn-up on land as well as more formal battles at sea, were happy to lend their skills and strength to her mad idea.

Another was Churath, the captain of the cargo-carrier *Kemekhta*. *Kemekhta* was one of just three cargo-carriers the ship-yard had built, and the only one of the three to survive the Battle of Tekhmet. She was a modified *khebek* with an especially long deck and large cargo door, built for the express purpose of transporting items too large for the ordinary *khebek*. Churath, Arabella knew, was a smart and ambitious khoreshte warrior who had been disappointed to be assigned such an unwarlike vessel. When Arabella approached Churath with her scheme, the captain was delighted to participate.

One man Arabella dearly wished could have accompanied her on this mission was her dear friend Gowse, whose ability to handle Isambard and other creatures was exceptional. But Gowse, sadly, had been lost along with Fox and the other Touchstones.

The hydrogen for *Kemekhta*'s descent and ascent would be supplied—just barely—by the small amount of excess gas that could be spared by *Diana*. This Arabella obtained herself, and in some ways it was the most guilt-inducing part of the whole operation. For not only was she compelled to steal a vital war material from her own husband in the brief darkness of Phobos's night, but—unlike *Kemekhta* and, for that matter, herself, she could not return it at the conclusion of her operation. On the other hand, she told herself, if the operation were successful there would be hydrogen to spare.

---

The smugglers' camp lay in the Sukhara desert some days' journey east of Sor Khoresh; local time there was about three hours later than here. These time calculations had become second nature to Arabella since her arrival at Phobos.

Thus it was that at midnight Phobos time, with Captain Singh fast asleep, Arabella slipped from their bed, collected the bag of clothing she had prepared from its hiding place, and made her way to *Kemekhta*'s berth.

Arabella finished buttoning her jacket, tugged on her cap, and turned back to Taylor. "How do I look?"

"Disreputable," he replied.

This was exactly as she had intended. Arabella was now costumed as a man, and quite a disgraceful man at that—exactly the sort of low type to be found consorting with Venusian drug-smugglers at an isolated camp in the sukharate wilderness. Her trousers and jacket were filthy and worn, her cap battered and pulled low to hide her face, and her features were further obscured with a smear of charcoal intended to resemble some days' growth of beard. Only her shoes might betray her origins as a young woman of quality—the one on her natural foot was half of the selfsame pair of sturdy Mars-made half-boots which had accompanied her to Earth, to Venus, and back, and the other was as close a copy as could be made—but on this point she refused to compromise, as she had seen many times that an ill-fitting shoe could lead to disaster if pursuit or escape were required.

"Thank ye, sir," Arabella replied in a gruff low voice. "I'll be making me way to Mars now."

"Very convincing." Taylor smiled briefly, then resumed a more serious mien. "We must depart right away."

"Aye aye, sir," she growled, touching her cap-brim.

———

*Kemekhta* was, like her *khebek* siblings, not much of a ship, having only one deck, two masts, and a single balloon envelope. But all the other parts were present, albeit sometimes in truncated form, and her crew of Martians—Captain Churath, her first and second mates, and five aerial sailors—was likewise somewhat abbreviated, but competent, sprightly, and enthusiastic. They all spoke very good English, and they were all very respectful of Arabella. "You are in good hands, ma'am," said the captain, holding her hand flat above her head as though to shield her eyes from the Sun. This gesture seemed odd, as the Sun was very low in the sky behind her—with Phobos's rapid pace through the air, it was very close to setting—but then Arabella realized that, given the construction of the Martian head, it was the closest Martian equivalent of a respectful knuckle to the forehead.

Setting off from Phobos was very much unlike launching from a planet's surface. The gravity being so weak, it was not difficult for the crew to simply shove the ship up from her berth with their hands. This initial push was not sufficient for her to escape Phobos's gravity, feeble though it was, but it gave her enough momentum that, in just a few minutes, she had drifted far enough away from her dock for the crew to take to the pedals without fear of damaging either the pulsers or any thing upon the Phobian surface. And the *khebek*'s five-sail pulsers were more than powerful enough to propel the ship to the moon's escape velocity.

The pedals were right on the main-deck—two rows of five, to accommodate the ship's usual full complement—and Arabella joined in pedaling along with Taylor, Mills, and the five sailors. The two officers and the captain were sufficient to handle the sails, and soon they were jouncing and jolting along through the rough tumultuous air of Phobos's little Horn, with *Kemekhta*'s automaton pilot helping to guide them in their course. It was not long at all before they had left Phobos well behind—or, to be accurate, Phobos left *them* behind, continuing to hurtle along in its path even as they pedaled and spread sails to shed their orbital velocity for a descent to the Martian surface. This maneuver also meant that when night fell, as it did very shortly after their departure from the dock, they remained within Mars's shadow thereafter rather than accompanying Phobos to its rendezvous with dawn a few minutes later.

Arabella and the others pedaled furiously, grunting in the dark, while the captain and her mates only muttered quietly to each other as they managed the sails. They were a tight and experienced crew, and furthermore the sort of boisterous, even joyful calls of command and response usually heard aboard a ship of the air might attract unwanted attention. So it was in darkness and near-silence that they fell toward Mars, while gray and rocky Phobos flared into bright visibility above and beyond their course.

For a tense dark hour they pedaled, working hard to bring

*Kemekhta* into an orbit that intersected the surface near the smugglers' port, and hoping to evade the English patrols which were a far-too-common danger. The Navy, even with the addition of the Ceres fleet, was not numerous, but Phobos's location was no secret; even under the cover of darkness an encounter with an English ship was a strong possibility. Thanks to the *khebeks*' maneuverability and the automaton pilots, the Martians escaped these encounters unscathed more often than not, but this outcome was far from guaranteed. But, by good fortune, they met no other ships before the word came down the line, passed quietly from mouth to ear to mouth to ear: "Raise the envelope!"

Mills and Taylor continued pedaling, to give the ship some steerage-way—theirs were the strongest legs in the crew, and they had no experience with the particular requirements of *khebek*-handling—while Arabella assisted in unpacking, unfurling, and rigging the ship's single balloon. This task was not easy in darkness, but the Martians knew their work, and once the envelope was properly spread out and positioned within its net of fine silk ropes, the captain turned the gas-cock and, with a hiss, the invisible, irreplaceable stuff swiftly turned the loose flapping circle of silk into a sphere. Almost immediately Arabella felt her weight return—the ship was no longer freely falling toward the surface, but buoyed up by her balloon—but though they had long since departed Phobos's little Horn they were still in the lower reaches of Mars's Horn, and she and the others must perforce return to the pedals, lest the ship be blown far off course by its strong and mercurial winds.

Eventually, though, *Kemekhta* drifted below the Horn and into the calmer, more predictable currents of the true planetary atmosphere. "'Vast pedaling," the captain said, to Arabella's great relief, and she and the other pedalers left the ship to drift in the current under balloon and sails alone. The danger of pursuit was much less, now; the velocities of the planetary breezes being so much smaller than those of the Horn or of the interplanetary atmosphere, if any ship should come into view they would have many hours to evade it.

Arabella, Mills, and Taylor lay panting on deck while the Martians put the ship in proper order for low-atmosphere navigation. "I do not believe," Arabella said when she had recovered her breath, "that I have worked so hard since Venus."

"That's the worst of it behind us, though," said Taylor. His eyes glimmered in the dark, reflecting the wan light of the stars and tiny Deimos. "All we need do now is find that creature, herd it aboard, and let the balloon carry us back up."

Arabella and Mills exchanged a look—there would certainly be much more pedaling in their future, not to mention many other difficult and dangerous tasks—but Taylor seemed sincere. "You are not concerned about the mission?" she asked him.

"Nah," he replied, drawing a snuff-box from his pocket and taking a pinch, followed by a stentorian sneeze. He offered the box to Arabella and Mills, who declined; he did not bother offering it to the Martians. "Handling a beast like Isambard is easy; all ye need do is tickle 'im just so and he'll do whatever ye require. And as for them smugglers, well . . ." He cracked his knuckles. "'Tis much the same. They require a harder touch, is all."

"I admire your confidence, sir," Arabella said with a smile.

Taylor lay back upon the hard bench, hands clasped behind his head and elbows akimbo. "Just leave it to old Taylor," he said, and promptly fell asleep.

Arabella, too, tried to sleep—there would be little enough opportunity for that once they landed—but though the night was dark and the ship rocked easily in the gentle current, sleep would not come.

"Landfall," said Mills, and Arabella's eyes blinked open. Somehow she must have slept, though she did not recall having fallen asleep.

*Kemekhta* now drifted very low over rolling dunes, gray in the starlight. No structures were visible, indeed no sign of life at all; the only sounds were the slight creak of the rigging and the hiss of the wind-driven sand below. Arabella joined Mills, Taylor, and three of the Martians at the pedals, bringing the ship to a halt, while the captain worked a hand-pump to draw the hydrogen out of the balloon and the rest of the crew threw out sand-anchors and hauled her down to the surface. Soon the ship's keel met sand with a soft *crunch* and she settled gingerly into a protected cove in the lee of a large dune, the still partially inflated balloon gently wobbling in the breeze above.

"Dawn is about three hours from now," the captain said. "We will await you here until one hour after dawn." They all understood that once the Sun was well up the chance of the ship being discovered by the smugglers was too great to be risked. "You have the signal rocket?"

"Aye aye." Arabella patted the satchel slung over one shoulder. Its contents included a fire-work whose bright blue flare would summon *Kemekhta* to their location—if she happened to spot it, and if her situation permitted it. Use of the signal rocket was a last resort and its success was not to be relied upon.

"Very well, then. Good luck." The captain gave another of those peculiar salutes. It seemed very apropos to the resistance, a combination of English gesture and Martian physiology, and Arabella returned it in kind, holding her hand horizontal at the level of her eyebrows.

---

Arabella, Mills, and Taylor set off across the sand, scuffing along through the dark. Almost immediately the habits of Arabella's youth returned, automatically directing her feet to the more stable sand at the windward base of each dune, and she soon began to outdistance her companions. She went back and pointed out the better path, but even with this advice they still struggled. Part of their problem was that they lacked Arabella's trained eye—she suspected that even in full daylight they would not be able to spot the subtle indications she could—and part of it was simply their greater weight. But even with her advantages, Arabella was out of practice and not so lithe as she once had been, not to mention that her clockwork foot was not designed for this activity, and she soon found herself slogging along at the same speed as her old messmates.

Following first the sounds of voices and then the smells of breakfast cooking, they eventually reached the smugglers' camp. Moving cautiously and quietly, they climbed a dune and looked down upon the camp from its summit.

The smugglers' ship stood on her sand-legs in the midst of the camp, with her mainmast fully rigged and three balloon envelopes already swelling in preparation for a dawn launch. The smugglers themselves—though the ship had come from Venus, they were all human—bustled about purposefully, plainly eager to be on their way. But, critically, the ship's equivalent of Isambard had not yet been loaded aboard. A huge creature, larger even than *Diana*'s own Isambard, he lay on his stomach in a pen near the ship, breathing heavily, ignoring the piles of fodder that two of the smugglers shoveled toward him with pitch-forks.

"Him" was the pronoun which Arabella mentally applied to the creature, the same as *Diana*'s Isambard. And though Ulungugga had used the same masculine pronoun, in Wagala Venusian as well as in English, he had assured Arabella that this would not prove an impediment to the successful mating of the new creature to Isambard. This seemed odd, but as Ulungugga himself had given birth to a fine healthy gaggle of young on the voyage from Venus to Earth, Arabella was prepared to accept his assertion with puzzled equanimity.

Arabella gave careful consideration to the creature as he lay prostrate, his thick black tentacles splayed out across the sand, which appeared gray in the dim light of the smugglers' lanterns. Mars's gravity was less than half that of Venus, Arabella knew, but this poor beast would have been cooped up in the ship's hold all the way from Venus, in a state of free descent without any possibility of healthful exercise. It was no surprise that he could barely move, and had little interest in food, though the smugglers were strongly encouraging him to eat by word and action. Shortly after launch they would require him to produce a large quantity of hydrogen, to make up the gas inevitably lost in inflating the balloons, and before this could occur he must be well fed.

The situation was beneficial to Arabella in that the creature would be more easily absconded with from his pen than he would be from the ship. But the smugglers were paying him the very strictest attention, and would continue to do so up to the moment of launch, and even if she could manage to get the creature away it would be extremely difficult to march him across the desert to where *Kemekhta* lay waiting.

The two smugglers feeding him, Arabella realized now, were not human like the rest of the crew. They were Venusians, and they were in a very bad way. For one thing, they were naked—Arabella had rarely before seen a naked Venusian, as they had both a very sophisticated sense of fashion and powerful taboos against nakedness. For another, their flesh hung in loose folds—they looked as though they were starving. And, perhaps worst of all, their skin was dry, cracked, and flaking in the Martian desert air. Venusians, accustomed to a very hot and wet climate, suffered terribly in the cold dry Martian air and must be wetted down several times a day. These poor individuals were being horribly abused!

Even the creature for which they cared, which did not look particularly healthy, was in better condition than they.

"We require a distraction," Arabella said to Taylor and Mills as they slipped back down to the base of the dune. "Something which will cause those smugglers to entirely abandon this camp—and their Isambard, and his handlers—and will last long enough that we can summon *Kemekhta* to this location."

A long contemplative moment passed, as all three of them considered this seemingly impossible problem. Then the darkness was split by Mills's broad grin, shining in his dark face in the starlight. "Their lanterns," he said. "Green. They fear fire."

"Of course!" Arabella replied. The red sand looked gray because the smugglers' lanterns were Venusian worm-lights, whose greenish light was dimmer than oil lamps but ran no risk of igniting the highly inflammable hydrogen. Between the Isambard and the slowly inflating balloons, the risk of explosion must be ferocious. "But how shall we make use of this fact?"

Mills thought a moment more before replying. "The gas rises," he said. "Light at top, burn from top down."

From that seed a plan quickly grew in Arabella's mind. The danger was enormous, and the chance of success quite small. But that seemed entirely apropos to this already outlandish expedition. "Very well," she said to Mills and Taylor, "here is what we shall do . . ."

———

To Arabella's dismay, the eastern sky was already beginning to lighten as she slipped over a saddle between dunes, sliding down toward the smugglers' camp as silently as she could. Mills's eyes blinked down after her for a moment, then quickly vanished; he and Taylor would make their way around to the camp's windward side and await her signal.

Moving quickly, using every means of stealth that Khema had taught her, Arabella slipped through the night to the dark space between the ship and the Isambard's pen. The creature now munched contentedly, rapidly diminishing the pile of dry vegetation before him, while the underfed handlers lay sleeping as though dead. Arabella crept to the large silk tube which stretched from the ship to the creature's lower abdomen, carrying hydrogen from the Isambard to the swelling balloons, and, carefully keeping the tube between herself and the smugglers, moved along it to where it entered a hatch in the ship's hull. There she cut several large slits in the tube with her pocket-knife. The edges of the slits fluttered in the exhalation of the colorless, odorless gas; they were not so large or so numerous that the tube sagged noticeably, but with luck they would be sufficient to cause the tube to part here once it caught fire.

With luck. She had no way of knowing whether she had cut enough slits, or too many, or even whether such a number existed. But she did the best she could, and once she adjudged her work complete she crept back the way she had come.

But she found her way completely blocked. While she had been busy with her knife, a line of men, extending from a tent pitched at the base of a dune to the ship's open cargo hatch, had formed across the path she had taken.

With quiet rhythmic grunts the men were passing a series of small caskets from hand to hand. From the sounds they were making and the set of their shoulders as they worked, the caskets—no more than a foot and a half in the longest dimension—must be exceedingly heavy, and there were dozens of them at least.

Trapped between the Isambard's pen, the ship, and the line of men, Arabella crouched in the sand, hoping against hope that an opening would appear before the rising sun revealed her. Yet the sky in the east was brightening rapidly. She might have only a few minutes of darkness left.

Arabella's heart hammered so loud in her ears she felt sure it would betray her position. But she held herself absolutely still, moving nothing but her eyes as she sought some opportunity for escape. A simple whistle from her would launch the attack, but for her own safety she dared not make that call until she had put much more distance between herself and the ship.

Alongside the line of laborers, a group of three men—better dressed than the rest, with the bearing of officers and gentlemen— moved with lanterns, following the progress of the caskets. One of them in particular seemed especially keen on making sure that every single casket reached its destination. He paced the first casket in line, drawing nearer and nearer her position.

He moved awkwardly, yet something in his carriage was familiar.

And all at once she realized what she was seeing.

He had but one leg. He walked with a crutch, clumsy in the soft sand.

He was her brother.

"Michael!" she cried. The sound was wrenched involuntarily from her throat.

Michael turned to her, and the shock on his face in the pale light of dawn matched her own feelings. "Arabella!" he said. "What are *you* doing here?"

*So much for my disguise,* she thought, and *I could ask the same of you.* But she did not bother speaking. For one thing she was, with deep regret, certain of the answer, and for another she was busy charging at him, sand chuffing beneath her boots. Without a word she slammed into him, carrying both of them some ten feet beyond the astonished line of working men, and landed heavily atop him on a small hillock.

"How *could* you?" she shouted in her brother's face, even as he lay stunned beneath her in the cool sand. "How could you throw in your lot with these villains?"

"Villains?" he replied, catching his breath and shoving her off of himself. "These men are on the King's business!"

"The King is mad," she said, scrambling to her feet. "These men serve Lord Reid, and Lord Reid serves only Mammon."

Michael struggled to rise, but his crutch was of little use in the soft sand. "We all serve Mammon, in one way or another. You yourself came all the way to Mars for the family fortune."

"I came for *you*!" she cried, but then a thud behind her caught her attention. She turned toward the sound, then immediately ducked—one of the smugglers had dropped his casket and was leaping toward her. But he was from Venus, and in Mars's lesser gravity he misjudged his leap; he sailed over her, crashing into Michael and knocking both in a tumbled heap.

Continuing the momentum of her duck, she curled into a ball and rolled away, springing to her feet some distance away. Several other men had dropped their caskets and were charging toward her, teeth bared and arms outstretched.

One of the caskets, she noted, had come open in the fall.

Gold coins spilled from the open lid. Hundreds of them.

Without hesitation she put both her forefingers in her mouth and gave a piercing whistle.

Immediately, with a rushing hiss, a flaring rocket rose from beyond a dune to her left.

Time seemed to come to a halt then, as every one—the onrushing smugglers, Michael, the two officers, and even Arabella herself—watched the rocket as it rose, caught the breeze, arced over in a fiery parabola, and met the top of the ship's main balloon, exploding there with an eye-searing flare of bright blue light.

Arabella, knowing what was to come, was the first to break this paralysis, throwing herself to the sand and clapping her hands over her ears. A moment later came a tremendous whooshing *bang* as the balloon's hydrogen caught fire, the envelope's silk shredding instantaneously into flaming strips. The rush of hot air from the explosion pressed Arabella's body into the sand and nearly deafened her, despite her hands on her ears, but she was better off than the men who had been standing, many of them staring at the rocket as it descended. They now lay stunned on the sand, with flaming fragments of silk, rope, and wood falling all around them from the lightening sky.

Arabella stood, ears ringing, and looked around. There lay the line of caskets—thousands and thousands of pounds' worth of gold coins, surely the ill-gotten proceeds of the *ulka* trade, bound for Lord Reid's coffers. There stood the Isambard, moaning in fear, swaying on his tentacles as he peered wide-eyed at the flaming wreckage all about himself. There stood the Isambard's handlers, blinking in astonishment. And there stood the ship, her rigging and both of the remaining balloons dripping with fire. The silk of one balloon envelope parted as she watched, relieving the pressure within . . . preventing an immediate explosion, but sending a pale jet of flame shooting off to windward.

But that jet of flame caught the breeze and bent back toward the ship, where it met the stream of hydrogen, lighter than air, that rose from the place Arabella had cut the silken tube. Flame instantly ran down that invisible stream like a midshipman sliding down a ladder. The tube immediately caught alight, then flared in a brief soft explosion . . . which severed the tube, extinguishing the flame in the process, and knocked down several smugglers who had just recovered their footing.

It was a better outcome than Arabella had hoped for. Better than she had deserved, she had to confess.

Now freed from the ship and spurred forward by the explosion, the Isambard bellowed and charged off, with the tattered, smoldering end of the tube still attached to his hindquarters. His tentacles, built for swampy ground, floundered in the soft sand, and the unfamiliar gravity hampered him still further—but all of this panicked him even more, driving him thrashing forward at considerable speed. His two handlers rushed after him as though their survival depended on the Isambard's continued presence and good health, which it no doubt did.

Arabella followed the Isambard and his handlers as best she could, even as explosions continued to sound behind her, sending flaming wreckage and panicked smugglers flying in every direction. But just as she was finding her stride, something snagged her ankle—the flesh and blood one—and she sprawled face-first in the sand.

It was Michael, who held her ankle in a death grip. "How can you betray your King?" he shouted at her from the ground. "Your family? Your very *planet*?"

"*Mars* is my planet!" she replied. "And as for my family . . . is this *your* money?" She gestured to the caskets that still lay in a line on the sand.

"This money came from the weak!" he spat back. "Martians and Englishmen alike, weak men voluntarily paying to weaken themselves still further, and it is bound for England!" He grinned then, and the flaring firelight and the rising sun made of his face a very devil's mask. "This gold will buy me the first Dukedom of Mars!"

"Then you are not my family!" She kicked at him then, the hard metal of her artificial heel knocking his hand loose from her ankle and making him cry out in pain. "And the Prince Regent is not my King!"

The remaining balloon burst then, in a tremendous roaring explosion that sent Arabella rolling across the hard ground and left her deaf and half-blind from the sand in her eyes. Shaking her aching head, spitting out sand and ash and wiping her face, she sat up . . .

. . . and beheld *Kemekhta*, settling gently to the sand in the path of the fleeing Isambard. Thank Heaven, they had seen the blue flare!

Even as the *khebek* touched the ground her great cargo door, which had been constructed for just this purpose, thudded to the sand, forming a ramp up which the panicked beast ran headlong. But the Martians waiting on deck were ready for him, and quickly surrounded him, petting his leathery hide to soothe his shattered nerves and giving him cool water to drink. The two starving Venusians followed, and the Martians gave them water as well.

But the mission was not yet over. "Mills!" Arabella cried, struggling to her feet. "Taylor! To me!" She stumbled back toward the smugglers' ship, now a nearly unrecognizable heap of flaming wreckage, continuing to call, "To me! To me!" as she went.

She found a casket in the ashy sand. It was terribly heavy, and shifted awkwardly as she lifted it, but she managed to clutch it to her breast and stagger toward *Kemekhta* with it. Taylor soon reached her, then Mills. "Gold!" she cried. "Bring as much as you can!" They immediately set to with a will, and once the Martians had the Isambard under control they joined in as well.

The surviving smugglers did not take this theft well at all. But the captain and officers of *Kemekhta* were looking out for Arabella, and two cannon-balls from that quarter soon put paid to the opposition, scattering the wreckage of the smugglers' ship still further across the blackened desert.

The last few smugglers were left waving impotent fists at *Kemekhta* as she rose from the desert, with dozens of heavy caskets safely stowed aboard and the Martians struggling to calm the still-agitated Isambard. Among the survivors below, Arabella noted, was one better dressed than the others, with only one leg.

This one did not bother shaking his fist at the rising *khebek*. He merely glared . . . directly at her.

She met his gaze and, without looking away, she untied her cravat, unbuttoned her shirt, took off her locket—the silver locket bearing Michael's portrait in miniature, which she had never once removed since she was sixteen years of age—and dropped it over the rail.

---

"You stole an Isambard," Khema said.

"I stole an Isambard," Arabella acknowledged.

"You risked your life," Captain Singh said, "and the lives of your friends, and an irreplaceable *khebek*. And her crew."

"I did."

Fulton's mouth opened, then closed, then opened again. "And to what end?" he managed eventually. "A single such creature cannot produce nearly enough hydrogen for our entire *khebek* fleet."

"A *single* creature, yes. But if they are *bred* . . ."

Lady Corey goggled at the very notion. "Do you propose to turn Phobos into a . . . a cattle-farm for these tentacled monstrosities?"

"If that is what is required to put our fleet back in the air," Arabella insisted. "And I did bring along the Isambard's handlers, Venusians who were very badly abused by the smugglers, to help care for the creatures."

Khema considered this intelligence. "Are they willing to join the resistance?"

"Ulungugga says that their health is much too fragile for that," Captain Singh said. "He says they were very close to death when they arrived, and their recuperation will require years. The only humane thing to do is to return them to their homes on Venus. It is, at least, approaching inferior conjunction." This meant that Venus was between Mars and the Sun, so the journey should not be unreasonably long.

Khema's eye-stalks pressed against each other. It was an expression Arabella had never before observed in a Martian. Aggravation? Exasperation? Wonderment? "I propose to delegate

Captain Churath and *Kemekhta* to this task," she said after a time. "She and her crew are obviously not happy in their role here, and I cannot think of any assignment which offers a more appropriate . . . reward for their actions last night." Now her eye-stalks directed themselves at Arabella. "And as for yourself . . . I cannot imagine what reward, or punishment, would be appropriate for you."

"I only ask to continue my work at the Institute," Arabella said, with complete sincerity. "There is considerable work yet to be done on the automaton pilot, and many new students."

Khema looked to Captain Singh. "Will you promise to keep her from getting in trouble again?"

"That is a promise no one can make."

Again Khema's eye-stalks pressed together. "I am afraid you are correct."

# 15

## THE FINAL ASSAULT

Arabella floated in her workshop, contemplating the automaton pilot which sat, more or less, upon the work-bench before her. The frame was fastened to the bench by clips, but as the air within the shop was quite still she had allowed some of the disassembled parts to float free. At the moment she was considering a revision to the arithmetic accumulator, which might permit a more rapid computation . . . sufficiently rapid, she hoped, to accommodate certain changes in the wind which the current version of the automaton could not predict quickly enough to make use of. But suddenly her ruminations were interrupted by two of the baby Isambards, which charged in the door squealing happily, chasing each other through the air.

"No!" Arabella cried, quickly shielding the floating mechanisms with her arms. "Shoo! Shoo!" She gestured ineffectually at the creatures, even as the trailing one caught up with the leader, grappling it with further happy squeals as they bounced off of a wall. Tentacles flailed every which way, and the sight was so endearing and ridiculous that, annoyed though she was, she could not help but laugh at the creatures' playful antics.

"Sorry, ma'am!" said Taylor, following his charges through the door and gathering them up in his arms. "These little'uns are hard to keep hold of!" These "little ones" were of the most recent litter, but even so had already grown to the size of large dogs. Taylor could barely hold on to both of them at once, and in a few days they would be too large for him to manage more than one at a time. Their older siblings were already hard at work in the pens, eating their weight in straw every day and producing thousands of cubic feet of hydrogen for the growing *khebek* fleet.

Arabella, still laughing, assisted Taylor in shepherding the juvenile Isambards out of the workshop, then straightened her dress and returned to her work. But though the playful creatures had, fortunately, done no damage to the delicate mechanisms, Arabella's concentration had been completely shattered. She decided to reassemble the automaton sufficiently for stability, then take a walk to clear her head.

A "walk" upon the surface of Phobos, of course, was more of a "drift." There was, to be sure, a slight downward pull, but for Arabella this amounted to little more than an ounce of weight, insufficient for a true walking motion. Instead, exactly as on the deck of a ship between planets, she propelled herself by gentle pushes from one place to another, using the guide ropes strung between the major structures to keep herself from drifting off into the air. Unlike a ship, though, if she did happen to drift away, Phobos's gravity would eventually return her to the moon . . . but it would take hours to drift back down, and she would most likely be intercepted by a passing *khebek* first. Thanks to Fulton's ingenuity and Michael's money, there were always at least two or three *khebek* visible on maneuvers close by.

The *khebek* fleet, indeed, had now grown to over fifty ships. With the destruction of Tekhmet, no more iron could be produced, but Fulton had managed to rescue several large loads of usable iron plate from the wreckage of the refinery, as well as an entire ship-load of Venusian silk fabric and cordage. And with the drug-smugglers' gold, they were able to purchase *khoresh*-wood, powder, and shot from Sor Khoresh. At this rate the resistance would be able to assemble and equip perhaps a dozen more *khebek* before the materials ran out.

Arabella had taken quite some time to come to terms with this "blood-money," which—despite Michael's insistence that it had been given voluntarily by weak men—she considered to have been stolen, or at least swindled, from victims who had been made dependent on the drug against their will. But Captain Singh had eventually convinced her that, rather than attempting to give the money back to those victims, the most appropriate use that could be made of it was to employ it to interdict further drug shipments and prevent the Prince Regent from taking complete control of the planet.

And, indeed, they had done so, or at least were attempting to do so. The growing *khebek* fleet made frequent sorties to Mars, generally under cover of night but some times, in groups, in bold daylight raids. There they met up with the even more rapidly growing number of Martians, and even some Englishmen, who had joined the resistance after the Ceres fleet's very public and quite destructive arrival. The *khebek* were invaluable in coordinating their activities and supplying them with arms, explosives, and other implements of sabotage. These were directed against the smooth operation of the Company and the Ceres fleet; the intent was to keep the English off guard and slow their consolidation of power in Saint George's Land and beyond. The less territory they controlled when the Prince Regent's armored fleet arrived, the longer it would take for them to overpower all resistance.

But though Arabella was doing all she could—as was, indeed,

every one on Phobos, including the twice-bereft Lady Corey—
she was forced to admit, if only to herself in the darkness of her
pathetic little shack, that a delay would be the best they could
hope for. The resistance was already able to do little more than
harass the Company forces, a well-armed and well-trained army
with the enthusiastic support of nearly the entire human population of Mars; with the addition of the Prince's fleet, she could
not imagine any sequence of events which did not end, sooner or
later, in complete defeat.

The resistance did hold a few advantages over the English. The
*khebek* fleet would be an unknown quantity to the Prince's fleet
when it arrived, at least at first, and they were drilling every day
and constantly improving the automaton pilots to consolidate
their skills in maneuvering and fighting within Mars's Horn, especially the particularly tricky winds around Phobos. They had the
sympathies of many Martians, perhaps even a majority, though
how many of these would take up arms in a direct confrontation
with the English was an open question. They had the advantage
of home ground; the Martians were supplied directly from their
own farms and plantations, while the English were forced to import much of their materiel all the way from Earth. And they
held Phobos as a base, and controlled the skies in its vicinity completely; the moon's ballistas made the region extremely dangerous to the English, and could also be used to drop boulders upon
Mars's surface. But though the boulders' impact was devastating
when successful, the tactic had proved not quite so decisive as
Arabella had hoped; most of Saint George's Land, including Fort
Augusta and Woodthrush Woods, was too far from the equator to
be reached from Phobos in its very low orbit.

But these advantages, Arabella believed, would not withstand
the Prince Regent's fleet when it arrived. They would be numerous, exceptionally well armed, trained and equipped specifically
for fighting at Mars, and entirely dedicated to their cause, with

the firm backing of the Regent, Navy, and Company behind them. Furthermore, the fleet would consist largely of armored first-rates, of an advanced design lacking *Victoire*'s fatal weaknesses . . . and, even with those weaknesses, *Victoire* had very nearly defeated Nelson's entire fleet single-handed. Captain Singh, she knew, had done his very best to prepare them for victory before turning his coat, and though he now found himself on the other side of the chess-board—which did give him some advantages, and he claimed confidence that the Prince could eventually be overcome— she was very far from certain that the resistance, even with Captain Singh's active participation, could overcome the Royal Navy with Captain Singh's strategies.

Once Arabella had awoken in the night to find her captain, still awake, contemplating a chart of the skies near Phobos, with small lead weights of various sizes, representing ships, floating above it. The number of large weights, representing the Prince's fleet, had seemed overwhelming, and his expression had been exceedingly grim. But when he had noticed her watching, his face had cleared, and he had reassured her that with luck they would win out in the end.

With luck, he had said. If even Captain Singh admitted to depending on luck, she knew their chances were very slim indeed.

But still, she reminded herself, pausing to watch a pair of *khebek* chasing each other through the Horn's tempests, firing their cannon in dumb-show with wad and powder alone, the Aerial Navy of the Martian Resistance—to give its perhaps somewhat inflated formal name—was not entirely inconsequential. They had already defeated the Ceres fleet once, outnumbered nine capital ships to two after a devastating ambuscade, and recovered brilliantly thereafter. Of course, that victory had been a Pyrrhic one—all nine ships of the Ceres fleet had limped away, whereas the Martian side had lost more than half its fleet, including dear *Touchstone*.

Sometimes she felt she must miss Fox just as much as Lady Corey did. At times such as this, alone with her thoughts and memories, she could almost hear his voice. Or voices, rather, as he had commanded quite a range of different voices due to his time in the theatre. His rumbling Scottish brogue as Macbeth, especially, had given her a most unseemly thrill. Macbeth's last speech seemed particularly apropos to this moment: "I will not yield!" he had cried, his full-throated captain's voice shaking the barracks' rafters. "Though Birnam wood be come to Dunsinane, yet I will try the last! Lay on, Macduff, and d—n'd be him that first cries, 'Hold, enough!'" And that dauntlessness had not been mere stagecraft, for even when the aerial kraken had first appeared—fading into view as though by fell magic, when Liddon and even Arabella herself had been paralyzed by fear—he had never quavered, simply leapt into action.

Birnam wood, she thought then. And the kraken.

The two memories, which had never happened to occur to her at the same time before, suddenly collided in her mind, and a new idea was born.

Reversing herself in the air, she swiftly pulled herself along the guide rope toward her workshop. She must begin work immediately.

———————————

Three weeks later, Arabella found herself aboard *Hetmesh*, one of the newest of the *khebek*, on maneuvers designed to test some recent changes to the automaton pilot. Her captain and crew, though well-seasoned individually, had all recently been promoted to their current stations and were just becoming accustomed to each other.

"Five points up," said the Martian operating the automaton

pilot to the first officer, who acknowledged and carried out the order with crisp precision. Arabella nodded and marked the exchange in her note-book, saying nothing . . . some of the changes were intended to make the automaton's more advanced operations more accessible to the operator. So far the new dials and labels seemed to be having the intended effect.

"Sail ho!" called the Martian at the masthead. "Many sail! Many, many sail!"

Arabella and *Hetmesh*'s captain exchanged glances and hurried to the larboard rail, each of them scanning the sunward sky with her own telescope. Arabella's instrument had a wider field of vision, but it was the captain who spotted the other ships first . . . and hissed something to herself in her own language. It was not a happy sound. Immediately she turned back to her first mate. "About ship!" she roared.

Even as the crew leapt to comply, Arabella continued to seek the other ships with her own instrument . . . and, forewarned though she was, she could not suppress a gasp when she found them. For the tiny white flecks she espied were practically too numerous to be counted, spreading in a very precise square formation that spanned the full width and height of her field of view. Even as she scanned the glass from side to side she could not encompass their number; so many were they, and so exact their formation, that it was nearly impossible to distinguish them one from another.

But though their numbers were uncertain, their provenance was not. Only the English used a square formation, and here and there among them Arabella spotted bright glints . . . the reflection of the Sun behind them from the polished metal of their armored hulls.

Arabella collapsed the glass and pushed off the rail, propelling herself to the nearest set of unoccupied pedals. There, without hesitation or commentary, she hitched up her skirts, settled herself upon the rough *khoresh*-wood of the saddle, and began pedaling.

No one objected. They all knew that every hand—and every pair of legs—would be needed from this moment forward.

---

The Council was already in session when Arabella entered, having been alerted to the arrival of the English by flag signals from *Hetmesh* and other vessels. "We must assume," Captain Singh was saying to the assembled group, "that they will proceed directly to Phobos, and will attack here before the day is out. How many *khebek* have we?"

By good fortune Khema had just recently arrived at Phobos from the Martian surface, and this was information she could recite from memory. "Fifty-seven all told," she said, "of which forty-four are in fighting trim. Thirty-eight of these carry Mrs. Singh's latest innovations"—she pointed with her eye-stalks to Arabella, who nodded in acknowledgement—"and the automaton pilots of the remaining six are at most two weeks out of date." Khema then returned her attention to Captain Singh. "Against how many English men-of-war must they sail?"

"Thirty, more or less, including some unknown number of frigates and other noncombatant vessels." These odds seemed reasonably good for the Martians, Arabella thought, except that each *khebek* had only two four-pound cannon whereas the English first-rates—and there would be at least five or six of these in the fleet—carried twenty-four eight-pounders, and all the men-of-war, even the second- and third-rates, were clad in steel armor which would be completely proof against a four-pound ball. "We await closer observation to determine the fleet's exact composition and armament."

"By which time it will be too late to do any thing about it."

Captain Singh inclined his head in acknowledgement of this fact. "But not, perhaps, too late to do any thing *with* the information, if you catch the distinction."

"I do." Khema sighed, a human habit she had picked up from Arabella's late father. "I wish we had had more time to prepare."

"We have done what we can with the time given to us," Captain Singh replied, philosophically. "That is all that can be asked of any man."

"Of any mortal," Khema corrected. "Which reminds me . . ." From the satchel she had carried from Mars, which still hung on her armored and spike-encrusted shoulder, she drew a large package wrapped in brown paper and twine. "Mrs. Singh, I have brought you a present."

"This scarcely seems the time for presents," Arabella said, even as she drifted over to Khema to accept the package. It looked incongruously like a dress from the high-street shops in Fort Augusta.

"For *this* present, there is none better." Without another word she handed it to Arabella, who immediately untied the twine.

As soon as she saw the material beneath the brown paper she paused. "This is impossible," she said to Khema. "My mother burned it."

"She did," Khema acknowledged. "This is a new one. Lady Corey gave me your measurements."

At once Arabella tore the remaining paper aside, heedless of its reuse, and shook out the garment within by its shoulders.

It was a *thukhong*. That beautiful, form-fitting, fur-trimmed leather garment which had kept her warm and uninjured through so many adventures with Michael in the desert, and whose shameful exposure of Arabella's lower limbs had been so hateful to her mother.

Those days seemed a lifetime ago. Ten lifetimes. *Every* thing had changed since then.

Arabella's eyes filled with tears and she clutched the leather—still carrying the chill of Khema's ascent from the Martian surface, but butter-soft and smelling wonderfully of itself—to her face. "I cannot accept this," she murmured into the fur trim, eyes closed.

"Winter will be upon us soon," Khema said gently. "And if I know you—and I do—you will require a warm and protective garment for your resistance work."

"Thank you, *itkhalya*!" Arabella cried, flinging herself heedlessly into Khema's arms just as though Khema were her nanny and not a hulking *akhmok*, leader of entire Martian nations.

Khema accepted Arabella's tearful and overly demonstrative thanks with admirable restraint. "You are most welcome, *tutukha*," she said, patting Arabella's back with one hard and spiny hand. "Now go and put it on. We have much to do, and you must be properly clothed."

"Yes, *itkhalya*," Arabella said, bowing in the Martian fashion.

---

Arabella was still in the grip of a thousand strong emotions as she floated beside her husband on *Diana*'s quarterdeck, clad in her new *thukhong*. Chief among these was anxiety, to be sure. No sane person could fail to be anxious at the sight of the rigorous square grid of sails, now plainly visible to the naked eye, which seemed to spread across half the sky—every one of those white flecks a fully armed man-of-war of the Royal Aerial Navy, packed with men and bristling with armor and weapons, and drawing closer by the minute. But that anxiety was joined by many other sentiments. Pride, for Captain Singh and for the work that he, and she, and all the rest of the resistance had done together to prepare for this moment. Hope, for despite the terrible odds against them, she still did find within herself some optimism that they might yet win out. Anticipation, for finally all their plans would now, at last, be put into action . . . and, win or lose, at least the interminable waiting would be over. And even that most peculiar emotion of all: love. Love not only for her captain, but also for Khema, Lady Corey, and every other member of the crew . . . even Aadim, though she had no idea whether his peculiar self-awareness included the ability to reciprocate. Indeed, she felt tenderly even toward hulking Isambard and his many children! They had all been through so much together, and she felt she owed them so much. In point of fact, she owed many of them her life, in some cases several times over.

*Diana's* people floated on the deck below, grouped by divisions and lined up nearly as tidily as though they had stood in gravity. Though the winds of the Horn batted them this way and that, they were all old hands by now and they moved with the ship almost unconsciously. Here were the waisters, including a few Martians, with dear old Faunt still scowling at their head; here the topmen, including Mills, once her messmate and now captain of the larboard top; there the gunners and the hydrogen hands, stalwart green Venusians in the main, led by Ulungugga; and all the rest, a veritable crowd of fierce determined faces. Lady Corey and Dr. Barry stood with Arabella on the quarterdeck, along with the other officers and idlers . . . including Watson, whose performance in the Battle of Tekhmet had been so exemplary that he had been promoted to second mate. Even Captain Fox was here, if only in spirit.

Captain Singh stepped to the forward rail, looking out over his ship and his crew and the English fleet beyond them, and the people immediately fell silent. "You have the honor to serve," he said in his ringing baritone which seemed to reach every corner of the deck without effort, "aboard a ship of impeccable distinction. The dear *Diana* was built in the Honorable Mars Company's yards at Blackwall. She served the Company well for twenty-eight years before being captured by the French and re-fitted as a man-of-war. Recaptured by Company forces, she acquitted herself admirably in the Battle of Venus, and had the honor of serving briefly as Admiral Collingwood's flagship before returning to England." The captain did not, Arabella noted, acknowledge his own part in any of this. "But England did not deserve her loyalty, and now she serves Mars." He straightened further. "As do we all." He stared out at his people, his piercing brown eyes seeming to meet every single gaze; they replied in kind, gazing back in rapt silence. "A great challenge has been laid before us this day. A greater challenge than any we have yet faced; greater, perhaps, than any single airship has ever faced at all. I cannot promise you that we will succeed, though we have done our best to prepare for this moment. But I can promise you this: I will do my utmost for you, if you will do the same for me. Do I have your assent in this?"

"Aye!" they cried in unison, and Arabella shouted "Aye!" as enthusiastically as any of them.

Once the cheering had died down, the captain stepped back from the rail and Khema stepped up. As head of the Council, and by dint of her brilliant strategic mind, she was also the Admiral of their fleet. As such she commanded Captain Singh as well as all the *khebek*, and was thus the superior of all the Dianas. Despite her continuing air-sickness, she carried herself with dignity as she looked out over the assembled Dianas in silence. "I am deeply moved," she said at last, in English, "by your eagerness and zeal. Looking at your faces—red, pink, black, brown, and green—I see that you have come from many places and many creeds, yet all willingly offer your efforts, perhaps even your very lives, to Mars. And Mars welcomes your assistance, no matter from whence you come. Indeed, your very differences are your strength; by bringing together many voices from different lands, we open ourselves to new solutions to the problems that face us." She raised a hand then, holding it horizontal above her eye-stalks in the peculiar gesture which had become an expression of respect for the entire resistance, whether Martian, human, or Venusian. "I salute you all."

With a great rustle of cloth and leather, every one on the ship, including Arabella and Lady Corey, returned Khema's salute in kind. And then little Watson leapt up from the quarterdeck, catching himself with one foot on a backstay, and from this vantage he cried out in his cracking voice: "Three cheers for the Admiral! Hip hip!"

"Huzzay!" responded every one in a full-throated roar, Arabella not least among them.

"Hip hip!"

"*Huzzay!*"

"Hip hip!"

"HUZZAY!"

Khema's eye-stalks trembled with strong emotion. "And three more for Captain Singh!" she cried, leading three more cheers, in which every one participated with even greater zeal.

Captain Singh appeared to take this praise with his usual equanimity . . . but Arabella, more sensitive than most to his moods after such long acquaintance, noticed him blinking rapidly, his eyes shining in the pale Martian sun. "Very well!" he called after the echoes had died away. "Run up the Company colors, idlers and waisters to the pulsers, and let us be off!" And as the tidy arrangement of officers and crew broke up, all moving to their stations in an orderly bedlam of sound, only Arabella heard him mutter to himself, "And may Heaven smile upon our efforts."

*Diana* approached the oncoming fleet under false colors, the Honorable Mars Company's ensign fluttering in the wind of her whirling pulsers. "I mean to sow confusion," Captain Singh had explained to the Council. "Though I am certain they are aware that *Diana* is no longer their ally, perhaps a few officers or gunners may hesitate to open fire upon the Company flag. Any delay or lack of commitment in a key moment could make the difference between survival and destruction."

Although such a deception seemed to Arabella less than sporting, she knew from her reading and personal experience that it was a common military tactic, with its own conventions and etiquette. And given her own contributions to the coming battle, she felt that she had no standing to complain. Even her own person was flying false colors, in a sense; her *thukhong*, as her mother would surely point out if she were here, gave her a distinctively masculine profile. Yet the fur and smooth leather that gripped her limbs so tightly—so scandalously—gave her solace and confidence. The very smell of this garment, so full of memories of happy adventure among the dunes, made her feel lithe and strong and capable of any thing . . . and it reminded her that she was, truly, a child of Mars, not of England, and indeed always had been.

No matter who her family might be. "Michael," she muttered to herself between gritted teeth. She had heard nothing from him and not very much about him since that day in the desert, but she knew that in the succeeding months he had become an even more prominent Tory—even standing for a seat in the colonial assembly, though he had lost out to the incumbent—and had thrown in his lot and his fortune quite publicly with the Crown, supporting the Company's new and harsher policies with

speeches, letters, and monetary contributions. He had also continued to participate in, and profit from, the *ulka* trade, though
the resistance—in large part thanks to the gold they had captured
from him—had seen some success in reducing it.

She had never, before this year, realized the degree to which
Michael took after their mother, even as Arabella had favored
their father. And to think she had risked every thing to save him.

Of course, had she not done so, who knew where she might be
to-day? It could very well be that at this moment she would be
languishing in some paltry cottage in Croydon, while her wicked
cousin Simon dined upon *gethown* and *khula* at Woodthrush
Woods. And in that case, might Captain Singh still be a prisoner
at Marieville? Might Napoleon, in fact, still rule France . . . or,
indeed, with *Victoire* and her deadly sisters, the entire solar
system?

If only things were not as they are, she reflected, they would
certainly be different. But that was no reason for despair . . .
quite the opposite, in fact, for the more she thought about it, the
more certain she became that any small change might eventually
lead to great effects, perhaps even to alter the course of history
itself.

So be it. She would do what she could, and if that failed she
would try something else. Again and again, if necessary, until
fate brought her story to a close.

Arabella blew out a breath through her nose, straightened in
her straps, and returned her attention to the present moment.
Captain Singh was peering forward with his telescope, scanning
side to side and up and down to take in the whole English fleet
and the air around it. Suddenly he paused, focusing the instrument carefully . . . and then a small sly grin crept onto his face.
"Oh ho," he chuckled softly. He moved the telescope slightly
to one side, repeating his careful inspection on a second target

and then a third. "Dundas," he muttered, "you are a fool . . . and worse, a *predictable* fool." He collapsed the telescope and tucked it into his jacket pocket, turning to speak with Khema.

After Captain Singh and Khema had discussed whatever it was he had seen, Khema spoke to the new first mate, a solid young man called Morgan. "Raise the red signal-flags," she said, "and ready the red rockets. The red, mind you."

"Signal officer!" Morgan called in a voice larger even than his captain's, but with its own unique accent. He was an American, a former officer of that country's small but resolute aerial navy; he had made his way to Mars for love, then joined the resistance at Tekhmet after his beloved had fallen to the curse of *ulka*. The signal officer soon appeared, and Morgan relayed the Admiral's instructions to him.

"What is it that you have observed?" Arabella asked Captain Singh in the lull that followed.

"The English vessels lack swivel-gun turrets," he replied with grim satisfaction. "They have a few chasers, but their great guns fire only directly forward."

"I am amazed!" Arabella said. "*Victoire*'s swivel-guns were nearly our undoing at Venus." Napoleon's flagship had been equipped with four large swivel-guns in armored turrets. Turning swiftly to meet any target, they had allowed a single armored ship to hold her own—better than hold her own—against Nelson's entire fleet.

"Dundas and his dunderheaded compatriots in the Admiralty considered those turrets a weakness," he fumed. "A *weakness*! They saw only that Nelson succeeded in disabling two of them, leaving an opening for *Diana* to destroy her."

"Only at the cost of his flagship, and his life."

"Indeed," the captain acknowledged. "But the Admiralty is too conservative to even consider such a dramatic departure from their traditional designs, no matter how well proven." He shook his head. "Still . . . under the circumstances, I suppose I have never been more fortunate to have a recommendation ignored. I may disagree with Fulton on many things, but in the matter of innovation in aerial men-of-war I must doff my hat to him."

The red signal-flags then flew up the mainmast, and the captain again took up his glass and peered into the distance. Though Arabella saw nothing with the naked eye, she was content with his pleased reaction and did not draw out her own telescope from her *thukhong* pocket. "How much longer?" she asked.

He turned his glass to the closest English man-of-war, a hulking armored first-rate which, by the quantity of flags and gold leaf she carried, must be the flagship, *HMAS Royal George*. The name, supposedly in honor of the King, was, Arabella was certain, actually an expression of Princely self-importance. "Perhaps half an hour. Certainly no more than an hour."

Arabella peered at the oncoming English fleet for a time, then looked all about. Apart from the English ships the sky appeared empty, with only a few bits of flotsam and scraps of cloud seeming to mar the clear blue sky of Mars, and nothing was visible abaft but the mottled, lichen-crusted, wreckage-strewn surface of Phobos. That motley surface hid much, she knew, including dozens of ballistas awaiting the signal to let fly their stones, but apart from the brave ballista operators themselves, mostly Martians and all volunteers, the structures which the resistance had occupied since the destruction of Tekhmet now stood vacant. Phobos, they all knew, was an open target—immovable, incapable of concealment, and defenseless save for its winds and its ballistas—and no matter what happened in the coming battle it would certainly bear the brunt of the English cannon. Those who were neither ballista operators nor *khebek* crew, including Fulton, had been evacuated to the Martian surface.

"I should get below," she said. Though she would much rather remain with her captain, her place during the battle was with

Aadim. At least they had opened a larger scuttle between the quarterdeck and the great cabin, to ease communication between the two, and added windows on either side so that Arabella could have some visibility of the battle as it progressed.

"Break a leg," he replied—a theatrical term they had both learned from Fox, and which seemed particularly apropos at this moment, with the curtain about to rise upon what would most likely be, for good or ill, their final performance.

"I love you." Then, not wishing him to see the worried expression on her face, she immediately turned, pushed off the after rail with her foot, and shot down the ladder toward the great cabin.

---

In the great cabin, Arabella made certain that all was in readiness for battle. Aadim ticked and whirred patiently, his gears all carefully oiled and his many springs wound to optimum tension. Charts were rolled in their pigeon-holes for rapid access, and boxes of tools and spare parts lay ready close at hand in case repairs should become necessary. A wet washing-leather was available to sweep splinters or shards of glass from the air. All else had either been cleared away or stowed securely.

She looked up through the scuttle to the quarterdeck, which from her current position gave her a vantage onto the ship's wheel. Watson stood there, gripping the wheel tightly, staring forward with a face so firm and determined that she felt her heart squeezed with anticipatory melancholy. So many had already been lost . . . she hoped that his young life would not be among those snuffed out this day.

Suddenly Morgan, out of sight above, called out a rapid series of commands: "Set jibs and spankers! Pulsers ahead, smartly now! Ready great guns and bow-chasers! And run up the colors!"

At once the ship surged to life around Arabella. Commands, responses, and the irregular thump of bare feet upon *khoresh*-wood planking sounded all about as the ship's people leapt into action, readying sails and guns for the coming battle. The pulsers beyond the great stern window rushed past with renewed vigor, propelling the ship forward and pushing Arabella and every other unsecured object sternward. And with a squeak and hiss of lines through blocks, the false Mars Company ensign at the stern came down, replaced by the flag of the Martian Resistance.

This was the resistance flag's first showing in battle. A great red circle on a field of sky blue, representing Mars, bore a small white oval at the top, representing Mars's north polar cap, and a network of fine white lines representing canals. The red disk was surrounded by a golden ring, symbolizing the united peoples of Mars and their vow to protect the planet from outside interference, and was bracketed by a swift *huresh* and a fierce *shorosh*, both rampant. Working out this design had taken far too much of the Council's time, but despite Arabella's misgivings—any declaration of Mars's unity seemed far more aspirational than factual—she had to admit that it was a very striking design.

But Arabella had no time to admire the great blue and red ensign which now fluttered abaft. Dashing all about the cabin—here taking a sighting upon Jupiter, there peering out the larboard window at the English ships ahead—she kept herself and Aadim busy, calculating sailing-plans and course corrections and calling them up through the scuttle. "Up a point," she called, then, "Larboard two points." Watson, at the wheel, kept pace with her rapid adjustments, steering the ship steadily through the Horn's capricious winds.

"Signal rockets!" cried Morgan. Immediately a triple *whoosh* sounded, rapidly diminishing in pitch and loudness, followed by three *bang*s and three blossoms of red fire, whose light danced across the great cabin's decks and bulkheads. Before the light and sound had faded, Arabella dashed to the starboard window and looked forward, where a remarkable sight met her eyes.

In the air between *Diana* and the nearest English man-of-war, a patch of sky seemed to crumple, shrivel, and involute itself. This peculiar sight swiftly resolved itself into a large painted-canvas bag—mottled gray forward, to match the surface of Phobos, and sky-blue aft—being struck and furled from about a *khebek* which had hung, silent and immobile, in that spot in the sky for nearly the entirety of the past day. The Martians performing this labor shielded their eyes against the sudden sunlight.

In every direction dozens more *khebek* suddenly appeared in this same manner—just as the aerial kraken had revealed itself by darkening its luminescent skin against the brightness of the Sun, and just as Malcolm's army had cast aside the concealing trees of Birnam Wood at the climax of the Scottish play. Most of the *khebek* thus revealed lay either between or behind the English ships . . . well beyond the easy reach of their forward-facing great guns. "They will almost certainly obey the dictates of their Admiral Nelson," Khema had explained to the assembled *khebek* captains before the battle, "who said, 'Never mind the maneuvers, just go straight at 'em.' If you can but restrain yourselves and wait patiently, they will charge straight at Phobos and pass you by, leaving themselves open to attack from behind."

And, indeed, the English had behaved exactly as Khema had expected, and once the *khebek* had freed themselves from their painted canvas masquerades they began firing. Their cannon were small, and not numerous, but they had drilled and drilled for months and their accuracy and rate of fire were second to none.

As Khema had directed, the *khebek* targeted the English pulsers. For though the English shipwrights had learned from *Victoire* and armored the ships' sterns more heavily, the propulsive sails themselves were, of necessity, exposed and lightly constructed, and a well-placed cannon-ball could do significant damage. For this reason no wise captain would let his adversary get behind him in battle . . . but the Prince Regent's captains had forsaken their wisdom through overconfidence in their indomitable commanders, their impregnable armor, and their inviolable sense of English superiority.

"Huzzah!" Arabella cried as she saw an English second-rate's pulsers tear themselves into fragments—the sails' own rapid rotation completing the job of destruction begun by a *khebek*'s cannon-ball. The ship, though otherwise undamaged, immediately lost steerage-way and began to tumble, seized by the Horn's constantly changing winds. Another ship, this one a first-rate with dual pulsers, suffered an even worse fate: with one pulser disabled and the other still driving at full speed, the ship spun out of control, flinging officers and crew into the uncaring air.

But though the *khebek* were clever, nimble, and had the advantage of surprise, they were still sadly surpassed in most respects by the heavily armed and armored English vessels and their numerous and highly experienced crews. More than half the English fleet survived the initial ambuscade unscathed, and these immediately turned to attack their much smaller adversaries. And though the *khebek* ducked and dodged, using their superior command of the Horn's variable winds to avoid the lumbering first-rates, the English threw such a weight of metal—twenty-four eight-pound balls in each broadside, with a broadside every three minutes or less—that by profligacy and chance, if nothing else, they were bound to strike their targets every once in a while. And as a single eight-pound ball, properly placed, was sufficient to devastate a lightly-armored *khebek*, these occasional successes swiftly added up. One after another, the plucky Martian ships were disabled or completely demolished, smashed into flinders or exploding in a sphere of pale hydrogen flame.

Even when the English great guns proved insufficiently adroit to swat away the flies which perturbed their flanks, they were still equipped with smaller swivel-guns which, while not so devastating as the thundering broadsides, could still do significant damage. And if that were not enough, every English ship carried great numbers of Marines, who sniped from the rigging at any Martian officer who held still long enough. These rifles, sadly, took many a brave Martian out of action.

The skies swiftly became a turbulent aerial charnel of smoke, floating wreckage, and drifting body parts. The view was never so obscured as it had been at the battle above Tekhmet, as the air here was constantly freshened by the Horn of Phobos, but navigation was still difficult, and Arabella and Aadim were constantly challenged to keep *Diana* and her great guns properly pointed at whichever English vessel was currently the greatest threat.

*Diana* herself was by far the most powerful ship in the fledgling Martian Aerial Navy, and with Captain Singh in command she had a devastating effect. Though only a single ship, and throwing much less weight of metal than even a third-rate, her command of the Horn's unpredictable winds was infinitely superior to that of her ponderous English prey.

The ballistas of Phobos took a toll on the English as well. The stones, slow and inaccurate though they were by comparison with cannon-balls, were so massive that when they did strike their target they destroyed it completely with a single blow. At one point Arabella found herself gaping in astonishment as an English first-rate folded like a clenching fist around the ballista-stone which struck her amidships, changed in an instant from a proud Naval vessel to a crumpled ball of floating wreckage. And even that wreckage was soon consumed by red and orange flame, with hydrogen and *khoresh*-wood and even steel armor burning fiercely in the whipping winds. But every stone launched from

Phobos inevitably betrayed the location of the ballista from which it had come, and the English guns soon hammered those sites into rubble.

As the battle progressed the English soon found their greater numbers and their magnificent, shining armor changed from intimidating advantages to stumbling-blocks. For the armored vessels, though highly resistant to direct cannon-fire, were heavy, slow, and cumbersome, and—especially with so many of them unable to maneuver properly, due to damage to their pulsers and the unpredictable winds—they frequently got in each other's way, and indeed collided with one another on more than one occasion. And as they blundered about, invulnerable though they might be in the main, *Diana* and the *khebek* picked at their vulnerable parts—their pulsers, their rigging, and their officers.

But even a lumbering, half-blinded giant is still a giant, and whether deliberately placed or not the sole of his shoe is still a force of inescapable destructive power. And the Prince Regent's fleet was a very large giant indeed. So numerous, so disciplined, and so heavily armed and armored were they that, even in disarray, they still took a heavy toll upon the Martians.

*Diana* too took significant damage from the English attack, with pulsers and sails shot full of holes and fractured masts held together with whipcord. One of her great guns had burst, doing terrible damage to the gun-deck and its largely Venusian crew, and half her rudder had been destroyed. It was only the skills of Chips and his men in patching her up in the brief intervals between attacks—and the skills of Dr. Barry in patching up the crew—that kept her flying at all.

At least, that was the hope. But as yet another broadside struck *Diana*, sending Arabella tumbling with a shriek and a painful thud against the starboard bulkhead, she knew that not even all Captain Singh's cleverness, the crew's bravery, and Aadim's calculations could keep one fragile wooden ship aloft forever . . .

not when her destruction was the intent of an entire fleet. "Are you well, ma'am?" called Watson through the scuttle, alarmed by her cry of pain.

"I am well enough!" Arabella replied, though her right elbow pained her fiercely from its impact with the wall. "Larboard three points, now!"

Again and again the hammer blows of English broadsides fell upon *Diana*, rattling Arabella in the great cabin and shaking her confidence. Aadim's workings stuttered and shrieked as some of the many cables, rods, and levers that extended throughout the ship were damaged . . . but after the Battle of Tekhmet she and the captain had fitted these extensions with special linkages which detached themselves if part of the mechanism became jammed, and he continued operating, albeit with reduced function.

But still the English cannon roared, and *khoresh*-wood shattered, and airmen of all races howled in frustration and pain, and little by little the sense Arabella had of the ship—"It is as though you can *feel* the ship," Captain Singh had said once, "whereas I must *think* of her motions"—told her that *Diana* was struggling. Penned up in the great cabin as Arabella was, she could not see the damage abovedecks nor the crew's expressions, but she could feel the pulsers slowing, the broadsides weakening, the ship maneuvering more and more sluggishly as, one by one, her sails and yards were shot away.

Grimly Arabella continued, pushing Aadim's mechanisms past increasing, grinding resistance, pushing her own body through fatigue and pain and despair. She would not falter, she would not fail . . . she would not stand down until all other alternatives had been stolen from her.

Then there came a lull—a pause in which, though cannon-fire still sounded all around, for the moment none of it seemed to be directed at *Diana*. Arabella took the opportunity to drain her water-skin, but even this brief respite was interrupted by a cry through the scuttle: "Navigator!" It was Morgan. "Report to the captain at once!"

"Aye aye," she replied automatically, and made sure to stow her tools and charts properly before complying. But even as she did so she wondered—worried, to be precise—what could justify pulling her from her post in the midst of battle.

———————————

Arabella came out on deck, squinting against the sunlight. Despite the miasma of smoke and wreckage all around, the light here was far brighter than that within the cabin, and for a moment it blinded her. But soon her eyes adjusted.

She wished they had not.

*Diana* was a wreck. Arabella had known she had taken serious damage, but she had not realized just how bad it was—certainly far worse than at the Battle of Tekhmet. Broken spars, tangled lines, and torn sails drifted every where, and tangled up in these like horrific fruit on some ghastly vine were bodies and parts of bodies, human, Martian, and Venusian. The mingled stinks of blood and powder were overwhelming.

Coughing, batting bits of wreckage from her face—some of these, disturbingly, were soft and moist—Arabella made her way to the quarterdeck. There, to her great relief, she found Captain Singh still mostly whole, though his hat had vanished and his coat was bloody, sooty, and torn. Khema, too, was battered but not seriously injured. But both of their eyes held such serious expressions that she immediately dreaded what was to come.

"Mrs. Singh," the captain said.

"Sir," she replied with a Martian salute.

There were so many other things she wished to say at that moment, but she feared that if she even attempted to articulate them she would break down in inconsolable, ineffectual tears.

"Our situation is . . ." He paused, swallowed, started again. "Our situation is . . . untenable. The gun-deck is entirely demolished—it is a wonder the fire was contained—and even the bow-chasers are out of action. Only three sails remain to our pulsers, we have barely sufficient sheets and yards to navigate, and casualties . . . casualties have been substantial." He swallowed again. "I have pulled *Diana* out of action momentarily, but the English flagship, *Royal George*, is in pursuit and will catch us up before long." He gestured sunward to a gaudy first-rate, speeding directly toward *Diana*, not very much damaged and with both pulsers whirling. "After consultation, the admiral and I . . ." He paused, swallowed, began again. "We have a very particular request of you."

Arabella could not frame any reply. She simply stared at her captain, her husband, her love, trying and failing to retain some fragment of hope that she and he might yet find some solution to the horrible situation in which they found themselves.

"I need you to ask Aadim to lay in a collision course with the English flagship." Ignoring Arabella's gasp, he continued, "Then take Admiral Khema, and as many of *Diana*'s people as you can, to safety in the captain's gig. You can easily tow two lines of people, at least twenty or thirty, behind the gig. The rest will be released from duty to fend for themselves. I will remain aboard with a minimal crew of volunteers. Then . . ." He paused and looked away from her, his eyes fixed on the empty space over her left shoulder. ". . . we will open the gas-cocks and drive *Diana* directly into *Royal George*. With luck the resulting explosion will destroy the *George*, damage several other English ships, and put the remainder into sufficient disarray that you can reach shelter on the far side of Phobos." He blinked and returned his gaze to her, though his attention still seemed distant. "Failing that, I am certain that if you are picked up by the English they will accept your parole."

Arabella could not bear her captain's earnest eyes, and dropped her gaze to his top coat-button. It was badly scarred, its metal torn to a dangerous ragged edge. "Is this an order, sir?" she whispered.

"I cannot order such a thing, Mrs. Singh. But . . . but I hope that you will find it in your heart to comply."

Miserably Arabella looked to Khema, hoping against all hope that her beloved *itkhalya* would have some word of advice, some reassurance that all would be well. But her eye-stalks were downcast. "We have discovered no alternative."

Arabella acknowledged this painful truth with a slight, slow nod. "I . . ."

But no following word would come. How could she obey such a horrific request? On the other hand, how could she deny her husband's final wish? Would it be selfish to insist upon dying at his side, when if she did as he requested Khema and many others might be saved? But how could she bear to lose her beloved captain . . . and Aadim as well? Should she argue in favor of honorable surrender? Or would that be a betrayal of the cause they had both believed in, and had worked so hard to bring about?

"I—" she began again, still not certain what would follow, but hoping her voice might find a solution when her mind and heart could not.

"Sail ho!" came a hoarse voice from the mainmast head, interrupting her before she could learn what she was about to say.

"Where away?" Captain Singh called back, drawing his glass from his pocket and scanning all about—sunward, skyward, east, west . . .

"North, sir! Eighteen sail of ship, two points skyward of due north!"

The captain turned his glass upward—a direction from which

no ship would normally approach Mars. "The Jarvis . . ." he breathed with wonderment.

Arabella's mind whirled at this unexpected statement. The Jarvis Current, she knew, was, like the Swenson, one of the recently discovered currents which ran perpendicular to the plane of the ecliptic. It was a wickedly fast current, unpredictable and hard to catch, but it did indeed flow near Mars at this season of the planet's year.

But who could possibly be making use of such an unusual breeze? And to what end?

Arabella drew out her own glass. Through it she saw not merely eighteen but twenty-four . . . no, twenty-*eight* ships, and possibly more behind them just coming into view, and the swift Jarvis Current was bearing them toward the battle at a precipitous pace. They were not capital ships, by the look of them . . . even without full detail she could see they did not show the typical hexagon of a British or French ship-of-the-line, with six or nine masts in alternating triads. Indeed, as they came clearer she realized that most of them were of an entirely unfamiliar design: two masts, one aloft and one below, with stiff, wing-like sails. But one . . . one was a four-master.

"No," Arabella said, focusing her glass. "It cannot be."

But it was.

"*Touchstone*," she said—quietly, to herself, as though she did not dare speak the word aloud for fear of contradiction. Then, gaining confidence, "*Touchstone*." Then she called out as loud as she could, "*Touchstone*! It is the dear *Touchstone*!"

"*Touchstone*! *Touchstone*!" The cry was taken up all across the deck.

The Venusians, too, were exceptionally pleased to spot the incoming ships. "Those are *muglugunggna*!" Ulungugga exclaimed. "Venusian traders!"

"I care not who they are," Arabella said, "so long as they are here to help!"

"Signal 'request aid,'" Captain Singh said to Watson, who immediately leapt to the mainmast to run up the appropriate signal-flags, and then to Morgan, "Ready the stern-chasers and distribute small arms. This battle is not yet over."

By now every one in both fleets had spotted the onrushing *Touchstone* and her Venusian companions, and the English ships were turning to face them—obviously assessing them, quite correctly, as the greater threat. But the *khebek* and game *Diana*'s little chasers continued to peck away at the English, dividing their attention. "Target *Royal George*'s quarterdeck!" Captain Singh called to the rifle-men, and though they were not the equal of the English Marines they did their best, harrying the officers and driving them to the cover of their armored great cabin.

Arabella, peering through her glass at *Royal George* as the two ships continued to draw nearer each other, spotted one officer descending the ladder whose silhouette was distinct, un-Naval, and curiously familiar. A grotesquely fat man, his coat was lavishly ornamented with braid and medals that glittered in the sun. His hat, too, was extraordinarily large and ornate, bearing a white fringe and a substantial cockade. And his feet . . .

One of his boots was black, the other white. No, not a white boot—a bandage.

"Prinny, you self-important b——d," Arabella muttered to herself as the Prince Regent vanished below. Immediately she shot across the quarterdeck to her husband. "The Prince Regent is aboard the flagship!" she informed him.

"I had suspected as much," he replied, "from *Royal George*'s curious unwillingness to engage until the battle was nearly won. We can use this to our advantage." He nodded to Khema.

Khema returned the captain's nod, then turned toward

Morgan. "Signal 'engage the enemy more closely,'" she said, "and bring out a white signal rocket."

Captain Singh then returned his attention to Arabella. "To your post, Ashby. We yet require Aadim's help to survive the day."

"Aye aye," she replied, and headed to the great cabin.

---

Even as she reached Aadim's desk, Arabella heard the *whoosh* of a signal rocket being fired, followed by cries of excitement and surprise. She put her head out the larboard window and looked forward, where the saw the rocket's trail diminishing rapidly in the direction of the English flagship, the line of smoke immediately torn and knotted by the Horn's winds. A moment later the rocket burst, a white flare of light so close to the flagship's deck that airmen there were forced to duck and put up their hands to protect themselves from the flying sparks.

"Lay in a course for *Royal George*!" called Morgan through the scuttle. "Bring us around behind her for a shot at her pulsers!"

"Aye aye!" Arabella responded, and immediately took up her sextant.

She and Aadim worked feverishly through the next few minutes, bringing the badly wounded *Diana* about and pushing her forward with all the speed her damaged pulsers could provide . . . *toward* the greatest threat in the vicinity. But the *khebek* fleet had seen the signal-flags and the white flare that Khema had sent up, and brought all their powers to bear upon that one ship. Harried from every direction, with her officers driven to ground by concentrated rifle fire, *Royal George* responded haphazardly, firing off her deadly broadsides at first one flitting target and then another. Several brave *khebek* were completely demolished in a single blow, but the others continued to press the attack at the risk of their own lives.

Despite the annoyance of the *khebek* fleet, *Royal George*'s captain clearly knew where his enemy's admiral was, and continued to attempt to pivot toward *Diana*. But Arabella and Aadim rode the wild winds of the Horn like a rearing *huresh*, dodging and weaving, drawing ever nearer to *Royal George* while avoiding the cone of death at whose apex lay her great guns.

Captain Singh's aim was to disable the English flagship's pulsers. But with only two stern-chasers and a few rifles remaining to her, *Diana* was operating at a distinct disadvantage. Nonetheless, Arabella persisted, and Aadim rose to the occasion, devising maneuver after unprecedented maneuver to bring *Diana* close enough that those small guns would be sufficient to achieve the required result.

And then, clearly audible over the tumult of the battle, came a sound dear to Arabella's heart: the distinctive octuple *ba-ba-ba-bang* of *Touchstone*'s great guns! For even as *Diana* darted and lunged closer to the English flagship, the powerful Jarvis Current had been working all the while to bring *Touchstone* and the Venusian traders closer to the battle.

Arabella dashed to the larboard window to risk a glimpse aloft. *Touchstone* was descending from northward toward *Royal George* with all sails set—a magnificent spread of silk to check the great forward velocity the Jarvis Current had given her—discharging broadside after broadside onto the English flagship's decks all the while. Her peculiar companions were doing the same, many of them directing their fire to *Royal George* but others, on the peripheries of the fleet, attacking the rest of the surviving English ships.

The Venusian traders were no match, nor even a serious challenge, to even a third-rate line-of-battle ship. Lightly armed, they moved in no formation at all, merely a rough untutored crowd of sails and hulls. But they did carry cannon, if only a few each, and they and their crews were fresh and uninjured, sailing into the fray with unexpected speed and from an unexpected direction. And out of the English fleet, there remained only a dozen or so still fighting, so the battle between the English and the newcomers was more evenly matched than it might at first have seemed.

Arabella knew *Touchstone* to be a fierce fighter, a bantam rooster of a ship, her crew well-practiced with their guns and her passage through the Horn's turbulent winds aided by an automaton pilot. The rest of the newly-arrived fleet were not so formidable, but what they lacked in speed and strength they clearly made up in enthusiasm. They fired with gusto rather than precision, but nonetheless disconcerted the English considerably. Their mere arrival, too, gave heart to the plucky *khebek* fleet, and these hammered their English prey with renewed vigor.

The English airmen were strong, experienced, and numerous, well-fed and well-trained into the bargain, and fought with the conviction that they served their King and the King served God. But though Arabella did not stand upon the deck as she had in some previous battles, she knew when this one was drawing to a close. She felt it in the creak of Aadim's gears as she guided his hand across the chart. She heard it in the grunts and muffled cries of the airmen on the deck above. She smelled it in the waft of powder and of splintering wood.

So, when Captain Singh's triumphant order to "stand down and make all fast!" came echoing through the scuttle, she was not surprised. She smiled as she drifted off to an exhausted sleep, right there in the great cabin, with Aadim ticking and whirring beside her and the cheers of the Martian Resistance echoing in her ears.

# 16

## VICTORY

The mood aboard the captain's gig was exceptionally mixed, despite the company being so small: Khema, Captain Singh, Arabella, Watson as coxswain, and two airmen at the pedals. There was jubilation, to be sure, at the rough and improvised Martian Navy's victory over the best the English had to offer; but there was also sadness, anger, and shock at the horrific losses the battle had incurred; quiet pride; vicious glee at the thought of *Royal George* and all her highly decorated officers being brought low; and simple exhaustion. Every person present, Arabella thought, must be feeling all of these sentiments in the same confused gallimaufry that she herself did.

Captain Fox had been invited, but had declined. "Some one must keep an eye on the fleet in Miss Khema's absence," he had declared, though every one present understood that it was he and Lady Corey who were keeping an eye, and possibly much more than an eye, on each other.

Arabella had received a most enthusiastic greeting from

Fox—though not quite so enthusiastic as his greeting to Lady Corey—when he had boarded *Diana* after the battle. "Your automaton pilot," he had exclaimed to Arabella, "was essential—absolutely essential!—to *Touchstone*'s escape from certain destruction at the hands of the Ceres fleet." The automaton, he explained, had permitted him to devise an apparently-fatal fall to Mars's surface, to pull out of it once out of sight, and to navigate his heavily damaged ship away from Mars.

"Our timely return to Mars was also your doing," Fox had continued, "albeit indirectly." For it was the cargo-carrier *Kemekhta*, carrying the two formerly-enslaved Venusian Isambard-handlers to Venus, that had encountered *Touchstone* drifting helpless and towed her to Venus for repairs. At Venus, Fox's persuasive skills, combined with the Isambard-handlers' effusive thanks to Arabella and Khema, had convinced a significant number of independent Venusian traders to take up arms in the cause of Mars. "And if you had not demonstrated to me at Mercury the navigational possibilities of the perpendicular currents, our return journey would have taken months longer."

---

Soon the gig arrived at *Royal George* and, under the silent stares of a hundred English airmen, the Martians disembarked. As soon as Captain Singh's toe touched the planks, some one shouted, "Admiral on deck!" Instantaneously every man on deck brought a knuckle to his forehead, a tune played on the bosun's pipe, and cannon boomed.

But Captain Singh waved away all these accolades. "I am merely a captain," he said. "*There* is your victorious admiral!" He indicated Khema, who, following Martian protocol, had followed him in descending from the gig to the English flagship's deck.

The English airmen looked at each other with confusion and

concern, obviously uncertain of the protocol of this situation. Finally one of the officers, wearing the uniform of a Royal Navy captain, cleared his throat, pointed to Khema, and cried, "You heard the man! Admiral on deck!"

The salutes, the bosun's pipe, and the cannon repeated themselves, albeit a bit raggedly, and Khema accepted the tribute with what seemed to Arabella more grace than it deserved.

Two straight rigid lines of Naval airmen awaited them. Had these men been selected for uniformity? They certainly did seem all of a height, with identical clothing and identical steely expressions, and they floated in strict parallel, looking just as though they stood in gravity. And at the other end of those lines floated a crowd of officers.

Among the officers Arabella recognized the uniform of a Royal Navy admiral—a dour apple-cheeked man with a high forehead, he must be Admiral Thornbrough, the commander of the fleet— but her attention was drawn to one who, though he floated in the midst of the group, stood out due to his elaborate costume, broad girth, and the wordless deference offered him by those about him. The Prince Regent.

The Prince was even more corpulent than he had been when Arabella had departed Brighton; though his uniform was very well tailored, his jowls still strained against his collar. That uniform, seen close up, was even gaudier than it had appeared through her telescope—a flamboyant confection of braid, medals, and brass buttons, embroidered with vast quantities of metallic thread and topped by a pair of elaborate epaulets so festooned with fringe they seemed two golden mops attached to his shoulders. And the hat was even more extravagant than the jacket. Knowing the Prince's tastes, Arabella was certain he had designed the ensemble himself.

The expression on the Prince's face was thunderous, and though his piggish eyes darted all about none of the English officers would meet them. The reason for this discord in the ranks soon became clear, for even as Admiral Thornbrough floated toward Khema, carrying his sword flat across his hands for a formal presentation of surrender, the Prince pushed through the crowd of officers and clapped the Admiral upon the shoulder, spinning him around in the air. "How dare you!" he spat. "This war is not yet over! Far from it!"

Most of the officers managed to contain their outrage at this violation of protocol—loyalty to the Prince Regent winning out over respect for Naval tradition. But the expression on Admiral Thornbrough's face was that of a nanny faced with the tantrum of a toddler . . . a nanny for whom such tantrums were a daily occurrence, and whose continued employment depended upon the approval of the parents rather than the child's good behavior in public. "The exigencies of war, Your Royal Highness," he explained, clearly not for the first time. "There is no dishonor in surrendering when one has been fairly bested. To continue this conflict would be a pointless waste of lives and treasure."

"Treasure!" roared the Prince, his already-red cheeks becoming still more florid. "Consider the *treasure* to be won if we press on!" He turned in the air, importuning his officers with his hands alternately extended in supplication and clenched in fists. "The cost of the war is *nothing* by comparison with the gains to be realized! You *cannot* surrender! We will not *permit* it!"

The English officers shifted uncomfortably, their eyes going every which way as they sought to avoid their sovereign's demanding gaze. Their admiral, she noted, looked to Captain Singh as though seeking sympathy . . . but found none.

Treasure, Arabella knew, was to the Prince the crux of the matter: the money to be made from the control of Mars. He had admitted as much to her in Brighton. But Lady Hertford had said, "He is manipulable. If you appeal to his self-importance, if you can convince him that his interests align with yours . . ."

"Your Royal Highness," Arabella said into the awkward silence.

At once all eyes went to her, and she suddenly realized the sight she must present—a slim twenty-three-year-old woman in a scandalously revealing Martian leather outfit, the only female among hundreds of English airmen, whose presence had been painstakingly ignored by every one up to this point.

"You!" spat the Prince, pointing at Arabella with astonishing ill manners. "You are the Jezebel, the virago, the *traitoress* who lured our commander away from us! You could have been the first Duchess of Mars!"

"It was for the sake of the Martian people that I departed your company," she replied evenly, bowing in the air. A curtsey might have been more appropriate, but could not be properly performed without skirts. "They are worthy of your respect, Your Royal Highness, and as you have learned this day they are formidable opponents. You may continue to battle against them if you wish"—here the Prince pouted still further and he nodded, as though she had conceded a point—"but Mars is their home, and no matter how many ships or guns or men you send against them they will always be more numerous, more spirited, and more knowledgeable of their native land. You can bomb them and shoot them and imprison them, you can try to crush their spirits with drugs, but in the end they *will* win out. And the cost of the effort will be . . . incalculable. Consider how much money your father spent fighting against the Americans . . . and still lost out in the end." The Prince's face seemed to swell as she spoke, like a balloon being overinflated toward the bursting point.

"But." She held up one finger to indicate a change of subject. "Suppose that instead of repeating your father's mistake, you *support* the Martians in their bid for independence. You would avoid the debt, the disruption of trade, the increased taxes needed to support a war . . . a war in which the transportation costs alone, to supply the troops at such an enormous distance, would be outrageous, never mind the cost of the war itself. And, afterward, instead of facing a hostile population determined to stymie your every wish—which is the best you could hope to achieve even if you somehow managed to eke out a temporary victory—you would have a willing trading partner, eager to sell you *khoresh*-wood and fine Martian steel and purchase English craft and manufactured goods."

The Prince, by now, was listening carefully, and Arabella set the hook. "Keep in mind that the Honorable Mars Company would take the lion's share of this increased trade. And I know that you, personally, would profit substantially, due to your holdings in the Company. These profits, by the way, would be entirely yours, and not under the control of Parliament. And you would be hailed by both Britons and Martians as the bringer of peace and prosperity to two planets."

Every eye on the deck was still upon Arabella's face, but she strove to ignore them and meet only the Prince's gaze. "Prinny," she simpered—hating herself for doing so, but knowing that it was necessary for the future of Mars—"I know that you are not a bad man. You only want what is best for your country. And all you need do, to bring about all of this peace and prosperity, is surrender this one small battle."

"Surrender?!" he spluttered. "By no means!" Arabella's heart sank. But then the Prince continued, "This is no surrender . . . this is a great victory for England!" And, again pushing several other officers aside, he seized his Admiral by the shoulder and snatched the sword from his nerveless fingers, offering it in turn to Captain Singh. "Pray accept this sword," he said, ignoring all protocol, "as a token of our great esteem for the Martians and our hopes for a great and very profitable future."

Captain Singh silently and smoothly redirected the offered sword to Khema. The Prince's eyes widened and his mouth gaped

like a fish, but he did not, as Arabella had feared he would, protest or snatch the sword back.

"I accept your surrender," Khema replied with more formality
and dignity than the graceless offer deserved, "on behalf of all
the peoples of Mars." She then bowed from the waist, in English
fashion—how odd it seemed after so many months of only
Martian bows and Martian salutes—and accepted the congratulations of the English officers upon her victory.

None of the officers seemed quite certain how to treat Arabella,
with her outlandish costume and habits. Many bowed, a few
shook her hand as though she were a gentleman, and some simply stared as though she were some talking dog. But she did not
care. She had won out, and with her husband alive and whole by
her side.

---

The Victory Ball was held at Mars House in Fort Augusta. Despite
the official name change, nearly every one still called it Government House; however, the fire-places which had formerly burned
continually in every room for the comfort of the English had
been extinguished. Company House, by contrast, was still Company House, and in fact had become so busy in recent weeks that
construction of an addition was being discussed.

The ball was a very strange affair in many ways, with some of
the defeated English plainly glad to see the end of the conflict
and some of the victorious Martians plainly concerned about
what the future might bring. It was also rather strained by the
fact that the Martians, the most numerous of the company, were
unfamiliar with the dances, games, and foodstuffs on offer, and
the Venusians even more so. The Martian victory celebration, or
*khapla lokhno*, had been held earlier in the week, and it had been
equally awkward for the human guests. The *shorokleth*, in particular,

a rare and costly crustacean considered uniquely propitious when consumed raw, had resulted in several very uncomfortable incidents due to its strong flavor.

Many of the Tories and other loyalists—including, to Arabella's surprise, several prominent Martians—had expressed their horror and dismay at the terms of the Prince Regent's surrender, vowing to take themselves and all their chattel back to England. Among these, sadly, was Michael, who had absolutely refused to speak to Arabella, conducting all negotiations via Mr. Trombley, the family solicitor. Under the terms of the treaty, Martian property held by English subjects—all of which, technically, belonged to the Crown and was only leased by its occupants—would return to Martian ownership, but those who wished to continue living upon it would be permitted to do so, under the terms of their lease, for the rest of their natural lives. Through the offices of Mr. Trombley, Arabella and Michael had worked out an arrangement whereby Arabella would inhabit Woodthrush Woods, while Michael would receive the proceeds of the *khoresh*-wood plantation. Until Michael vacated the property, though, she and Captain Singh were living in rented rooms in Fort Augusta.

After being handed down from her carriage by Gowse— having survived both the Battle of Tekhmet and the Battle of Phobos, he had loudly sworn off aerial service forever and taken a position as Arabella's *huresh*-groom—Arabella accepted a glass of *lureth*-water from a passing servant, and strolled about the gathering for some time. Khema and her fellow *akhmok* were holding court, but many of the other guests had not yet arrived . . . including Captain Singh, who was engaged in negotiations at Company House. Now that the fighting was over, his background had made him the obvious choice to represent the new Martian government to the Company, but the discussions often ran long and this was far from the first time he had been late to an important event.

"Mrs. Singh!" Arabella turned to the familiar light voice to find, as she had expected, Dr. Barry. He raised his glass to her as he approached. "Sherry?"

"I am drinking *lureth*-water," she said, raising her own glass. "But thank you." She paused, considering. "I had thought you did not partake of strong spirits?"

"Not usually," he said. "But I have had news to-day, both bad and good." She realized from the surgeon's careful diction that he was, in fact, already slightly tipsy, a state in which she had never before observed him. "My patient Mr. Young has passed on."

"Young? Oh, my goodness!"

"You knew him?"

"He was a shipmate of mine." He had been a member of her mess when she had first joined *Diana*. They had, in fact, shoveled coal together on her very first ascent as *Diana*'s captain's boy, and his loss, even on top of so many others, pained her extremely.

"My condolences. I am sorry to be the bearer of bad tidings." He bowed.

"I had thought he was discharged?"

"He had been, but there was a deep and hidden infection which, apparently, his powers were insufficient to defeat. He returned to hospital yesterday and died early this morning." He shrugged. "He was sixty-eight years of age. Not a bad run, in his profession."

"Not bad at all, no." She sipped at her *lureth*-water and seriously considered taking Dr. Barry up on his offer of sherry . . . or perhaps even brandy. How she wished Navy grog were on offer! *That* would be a proper toast for Young. "You said you had good news as well?"

"Indeed, and yet it is the very same news. Young was the last of the casualties from the Battle of Phobos in my care. Now the battle is truly over. Though some will suffer from their injuries for the rest of their lives, of course." He raised his glass again. "To the invalids."

"To the invalids." They drained their glasses, and Arabella considered her own injury. Her artificial foot functioned well enough that many people did not even know she had one, but her stump still did pain her from time to time. And that pain, she had been warned by many a wounded airman, would only worsen as she aged.

The planet Mars, too, bore scars from the battles just past which would take a long time to heal, if ever. Although Lord Reid had been expelled from the Court of Directors of the Honorable Mars Company—one of several prominent men to lose his position in the purges following the failure of the Prince's scheme, though of course the Prince himself was immune to any such— the drug *ulka* had taken root among the Martian population and other suppliers had arisen to meet the demand. This was an ongoing problem and, according to the Venusians, it might never be completely eradicated.

"I am disappointed, Mrs. Singh," the surgeon said, interrupting her thoughts. She returned her attention to him and saw from his mien that he was not, in actuality, very disappointed at all.

She returned his smile. "How so?"

"I had hoped to see you in a dashing cutaway coat this evening." He gestured to her dress, a lovely frock of white figured gauze with slashed sleeves, which Lady Corey had helped her select. "You made a very handsome gentleman, you know."

Arabella found that her emotions in response to this compliment were surprisingly complex, and she took a sip of her water to hide her discomfiture. "I thank you, sir. But I suspect that I shall not be donning any of my brother's old outfits again. I shall certainly wear my *thukhong*, of course, for expeditions into the desert, but despite its silhouette—rather shocking though it may be to those of conventional mind—it is in fact a woman's garment just as much as it is a man's."

"Thank you for enlightening me." He seemed to inspect her form very carefully. "A word of advice?"

"Hm?"

"Even when costumed as a gentleman, your posture is very much as it is now, quite straight and prim. You should strive to take up more space." He angled his feet slightly outward and put his arms akimbo, suddenly seeming several inches larger. Though in fact he was quite a small man, slight as well as short . . . and now that she looked at him carefully, his hips were rather rounded as well. And his voice was quite light and high for a man. Somehow she had never noticed all of this at once before.

Suddenly she marveled at just how much difference a person's costume and posture could make . . . and wondered whether, in fact, the difference between a man and a woman were as ineffable as she had been taught. But that was a conversation for another day. "Thank *you* for enlightening *me*," she said.

"You are welcome."

"Mrs. Singh!" came another voice, this one deep and carrying— the voice of an experienced aerial captain. It was, of course, Fox, with Lady Corey on his arm. The two had been inseparable ever since his dramatic return from the dead, as he put it. "Will you please explain to these delightful gentlemen the principles of operation of your automaton pilot?"

"But of course." She made her way over to them, where she found that Fox had been regaling a small crowd of Fort Augusta's leading citizens with the tale of how he had escaped from the Ceres fleet. It was a story she had heard many times before, of course, and though Fox always acknowledged how invaluable Arabella's contributions had been to his survival, somehow Fox's own role grew more heroic with each retelling.

"The use of the perpendicular current may have been my idea," Arabella said to Fox, "but it was your own navigational skill which made the course possible. And it was your recruitment of the Venusian traders to our cause which truly saved the day, in the end."

"Your rescue of the Isambard-handlers played a large part in that," Fox replied. "But I must also acknowledge my dear wife." He gave Lady Corey a squeeze which was just barely within the boundaries of propriety. "Though she was not present, her example was constantly on my mind during my talks with the Venusians. And, of course, her role in negotiating the treaty just concluded with England is known to all."

"The meeting of the mutual admiration society," Lady Corey said, chuckling modestly, "will now come to order. But it was primarily Miss Khema"—she pronounced the *kh* perfectly— "whose combination of firmness and flexibility permitted the success of those negotiations. Have you met her?" Several of those present had not, so Lady Corey called Khema over for introductions. "It is truly you, not I," she said to Khema, "who should be the hostess of this event."

"This Victory Ball is your affair," Khema replied modestly, "as the *khapla lokhno* was mine, and I am happy to attend it as your guest. In any case, I believe that one of the primary duties of the hostess of an English ball is to lead the dances, and this is an area in which I am sadly ignorant."

As it happened, the band leader then announced that the dancing would shortly commence, and Arabella glanced about for her husband . . . only to see him just entering the room. "So good of you to join us," she said as he took up and kissed her hand.

"I would not miss this for all the worlds," he replied, and led her into the dance.

# EPILOGUE

MARS, 1828

## AN EXPECTED PACKAGE

"Devi!" Arabella cried. "Be careful!"

"Oh, Mother! Do not be such a fidget!"

Devi, her long brown arms thrown wide for balance, was walking atop the fence surrounding the manor house at Woodthrush Woods, which divided it from the *khoresh*-tree plantation. That fence, Arabella reflected, was almost exactly the same age as Devi herself.

How on Mars could she be eight years old already?

And how could Arabella be thirty-three?

"Mummy?"

Arabella looked down, concerned that little Gonekh might have found some poisonous creature, as she so often did. But no, she was merely holding out her chubby little arms for a hug. Those arms were not merely shorter and plumper than her elder sister's, but far paler . . . for some reason her color favored her mother more than her father. Or perhaps it was merely that she spent less time in the sun, as for some reason she generally preferred indoor pursuits more than her sister did. How different two siblings could be!

Arabella picked Gonekh up, snuggled her, and then settled her on one hip, where she toyed contentedly with the hem of her mother's sleeve. Devi clambered down from the top of the fence, to Arabella's quiet relief, and proceeded to dig for *gethown* in the sand at the base of it instead.

It was such a delight, Arabella thought, to have a moment of peace. Between Captain Singh's negotiations with the Company and the Martian and English governments, Arabella's work at the Institute, and the never-ending small crises of any household with two children, such moments were exceedingly rare.

And, true to form, this scene of quiet domesticity was interrupted by a voice from the front gate. "Mrs. Singh!" cried Gowse, excitedly. "It's here!"

"I shall be there momentarily," Arabella called back.

Setting Gonekh down, Arabella took both her daughters' hands and ran with them back to the manor house. It was rather smaller than it had been in her own childhood, and that was not merely because she herself had grown larger . . . they had torn down an entire wing, most of which was dedicated to the processing of *khoresh*-wood, after Michael had ordered the construction of a new drying-shed and offices in the north field. The two sides of the property—Arabella's residence and Michael's plantation—were growing more and more separate from each other with time, even as Mars and England were also settling into a more independent relationship.

She found Captain Singh in the parlor, eagerly prying with a crow-bar at the lid of the large crate which had just arrived. Even as she entered the room, the lid came up. And beneath it, peering up at them from a nest of wood shavings, lay a very familiar face.

Aadim.

Arabella seized a claw-hammer and joined her husband in removing the rest of the crate.

They had boxed him up themselves three days earlier. Due to the great complexity of Aadim's connections with the ship, the process of separating him from *Diana* had taken more than a week—a week full of memories and tears, both joyous and sad—but the three endless and unexpected days it had taken to locate, hire, and await the arrival of a suitable wagon after that job was done had been far worse. Now, at last, he was here.

When Captain Singh had finally presented *Diana* to the Museum of the Martian Resistance, after years of polite but persistent requests, the curators had been greatly disappointed to be deprived of this most significant part of the donation. But Arabella and Captain Singh had both been quite insistent: you will get him only after we have both passed on. Until then, a wax-work dummy would occupy his place in the great cabin, along with waxworks of Captain Singh and Arabella.

They had met with the wax artists several times already. Arabella looked forward to meeting her own wax twin with a mixture of amusement and dread.

Soon they had torn away the planks, paper, and wood shavings and Aadim stood completely revealed. The girls, uncharacteristically shy, stood back and stared at him from the far side of the room, Gonekh sucking her thumb nervously. "There is nothing to fear," Captain Singh told them, folding his considerable length down to their eye level. "He is your brother, in some ways. You will like him, I assure you."

With the help of Gowse and several other members of the household staff they moved him to the space before the front window which they had selected and prepared for him even before Captain Singh had signed the donation papers.

They set him up facing the window. "The view is not so changeable as aboard *Diana*," Arabella told him, "but the weather is generally pleasant, and rarely includes bullets or cannon-balls."

"Never," amended Captain Singh, forcefully.

"There have been a few occasions in the past," Arabella admitted. "But we can hope that these are not repeated." She brushed a bit of wood shaving from Aadim's cheek.

The paint on the automaton's face was rather scuffed and chipped, but they had no intention of renovating him. All of those marks were very familiar to Arabella—she had been there when most of them had occurred, and in several memorable cases she had inflicted them herself, through accident or annoyance—and to remove them would be as unreasonable and inappropriate as to remove the wrinkles from Captain Singh's face. He might, just perhaps, be more conventionally attractive without them, but they were well-earned, distinctive, and essential to his personality.

It took some hours to get Aadim properly settled in his new home. Although they had taken as much care as they could when they had disconnected him and boxed him up, his mechanisms were so complicated that a certain amount of disruption had been inevitable. But soon, just before sunset in fact, they inserted his mainspring key and, with both their hands on the key, wound it together to just the proper point of tension.

The mechanisms within Aadim's desk and torso began to tick and whir, a sound foreign to this place and yet delightfully familiar and homey. And his green glass eyes, although impassive as ever, filled once more with vibrating near-life. The golden light of the setting Sun refracted through the green glass.

"Welcome home," Arabella told him.

"Aadim?" asked Gonekh, clambering up on the automaton's desk and extending one plump little hand to touch his nose.

"Aadim," Captain Singh acknowledged.

"He live here?"

"He has come to live here, yes," Arabella said.

Gonekh's smooth, translucent brow furrowed then, and her dark eyes turned to her parents with concern. "Is he alive?"

Arabella smiled and turned to Captain Singh to see his reaction, but was surprised to see his eyes widen as though in shock. Immediately she turned back, following his gaze.

Perhaps it was only some minor misadjustment in the automaton's recently-disrupted mechanisms.

Perhaps it was something Gonekh had done while Arabella's back was turned.

Perhaps it was a trick of the light, which was just fading as the Sun slipped below the horizon.

But it certainly seemed as though Aadim were nodding.

# ACKNOWLEDGMENTS

This novel was written under difficult circumstances. Although grieving a dead spouse is not as much work as caring for a dying one, it is still very hard, and if it were not for the support of my family and community there is no way I would have been able to finish this book.

I would like to thank everyone who sat and wrote with me in coffee shops, living rooms, libraries, and airports, including but not limited to K. Tempest Bradford, Robin Catesby, Sara Mueller, Mary Hobson, Felicity Shoulders, Mark Ferrari, Lucy Bellwood, Rachel Swirsky, Aimee Amodio, Alex C. Renwick, Tina Connolly, Grá Linnea, Thorn Coyle, Mary Anne Mohanraj, Mary Robinette Kowal, and most especially Shannon Page. Also the whole Portland NaNoWriMo crew and everyone on the 2017 Writing Excuses Cruise.

I would like to thank everyone who offered moral support, provided a shoulder to cry on, went to a show, or shared a meal, including but not limited to Michelle Franz, Sue Yule, Marc Wells, Patty Wells, Wendy Ice, Teresa Enigma, Jacob Engstrom, Mark Stein, Tim Learmont, Amanda Clark, Kate Schaefer, Glenn Hackney, Bo O'Dell, Don Hicks, Debbie Notkin, Alberto Yáñez, Debbie Cross, Paul Wrigley, Andrine de la Rocha, Howard Patterson, Diane Chaplin, David de la Rocha, Rhiannon Marie Louve, Goldeen Ogawa, Lee Moyer, Venetia Charles,

Allan Hurst, Will Martin, Ellen Klages, Elf Sternberg, D. Omaha Sternberg, Eleri Hamilton, Carmen Risken, Gina McCarrig, Alisa Wood-Walters, and especially Cynthia Nalbach. Special thanks to Clare Katner, Daniel MacLeod, and Kay Gage for service and friendship.

I would like to thank—seriously!—Liz Bourke and Sylvus Tarn for their critical comments on colonialism in *Arabella and the Battle of Venus,* and Aliette de Bodard and Grace Fong for their similar critiques on an unpublished Arabella short story. It's never fun to receive a negative review or critique, and I must admit that at first I didn't want to hear it, but in the end I came around to understanding and appreciating the issues they raised. I have attempted to address their concerns in this volume; whether or not I succeeded is not up to me to determine, but I thank them for taking the work seriously enough to critique it.

And last but definitely not least, I would like to thank my editor, Christopher Morgan, whose efforts improved this volume immeasurably; my agent, Paul Lucas of Janklow & Nesbit; and the team at Tor: head of publicity Patty Garcia, art director Irene Gallo, and publicist Desirae Friesen. It's been an amazing journey and I'm proud and pleased to have taken it with you all.

# ABOUT THE AUTHOR

DAVID D. LEVINE is the author of the Andre Norton Award–winning novel *Arabella of Mars* and more than fifty science fiction and fantasy stories. His story "Tk'Tk'Tk" won the Hugo Award for Best Short Story in 2006, and he has been short-listed for others, as well as the Nebula, Campbell, and Sturgeon. His stories have appeared in *Asimov's Science Fiction, Analog Science Fiction and Fact, The Magazine of Fantasy & Science Fiction,* numerous Year's Best anthologies, and his award-winning collection, *Space Magic.* He lives in a hundred-year-old bungalow in Portland, Oregon.